REPUBLIC

THIRSK

STONINGTON

ALLIUM

AURONE

FENNIS END

WAYSTRELL

SARASK

SIMTA

THE ARDENT SEA

NIGHTBIRDS

NIGHTBIRDS

KATE J. ARMSTRONG

 Nancy Paulsen Books

NANCY PAULSEN BOOKS
An imprint of Penguin Random House LLC, New York

First published in the United States of America by Nancy Paulsen Books,
an imprint of Penguin Random House LLC, 2023

Visit us online at penguinrandomhouse.com.

Library of Congress Cataloging-in-Publication Data
Names: Armstrong, Kate J., author.
Title: Nightbirds / Kate J. Armstrong.
Description: New York: Nancy Paulsen Books, 2023. | Series: Nightbirds; book 1 |
Summary: "In Simta, the magic of women is outlawed, but four girls with unusual powers
have the chance to change it all"—Provided by publisher.
Identifiers: LCCN 2022037458 (print) | LCCN 2022037459 (ebook) |
ISBN 9780593463277 (hardcover) | ISBN 9780593463284 (ebook) |
Subjects: CYAC: Magic—Fiction. | Friendship—Fiction. | Fantasy. |
Fantasy fiction. lcgft | Novels. lcgft
Classification: LCC PZ7.1.A7479 Ni 2023 (print) | LCC PZ7.1.A7479 (ebook) |
DDC [Fic]—dc23
LC record available at https://lccn.loc.gov/2022037458
LC ebook record available at https://lccn.loc.gov/2022037459

Printed in the United States of America
ISBN 9780593463277 (hardcover)

1st Printing

LSCH

Edited by Stacey Barney
Design by Suki Boynton • Text set in ITC Galliard Pro

To my mom,
who makes everything feel magical

THE MAGIC IN A KISS

ALL HIS LIFE, young lord Teneriffe Maylon has heard whispers. They circled the edges of ballrooms and slithered through hushed conversations over port. *The Nightbirds will change your fortunes,* the whispers promised. *Their magic can be yours with just a kiss.*

If you can find them, that is, and meet their requirements. They are a privilege he's about to pay quite dearly for.

At last, Tenny is allowed to remove his blindfold. For a moment, all he can make out is the bright burn of candles painting circles on the deeply purple walls. Then a woman perched behind a desk comes into focus, wearing a gown of fine velvet and a darkly feathered mask. It shrouds her face, mesh stretched over the eyeholes. He knows her only by her code name: Madam Crow.

She holds out a gloved hand, letting it hover. "Your payment."

Tenny's fingers shake a little as he extends the string of rubies. That shake is what gets him into trouble at the krellen tables—it's such an obvious tell. Tenny is used to seeing money leave him, but it usually flows in the form of coins, not treasures pilfered from his dame's jewel box. The shame of it tastes like the last dregs of bitter wine. He is tired, nerves tattered from avoiding his rather nefarious creditor and his sire's certain wrath if he finds out about his son's growing debts. Tenny's had a poor run of luck, is all, but tonight, that all changes.

Madam Crow winds the rubies around her fingers. The dark gems seem to swallow the light.

"And your secret?" she demands.

Sweat slides down Tenny's collar. "The jewels are payment enough, don't you think?"

She arches a brow. "Secrets protect my girls better than gems, however pretty. I will have your secret, or you'll have nothing at all."

Tenny sighs and hands her the note he wrote that afternoon, explaining it was he who took his dame's rubies. He threw in the extent of his debts and the dalliance with his family's maid for good measure. It's a risk, to put these secrets into Madam Crow's keeping, but he knew money wouldn't be enough to get him through this door.

The Madam reads his secrets, then folds them up again. She holds a stick of purplish wax over a candle flame until it drips. His pulse picks up as she pours it onto the paper's folds and slides it toward him. He presses his House Maylon ring into the wax, marking its contents as authentic. Ensuring he will never tell a soul of what he sees tonight.

That business done, the Madam smiles. "Which Nightbird are you seeking?"

Tenny licks his lips. A few of his friends have boasted vaguely about their time with a Nightbird, but the magic they spoke of seemed too fanciful to credit. Wild tales to trap desperate fools like him.

The Madam lays down three cards on the desk between them. They look like krellen cards, but instead of mythical beasts and kings, they hold finely drawn birds.

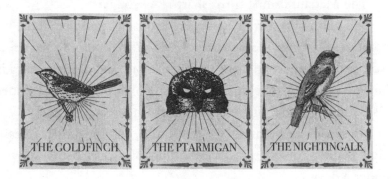

THE GOLDFINCH | THE PTARMIGAN | THE NIGHTINGALE

"No Nightbird's magic is the same," she explains. "They are each a different vintage. The Goldfinch will help you change your feathers, making you look like someone else. The Ptarmigan gives the gift of camouflage— near invisibility. The Nightingale will let you manipulate someone's emotions, smoothing them in whatever direction you desire."

Tenny's mouth has gone dry. All magic is illegal in the Eudean Republic, but this kind is also incredibly rare. He's tasted plenty of alchemical magic—the kind that's mixed into cocktails in Simta's speakeasies and ground into powders in alchemists' back rooms. Such concoctions will let you speak another language for a handful of minutes or make your skin glow in the dark. But a Nightbird's gift is purer, and so much more precious. It is what those alchemists and barkeeps try so hard to imitate.

"The gift only tends to linger for a few uses," the Madam says. "So choose wisely."

Tenny is tempted by the Nightingale, who might help him sway the outcome at the krellen tables, but he doesn't want to cheat his way out of his trouble. He wants to win his fortune back by himself.

He points to the Goldfinch.

The Madam's smile turns sharp. "As you wish."

She gives him the rules: no lasciviousness, no demands, no pointed questions. He is too nervous to take in more than a few words. Then the blindfold goes back on, and someone leads him down a hall that smells of lilies. Thick carpet gives under his boots as slender fingers tug him by the wrist.

After a few twists and turns, they stop, and the fingers release him. Paper shuffles, the covert sound of a card being shoved under a door.

Sweat dampens Tenny's cuffs.

"Ah . . . how should I address her?" he asks the darkness.

There is a pause, then a scratchy male voice that makes him jump.

"By her code name. Otherwise, you don't need to address her at all."

More silence. Guilt prickles at the back of Tenny's neck. His sire supports the Prohibition and is a staunch abstainer. What would he say if he could see his son buying such magic with some stolen family jewels?

Tenny sighs. He doesn't know why krellen calls to him so strongly. Just that he loves how it offers players a chance to be pauper or king, god or mortal, a thrilling brand of risk. This night is a risk, as dangerous-sweet as any. He turns his thoughts away from his sire and toward the Goldfinch—only the Goldfinch. The mysterious, miraculous magic to come.

Tenny straightens his tie as a door clicks open. Light flickers through his blindfold, soft and warm. He is pushed forward, and then the door shuts behind him.

"You can look," the Goldfinch says. "It's just us now."

Her voice is soft. No, rich, like blush wine from the Farlands, but strangely distorted. She must be burning some sort of voice-altering alchemical. Another layer of disguise.

He takes off the blindfold. The room is dimly lit and richly furnished, dark wood draped in velvet and wine-colored rugs. Two chairs sit near the fireplace, deep and beckoning. Amidst it all is a girl in a mask. Hers is like Madam Crow's, covering most of her face in gold-edged feathers that catch the light of the candles on the hearth. The mesh over her eyes makes her anonymous, but he guesses she must be his age, perhaps younger. Though her smile speaks of a wisdom that is well beyond her years.

She isn't a courtesan—he would be foolish to think it—but it's hard not to stare at those full, generous lips. Has he seen them before? It would be dangerous to put a name to them. There is a reason for the code names and the masks. Some would kill to have unfettered access to such magic. The church, and many of the city's staunchest abstainers, would likely kill the girls outright. No: It's better that she just be the Goldfinch. Tenny doesn't need more trouble than he has.

He bows deeply. "Welcome evening, Young Lady Goldfinch."

Those lips curl, coy and playful. "Young Lord Maylon. Aren't you a pretty surprise."

His eyes follow the golden chain around her neck, traveling downward. Why do they call it a neckline when it tends to hang so much lower? He looks up, hoping she hasn't noticed. With the mesh over her eyes, it is impossible to tell.

"Let's have some wine," the Goldfinch says. "Or perhaps something stronger?"

He nods, though his stomach is twisted. "Lady's choice."

The Goldfinch goes to pour their libations. The dark sequins of her dress wink as she moves. Truth be told, he isn't clear on the finer mechanics of the evening he's purchased. How will it start? How will it feel?

She hands him a glass full of amber liquid that smells of pine resin and thunderheads.

"Fortune favor you," she says, tilting her glass to him.

He swallows hard. "And you as well."

They drink. Tenny finishes his in one large gulp. He sits in one of the chairs, expecting her to perch on the other. Instead, she settles on his lap.

"Are you ready?" she purrs.

He nods, willing his hands to stop shaking.

The Goldfinch pulls out a simple black mask and fits it to the top half of his face.

"This is what will call up the magic," she says, "when you're ready to use it. Just tie it on and envision the person whose face you want to wear."

He leans into her touch, her skin as soft as petals.

"You will need to hold something belonging to the person you want to look like. A kerchief is fine, if they've recently held it, but hair or fingernails are better."

He nods again. His heart is thumping wildly. It feels like the moment just before he lays out his krellen cards, not knowing if he's won or lost.

"Now imagine how you will use my gift," she says. "Put the image in your mind, strong and clear."

It isn't hard—the images are there already. He sees himself walking into the Simtan Bank wearing his sire's face, his voice, his manner, accessing the funds he needs to win his way out of the shadows. Money drips from his pockets, and once again he is golden. The son his sire expects him to be.

The Goldfinch tilts up his chin and kisses him.

Tenny has kissed girls before. Boys, too, for that matter, but those were only sparks compared with this fire. Her magic spills from her lips and past his, warm and heady, twining itself around his bones. He is drunk with it. It makes him feel like a king—perhaps a god.

His arms go around her. He understands now why this girl is such a secret. To hold on to her, he would pay any price.

PART I

A
THOUSAND
LAYERS
OF
SECRETS

Darling Matilde,

This dress is old, yes, but it's a fine vintage—one I believe will suit you well. I have had it re-charmed so its jewelflowers unfurl as they did when I was in your shoes, with all the world shining before me. Let it be honey that lures in only the worthy. Let it be your armor, too.

Fly carefully.

My deepest love,

Gran

—A NOTE FROM LADY FREY DINATRIS TO HER GRANDDAUGHTER

CHAPTER 1

JEWEL, STAR, AND SEA

MATILDE IS A thousand layers of secrets. Some sit against her skin, there for anyone who knows how to read them. Others are tucked into a rarefied language only a few girls can speak. Still others have wings, and they are hidden inside her.

She smiles to herself behind her mask.

As Matilde descends the stairs into the ballroom, heads swivel. This is precisely why she made her family wait for over an hour before leaving for Leta's Season-opening ball. Grand entrances, she finds, are the only kind worth making. Especially during the summer season, when Simta floods with people from all over the Eudean Republic, come to make matches, deals, and fortunes in the City of Tides.

The room is full of finely dressed people, talking and swaying to a tasteful string quartet. It's clear that many of them have been to Simta's best trickster tailors, who have outdone themselves enchanting their outfits for the evening. The seed pearls at one girl's neckline unfurl into flowers. A boy's evening coat sparks every time someone touches it. Masks smoke, lapels bloom, gloves glow. Matilde is sure there are alchemical potions she can't see, hidden inside watch fobs and hollowed-out canes. Leta's added some to her candles so they flame cerulean and emerald and black, her House colors.

Standing here, you would never know that magic is illegal. In the circles Matilde swims in, such laws barely apply.

Her brother, Samson, gazes longingly at Æsa, their pretty housemate, but she is busy staring wide-eyed at the room. After a sidelong glance to make sure their dame isn't watching, Samson snags a few drinks from a passing waiter and holds one out to her. Æsa shakes her head—the newest Nightbird seems too nervous to enjoy her first proper Great House party. Matilde will have to work on that.

"I wish you had worn what I laid out for you, Matilde," her dame says.

A dress with frothy skirts, like Æsa's, and a far-too-tight bodice. The one that made Matilde look like a present wrapped for someone else.

"Really?" Matilde does a twirl. "I'm rather pleased with my choice."

Her gown is a columnar sheath, with beaded jewelflowers shimmering darkly against wine-red velvet, gathered up at one hip with a golden clasp. She likes how it's somehow both loose fitting and suggestive. It's her gran's from when she was a Nightbird, made over in the newest style. Perhaps that's why her dame doesn't like it—she thinks it's something Gran should have given her instead, just like her Nightbird gift. Intrinsic magic runs through most of the Great House bloodlines, passed down from woman to woman, but sometimes it skips a generation. Matilde doesn't think her dame has ever gotten over it.

Dame purses her lips. "It's just the cut is rather . . ."

Matilde smiles. "Rather ravishing?"

"I was thinking more along the lines of risqué."

Gran smiles in a way Matilde has practiced for endless hours but has yet to master.

"Good fashion is never risqué," she says. "Only a little daring."

Dame's lips pinch together even tighter.

Matilde runs a gloved finger down one of the jewelflowers' beaded petals. It curls, trickster-kissed to open and close as she moves. Gran has tried to grow real jewelflowers in their garden, but they don't do well outside the swamps of the Callistan. One bloomed last summer, though, its near-black petals begging to be touched. Gran caught her hand before she could. *This jewel's beauty is her trick*, she said. *She lures in prey by looking soft, and once they're close* . . . She let a ribbon fall, and Matilde watched the flower swallow it, sizzling as the fabric turned to ash.

She thinks of it often, that flower with a secret. Poison in the guise of something sweet.

"Let's get to our table," Dame says. "We must survey the Season's prospects."

Prospective suitors, she means. The army of bores she will pour onto Matilde's and Æsa's dance cards, trying to push them both into an advantageous match.

"Really, Dame," Matilde says. "We only just got here."

Her dame lowers her voice. "You've already had too many single Seasons. People are starting to talk of it."

Matilde rolls her eyes. "I'm not a prime cut of meat at market. I won't start to stink if you leave me in the sun."

She doesn't know why Dame froths over the issue—most

Great House boys would eagerly wed a Nightbird. They apply to Leta, their Madam, for the privilege, even though they don't know who they're getting engaged to. From what Matilde has seen, they don't seem much to mind. The suitors are Great House born, and always diamonds. But choosing from a small, curated jewel box isn't the same as choosing for yourself.

She goes to hook an arm through Æsa's, but Dame beats her to it. Æsa looks like a fish caught on a line. Matilde has the notion that her dame is pushing Samson toward Æsa—not that he needs the encouragement. With red-gold hair, lush curves, and green eyes, she is stunning. She has no money, but being a Nightbird is a dowry all its own.

She wonders if Æsa can see her dame's machinations. Since she arrived, she's seemed too homesick for the Illish Isles to see much at all.

"I'll take a turn first," Matilde says. "Do a bit of my own surveying."

Dame frowns. "The last thing we need is you causing mischief."

Matilde tugs at one long, silken glove. "I wasn't planning on it."

Dame sniffs. "You never do."

Samson closes one eye behind his umber-colored mask, as if he might block out the brewing argument. "Really, ladies. Must we?"

Samson won't be chastised for the cut of his outfit or made to dance with some sweaty lord with an underbite. Resentment burns hot on her tongue.

"Never fear," Matilde says. "I don't imagine I'll break any rules between here and the refreshments table."

Dame is clearly about to argue when Gran cuts in.

"Oura, it's Matilde's first party of the Season. Let's allow her to enjoy it."

Matilde waits as her dame pretends to consider it. She is not the head of House Dinatris, after all.

"Fine," she says at last. "But don't be long, Matilde. And no cocktails. I mean it."

With that, she heads toward their table, tugging Æsa along with her. The girl looks back with *don't leave me* eyes, her bright hair burning in the shifting light. Matilde should rescue her from Dame's clutches, and she will—eventually. Samson follows, swiping a glass of Leta's signature cocktail and raising it in a mock toast to Matilde.

Gran turns toward her, the grey-blue sequins of her simple mask winking. "Don't mind your dame. You know how she worries."

Matilde adjusts her own mask. "I've forgotten what she said already."

It's a lie, of course. Dame's words from that afternoon are still circling. *You cannot fly free forever. Eventually you must settle down and build a nest.* Matilde doesn't want to *nest* with someone who only wants her for her magic. She wants the freedom to choose a future for herself.

"She's right, though," Gran goes on. "You will have to choose soon."

Marriage is expected of a Nightbird, so she can pass on her gift to a new generation of Great House girls. It's practically demanded. The thought makes something tighten in her chest.

Gran adjusts Matilde's corsage of winglilies, their House's floral sigil, and gives her a secretive smile.

"I had adventures in that dress, you know. It has tricked many into thinking the girl beneath was soft and biddable."

Matilde's lips tilt. "Are you saying you got up to *mischief* in it?"

"Perhaps." Gran taps the back of her hand with two fingers. "Fly carefully, my darling."

Matilde smiles at the Nightbird watchwords. "I'll do my best."

She weaves through the room, guessing whom she might know and whom she should want to. Matilde enjoys secrets and puzzles, and so she loves the Houses' penchant for throwing masked summer balls. People grow bolder with their faces covered; they gamble with fortunes and with hearts. It's easy to tell who isn't from Simta: They have a shine in their eyes like the wings of newborn flamemoths, dazzled to see so much magic on display. Simta boasts the Republic's best trickster tailors and alchemists, and those with coin and connections know where their illegal concoctions can be found. Such powders and potions are coaxed out of herbs and earth, crafted by clever hands, and they make wonderful illusions, but it isn't like the magic that runs through Matilde's veins. Hers can't be brewed: It lives inside her, rare and unfiltered. She loves being a secret glittering in plain sight.

She takes a deep breath. The air tastes of flowers and champagne, and the beginning of the Season. It's a flavor that Matilde knows by heart. If this is to be her last summer as a Nightbird, she's going to drink in every drop of it.

She reaches for a coupe glass full of Leta's signature cocktail, Sylva—*Dreamer*. The magic in it makes it taste of nostalgia: a favorite childhood treat, a sunny field, a stolen kiss. But as it slides across her tongue, her thoughts turn toward the future. In just a few hours, she will be the Goldfinch for someone.

Whose jewelflower will I be tonight?

SAYER STALKS THE edges of the ballroom. She is used to being the watcher, not the watched, and it feels like half the dashed room is staring at her. She stares back, fighting the urge to bare her teeth.

Leta's ballroom reminds Sayer of a mini version of Simta: a series of rings that get prettier and richer as you make your way in. Servants, guards, and butlers stand by the walls, not really a part of things. They're the Edges. A few steps in you find the strivers trying to look like they belong. They're the Fringes. A few steps more and you arrive at the Great Houses that form the privileged center of it all. Her dame was one of them once, glowing like the flamemoths that fill lanterns in the Garden District. Of course, that was before she tripped and fell out of their light.

Sayer is supposed to be mingling, but all this glitz and empty talk is making her restless. The bootleg in this ballroom could probably buy a fleet of merchant ships. These people flash magic like gems, a status symbol. Only the best for Simta's brightest young things.

As a man tries to sneak a peek down her dress, she's sorely tempted to try and slip something out of his pocket, just for practice. Since leaving Griffin Quarter, she hasn't had much chance to use her cutpurse skills, and no real need. Leta, her guardian, has been more than generous. Leta's told everyone that her prickly new ward is some distant cousin from the country. No one seems to have guessed she's the daughter of the late, disgraced Nadja Sant Held.

Unlike her dame, Sayer grew up across the canals in Griffin's. They lived above a silversmith's, in four rooms that smelled of metal polish and dusty castoffs from friends who never came to call. Until a few months ago, Sayer had barely set more than a foot in Pegasus Quarter, even though it was just across the water. It was another world, made wistful by her dame's rosy stories that all seemed to begin with *if only*. If only she had waited for Wyllo Regnis to propose instead of giving in to his desire for his favorite Nightbird. If only he would regain his senses and come to claim them as his own.

Sayer's magic first started stirring late, for a girl like her: only six months ago. Dame wanted to take her to the Madam to be tested, but she refused. Until her dame's coughs started bloodying whole kerchiefs, and her *if only* words turned slurred and urgent.

If only you would join the Nightbirds. You could bring us back into the light.

Sayer had no interest in joining her dame's old club, but she promised she would, hoping it would revive her. It didn't. And then she died, and Sayer found herself alone. Even then, she wasn't sure she would become a Nightbird. But what else was there? Her options were to scrape together coins as a coffee girl, join a gang, or go to her estranged sire: impossible. So here she is, at the heart of all her dame yearned to get back to. And all she wants to do is tear it down.

She stops to watch a maid set up a coffee service on a side table. The smell takes her back to her days at Twice Lit, where she worked despite her dame's protests. After all, they needed the coin. She liked the smell of roasted twills and the sound of students at its tables, debating the movements of politics and stars. She liked the urchins and the sandpiper gang boys who hung around the shop even better. They taught her more useful things: how to blend into a crowd, wield a knife, steal with a smile.

A partygoer brushes past the maid, making the stack of plates she's holding wobble. He uses steadying her as an excuse to move in close. Sayer can't see his hands, but the maid blushes fiercely at whatever part of her he is touching. The girl won't complain, though: The man's a lord. Sayer grimaces. In Simta, all the wrong people suffer.

Sayer steps in. "She doesn't need your help. Move along."

The man makes an affronted noise but moves on without protest.

"Oh," the maid says. "Thank you, miss."

She bobs a curtsy. The gesture makes Sayer feel annoyed.

"Can I help you set up?" Sayer asks.

The girl's eyes widen. "Such work isn't meant for ladies."

It's the same thing Dame said when she first got her job at Twice Lit.

Words Sayer will never hear her say again.

She clears her throat, swallowing down the painful weight there. The maid's refusal is just as well, as Sayer isn't sure she can bend down in this dress. It's in the latest style, its drop waist falling just below her hipbones, clinging to her in a dark, blue-black sheath. A capelet drapes down her back, shimmering with tiny beads some tailor's trickster-kissed to shoot like stars across it.

Smile, my girl, Leta said when she presented it. *You are a walking constellation. One that everyone will want to wish on.* But shining brightly only makes people want to steal your glow.

Later tonight, she'll become the Ptarmigan: a code name Leta chose for her because of that bird's adroit camouflage. Sayer's magic has the power to help someone blend into their surroundings, letting them walk through the world unseen. She doesn't want this life, but she made her dame a promise.

For a summer, at least, she'll see it through. Leta swore she could keep the Ptarmigan's earnings; a couple months' worth will equal more than she could make at Twice Lit in a decade. It will set her up so that she never needs help, or this place, again.

From across the room, Matilde catches Sayer's eye, crooking a finger. She seems to want the three of them to be a pretty flock of fledglings, sharing outfits and secrets and dreams. *Nightbirds are like sisters,* Dame told her once. *They are the only ones who will ever truly know you.* But where were they when her dame needed them? Probably laughing around a table at some gilded party like this.

Sayer didn't come here for sisters. She came to pick these people's pockets for all they're worth. After all, she is not a star made for *if only* wishes. She's the kind of star that burns.

ÆSA'S GRANDDA USED to say she had a sheldar within her. It's an old story, whispering of a time when the windswept Illish Isles held not just fishing nets and rusted tills, but strength and a deep, resonant magic. That one day it might come back again.

They were always women, the sheldars, he would say, stringing the day's catch up by the fire to cure. *Touched by the Wellspring, they were. Witches fierce as the sea, and just as fearless.*

They shot their foes with magic-kissed arrows, her gran would add, jabbing at his fancies. *And rode bears with antlers.*

They needed no steeds, he corrected, *as they had wings.*

Æsa liked their intricately braided hair, woven with bones and sea glass wishes. She longed for their fearlessness as well.

Remember, my girl, Grandda would say when the crops died,

or the rent came due. *You have a sheldar singing through you. Just listen for her tune and have the courage to answer.*

Sometimes, when she stood on the beach, its dark blue sand sucking beneath her, she thought she heard it—a song inside, deeper than want, stronger than fear, but she isn't a sheldar. After all, she is only a girl.

Grandda died last winter, and after that Æsa heard no more stories. Her own da thinks they're just blasphemous tales. He is an abstainer and regular churchgoer, and the Church of the Eshamein—the Ones Who Drink—preaches that magic is holy, not to be grasped by mortal hands. Certainly not by women. They corrupted it once, poisoning the Wellspring from which all magic flows. That is why the church's paters once hunted the sheldars. They think they rid the world of girls with magic running through them long ago. Yet here she stands, trying not to lose her nerve.

Æsa positions herself against the wall beside a potted featherfern, relieved to be away from the Dinatris table and Oura's oppressive attentions. She still can't picture Matilde's dame and her own being friends, but they grew up in Simta together. Nothing Mam told Æsa prepared her for this raucous place. The city's full to the brim with people speaking tongues she's never heard before, having many-layered conversations that she struggles to take in. Even after a month of living with the Dinatrises, she feels overwhelmed by it, this ballroom especially. Its cream-colored marble floor twisted through with red waves is nothing like the earthen one in her family's cottage. The stain of it won't leave her feet, no matter how hard she scrubs.

Her frothy gown billows around her, its tulle the pale green blue of the ice moss that grows along cliffs back in Illan. It's more modest than most, and yet she still feels exposed by it. Mirrors fill the room, but she can't bring herself to look.

She needs to find one of her fellow Nightbirds. Surely her first ball will be less terrifying with them beside her. But they are still mostly strangers: Matilde, bright and impatient, and Sayer, all shielded eyes and sharp-edged words. Anyway, they are from Simta. They don't understand what it means to be an outsider, full of a homesickness that surges every time you take a breath. She misses her family, her wild cliffs, the familiar crash of the ocean. All she wants is to go home.

You're here now, Matilde said just days ago as she painted Æsa's nails the palest blue. *No more dirt floor and fish cakes. Why not let yourself enjoy it?*

How can she, knowing what lives inside her? That soon she will have to let it out?

She remembers the night Leta came to their cottage. Da was gone on a trip to Caggan-Way, hunting for work. The autumn fishing had been bad, and their table held little but sourcakes and a jug of swiftly turning milk. Until she came, Æsa didn't see how thin Mam was, her clothes like ill-fitting sails, hanging windless. Hungry for more than their life could give.

At first, Æsa thought Leta was one of Mam's old friends come to visit. But then why did Mam keep wringing her hands, eyes darting to the door?

In the end, the deal was simple: Æsa would have lavish room and board and an advantageous marriage into a Great House. Her family would be taken care of, their future secured.

Will she be safe? Mam asked Leta.

She will be a secret. All secrets in my care stay safe.

What must she do to give her magic to someone?
It's just a touch. Just a kiss.

Later, when Æsa asked Mam if Da knew, she said he couldn't. She would tell him that an old Simtan friend offered to sponsor their daughter, and he would take her at her word.

When Æsa asked if she had to go, Mam said yes, because she wanted better for her.

You need this, Æsa. We all need this. And we both know that you cannot stay here.

Even now, she isn't sure if she chose to go or if Mam sold her. It shouldn't matter if it means they won't ever have to struggle again.

Dancers twirl around her: an older couple, a group of girls, two young men holding each other close. It hurts her eyes, the way their clothes shift colors and move in phantom winds. She has never seen such wanton displays of magic. In his sermons back home, Pater Toth rails against such uses of magic, preaching that it's a moral duty to abstain.

Guilt stings. What would he say about *her* magic? Probably the same thing he says about vice, and the scarlet moss that grows amidst the jinny fields. *Such things must be ripped out before they spread.*

Oh, but she tried. After what happened with Enis Dale, she prayed to the Eshamein to take the magic out of her. She filled her hair with sea glass and made wishes on them all.

A man steps in close, blocking her view of the dancers. He has bronzed olive skin, like most Simtans, and is many things: very round, very red, very shiny. A sticky-looking mass of flowers hangs from his lapel.

"Good Season, Young Lady."

"A-and to you," she stammers. Is that right? Her Simtan's rough when she's nervous.

His mask gleams copper against his wine-flushed cheeks. "How fares your evening?"

She grasps for words she learned during Oura's etiquette lessons. "Favorable, I thank you."

He smiles, lips wet with grease from the plate of meat he is holding. The nearest table of food has gone mostly untouched. Such a waste.

"Is that an Illish accent I hear?" he says. "How charming. Whereabouts?"

Æsa sighs, grateful to speak about something familiar. "Adan-Way. At the edge of the Faire."

"Ah, of course."

He launches into a story she struggles to follow about his granddame's country house, with charming chimneys that smoked and a redheaded maid. And she wonders: Will he be at the Nightingale's door later tonight, demanding kisses? Asking for things it feels blasphemous to give?

His hand finds hers, his gaze too hungry. "Dance with me."

She wants to pull away, but feels frozen. "Really, I . . . would rather not."

He doesn't seem to hear her. "Come, now. You're too lovely to hide against the wall. Let the room enjoy you."

She swallows. Matilde says her beauty is an advantage, but it makes her feel like a target. Sometimes beautiful seems like a dangerous thing to be.

Someone steals her gloved hand from the shiny man's grip. Æsa exhales.

"Darling," Matilde says. "Where have you *been*? I've been desperate for you."

The man puffs out his chest, clearly affronted by the interruption.

"Young Lord Brendle," Matilde says. "Is that you?"

He lets out a braying laugh. "Not even a mask could make me look like my son, Young Lady Dinatris."

She bats at his arm. "It wipes years from you, Lord! I swear it. You had me utterly fooled."

Matilde is so elegant, all chestnut waves and sparkling amber eyes. So at home in this world—she doesn't seem afraid of anything.

The man looks back at Æsa. "And what business have you with this dazzling creature?"

"It's quite scandalous," Matilde says, smiling wickedly. "Not fit for your innocent ears."

He grumbles, but Matilde is already looping her arm through Æsa's. At the press of skin to skin above their gloves, something tingles. It's always like this when they touch: a call and response in some unknown language. Æsa assumes it's the magic within them. It makes her want to both pull close and pull away.

"That man is odious." Matilde's nose wrinkles. "More ferret than lord."

Æsa tries to answer, but her breath is a wave that won't come back to her. The room is spinning, the lights like spirits in mist.

"Air is made for breathing, darling." Matilde hands her a glass of something cool. "So breathe. And drink this."

Matilde is not one to take refusal lightly, so Æsa tips the cocktail back. It tastes of ocean spray and the cakes Mam used to make on harvest Sundays. She tries not to let a sob rise in her throat.

"You don't need to be nervous," Matilde whispers. "There's nothing in this room to fear."

But this place is full of sharks, and she is a minnow. She feels certain it will swallow her whole before the Season's done.

MATILDE SIGHS. IF Æsa's going to thrive, she needs to learn how to deal with lecherous weasels like Brendle. The trouble is that she's a terrible liar. Matilde has tried to teach her the art of deception, but she's frightened of everything, and her pale Illish skin does her no favors when it comes to hiding blushes.

"You do know this is a party, don't you?" Matilde asks. "It's meant to be enjoyed."

"I know. It's just that I have a feeling . . ."

"What kind of feeling?"

Æsa bites her lip. "That something bad is going to happen."

It's a good thing Tenny Maylon didn't choose the Nightingale the other night—in Matilde's opinion, the girl doesn't seem ready to see clients, but the first night of the Season is a time of high demand.

She pushes an errant lock of Æsa's hair behind her ear. "We're well guarded. You don't need to worry."

Æsa doesn't look convinced. "I just wish . . ."

She lets her wish hang unfinished, so Matilde casts her eyes over the crowd. Distraction is in order.

"Let's take a turn."

As they circle the room, Matilde explains who is who amongst the dancers. She doesn't point out her past clients or tell Æsa what the Goldfinch made possible for each. The lord who impersonated a business rival to discredit him in front of associates; the young lady who made herself look like a certain sailor so she could sneak her way onto a naval ship. What some do with her gift she doesn't know, and doesn't want to, truly, but she thinks it must be thrilling to wear so complete a mask.

She wouldn't know. Nightbirds can only gift their magic to others, though family lore says the women she's descended from could use it for themselves. She grew up with bedtime stories about the feats of the powerful girls they once called Fyrebirds. They sound like goddesses, parting seas and moving mountains. Tempting tales that seem too good to be true.

A House matron glides by them, leaving a trail of trickster smoke behind her.

"So much magic," Æsa whispers. "Don't any of them fear the law?"

Prohibition, she means, championed by abstainers and the church, whose paters do love to drone on about how magic is a holy thing, not to be touched.

"Leta's parties are very exclusive," Matilde says. "There aren't any abstainers or Wardens here."

For coins and favors, many of them will avert their gazes from parties like this one. None would dare break down a Great House door, anyway.

"And you don't fear them?" Æsa asks.

Matilde twirls, and the jewelflowers on her dress all snap closed. "Oh, please. If a Warden saw me in this dress, he'd only slap my wrist."

"No, I mean . . . because of the other kind."

Their intrinsic magic? Matilde smiles. "Of course not, darling. According to the church, girls like us don't exist."

Prohibition's a bore, but it's never really felt like it applied to her. Matilde finds there's something of a thrill in breaking rules.

She taps a foot. "Where has Sayer skulked off to?"

"Missing me already?"

Matilde and Æsa both jump.

"Dirty shills, Sayer," Matilde swears. "What have I told you about sneaking up on people?"

Sayer gives her a pointy smile. "It's not my fault you're easy to scare."

Her golden eyes shine out from her midnight mask, her near-black, bobbed hair slicked back in fetching waves. The new fashions suit her long, lean frame. But even in fine fabric, Matilde would know she didn't grow up in Pegasus. It's something in the way she prowls, a hungry cat.

"And what have you been up to?" Matilde asks. "Picking pockets?"

Sayer's expression doesn't change. "Only the loose ones."

Leta wouldn't tell Matilde where Sayer came from, but Dame says she has Nadja Sant Held's golden eyes. Nadja Sant Held, who it's said lost her place as a Nightbird because of some clandestine love child. Matilde would do a saucy dance for Lord Brendle if it meant gaining access to *that* secret, but Sayer's lips are closed tighter than a Farlands oyster shell.

Matilde pulls them both close.

"Let's play a game."

Sayer groans. "Not this again."

Matilde stifles a frustrated sigh. She misses being a Nightbird with Petra, Sive, and Octavia; misses the easy gossip and secrets whispered over pilfered wine. Nights with them used to sparkle, full of promise. But Petra has been busy since she got married this past winter, as have Sive and Octavia, married a few months before that. Their magic dims after a decade or so, sometimes two, which is why Nightbirds tend to marry after only a Season. From then on, they reserve their gift for their spouse. Matilde was alone until a few months ago, when Sayer came, Æsa arriving some weeks after. Sometimes it's worse than being a party of one.

"We each tell one secret," Matilde continues. "And the others have to guess if it's true."

"Fine." Sayer tilts her head, making her mask's sequins wink. "I've got a knife under my dress."

Matilde arches a brow. "I very much fear that one's true. But where in the dark depths do you hide it?"

"You said *one* secret. Now it's your turn."

Her lips start to curl—why not have fun with it? "I've developed a fancy for an alchemist's apprentice. We talk of running away into the sunset."

"False," Sayer shoots back. "You're too in love with the high life. You'd never dream of flying out of your gilded cage."

Matilde stiffens, but Sayer is all sharp corners with no desire to be blunted. She has a way of making Matilde feel weighed and judged.

"It's not a cage we're in, darling. It's a club—something I think you desperately want to belong to."

Sayer's golden eyes glimmer. "The girls at the Purple Pony are a club, too. You don't see me lining up to join it."

"Don't fight," Æsa warns. "Not here."

Matilde ignores her. "Must you say it like that?"

"Like what?"

"Like what we do is whoring."

"Well, isn't it?"

Anger flares. "You would think that, given who your dame is."

Æsa gasps. Something shoots through Sayer's eyes like a star, too fast to catch. She storms away without another word.

"Matilde," Æsa intones. "That was unkind."

Matilde tugs at one of her gloves. "Was it?"

"Her dame only passed away a few months ago."

Her cheeks flame. "Dash it, she started it."

"Still," Æsa says, gaze trailing after their fellow Nightbird. "Sayer's hurting."

How would Æsa know that? Are they having deep chats when Matilde's back is turned?

Love your sisters, Gran used to say when she and Petra argued, or Sive acted jealous, or Octavia threw a shoe. But these two, guarded and timid, don't appreciate what it means to be a Nightbird. They don't seem to want to know her at all.

She turns, looking for a diversion, and catches sight of Samson walking toward them, a friend in tow. It's Teneriffe Maylon. She knows it's him, despite his bright mask. They grew up in the same circle, playing in drawing rooms while their dames plotted social domination over brunch. But that's not why she knows him in this moment. This tingling recognition always lingers after someone comes to see the Goldfinch. For a week or more, she could find them anywhere in Simta. Her magic glows in him like a flamemoth, a light only she can see.

The boys are in front of them now, bowing. Samson smiles, swallowing Æsa with his eyes.

"Æsa, may I have the honor?"

After a moment, she nods. They swirl off, and suddenly it's just her and Tenny. He reaches for her.

"Young Lady Dinatris, will you join me?"

She's not nervous. Clients never seem to look at Matilde and see the Goldfinch. People only see the parts of her she wants them to.

"Since you asked nicely."

His hands go around her. "You look wonderful, Matilde. But then you always do dazzle."

"You look rather handsome yourself."

Tenny looks much better than he did when she kissed him a week ago. He must have used the Goldfinch's magic to advantage. What she can see of his face is flushed with drink and triumph.

"Samson tells me you've been rather lucky lately."

He puffs out his chest. "I've had a few good turns at the krellen tables. My skills are improving. I might even be able to beat you."

At krellen? Please. "A boy can dream."

She doesn't know how, but she is sure it's her magic that helped turn him so golden. And yet how easily he pretends he did it all on his own.

He pulls her in. The scents of clove smoke and the honeysuckle pinned to his lapel are overpowering.

"That's not the only thing I've been dreaming of," he says.

"Is that so?"

"My sire says it's time for me to find myself a wife, and it strikes me you would make an awfully fine one."

The way he says it, as if it's a foregone conclusion, sparks an angry heat inside her chest.

"That's a little presumptuous."

He laughs. "Ah, come now. I'm not so bad a catch."

Tenny isn't the brightest flamemoth in the lantern, but he is handsome, and from a prestigious Great House. On paper, he is as fine a match as any. But she isn't going to be anyone's pretty decoration. She is poison in the guise of something sweet.

She smiles, flashing teeth. "I'm not sure you could afford me."

He mistakes her meaning—of course he does.

"Oh, I'm sure I could keep you in style."

Over his shoulder, Matilde glimpses her dame watching them, face alight—no doubt she's already planning the reception. How she would love to see Matilde on Tenny's arm, walking toward a future full of tasteful dinners and putting someone else's wants before her own.

All at once, Matilde feels mutinous. That angry spark is now a leaping flame.

She leans in close. "I hope you've held on to your mask."

He touches his face, nonplussed. "Aren't I wearing it?"

"Not that one," she purrs. "The one you got from the gold-feathered bird."

His mouth drops open. She should stop, but the words are tumbling off her tongue.

"You wouldn't want to lose so precious a souvenir, would you? Who knows if you'll ever taste such riches again."

The song comes to an end, and she turns to leave him, pursing her lips into a shape he will remember and blowing him a kiss.

His eyes widen, recognition blooming in them.

Matilde walks away, heart pounding hard.

Did she really just reveal her secret to Tenny Maylon? She doesn't know what possessed her to let it flow. She just wanted to wipe that assured smile off his face, destroy his certainty. It did that, at least. But ten hells . . .

She grabs another cocktail and takes a deep, steadying sip. The music flows in liquid streaks around her. She knows each step the dancers will take, every gesture. Watching them move is a reassuring thing. After all, this is her world, her rules—she owns it wholly. Nothing can hurt her in this game she knows by heart.

One never forgets his first taste of a fine alchemical. It sparkles on the tongue like bubbly wine. But that is nothing compared to how it feels to kiss a Nightbird. Alchemicals are a blend of ingredients, and they require a set of human hands to craft and distil them, while a Nightbird's magic is the finest spirit drunk neat. Alchemicals fade, but those girls are bottles you can continue to drink from. One can see why they are worth such a heavy price.

—AN EXCERPT FROM THE PRIVATE PAPERS
OF LORD EDGAR ABRASIA

CHAPTER 2

MIDNIGHT VISITATIONS

MATILDE SLIPS ON her Goldfinch mask. It's like a second skin: her truest face and best lie.

It's late, and she is perched high in a mansion in the Garden District. Leta moves their location now and then to ensure no one finds the Nightbirds except through the Madam, but the room is always the same: luxe furnishings, two chairs, the feathered mask.

Anticipation flutters. Who will her client be? Young or old, man or woman, they will be from one of the Great Houses. Theirs is an exclusive, high-end club. At least she can be sure it won't be Tenny Maylon, thank the Wellspring. Leta only lets a client see a Nightbird once or twice a year. *Too much of a drug leads to addiction,* she is fond of saying. Another favorite: *Anything can be had for a price.*

What will that kiss she blew to Teneriffe Maylon cost her? It's been a few hours since Leta's party, but her nerves are still fluttering like wings, unable to settle, even as she tries to put it out of her mind. It's not as if she explicitly *said* she was a

Nightbird. Wine-fueled Tenny might not have understood . . .

And even if he did, he has no way to prove it. Surely he won't speak of it at all. He's a puppy, eager to follow the rules—the ones the Houses set up long before him.

Long ago, when the church was still hunting down witches, the strongest of them hid in what was then the small port town of Simta. A few of its families sheltered the Fyrebirds, keeping them safe from those who meant them harm. In thanks, they started gifting their magic to their protectors. Over time the practice formalized into a kind of club. Fyrebirds became Nightbirds, so called because they only work in darkness: a little inside joke.

The Houses keep the girls safe from those who might harm them. In return, they get exclusive access to their gifts. It's a system that benefits all—Tenny knows it as well as she does. Just as he knows that if he spilled, Leta would send whatever secrets he gave her flying to places he doesn't want them to go. His sire is an abstainer: Such people think it's sacrilegious to use magic for personal gain or pleasure. Tenny wouldn't risk him finding out, surely. There isn't anything for her to fear.

Matilde looks down at her locket, Gran's from when she was a Nightbird. The candles make it look like liquid gold pooled in her palm. Its contents are a secret, like so much else about her. Usually, she prides herself on how many she keeps.

Never take off your mask. A Nightbird rule. *Never let them see you.*

What would Gran think if she found out that Matilde let hers slip?

A knock comes. Two short taps and a cascade of fingertips, clicking against the door like rain. Matilde slips her locket back under her dress, clearing her thoughts.

A note is passed under the door. She picks it up and reads the name:

Lord Dennan Hain of House Vesten

Matilde's breath flies away.

Dennan Hain is at her door?

She's surprised that Leta would admit him. He is Great House born, yes, but his sister is the suzerain—the Eudean Republic's chief magistrate, and a powerful member of the Table that governs it. She is also a staunch supporter of the Prohibition, which became law some five years ago. Leta would never let Epinine Vesten see the Goldfinch, that's for certain. But Dennan isn't truly a Vesten. Most people call him the Bastard Prince.

The last time she saw Dennan Hain was three years ago, at a reception at the Winged Palace.

The last time she saw him, she made a terrible mistake.

She rushes around the room, blowing out some of the candles. The light was dim to begin with, but she wants it dimmer still. She only stops to peer into the mirror above the mantel. Her feathered mask is straight, her lips painted. The costume is complete, and yet . . .

She takes a steadying breath. She could send him away— Leta warns clients it's a Nightbird's choice whether to admit them. And yet she finds herself reaching for the door.

When it opens, she sees her little Sparrow, the girl who guides clients to her, and the hulking Hawk who guards her, faces covered. Dennan Hain is between them, wearing a dove-colored suit and a blindfold.

Matilde nods to the Sparrow. The girl pushes him forward, and suddenly it's just the two of them. The drip of wax on the mantel seems too loud in their silence, drowned out only by the sound of her heart.

She takes her time soaking him in. His finely cut suit and slicked-back hair make him look older than she remembers—but then, he is older. Taller, too. Lean and deeply tanned, he looks like the best kind of mischief. The curve of his lips holds a spark she can't quite name.

His voice is a spark, too. "May I take off the blindfold, my lady?"

Sometimes the best way to own the room is to remind a client that they're there at her pleasure. "Not yet. I like you better in the dark."

He slides his hands into his pockets. She wills her own to unclench. The Vox oil she's burning will change the timbre of her voice, making it sound like someone else's, but the true key to playing the Goldfinch is confidence. She gives her words a playful tilt.

"I suppose I should welcome you home, Lord Hain. How long has it been? Years, surely."

He tips his head, a small bow. "It's nice to be remembered."

Oh, she remembers. They used to be friends, but she's heard nothing from him in the last three years—only *of* him.

"Yes, well, stories of your exploits precede you."

"I see. And are the stories good?"

"They've certainly won you a fair number of Simtan hearts."

The stories tell of an up-and-coming sea captain, securing new trade routes with the Farlands, fighting pirates, and leading the charge in the trade wars with Teka. Bastard or no, the people consider him a member of House Vesten, whose members have served as Eudea's suzerain for so long.

But before that, Dennan was the boy she used to play with

at the edges of parties. As Marcus Vesten's son, he was always invited, but because his dame was no-one-knew-who—certainly not Marcus's wife—he was a scandal. Matilde's dame demanded she keep her distance, but that only made her want to chase him. Forbidden fruit is so much sweeter than the rest. She followed him into closets and dark corners, where they made up complicated games together. They wrote each other notes in a code only they knew.

Their connection is one of Matilde's favorite secrets. Or was, before he left without a word.

"Tell me," she says. "Is it true that you spent your days fighting pirates, or did you become one?"

"That depends on whom you ask."

She should probably make him leave on the blindfold, but she has the sudden urge to see his eyes. She used to wish she could bottle their vivid blue purple, like sweet crysthellium syrup from the Jewel Isles. Are they the same as she remembers? Is *he*?

There's only one way to find out.

"Well, then. You might as well make yourself comfortable."

He peels the blindfold off, blinking into the dimness. Even in the low light, his eyes glow.

For a few long breaths they just stand there, watching each other. She makes sure to keep her posture languid, as if this is all a lark to her. Let him think she has no real stake in this game.

"Shall we have a drink, Lord Hain? A toast to your fortunes."

He nods. "I'll have whatever you're having."

Matilde turns her back and goes to the sideboard, discreetly pulling out her locket. Once unscrewed, the top becomes a golden dropper, dispensing the alchemical liquid inside. Estra

Doole, it's called. *Deep Ease*. It makes clients calm and pliable, which is good, because they sometimes get overexcited. Magic— all magic—has an intoxicating effect. A Nightbird's gift can't be taken by force, and her Hawk is there to ensure clients don't try it, but one can never be too careful. Besides, Matilde is a collector of the clandestine, and this is often how she finds it. Estra Doole has the delicious side effect of loosening lips.

She finds herself wanting some of Dennan Hain's secrets quite badly.

Matilde watches the potion bead at the dropper's end.

Drugging clients? Sayer's voice is like church bells on an Eshamein's day, annoyingly insistent. *I hear the girls at the Purple Pony do that, too.*

Matilde silently snaps back: *This isn't a Smoky Row brothel.*

But Sayer's words from earlier haven't left: *Well, isn't it?*

Matilde pulls the dropper back from the wine she's poured them, screwing the locket closed before she can second-guess her choice.

"I must admit," Dennan says behind her. "Growing up, I thought the Nightbirds were just a flight of fancy, invented by men in their smoking rooms."

She turns. "And yet here I am, dream made flesh."

Matilde hands him the drink. This close, she can see a pale scar cutting through his lip that wasn't there before. It makes him look like a rough-cut rogue.

"What shall we toast to?"

He smiles. "My crew likes to toast to good friends, both old and new."

It takes an effort not to choke on her wine. "To friends, then."

They toast. She sits on one of the chairs, and he does likewise, swirling the contents of his glass. His hands are calloused—

a sailor's hands, no doubt hard-won on the ocean. She wonders what they would feel like on her skin.

She takes another sip. Usually she enjoys this moment, anticipation in the air, made into a thrill with playful banter. But with him, the usual script doesn't feel right.

"Tell me," he says at last. "Do you like it?"

He says it the way you might a lover's confession. It makes something quiver in her chest.

"Like what?"

"Being a Nightbird."

Truth to tell, no one has ever asked her that question. She wonders what kind of game they are playing.

"It has its moments."

"You don't mind having strangers at your door, demanding kisses?"

"No one can demand things from a Nightbird. And you and I won't be strangers for long."

A candle pops. The air seems to be getting warmer. She's good at playing silences, but his wears away at her, making her want to say something—anything.

"There just seem to be a lot of rules," he says. "That doesn't bother you?"

Matilde bristles. "They are there to protect us."

"Rules can also keep you in the dark."

Behind her mask, her cheeks flush. He is clearly trying to rile her, but why?

She makes her tone light. "As scintillating as this discussion is, we have business to attend to."

He puts his elbows on his knees. The gesture makes him look more like the boy she remembers.

"I didn't come here for a kiss."

Her breath catches. "Then what did you come for?"

The playfulness falls away. "I came to warn you about the suzerain."

His sister? She fights to keep her voice smooth, unreadable. "Go on."

"She wants to steal the Nightbirds. All of you."

That knocks Matilde speechless. Suddenly there isn't enough air in the room.

"As I'm sure you know," Dennan says, "when our sire died, Epinine became the suzerain on something of a technicality."

The suzerain is elected by the Table, the governing body that keeps the Republic running smoothly. Made up of a handful of Great House members, the suzerain, and the church's Pontifex—all men—they share power. There was a time when the suzerain ruled as monarch, but these days she is more figurehead than sovereign. That doesn't mean the position has no teeth.

"The suzerain serves for life," he continues, "and so a vote should have been called the year he died. But we were at war with Teka then, and such votes can't be called during wartime. So our sire's wish to have Epinine take his place was honored. But the summer meeting of the Table is coming, and with the peace assured, they mean to call the vote at last."

Matilde frowns. "Surely the Table will vote her in. She's a Vesten."

The position is open to any Great House member, but it has always been a Vesten. They aren't royalty, but something almost like it.

"The Pontifex supports her, and the church holds plenty of sway on the Table. But she's convinced the other Houses are going to vote against her. They've accused her of mishandling things in the war with Teka. And some of them don't like how cozy she is with the Pontifex, supporting his crusade on magic users. They think it's draining Simta's resources and only emboldening its gangs."

But would they really break with tradition and vote someone else in? It seems bold, but Matilde has eavesdropped on enough conversations in her lifetime to know the balance of power is never easy. Everyone wants a bigger slice than they have.

"Epinine wants to shore up her position before the vote is called," Dennan continues. "She wants to weaken the other Houses by taking away the thing she thinks makes them strong."

Matilde swallows. "The Nightbirds."

Dennan nods. "She says she wants to hold you hostage until the vote is over, to ensure it goes her way. But I think she's just as likely to hand you over to the Pontifex. It would cement their favor and her commitment to the Prohibitionist cause."

But Epinine must know what the church paters once did to girls with magic inside them. Those stories, true or not, give Matilde nightmares even now.

His words ripple through her: *She says*. How would he know about her plans unless she told him?

She stands, taking a few steps back. "Is that why you're here? You want to collect us for her, like spices from some foreign port?"

"Of course not." Frustration ruffles his features. "I want to save you from her."

Matilde prides herself on being able to read people. It is why, when she plays games, she always wins. But there is too much in Dennan's eyes to sift through. Fixed on her, they burn blue, like the heart of a flame.

"Why bring this to me? Why not just tell Madam Crow?"

He lets out a rough breath.

"Because I didn't think she would trust my good intentions."

"And you thought I would?" After all, he has given her no proof of what he claims. "Epinine is your sister."

"Why would I make up such a story about a member of my own House? What would I stand to gain?"

She doesn't know, but that doesn't mean she should believe him.

"I want to be your ally," Dennan says, "but you would have to trust me."

She tilts her chin up.

"Trust is something to be earned."

His voice is soft. "I like to think I earned it long ago, after you kissed me and I never told a soul."

Her heart is in her throat. He knows. Ten hells, he *knows*.

She was fourteen when she kissed him—not yet a Nightbird, but she knew about the magic that ran in the Dinatris blood. She felt it stirring, a restless warmth beneath her skin. When he dared her to kiss him at that party, she didn't want to back down. She thought she understood how to keep the magic in, but she didn't. It spilled from her lips and onto his.

Later, she convinced herself she imagined it. Some truths, buried deep, will break down and disappear. Clearly she was wrong, but she won't admit it—can't admit it. She has risked too much tonight as it is.

"I don't know what you mean," she says. "You must be confusing me with someone else."

He stands.

"We played together in shadows deeper than these, Matilde. I would know you anywhere."

Her true name on his lips is like an incantation, freezing her in place. He steps closer, until she can feel his breath against her neck.

"You trusted me once," he says. "But I know that there's only one way to prove you still can. It's to walk away with your secret and continue to keep it. When you're ready to talk, this is where I will be."

Something is pressed into her palm: a calling card, with an address in Dragon Quarter. Then he turns away, toward the door. Matilde feels like the ground has gone soft beneath her. She needs a way to make it solid again.

"Lord Hain."

He turns. She points to her lips.

"Haven't you forgotten something?"

The comment was meant to throw him off-balance, but as he closes their distance, her thoughts become a cloud of frantic birds.

"I'd love nothing more." He takes her hand and brushes his lips against it. "But I would rather you kiss me of your own free will. And as yourself."

His blindfold goes back on and he's gone, leaving her dizzier than the wine did, and with the taste of danger on her tongue.

She should call for her Hawk, or go get Leta, or . . . something. But what would she say? *I've spilled our secret to not one but two boys, alas?* Unfathomable. Just like what Dennan told her about Epinine Vesten. What to make of what he said—what to *do*?

Minutes pass. She turns toward the fireplace. Her hands have started tingling, and she has the sudden feeling that she has forgotten something important. Then she thinks she hears a muffled cry behind the wall. She strains her ears, but no . . . There's nothing but the dripping of her candles. Dread blooms deep inside her just the same.

Something is wrong.

SAYER'S PTARMIGAN DRESS is a black tulle monstrosity. The dark, starry sheath from the ball is gone, replaced by a thing her Sparrow had to cinch her into. How is she supposed to move in this? Leta says pageantry is part of the deception, but the whole thing sets her teeth on edge.

Worse, the mask smells of the girl who wore it before her. Its feathers have held on to the cloying scent of her perfume.

She has seen a few clients in the past few weeks—an ancient lord who didn't say one word during their entire exchange, a chatty woman whose lipstick tasted unpleasantly of roses—so this evening's events aren't anything new. Still, she has to fight the urge to prowl the room, palms sweating. She thought after the first few times, being a Nightbird would get easier. Instead it only seems to get worse. She hates that she's giving any part of herself to these people. She hates how good using her magic feels. *It's like slipping into a hot bath on a cold day* is how Dame once described the feeling. Sayer thinks it's more like popping a blister: a sick sort of relief. It makes her stomach twist, imagining her dame in the mask, smiling sweetly. Her doomed affair with Sayer's sire started in a room just like this.

Nadja Sant Held was always full of sunny descriptions of Wyllo Regnis, the young lord she fell hopelessly in love with. She had to describe him, as Sayer still has no idea what he looks like. It's not as if he ever came to call. But Nadja would never tell Sayer the full story of what happened—how a Nightbird ended up in a dusty apartment in Griffin's. She suspected her dame preferred the stories she conjured for herself. Sayer stopped caring if her sire showed up—she wants nothing to do with him—but Dame believed he would come and make things right between them. He never did, but other men came in his stead.

Sayer discovered this when she was thirteen, fresh back from one of her first shifts at Twice Lit, and she heard noises coming from the back bedroom. She crept through the dim light, hid behind a curtain, and watched as a posh-looking man kissed her dame against the wall.

Little dove, he said, eyes glazed. *Nothing tastes as sweet as you do.*

Before he left, he put a satchel of money on a table. It took her days to understand what it was for. Sayer never asked, but she knew he had come for the last dregs of Dame's magic. And she had let him take it, time and again. That's why Sayer was so resistant to becoming a Nightbird. She vowed long ago never to make the same mistakes.

And yet you're here, she thinks. Matilde's irritating words from the ballroom float back to her. *It's a club. Something I think you desperately want to belong to.* But she has no interest in getting tangled up with anyone. She doesn't plan on marrying any of these puffed-up peacocks, and she didn't come here to make nice with her sire. She's here to take her clients' money, then walk away, perhaps out of Simta entirely. She can see herself in the river-wrapped city of Sarask or one of the mountain towns of Thirsk, renting some quaint stone cottage. Perhaps set up her own coffee shop. She imagines herself in a kitchen, warm and smelling of starcakes, someone's hand wiping a streak of flour off her cheek. The person smiles at her around a dark green eyepatch. It's Fenlin Brae, and suddenly she's leaning closer . . .

A soft knock shakes her from her thoughts. A note appears under the door, glowing against the dark carpet.

Lord Robin Alewhin of House Rochet

The name is a stranger's. But then, aren't they all?

She wipes her hands on the dress, remembering the mantra Fen taught her during one of their sparring lessons. *Smile on your face, knife at your back.*

The door opens, revealing a blindfolded man about her height. With a head of dark hair and olive skin, he could be almost any man in Simta. She notices he isn't smiling.

She can see her Hawk in his beaked mask in the shadows, looking thuggish. It would be so much better to have a friend from Griffin's standing there—someone she trusts. She thinks of Fenlin Brae's wild flame of hair, her sharp humor, her lithe and brutal grace. Suddenly Sayer misses her so fiercely that she's breathless with it. Guilt stabs: She didn't even say goodbye to Fen . . . but now is not a time for thoughts like that.

She makes herself smile, though the client can't see it. Dame always said you can hear a smile in someone's voice: a pretty lie.

"Welcome, Lord Alewhin."

She sizes him up. A girl from Griffin's has to know how to tell a fool from an actual threat. He's thin, and sinewy as a sailor. He stands motionless in his suit, but something about him feels restless, a kettle simmering close to a boil.

The client's pushed into the room, and the door closes. A corner of his mouth ticks. "May I take off the blindfold?"

Matilde thinks she doesn't listen during their informal Nightbird lessons, but Sayer hears her. *That room is your world. It's best to quickly let them know it.*

"In a moment." Sayer goes to the sideboard and takes a

liberal sip of Illish whiskey out of the crystal decanter, burning with the taste of brine and smoke. "Now you may."

His eyes are the brown of weak coffee, and his eyebrows look like they were recently shaved.

"What happens next?" he asks, hands stiff at his sides. "I confess I'm not quite clear on the particulars."

Sayer gestures to one of the armchairs. "You can start by taking a seat."

As he sits, the dim light draws sharp lines across his features. He smells of something earthy, like the jawbone algae in Simta's canals, but charred.

"Would you like a drink?"

"No," he says, teeth clenched. "I thank you."

It seems he wants this transaction over with. Happily, so does she.

"For the magic to work, you need a way to call to it," she says, picking up a gauzy grey mask on the mantel. "When you're ready to call it up, just put this on."

She holds the mask out, but he only grips the arms of his chair.

She tries not to sound annoyed. "You'll need to wear it when we kiss."

He frowns. "Kiss?"

Blazing cats, did Leta tell him nothing? "Never you fear. I won't bite."

He puts on the mask and clamps his eyes shut. She thinks about taking another swig of whiskey, but instead she goes to stand in front of him. You're supposed to close your eyes for a kiss, she supposes, but she could never trust a man who would pay for one. So as she bends down, she keeps them open. That is why she sees the metal flash.

She leaps back, but her dashed dress is tangled up around her legs. She stumbles. The man stands fast and spins, one arm cinching tight around her ribs.

"Scream," he snarls, pressing a knife to her throat, "and I will snuff you out."

She fights against his hold. Blazing cats, he's strong. She just needs to make some noise, knock something over, but it's hard to breathe and her feathered mask makes everything a shadowed blur.

"Your guard can't help you," he whispers. "I've made sure of it."

A moment later, she hears something heavy hit the floor out in the hallway. Her Hawk—it must be.

The client pulls a vial from his coat.

"Drink this," he says, "and no one else will get hurt."

She struggles as he unstoppers the vial, its contents smelling like pond scum, and tries to press it to her lips. Panic fills her, but Fen's voice breaks through with her advice about fights: *Be unpredictable.* Swift as lightning, she brings her heel down on his foot. He stumbles but recovers quickly, grabbing for her arm as she lunges for the door. She spins, but her dress is a snare they both get caught in. They fall to the rug, twisting and grappling. There's a crunch as someone rolls over the vial.

Lord Alewhin—if that's even his name—must have dropped his knife because both hands are on her now, choking. His hot breath is on her face, and she has little of her own. The dress hitches up around her thighs as she bucks beneath him. For a wild moment, she wants to laugh: *If you came for a courtesan who takes her clothes off, you're in the wrong place.* But that can't be what he wants, because he's holding her like he can barely stand to touch her. It's the only reason she can still breathe at all.

"Get off me," she croaks, straining for her knife. It's strapped to her thigh, trapped under feathers. If she can just get her hand down a few inches more . . .

"You are proof," he whispers, "that witches live amongst us. The kind who will poison the world if we let you. For bringing you in, I will be rewarded."

Bring her in to who? She doesn't know, but it's clear he means to hurt her. Something's building in her chest, tasting of storms.

His spit hits her cheek. "Sant catchta aelit duo catchen ta weld."

She strains, but she has no breath left to shout. No one is coming to save her. She's going to die at some man's whim after all.

The door to the hidden passage that connects the Night-birds' rooms bursts open. Matilde tumbles through it. When she sees them, she screams.

The client's head whips around, hands loosening for just a second. It's long enough for Sayer to pull her knife out of its sheath. She swings it up and into his arm. He tumbles off her, shouting obscenities. Sayer grips the bloody knife and stands up.

"Move and I'll slice you where it counts," she growls.

He goes to lunge for her, but someone else keeps him back—Matilde, brandishing a fireplace poker. Surprise flashes through Sayer to hear such rage when she speaks.

"Don't you dare."

The main door into the room flies open and a Hawk is there—not hers—grabbing the client roughly. They wrestle briefly, but the wound in his arm seems to have doused some of his fire. In the struggle his jacket is ripped away, exposing some of his chest. Dark lines are etched there, a tattoo made up of an oblong diamond framing a sword on fire. It feels familiar, but she can't quite place it.

Matilde nudges her. She is still clutching the poker like a sailor about to harpoon an octopus. "Please tell me you didn't start it."

Sayer wipes her knife on her dress. "No, he did. I just made him bleed a little."

The Hawk has the client now, hands pinned behind him. Something wet is coating Sayer's hand, dripping onto the carpet. It's his blood, she thinks, but who knows . . . It could be hers.

She steps toward him, voice low but clear. "Who sent you?"

"I do Marren's work," the client gasps. "He gave me my mission. And where I failed, know that my brothers will not."

What had he said before? *Sant catchta aelit duo catchen ta weld*. They're the words paters use at the beginning of a candle prayer. *A cleansing fire to cleanse the world*. Cleanse it of what?

"And what is that mission?"

He smiles, but his eyes are far away. "To wipe your kind from the earth."

Something crunches. Black blood spills over the man's lips. Ten hells, Sayer almost kissed them.

The Hawk swears, trying to hold him as he shakes. "He ate a glass bead."

She's heard stories of glass beads: Soldiers hold them in their mouths and break them if they're captured. Better to die by poison than be tortured and shamed. Why would he want to die here, rather than be questioned? What is he hiding?

She grabs him by his lapels.

"Who sent you? Tell me. *Tell* me."

Black spit hits her neck, burning hot. "Soon enough, you will see."

She backs away as the Hawk lays the client down. They watch, frozen, as the light fades from his eyes.

She is from Griffin's: She's seen people stabbed, and dead bodies besides. But none of them ever tried to drug and abduct her. She shudders.

Matilde's face, still masked, is turned toward Sayer. Sayer is glad the girl can't see her eyes through the mesh.

Matilde touches her arm. "Did he hurt you?"

Something whispers through Sayer. Her skin tingles, tongue tasting of lightning. Between them she feels a strange sort of charge.

She pulls away, fast, and the feeling fades. "I'm fine. Though this isn't exactly how I thought I'd spend my evening."

"I'll bet." Matilde shakes her head a little. "Me either."

Sayer rubs at her neck, trying not to look at the client. Her eyes land on his palm, shiny with an old burn. "How did you know I was being attacked?"

The Goldfinch's room is in the opposite corner of the house: Surely she couldn't have heard them.

Matilde is looking down at the hand she just had on Sayer's arm. "I suppose I had a feeling."

Sayer frowns. "What do you mean, 'a feeling'?"

But then she gets one of her own. It's a tight, frantic fist around her heart. What's going on? Her thoughts are so jumbled.

Matilde gasps, spinning toward the back wall.

"Where is Æsa?"

ÆSA STANDS BY the window, gulping down air. In, out, but the fear still won't leave her. She pushes the window wider, its rose-tinted glass turned almost purple by the moonlight, and tries to peer through to the port. She can see the ocean twinkling in the distance, but she cannot smell it. Simta's city scents smother all else.

She never realized how constant the sound of the sea was in her life until she came here. Her home is a harsh place, but she knows its rhythms, its many moods and quietest cries. She belongs there.

Her client will arrive soon—her first as a Nightbird. She is already wearing the dark wig Leta picked to disguise her distinctive red-gold hair. All she needs is to fit the feathered mask to her face and she will be the Nightingale, a code name chosen for the way that bird's beautiful song entrances its audience. Though her magic is less about charming people and more about controlling how they feel. She shivers to think about what a client might do with such power, though she doesn't have to imagine—she has seen it. A tide of guilt rises swiftly in her chest.

The first time she kissed Enis Dale behind his da's drying shed, she didn't know about the magic. Her mam never said it ran in their family's blood. She remembers the feel of it leaving her lips like breath on a cold morning, soft and silent. It felt better than she thought a clandestine kiss probably should.

Did you feel it? he whispered after, breaths ragged.

Feel what?

It was like a wave coursing between us. A rush.

He looked drunk, or awed, and it made her feel as powerful as one of the sheldar. So she pulled him in and kissed him again.

Later, she told Mam about the kiss, thinking of how Pater Toth always preached that lying made the crops go bad. She told her about the feeling it gave her. Mam told her that Pater Toth wasn't to know, or her da. Æsa was ashamed of her wantonness, swore she wouldn't give in to it. But then Enis sought her out again. *Inger gave me his best horse,* he said, eyes fever bright. *I made him want to give it to me. Magic, Æsa. And I think it came from you.*

He kissed her again, and gods help her, she let him. The magic spilled from her, eager and flushed. Their kiss fed something inside her—a hunger. A hollow ache she still can't name but knows to fear.

She reaches up to touch one of the sea glass wishes braided into her hair where no one will see. Would her magic have lain dormant or gone away if she hadn't given in to temptation? Could she have changed her future if she'd prayed more and hungered less?

It doesn't matter. She's here now, and it's where Mam wants her. She goes to the mask on the mantel and tells herself to pick it up. But such magic is meant for the Wellspring and the four gods, not country girls. She thinks again of Pater Toth's sermons: *In mortal hands magic turns into a vice, and then a poison.* Mam wouldn't have sent her here if that were true, surely. But still she wonders: Is it wrong, to be a Nightbird? Will giving this magic away corrupt her soul or someone else's?

There is a soft creak behind her. She turns to see the rose-glass window swinging wide. Her skin prickles as someone climbs through the opening. She jumps, ready to shout, but then the intruder looks up.

She gasps. "Enis?"

His smile is wide. "Æsa. At last."

He looks the same as when she left him: dark red hair, pale cheeks made ruddy by sea winds. A piece of home.

She throws her arms around him, her relief so thick it's hard to speak. He holds her close, pulling the wig from her, fingers sliding through her hair.

"I can't believe it," she says. "How did you find me?"

"I had to find you."

Something in his voice makes her pull back. "But how, Enis?"

His eyes are the same blue, but deep shadows pool beneath them.

"I worried for you. Your mam said you sailed to Simta to stay with some relative, but I knew you wouldn't leave me. Not when we belong together."

Her breath catches. There was a time when she would have relished these words from him, but all she feels in this moment is dread.

"I couldn't sleep, after they took you. Couldn't eat." Enis strokes her arm, her hair, like he can't get enough of her, but his eyes don't quite seem to see her at all. "Since our kisses, I've felt this pull toward you. A mooring rope the Wellspring tied between my ribs and yours. I bought passage to Simta and I wandered, following that pull until I found you. When I passed beneath this window, I knew. So I climbed."

Matilde has said that Nightbirds feel a connection to their clients for a time, after the kiss, but she never said anything about this.

"I don't understand."

"Don't you see? The gods mean for us to be together, Æsa. I know it. I *know*."

He smiles again, but this time she sees something manic in it.

"Someone will come any minute," she says. "You can't be here when they do."

But he doesn't seem to hear her. Just draws her close, rough in his haste.

"Let them try to take you from me."

He starts pulling at her Nightingale gown. At first, she thinks he is just trying to hold her, but his urgency feels dangerous and dark.

"Enis." He is her friend—this isn't like him. "Stop it."

But he doesn't and she freezes, too terrified to break away.

His lips seek hers. Something rises in her chest, cool and crashing. It frees her voice. At last, she cries out.

The door flies open and her Hawk is knocking Enis sideways. He is much bigger than her friend, but Enis fights like a half-crazed dog. They roll across the room, tumbling a vase, a chair. Æsa presses herself down next to the fireplace, eyes screwed shut. There's the sound of fists on flesh, then a crumpling. She wishes she were truly a bird so she could fly away.

Someone crouches before her, slow and quiet. She hears his breath catch as if in surprise or pain. Her eyes open, but she can't bring herself to look up at her Hawk, the boy tasked with protecting the Nightingale. Her shadow, though she doesn't know his face or name.

He doesn't touch her—it's forbidden.

Instead he says, "Kilventra ei'ish?"

The words are Illish, their meaning as many-layered as the sea. On the surface, it means *are you well, friend?* But his twist on the word—*ventra*, not *ventris*—makes it into something dearer. *Are you well, heart in mine?* That is what he just asked her.

She looks up. His mask is gone, revealing brown skin and eyes the blue-green-grey of Illan's coastline. In the dark, they almost seem to shine. They are wide, as if he's as surprised by what he just said as she is.

It strikes her, all at once, that both their faces are uncovered. This is a rule they aren't supposed to break.

"I'm sorry, lass," he says in flawless Illish. "I don't know how he got past me."

She looks to Enis, sprawled and still on the floor. "He came through the window."

The Hawk frowns. "I'll give him points for bravery, at least."

He leans forward, just slightly.

"Did he hurt you?"

She shakes her head. Her lips won't stop trembling.

"Don't worry. I'll take him down to the Madam. She'll sort it out."

She grabs his hand—another rule shattered, but Æsa has lost too much of home already.

"You can't."

The Hawk frowns. "Why not?"

"Because it's not his fault," she blurts. "It's mine."

The Hawk frowns. For a moment he just stares, like he is trying to read the depths of her. Then there's a noise behind one wall that sounds like footsteps, growing closer. He reaches for her mask where it's fallen to the floor.

"Put this on, quickly."

She ties it on with shaking fingers as he straps on his own.

Sayer and Matilde burst through the hidden door, both holding pointy objects.

"Dash it," Matilde pants, looking between the Hawk and Enis on the rug. "What happened?"

Æsa can't think. She has never seen the other girls with their masks on. The mesh makes their eyes into strange, dark pits.

"All's well," the Hawk says smoothly. "Her client got over-excited, is all."

The lie is well told, but she doesn't know how they're going to keep it. Any second her real client's going to come to the door.

"He attacked you?" Sayer says, pulling Æsa to her feet.

Panic floods. "No . . . well, yes, a little. But—"

"Two attacks in one night," Sayer interrupts. "That can't be an accident."

Matilde pokes Enis's foot with what appears to be . . . a fireplace spit? "This one doesn't look like a zealous pater, but I suppose—"

Æsa's hands become fists. "Will you two *listen?*"

Both girls fall silent.

"He isn't my client. He's my friend from back home."

There are noises in the hall. Æsa takes a shaky breath.

"I need you to help me hide him."

The masks shroud their expressions, but she can almost feel their shock.

Matilde starts to speak, but Æsa cuts her off.

"Questions later. Please just help me. *Please.*"

There is a beat, and then her Hawk goes toward the door. Her heart sinks. But then he makes a gesture with his left hand: fingers curling like waves, thumb pressed down against them. Illish sailors use such symbols when the wind is too high to talk. It means *we sail for home*. It means *trust me*.

"I'll deal with them," he says, pointing toward the outer hall. "Put him in the secret passage. Make sure to tie and gag him."

He slips out of the room. For a moment, all is silence. Æsa's heart is pounding hard enough to break a rib.

Sayer rushes forward. "Matilde, grab an arm. Æsa, grab some linens and the door."

She pulls down the thin curtain from the window. Her fellow Nightbirds drag her friend across the floor. Even unconscious, Enis has a worried wrinkle fixed between his brows.

"Honestly," Matilde grunts. "How can one redhead be this heavy?"

Sayer scowls. "Blazing cats, you're barely pulling him at *all*."

Once they have him in the narrow, hidden hall, they use what little light there is to bind and gag him. They've barely closed the secret door when Leta comes into the room. Even with her Madam Crow mask on, Æsa can tell she is livid.

"Here you are. All right, ladies?"

Æsa thinks she nods, but her thoughts have gone fuzzy.

"Stay here," Leta says. "I'll return shortly."

As she leaves, Æsa slides down the wall and to the plush carpet. Sayer tilts her mask back and sits down beside her. Her hands are stained, streaked red and black.

Æsa sucks in a breath. "Is that . . . blood?"

Sayer nods, clutching her knife. "Probably."

Matilde sits on Æsa's other side, mask off, wine decanter in hand. With both girls so close, she feels that tingling sensation she always does when they touch. They're like birds on a line, something inside them each calling to the others. And yet it doesn't make her feel any safer than before.

"Well," Matilde says, voice just slightly shaky. "That was an adventure. I think we could all use a fortifying drink."

Æsa takes a huge swig, coughing at the sudden burn. It's not wine—it's Illish whiskey.

"The redhead in the passage," Matilde says, taking back the bottle. "Are we sure letting him go is a good idea?"

"My Hawk will take care of him," Æsa says, hoping it's true. "Enis isn't a threat to us. Like I said, he is my friend."

"Friends don't grope friends," Sayer grumbles, pointing at Æsa's torn bodice.

Æsa reddens. "I know, but . . . he wasn't himself."

Both girls are looking at her, expectant. Her throat has gone uncomfortably tight. They aren't really her friends, and yet they just helped her without question. She owes them something. But when they ask her how Enis knew where she would be, Æsa lies. She says they have been sending each other letters, and in a moment of homesickness she told him where to find the Nightingale. *Don't tell Leta,* she pleads. She will send Æsa home, and her family needs her to stay here. It feels wrong to deceive them, but it is safer than the truth.

I couldn't sleep, after they took you, Enis said. *Couldn't eat.* It wasn't love that drove him. All those kisses back in Illan— her magic—did something to him. She saw it in the way he looked at her, eyes glazed like the men she's seen stumbling out of the Hollow Tree Inn. Empty of soul, full of nothing but want. An addiction.

Her kisses might be poisonous after all.

IN A SECRET room in Phoenix Quarter, candles flicker. They lean toward Eli where he kneels on the floor. Eli hasn't spent much time in churches—until a few weeks ago, he spent most of his nights sleeping under stairwells, hoping not to get chased away. But then a pater came and gave him a bed, hot meals, and a purpose. The one that's brought him here tonight.

His eyes are level with the old stone altar. Two other boys kneel there too. Soon they will wear grey, like the men standing around them. It's the color of the ashes from a fire that once burned hot.

The chanting begins, deep and rhythmic. Eli shivers hard, but not with cold. He can only hope he is found worthy. He's never wanted anything as badly as he wants to be En Caska Dae. The Caska aren't like other paters he's met, all velvet robes and empty promises. They aren't afraid to fight for what is right.

A man in grey steps forward, out of shadow. His head and eyebrows are shaved, just like the rest, but his face is shiny with scars. Eli stares at the blood-colored handprint stretched across his cheek like war paint. The Red Hand is the reason he's come here. He is their general in the war against sin.

He spreads his arms. "Eshamein Marren, we make of these boys an offering."

The Red Hand's voice reminds him of the ocean, which Eli sees often as he combs the muddy pylons of the port at low tide for scraps to sell. It's cleaner, that voice, but just as powerful. It pulls as surely as a current on the shore.

"Give them the light of your flaming sword. Accept their pledge."

The Red Hand cuts his palm. Blood wells and is caught in a wooden goblet. Once they've all been cut and bled, he pours the fluid over the altar, where it drips down the stone. A sacrifice to their god.

"We have let the Wellspring's gifts be abused for too long," the Hand rumbles. "We have allowed the people to flout Prohibition, using what's meant only for the gods. And what has it brought us? Corruption. Our once-great city made a den of vice and sin."

Eli's fists clench. He knows the kind of damage bootleg magic can do. It killed his dame. Not that the sandpiper who sold it to her cared. Those who run this city don't, either. They take and take, never caring about those who live below them. But the Red Hand sees—he understands.

"What's worse, we have let witches rise again," the Hand says. "Our complacency has left a crack for such evil to slither through."

Eli shivers again. *Witches.* Girls who've stolen magic from the Wellspring, a holy thing that isn't meant to be theirs. The Red Hand says they hide in plain sight, looking as innocent as any other girl in Simta, but they are dangerous. Poisonous. Eli won't let himself be fooled.

"They are a wound, and we cannot let it fester. We must be the ones to rinse it clean."

The Red Hand closes his eyes, facing the altar.

"Marren, you once gave your life to banish witches.

Now these boys offer themselves as your soldiers in the fight against this rising tide. But first, they will prove their devotion."

Eli is the first to stand—he makes sure of it. He holds his palm over the Red Hand's flame. The men around him chant as his skin crackles. It hurts even more than the tattoo they inked into his chest, but he won't pull away. Not with the Red Hand's eyes on him, burning so bright.

"Will you cleanse this city of blasphemers?" he asks them.

Eli repeats the words as a statement—a promise. Together, they all recite Marren's prayer.

We light Marren's candle
and kindle his sword,
flames chasing shadows,
burning darkness away.
We make a fire,
a mighty fire,
a cleansing fire to cleanse the world.

CHAPTER 3

TRUTH OR LIE

T HE FIRE IN Leta's inner room is stifling. Matilde usually finds it a neat trick, the way she keeps it hot enough to ensure everyone's a little bit uncomfortable, making them more likely to spill truths. This morning, though, she has too much to hide to appreciate it.

Everyone is here: the Nightbirds perched together on a chaise, her dame and gran behind a painted screen, and Leta behind her desk, facing down their Hawks and Sparrows. Everyone is wearing their masks. She can't see their eyes, but she imagines they're as red-rimmed as hers are. After last night's excitement, she didn't sleep a wink.

Matilde reaches for more coffee as her Hawk makes his report. He is brief and brusque, as always. He's been with her for years, but she knows little of him outside his fondness for heathermints. Sayer's Hawk can't report, as whatever that horrid client managed to slip him knocked him out for most of the night and this morning, so Æsa's tall Hawk steps forward. Matilde is eager to hear what lie he'll spin.

His story is straightforward: He was waiting for the client to arrive when he heard a sound of distress from the Nightingale's room, so he entered. She was nervous about the evening, and he tried to calm her down. Then the Goldfinch and the Ptarmigan came in saying something about intruders, and he went to investigate. He's a much better liar than Æsa—smooth, unhurried. Not one word about the redhead they stashed behind the wall. Who knows what the Hawk did with him. He seems loyal to his Nightbird, at least—more so than to Leta, which is noteworthy. Æsa's tension as he speaks, hands bunched in her skirts, makes Matilde suspect there's more to the story than either of them have said. Æsa's broken the rules—that much is certain. But it's not as if Matilde can throw stones.

After last night's events, the kiss she blew to Tenny Maylon seems like a trifle, and yet it isn't settling well. What would happen if she told her family what she did? At best, they would be disappointed. At worst, Dame might try to use her boldness as a way to make her marry him . . .

She shakes off the thought as the Hawks and Sparrows file out, closing the door behind them. Her dame steps out from behind the folding screen.

"Any of them could have been involved," she says. "We should dismiss them all and get new ones."

"They are loyal," Leta says. "I've made sure of it. Do you imagine such a flock is easy to replace?"

Leta takes off her Crow mask. She is stunning still, with bronzed skin, shining brown curls and the sweet face of a doll, though no one who knows her would dare think she's safe to play with. Matilde's heard she was born not a Great House girl but a dockworker's daughter: the product, perhaps, of some House girl's wild youth. It isn't common for a Nightbird to crop up outside the Houses, but it happens. She's also heard that Leta once worked in a Smoky Row pleasure house, but it's hard to believe that rumor could be true.

Gran sits in a chair near the fire. "Even so, Leta. What happened last night was deeply troubling."

It also makes no sense. There has always been a madam tasked with protecting the Nightbirds, but Leta is particularly fastidious. She's the one who introduced strict limits on how often a person can visit a Nightbird, despite continued protests from the House lords and ladies. She's the reason the Nightbirds change locations and why clients come to see them blind. Madam Crow *loves* her rules, and she guards them fiercely. So how did such snakes find their way into her nest?

"An attack on a Nightbird," her dame spits. "It's inexcusable."

Leta's expression hardens. "Lord Alewhin was Great House born, some country cousin of House Rochet. He had his sigil ring, and I had no reason to suspect him. These are the rules the Houses set."

"You're supposed to protect them. How could you have let this happen?"

"What I want to know," Gran interjects, "is why the man did what he did."

Sayer rips off her mask and stands up, stalking the purple rug's edges. She doesn't seem to like to sit still.

"He was a pater," she says. "He must have been. His eyebrows looked like they'd been shaved recently, and he kept speaking of Marren."

Leta nods. "The tattoo on his chest looks very much like a

piece of the four-pointed star of the Eshamein. The one with Marren's symbol."

Sayer stops pacing. "I knew I recognized it. The flaming sword."

Matilde has never been fond of the Eshamein, who form the cornerstone of Eudea's official religion, but Marren is by far the most odious. Long ago, preach the paters, four men were given magic from the Wellspring to accomplish miracles before they died, becoming gods. Marren used a flaming sword to burn the magic out of witches. Such girls poisoned the Wellspring, apparently. What flotsam. Any excuse to bring a strong woman down.

Æsa frowns. "But the paters don't mark themselves with ink. Pater Toth always says it taints the blood."

Matilde scoffs. "And anyway, he was House Rochet. Surely no House boy would spout that kind of fire and brimstone. He knows better."

After all, the Houses have always protected the Nightbirds. There may be some abstainers amongst them, but they would never hurt one of their own.

"He was a zealot, for certain," Leta says. "But it's hard to say if he was acting alone or under orders. Unfortunately, dead men tell no tales."

Before last night, Matilde had only seen a dead body once, when her sire went to the waters. But where his face was placid in death, that client's was all malevolence, cheeks speckled with black spit and froth. She shudders. Beside her, Æsa does the same.

"He clearly didn't want to kill her," Gran muses, "which means he wanted something from her."

Sayer is staring into the fire, her golden eyes bright.

"He wanted to take me somewhere," she says. "He said I was proof of witches, and that he would be rewarded for bringing me in."

Leta's expression tightens. "Did he say to whom? The Pontifex?"

"No, but he tried to drug me."

She looks . . . not scared. Perhaps haunted. Matilde finds herself wanting to lighten the mood.

"It's a good thing you were armed," she says. "And that I'm so very good with a poker."

Dame makes a scandalized noise, but the comment provokes a small grin from Sayer.

"I'm not convinced you knew what you were doing with it."

It isn't a thank-you, but Matilde will take what she can get.

Leta gives them a pointed look. "How is it that you knew something was wrong in Sayer's room, Matilde?"

Matilde fights the urge to fidget. "I heard a noise."

"Your Hawk didn't hear it."

"Perhaps his mind was on other things. I don't know."

She isn't about to tell them all *I had a tingly feeling*. Not when even she doesn't know what it was. It was as if Sayer's distress made something rise inside her, charged with an echo of the fizzing sensation she gets when she touches either of these girls. It's puzzling: She never felt this with her past Nightbird sisters, and they were her friends, unlike these two.

Leta drums her dark-painted nails on the desk. "I will be questioning the head of House Rochet, but I would be surprised if he knows anything useful. And I will be getting some eyes and ears into the halls of Augustain's. If the Pontifex did send that man, the danger could be greater than we think."

Sayer and Æsa both stiffen, and no wonder. Every Nightbird hears the stories of what the church did to the Fyrebirds of old. Their zealous persecution is why there are so few girls with magic in them now. What would happen if the Pontifex and his Brethren found out about the Nightbirds? Would they start pulling House girls in for inquisition one by one?

Matilde banishes the thought. The man was probably a rogue—an anomaly.

"He didn't succeed, at any rate," she says, crossing her legs at the ankle. "And whoever sent him can't know our true identities, or else they would've come for us directly."

"True." Gran stacks her hands in her lap. "Are we sure none of the other clients were involved?"

"Æsa's seemed oblivious," Leta says. "And as her Hawk said, the client never reached the Nightingale's door."

Matilde looks to Sayer, who is looking at Æsa, whose gaze is fixed on the mask in her lap. Surely if the boy they helped her hide was a threat, she would say so? She seems determined to keep her redhead friend a secret. Matilde wants to trust Æsa, so for now, so will she.

"And what of Matilde's client?" Dame asks.

Leta's expression is hard to read. "By the time of the commotion, he'd been and gone already."

Gran's gaze sharpens. "Who was he?"

For a moment, it looks like Leta isn't going to answer, but Matilde knows this isn't a secret she can keep.

She puts down her coffee. "Dennan Hain came to see the Goldfinch. He's back in town, didn't you know?"

Teacups clatter. The silence that follows hangs, thick enough that she could slice and serve it alongside the cake no one has touched.

Her dame speaks first. "Am I to understand that you let the Bastard Prince see my daughter?"

"He is Great House born," Leta says. "It's his right to ask for access."

"But he's a *Vesten*. You know their stance on magic."

"He is not the suzerain. Matilde could have turned him away, had she wished."

Her dame's gaze swings back to Matilde. "What were you thinking?"

Annoyance flares. "I thought you wanted me married. Isn't the Goldfinch meant to be showing off her wares?"

"Not to him," she says, aghast. "He isn't even a true Vesten."

"Oura," Gran warns. "What's done is done."

Her words defend Matilde, but the censure in her gaze speaks volumes. *You should never have let him through the door.* Gran knows: Matilde confided in her all those years ago about kissing Dennan. When he disappeared, Gran told her to put it out of mind, but now . . .

Gran asks, "Matilde, did you sense any threat from him?"

Another, silent question crouches behind. *Did he know it was you behind the mask?*

She should confess, she knows. It's their rule: Lie, but never to each other. Not here, though. Matilde doesn't have the patience for one of her dame's tirades, and she doesn't want the other girls to know—not yet. She wants more time to think about what Dennan told her. She can believe that Epinine Vesten might be a threat, but not him. He's known about her magic for years and never told, and that counts for something.

They were friends once. She wonders what they are now . . . what they could be.

"No." Matilde palms her golden locket. "He seemed like any other client."

Leta doesn't press, but Gran's gaze says that she plans to. Matilde dreads it. She wants Gran's counsel, but not her censure. Still, she will tell her everything that Dennan told her. She will know what to do.

"This is outrageous." Dame's voice is rising, high and shrill. "Letting in zealots and Vestens and who knows who else. It's as if you *wanted* them in danger."

Leta's expression goes sharp. "And why would I want that?"

"So you can charge a higher price for access to them. Raise the prices of a business that you profit from so well."

"That is quite a slanderous accusation."

And it's ridiculous. Leta wouldn't let a religious zealot in on purpose. Would she?

Perhaps, if someone offered her the right price.

Trust can't be bought, Leta often says. But can she?

"Say what you like," Leta says. "I know what you whisper when you think my doors are closed. But I've been one of these girls, and I would never hurt them. I've seen what happens when Nightbirds don't look after their own."

Leta glances right at Sayer, who stares back with a look that's almost mercenary.

Leta stands. "I will get my spies hunting for answers. Until we get them, you will see no more clients."

Her dame's eyes flash. "The Houses won't like it."

"We are exposed," Leta says slowly, as if she's talking to a child. "I will not compromise their safety further. Not until we understand the threat and can control it."

Gran speaks again. "Just remember, Leta. Closing to clients also has its dangers."

She gives Leta a speaking glance. Matilde tries to grasp the meaning behind it, but it's like smoke, slipping through her fingers. One thing is clear enough: The matriarchs are keeping secrets. There are things they don't want the girls to see.

– ESTRA DOOLE –

5 spoons henbane
3 pinches letha, dried and ground
2 shakes powdered sleepweed (Callistan variety preferred)
12 chokeberries, fresh
a slug of flavien syrup, aged 3+ years in clay
half a bowl of coastal water (from north of the Neck)
a pinch of cold ashes
2 fresh tears

Grind the dry ingredients. Break open the berries with your hands (wear gloves unless you want blue hands for eternity) and combine them with the powder in a kettle. Stir slowly over medium heat, counterclockwise, until it starts to smell of forgetting. Add the syrup and the water, then ashes, then tears.

Most of the books you find on sleeping potions will stop at that. But this recipe is old, made for dreams and confessions. As you stir in the tears, cast this spell:

> *Fix your stare, stranger,*
> *And close your eyes,*
> *Drift slowly, friend,*
> *But do not lie.*

—FROM THE YELLOW ALCHEMIST'S
RECIPE JOURNAL

CHAPTER 4

ALL THAT'S GOLDEN

M ATILDE WINDS HER way through Brightwater Market. She used to come here with Gran, smiling at vendors until they gave her something sweet or shiny. They smile at her now, but she doesn't feel as soothed by it as she had hoped.

The market is crowded, the afternoon so steamy that sweat is trickling down her back, but it doesn't matter. It feels good to be out from under Dame's thumb. It's been two days since what she is calling Leta's Disaster, and this is the first time Matilde has been let out of the house. She's argued that the zealot is dead, and thus can't tell whoever sent him their true identities. It made no difference—everyone is on edge.

She agreed to let two House Dinatris bodyguards trail her at a discreet distance. Unlike Dame, they won't chastise her for eating in public or laughing too loud. Not that she feels much like laughing. A shadow has dogged her steps since that night they saw their clients. She pretends, for the girls, that she isn't dwelling on it, but she keeps having dreams about that horrid man on Sayer's floor. In them, he grabs her Goldfinch mask, yanking it away, leaving her bare faced. *I see you.*

She shakes her head, forcing the image away.

She returns her attentions to the market stalls, eyeing their treasures: lacework from Stray, stone trinkets from Thirsk, fragrant tea from the Callistan, bright spices and perfumes from the Farlands. There is no magic for sale, of course—not these days. She remembers how it was before Prohibition, with stalls selling potions that would give you a full beard for an evening or keep you dry on a rainy night. Not now, though: Those caught with bootleg risk the stocks and a thorough inquisition. No one would dare sell such things in the open.

She stops at a stall stuffed with buckets of flowers. With so few green spaces in Simta, such blooms are a luxury, and a status symbol. She names them silently: estaflower, larkspur, winglily. That last is her House's floral sigil, its winglike petals pale and lovely. She picks one up, breathing it in, but another scent cuts through its sweetness. Someone is burning incense, all smoke and char, and it reminds her of something . . .

A nasty feeling slithers down her spine.

I see you.

A clatter makes Matilde jump, heart pounding.

"Keep sharp, Basil!"

Matilde turns at the familiar voice. It's Brix Magna, scowling down at a boy and a pile of dropped baking trays. Just baking trays. She takes a deep breath, telling her nerves to behave.

"Hello, Brix."

The woman grins. "Pleasant morning, Young Lady Dinatris. You're getting more beautiful by the day."

Matilde poses in her cloche hat. "Watch out, now. I might forget how to be humble."

"Humble? You? If you say so."

That makes Matilde smile.

"How many today?" Brix asks.

"Six, please. You can't have just *one* of the best starcakes in Simta."

Brix winks. "Flattery gets you the best of the batch."

She hands over a box of yellow squares, still warm. Even through the dusting of sugar, Matilde can see the swirls of labnum seeds. Fortune seeds, they're called—it's said that getting one stuck between your teeth brings good luck.

"No charge," Brix says, like always.

Matilde pays her triple what they're worth, like always, and she tells herself that everything is fine—it's as it should be. But as much as she lies, she doesn't often fool herself.

She stops at the edge of the market, looking out over the Corners. It's her city's beating heart, its center of power. The Corners is where Simta's main canals cross, slicing the city into four distinct quarters named for creatures they say once flew through these skies. At her back is Pegasus, her quarter, and the Merchant Bank where much of Simta's money is kept. To her right is Phoenix Quarter and Augustain's church, where the Pontifex and his Brethren have their headquarters. Across the way is Griffin Quarter, home to some of the things Simta is most famous for: artisans and craftsmen, fast jazz, illicit clubs, sandpiper gangs. To her left is Dragon Quarter and the Winged Palace. The suzerain resides there, and it's where the Table holds all its important meetings. Matilde imagines it's where they will hold the vote just after Leastnight, some three weeks from now.

She usually loves standing here, watching boat runners throw out jokes and rude hand gestures, rowing their vessels full of dreamers and schemes. But today she can't stop staring at the palace and wondering . . . is Dennan Hain there, discussing the Goldfinch with his sister? She doesn't think so. Still, his warning about Epinine is never far from her mind. Since the Nightbirds meeting in Leta's parlor, an idea has taken hold: She can't believe how long it took her to see it. What if the suzerain is the one who sent that zealot to take Sayer? Dennan said she wanted to take them from the Houses. The zealot said that someone would reward him for dragging Sayer away. Would Epinine Vesten do something so bold? Such an act would tear a rift through the Great Houses—it might even start a civil war between them. It certainly wouldn't win her their allegiance in the long run. A week ago, Matilde would have laughed at the notion of anyone trying to steal away one of the Nightbirds. But that was before she fought off a zealot with a fire poker and dragged an unconscious redhead across a floor.

She told Gran what Dennan Hain told her, later that evening. She can still feel the displeased cut of Gran's pursed lips. Matilde thought she'd get a scolding. Instead, Gran asked a heap of questions, then spent half a lifetime staring into her wine. *Never fear, darling,* she said at last. *I will take care of it.* But can she, when there is so much they don't know?

Dennan Hain and his warning, the attack on Sayer, Æsa being groped by some half-crazed friend from home . . . they feel connected, like cracks in a wall branching from some unseen fissure. But cracks can be patched—they must be. Things will go back to how they are meant to be.

She turns, ignoring her guards as she walks back onto Pegasus Way, the thoroughfare that cuts through the middle of the quarter. It's full of pretty rowhouses, their balconies decorated with pots of trailing bottlevine and framed with intricate wrought iron. She doesn't know how they can stand to have their front doors open onto the street, with no garden to shield them. But then, most people don't have gardens like hers. She passes under a mothman and his long-handled broom, which he's using to sweep last night's flamemoths out of a streetlamp. They burn themselves out quickly, but their wings cast such a stunning glow.

One turn, two, past fine tailors and perfumers who cater mostly to the Great Houses. Finally, she reaches the gaudy yellow shop. A large sign hangs above it: *Krastan Padano's Alchemical Emporium*. Everyone calls him the Yellow Alchemist.

The door's bell chirps as she opens it. She doesn't bother looking back—the guards won't follow. They know this shop's owner poses no threat. Behind the long counter, shelves are filled to the brim with jars of herbs, feathers, gemstones. Skulls of various sizes glare down from the mantel, baring their teeth. The large yellow-glass window lays a golden blanket over everything, including Alecand, Krastan's apprentice. It gilds his mess of soft, dark curls.

She pauses, inhaling sweetness and smoke. If anything can settle her nerves, it's being at Krastan's. Some of her earliest memories are of spending afternoons with Gran here, chatting with Krastan as he mixed up his concoctions and fighting with Alec over who got to help him stir. Alec is looking down at whatever he is grinding in his mortar, studiously pretending he hasn't noticed her. A mug of frennet tea is set beside him, as always—he needs it to manage his sugar disease.

She sashays over, putting the starcakes down beside it.

"Who are we poisoning today, then?"

Alec blows a curl out of his eyes. "You, if you inhale too deeply, so lean back."

She tilts closer. "And deprive you of a sneaky peek down my dress?"

He smirks, coaxing out a dimple. "I've already peeked and seen better, I thank you."

It's always been like this between them, their friendship made of sharp jabs and playful barbs. As Krastan's adopted son, raised outside the Great Houses, he and Matilde have little in common, but she likes that. Just as she secretly likes how he doesn't let the difference in their stations stop him from telling her what's really on his mind.

He was gangly, growing up, and he's still lean, but now the muscles in his forearms stand out as he grinds, his mustard-colored vest wrapped taut around him. It's a shame he's so good-looking when he has no idea what to do with it. Her traitorous cheeks flush to have noticed.

"So what are you making?"

He glances up. Alec's close-set brown eyes are rich, classically Simtan, but so dark they are almost black.

"A sleeping tonic. Nothing fancy."

She leans farther over the counter. "Not a love potion, then. Shame. How are you ever going to find yourself a lady?"

"You know I only have eyes for you."

She wants to laugh off his words—they're absurd—but it didn't sound like he was joking. Alec has never been one for games, anyway.

Krastan sweeps in, dispelling the moment. He's got his steely grey hair swept back and tied with cord, his canary yellow cap pulled down over it. He smiles at her with crooked teeth.

"Stella," he says: *little bird*. An inside joke. "What a pleasure."

"You say that now," Alec quips. "Wait until she starts a fire."

"Oh, please." Matilde rolls her eyes. "That was *one* time."

She watches Krastan reach to put some vials up on a high shelf. His hands shake a little more than they used to, but he's still the best alchemist in Simta. The others have taken to painting their shops in bright colors to try to grab some of his renown. Most of what he makes is magic-free and perfectly legal, but he does plenty of clandestine trickster work for the Houses. At least, he does for hers.

His eyes roam over to the shop's closed door. "Where is Lady Frey?"

"Gran's at home today. She sends her best and warmest, as always."

"That woman," he sighs. "She's the love of my life, you know."

"So you always insist on telling me."

When Gran was a Nightbird, she walked into this shop demanding Krastan—then an apprentice—make her something without asking questions. He obliged by brewing her some Estra Doole. They became fast friends, despite the gulf between their stations. Eventually, she even told him what she was. Matilde has always wondered what made Gran trust him with such a thing, and yet she's never doubted him. Alec and Krastan know more about her than many of her blood relations. Krastan is like a grandsire to her, truly. And Alec is . . . well, not a brother.

"Have you come for something specific?" Krastan asks. "Or just to say hello?"

The shadowy dread starts to creep back in.

"Oh, Dame has been keeping a tight leash since the Season started. I needed an excuse to get out of the house." It's not a lie, exactly. Her fingers find her locket. "I thought we could brew something together. It's been too long."

Krastan shakes a gnarled finger. "As long as you follow my directions."

She makes a mock-affronted face. "Don't I always?"

As she skirts behind the counter, Alec puts a foot out, almost tripping her.

"Don't blow up the shop," he says. "I live here."

She stops. "You're the one with a penchant for making things combust."

She bumps her hip against his. He stiffens. These days, he always does when they touch. It's proper, she supposes. He is an alchemist's apprentice; she's a Great House daughter, and a Nightbird besides. Nothing but friendship has ever been in their cards. Still, his distance grates, so she leans even closer, taking a sip of his tea. It tastes like frennet and rumfruit—of Alec.

"Be nice," she teases. "You never know what I might tip into your cup when you aren't looking."

He doesn't answer—just stands there like a handsome piece of driftwood.

She steps away. "Honestly, Alec. It's not as if I have the pox."

With that, she follows Krastan down a narrow back hall. Clients aren't allowed back here for many reasons, chief amongst them the tidy bookshelf along one wall. One never knows when someone might try to pull down *A Compendium of Old Eudean Creatures*, as Krastan is doing, and find the bookshelf swinging open to reveal a hidden door. Matilde thrills at the sight, reaching for the door's yellow cut-glass handle. In her opinion, hidden rooms are the very best kind.

The back workshop is much like the front one at first glance. The shelves are packed with jars and vials, shiny bowls, small flasks and burners, all part of any alchemist's trade. But look closely and you will see the illicit. Powders that glow, potions that smoke, salves that glimmer. Alchemical magic has a scent to it, almost like burnt sugar. Unlike hers, which smells of nothing at all.

Few of Eudea's plants and minerals are magical on their own, but they have fragments of the Wellspring stored inside them. Mixed and processed by a practiced hand, they become concoctions people are willing to shell out for, though of course they can't offer the kinds of gifts a Nightbird can. Good potions are difficult to make, their ingredients expensive, and their effects fleeting. Still, Krastan is the best in Simta. It's astounding what he can do with those gnarled hands.

He pulls out bags and vials, arranging them around a small burner.

"So how goes the Season thus far?" he asks. "How fly your wings?"

She reaches up to the garden of dried herbs hanging from the ceiling, pinching some between her fingers. "It's been . . . strange."

He raises a bushy eyebrow but asks nothing. He knows her stories aren't ones he can demand.

She watches him crush a handful of grimmberries. When he breaks them open, garnet-red juice runs over his hands. You are supposed to wear gloves, but he doesn't. *My hands are a map of my accomplishments,* he once told her. In Simta, such marks can be dangerous to wear. Those caught with bootleg potions are scolded or fined, and sometimes pulled in for inquisition by the Wardens. Those who make it . . . well, that is another thing entirely. Still, Krastan has never been arrested. The Great Houses and his own savvy keep him safe.

The red juice hits the copper bowl, dark against the metal. Sometimes she wishes she could brew up her magic like this.

Krastan's potions might not have the same potency as what lives within her, but he can use what he creates in ways she can't.

"Are you going to ask me your question, Stella?"

She starts. "What makes you think I have a question?"

He gives her a knowing look. "Lucky guess."

He's right, of course. It's part of why she came here.

"Do you have potions that can alter someone's memories?"

He frowns. "Alter a memory, or erase it?"

She crushes the dried flower—bleeding heart, she thinks—against the counter. "Either one."

He puts the bowl over a small burner, stirring the juice slowly with a little wooden spoon. "I have potions that can sharpen someone's perception or enhance their recall. But alter memories already made? Remove them entirely? That is a dangerous proposition."

She swallows. "But could you do it, if I asked?"

There is a loaded pause. "Such things are not within my power."

Frustration flares. She feels fairly certain Tenny won't tell anyone about the Goldfinch, but with so many threats on the wind, she would feel better if she could take the secret back from him. She doesn't like knowing he has that coin in his pocket, even if it's one he'll never spend.

Krastan's forehead wrinkles. "I know that look."

"What look?"

"That look you get when you mean to cause mischief, or you have already."

"Oh, please," she quips. "I'm a paragon of good behavior."

He doesn't smile. In the silence the burner hisses softly, just a whisper in the muted golden light.

"Are you going to tell me what it is you want someone forgetting?"

The room feels like one of the too-tight corsets Dame tries to make her wear, but the lie still comes easily. Sometimes she dons a mask even here. "Oh, it was only a passing fancy."

Krastan doesn't look like he believes her. Steam curls up around his yellow cap.

"You must be careful, Stella. Things are tense in Simta just now. Things are changing."

She frowns. "What do you mean?"

"The Wardens are performing more raids than ever. The punishments for having or conjuring alchemicals are growing worse. They say it's to tackle the growing boldness of the sandpipers, but that is not who they punish. They pulled two girls in for inquisition just for selling enchanted flowers."

"Yes, well." The Wardens tasked with enforcing Prohibition can be a pain, though she rarely has to deal with them. "That's nothing new."

"It is, though," Krastan says. "It's as if they are looking for something specific. Perhaps *someone*."

She thinks again of the zealot. Did he tell anyone about the Nightbirds before his ill-fated visit? Could the Pontifex and the church have the Wardens combing Simta for *them*?

She makes her voice firm—sure. "The Wardens won't find us. And anyway, the law wasn't meant for girls like me."

"You only think that because you've never had occasion to be stung by it."

Matilde jumps. How long has Alec been hovering inside the doorway?

"It's never House lords and ladies who get brought in for

questioning," he goes on, crossing his arms. "Money buys them the gift of doing what they please without fear."

They've had this argument before. "I'm not in the mood for a lecture about privilege, Alec."

"You think alchemicals are just party favors, but the ingredients that go into them aren't just for fun. They go into medicine, too—things people need. The law and the gangs make sure they stay unregulated and expensive. If I didn't have an honest local supplier, do you think I would be able to afford to buy my frennet?"

"I don't make the rules," she snaps.

"But you shouldn't ignore them," Krastan says. "I think you forget, sometimes, how many people in this city fear magic. The church has taught its lessons well. It isn't just Wardens who would like to see us punished, who comb the streets for transgressors. It's getting harder to hide . . . for all of us."

His words carry an odd sort of weight that unnerves her.

"You needn't worry," she says. "The Houses will protect the both of us."

Alec shakes his head. "You really are a sheltered bird."

"Alecand." There is a sharp edge to Krastan's voice where usually there is only patience. "You mustn't neglect your herbs. They will feel it."

Alec slips back out the door, but his words have put another crack in her foundation, adding to her growing dread.

In the silence, she watches Krastan slowly measure out one of his powders. Perhaps measuring his words as well.

"The 'spring-touched girls of old weren't just vessels, you know," he says at last. "They could wield their magic. The most powerful of them shaped the way Eudea was run. There were Fyrebirds, they say, who could part seas and move mountains."

She smiles, used to his sudden changes of subject. "The legends say they could fly, too. What a sight."

Sheldars, flaetherin, Well women. Every corner of Eudea has a name for the most powerful magical girls of old, but Matilde has always liked Fyrebirds. *Fyre* is the old Eudean word for *wild*. Wildbirds, free and fierce, answering to no one. At some point, every Nightbird imagines being like them. But such dreams are like tossing a coin in a canal and making a wish on it: wasteful.

"Lately, I wonder if that old magic isn't gone," Krastan continues. "Just sleeping. If perhaps, one day soon, it will wake up."

Matilde sighs. "You know I can't use my own magic."

"Not yet, Stella. Not *yet*."

Again, that weight in his words, heavy with meaning.

"What are you trying to tell me?"

He surprises her by wrapping his berry-stained hand in a kerchief and cupping her cheek with it. "Just that if ever you feel out of your depth, I hope you come to me, Stella. We will always be your port in a storm."

But there's something else, a truth he is not sharing.

A while later, she returns to the shop's front room, squeezing past Alec without saying a word to him. Sadly, it seems he isn't ready to be done.

"Doesn't it bother you that your clients are Simta's most advantaged? Already rich and getting richer?"

She faces him. "Would you have me hand out kisses on the corner to anyone who might want one?"

He leans closer. "I would have you look over your garden wall and see what's happening beyond it."

His gaze pierces her skin, seeing through her. To her horror, she feels the sting of unshed tears.

"You think all I do is eat cake and go to parties," she says. "But believe it or not, I have problems of my own."

She goes to turn away, but he grabs her hand. His is calloused but delicate: the hand of a spell worker. She can feel his pulse against her palm.

"Tilde, wait."

Her heart jumps at the pet name, but she can't show it. She forces her voice into lightness instead.

"Have you changed your mind about that peek down my dress, then?"

"I just . . ." He runs a thumb across her skin, so light she thinks she's imagined it. "I didn't mean to upset you."

His cheeks are flushed. Why does arguing make him grow more dashed handsome?

"I'm not upset," she says. "I'm . . . vexed. There's a difference."

He lets go of her hand. "Before you leave, I have something for you."

He pulls a vial from his vest pocket.

"It's for the . . . feminine pains you spoke of," he says, loud enough for Krastan to hear if he happens to appear. "Just make sure you read the note before you use it."

She flips over the bottle to read the note glued to its bottom.

NIGHTCLOAK. Throw down hard—the bottle must shatter. It will envelop you in a dark as thick as ink. (Take care: It stings the eyes worse than a river jelly.) In case you need an escape from your gilded cage. ~A

Her mouth drops open, but he puts a finger to his lips.

She knows he dabbles with concoctions that Krastan doesn't know about. Last summer, she used one of his experiments to turn Samson a rather horrid shade of green. But this is serious magic—it's a weapon. The kind that would get him noticed by Simta's more nefarious characters and probably get him hanged if he was caught.

She shouldn't risk even having it on her, and yet she finds herself opening her purse's false bottom.

"Alecand Padano. I didn't think you had it in you to live quite *this* dangerously."

That gets a smile. "Just don't do anything rash before I see you next."

The bell jangles as she leaves. Hester Street looks the same, but it feels like something's changed. Krastan thinks she should be on her guard. Alec gave her a weapon. It's troubling, and they don't even know about what happened to the Nightbirds two nights ago. This little trip was supposed to soothe her, but if anything it's made her more on edge than before.

Unrest in the city, Dennan's warning—now Krastan's— Sayer's client, Æsa's friend, Gran's and Leta's loaded looks. It's a puzzle, but she can't quite see the picture it's making. Too many pieces are still hidden in the shadows, out of sight.

Her hand reaches into her purse, curling around the card Dennan gave her. She isn't a sheltered bird, whatever Alec might think of her. Perhaps she should seek out some answers for herself.

Down in Griffin's bowels, past the Trill and to the right,
You'll find us making merry almost ev'ry night,
Our secrets are hidden deep
But with the right words, all right,
We might just let you down
Down
Down.

———

Hot-sweet music, bootleg shine,
Hug it tight, I'll make you mine,
Pay the price and you will find
That sweet place where it never runs dry
Dry
Dry.

—"THE PLACE WHERE IT NEVER RUNS DRY,"
A SIMTAN JAZZ SONG

– CHAPTER 5 –
SHADOW AND SHINE

S AYER SECURES HER flat cap as she's rowed across the water. She's glad for her hair, cut short enough that she didn't need to pin it, and the workman's clothes she found in a closet full of what looked like the remains of Leta's conquests. She doesn't want to look like a Great House girl tonight.

In the two days since they saw their clients, Leta's kept her close—almost smothering. She isn't supposed to go out alone, and certainly not at night. But she didn't cross the canals to be coddled, or told to sit tight and wait for other people to make things safe for her. If you want something, sometimes it's best to find it for yourself.

The boatman doesn't talk as he rows them across the Corners. The moon sits on the water, shifting with the subtle tide. It's a typical Simtan summer night: hot and still, the air thick enough that you could eat it, smelling of salt and the jawbone algae that clings to the sides of the canals. The last time she took this boat ride was months ago, after her dame died. She hasn't been back to Griffin's since.

She looks over her shoulder. She used to stand on Griffin's

corner, sometimes, and stare over at Pegasus, wondering what life was like on what seemed to her then like a distant shore. Now she's seen how wealth, lavish gardens, and flamemoth lanterns cocoon girls like Matilde from Simta's realities. It's easy to believe life is fair and everyone's chances are equal when you grow up wrapped in broad, sheltering leaves.

They dock, and Sayer steps out of the boat into Griffin's. It smells as she remembers: bread, paint, and old blood. Gallows Row is empty but still foreboding—a warning to lawbreakers, especially bootleggers. Not that the worst of them take any heed.

Sayer stalks down Griffin Way, into the bowels of the quarter. There are no flamemoth lampposts here, making the shadows twice as dark. The row houses close to the Corners are neat and brightly painted, but farther in they grow smaller and grimier. Cracks creep across some of their faces despite the paste of herbs and mud residents use to patch them. Lines of laundry stretch between windows, ghostly in the dark. She sees a few scruffy urchins hovering under a stairwell. She used to give kids like them day-old starcakes when Twice Lit's owner wasn't looking. She wonders if anyone is feeding them now.

There: A pater is trying to coax them out with hot loaves of bread. He'll try to coax them into a pater-run orphanage or school, too. The church does some good work, she knows, but they're the reason so many Simtans think magic corrupts souls and morals. They tell people that girls with magic are—or rather, were—something to fear.

The zealot's words come back: *You will poison the world if we let you.*

She shakes them off, refusing to let them follow her here.

As she heads toward the Trill, the light changes. Colorful lanterns hang from balconies and swing above every door. This slice of Griffin's likes to stay out late, for both business and pleasure. She heads down Bayard Lane, stopping at the edge of the Scholars' Pavilion. Twice Lit coffee shop has its doors thrown open, letting out its roasted sweet scent. A brass street band wails in the courtyard as drunk students flirt with coffee girls under the twinkling lanterns.

Blazing cats, she missed this place.

Matilde would laugh: It's dirty and crass compared to where she just came from, but Griffin's doesn't pretend to be anything other than itself.

She skirts the pavilion, sticking to the shadows, not wanting anyone at Twice Lit to recognize her. Not that they're likely to in this getup. People only see what they want to see. If she looks up, Sayer will see her dame's old bedroom window, dark and empty. Deep in her chest, something constricts.

She waits until the band gets to the end of their song, the shop's patrons all clapping, before pinching the arm of the trumpet player near the back. Rankin whirls, then smiles under his moth-eaten flat cap, revealing a gap between his front teeth.

"Sayer?"

"Shh. You'll blow my cover."

She tugs him away before the band can protest, around the side of the shop.

Rankin looks up at her, but only a little. He's grown since she last saw him. "Where you been, Say? I been looking."

She swallows past the lump in her throat. "I live with friends in Pegasus now."

He makes a face. "So you're a fancy lady, then."

Not really. "A little."

"Too fancy for the likes of us."

She wipes a sooty smudge off his cheek. "Never."

Rankin straps his trumpet to his back. He's thirteen, she knows, but sometimes he looks older. Griffin's streets aren't an easy place to be a child.

"Watcha doing back here, then?"

"I have business with Fen." Sayer's palms have gone sweaty. "Where is she, at the clubhouse?"

Rankin touches the pin at his lapel, all orange and gold ribbons. "Nah. The Throne Room."

Sayer knows it, of course, but has never been. It's stuffed with sandpipers. Something flutters in her stomach at the thought.

"Do you know tonight's password?" she asks.

"Yeah, but I'm not telling you."

"Why not?"

He tugs on his loud orange vest. "Cuz it's been extra rough-and-tumble through the Green Light lately. Fen wouldn't want you going in without an escort."

"You?" She taps his cap's brim. "Are you even tall enough to see through the peephole?"

Rankin scowls. "Mind your manners, there, mate."

They wind together through narrowing streets, bathed in the glow of green-glass lanterns. Griffin's music is louder here: jazz pouring off vine-covered balconies, hawkers selling cups of sweet citrine and trying to lure revelers into their clubs. Its wild speakeasies make the Green Light District Simta's unofficial party center, at least for a certain type of clientele, but it has its dangers. It's crawling with sandpipers, so called because of how the gangs move illicit substances out and around the city, skirting close to the edge of the tide.

They pass a girl in a shadowy alcove, furtively handing some coins to a boy in a vest and flat cap. She has the burnt-sugar reek of someone who takes too many potions. The piper boy passes her a slender vial. Mermaid's Dust, Sayer wagers—an alchemical that enhances the senses. For the girl's sake, she hopes it's decent stuff. All magic is addictive, but Dust is especially so, and it's often cut with cheap additives. Bad bootleg is easier for the Wardens to trace, and it can make people sick or go blind.

Rankin breaks the silence. "Why'd you leave, anyway?"

She tries to smile. "My dame's friend offered me a place. I had to live somewhere."

"You coulda moved in with us. The Stars would've taken care of you."

Sayer knows. Fen and her crew, the Dark Stars, would have welcomed her, but Dame would roll over in her forever sleep to know her daughter joined a sandpiper gang. "I had things to do over the water. Money to make."

He gives her a judging look. "Sain minth tu gansen."

The Dark Stars oath: *Like shadows stick together.*

Sayer has to look away.

"Well, Fen's been testy since you left, anyway. She misses you. She doesn't say so, but I know."

Sayer swallows hard. She longs to see Fen, but it also makes her nervous. After the way she left Griffin's, she isn't sure how their reunion's going to play. Will she be angry? How will it feel to see her again?

Sayer tugs at her vest. This is no time for feelings. She has to keep her wits sharp tonight.

They stop at a turn in a shadowy laneway. There is no sign to announce the Throne Room—just a rusted, nondescript door. Rankin knocks five times: three short raps, two long scrapes with his knuckles. A little hatch slides open, framing two unfriendly eyes.

"Password?"

Rankin says, "Filly May."

The door opens, revealing a man missing a few teeth and a green vest struggling to contain him. "And what do you think you'll be doing in here, Rankin?"

The boy puffs out his chest. "We got business with the Fox."

The guard looks unimpressed. Sayer fears he isn't going to admit them, but then he puts out a meaty hand.

"All right, then. Weapons out."

Rankin pulls three knives out of nowhere, one half as long as his leg, and a few vials that Sayer doesn't like the look of.

The guard narrows his eyes at her. "Taking your time, mate?"

She shrugs. "I'm not carrying."

He waggles his giant paw. With a sigh, she pulls out a swan-handled letter opener. Leta took Sayer's knife, and she wasn't about to come here empty handed.

"What were you going to do with this?" he says, pinching it between two thick fingers. "Pick your teeth?"

Rankin brays out a laugh. Sayer elbows him.

"It has a pointy end, doesn't it?"

The guard ushers them in, still chuckling, and locks the door behind them. Rankin leads her up some dark, narrow stairs. The only light comes from green-glass lanterns in the hallway. She can barely see her hands and the sign beside her head:

– HOUSE RULES –
NO OUT-OF-HOUSE POTIONS.
NO WEAPONS.
NO BRAWLS.

Jazz winds through the air, beckoning them forward. A shimmering curtain parts and they're inside.

Her first glimpse of the Throne Room makes her think of Leta's ball: high ceilings, bright colors, mirrors lining the walls. But where that was masks and posture, this place doesn't pretend to be anything but wild. The jazz is hotter, a sensuous promise. The burnt-sweet scent of magic floats on the air.

Rough-cut chandeliers hang down, enchanted by some trickster tailor to glow without candles, gilding the teeming crowd. The place is packed with sandpipers, their gangs marked out by the flowers pinned to their lapels. Blue river fern for the Kraken, dark red freesias for the Quick Cuts, purple heart's blood for the Deep Seas. This is a place they can mingle, no business, all pleasure. Here they all rule, hence the name.

She didn't expect to see so many girls here. Most of the pipers won't let them join. They're clinging to each other on the dance floor, doing the scandalous Deepwater Creep. Magic is everywhere. It twists and twinkles on their trickster-kissed dresses, whose patterns change with every swing of their hips. She sees teeth made pointy with a swipe of Wolf's Grin, nails made talons after being dipped in some Sharp Claw, hair turned bright colors with Four Seasons balm. The singer onstage has a voice like smoke, amplified by some alchemical, and at the bar, the 'keeps are making magical cocktails. Dark green Viper, which makes someone's tongue appear forked while they drink it, and frothy Clockman's Bane, which makes everything seem to slow down. The piper in the corner's clearly been drinking Fair Maiden: His skin glistens. The boy slipping him tongue seems to like it just fine.

The bootleg in this room must be worth a fortune, but then the pipers run most of the city's underground alchemical market. Illegal magic is their stock-and-trade. The church and Simta's Wardens would kill to bust this club and hang most of the people in it, but no one in Griffin's would ever point it out to them. The sandpipers run this quarter just as surely as the Table . . . maybe more so. There's a reason the piper bosses call themselves lords.

The crowd parts, and she gets a flash of Fen at a corner table. Sayer's heart seems to get caught in her throat.

At first glance, Fen looks like any other piper—an arrogant boy, ruthless and hungry—but Sayer knows better. She drinks in Fen's sharp-cut cheekbones and short hair that twists up like a flame. It's the same warm shade of brown as the burnt caramels at Twice Lit, but nothing about Fen speaks of softness. Life as Simta's only female gang boss has taught her to be hard.

When they were both fourteen, Fen showed up bleeding at Twice Lit's back door. Sayer knew from the eyepatch she wore who she was. Fenlin Brae: *Sly Fox*. That was before she started the Dark Stars, but she was already making a name for herself amongst the gangs as someone with quick hands, a quicker mind, and a skill for cracking safes no one else could get into. Sayer expected her to bark out an order, like other pipers she knew, but instead she smiled. *I hear you give urchins treats,* she said, blood in her teeth. *How about a treat and some stitches?*

Sayer laughed. They became fast friends after that. Best friends. But are they still?

"Fen! I found her!" Rankin shouts when they get to the table. "You owe me ten shills."

"So you did," Fen says. "And so I do."

Fen leans back in her chair, relaxed yet somehow predatory. Her green velvet eyepatch doesn't make her gaze easier to hold.

Are you ever going to show me what's under there? Sayer used to tease during their sparring lessons.

Fen would just smile. *I'll show you mine if you show me yours.*

But they've never been that kind of friends, and Fen isn't one for letting her guard down. Except for that one time . . . Her mind flies back to the night Dame died, when Fen held her so tightly.

I'm alone, Sayer choked.

Fen wrapped an arm around her waist. *That's not true.*

That was the night Fen pulled her close, lips parting. That was the night they almost—

Olsa, Fen's second in command, clears his throat.

"Right, ah . . . the runt and I'll go get another round, then."

Fen's gaze never leaves her. "No cocktails for Rankin. Don't want to stunt his growth any more than we have already."

Rankin curses. "One day I'll be tall enough to squash you."

Not that he would. Rankin worships Fen—they all do. She named her crew after their city's local starfish: an unassuming thing, but tenacious. It clings to the rocks so tightly no storm can pry it off. The Dark Stars became a rock for kids the other gangs overlooked or deemed unworthy. Fen has a way of seeing the hidden strength in people. But she has a knack for finding their weaknesses, too.

Sayer sits. Fen looks her over, weighing and measuring. Sayer fights not to look at her full, plush lips. Scars peek up over her shirt's standing collar, much paler than the Dark Stars sigil that blooms from Fen's vest. She hasn't had the orange foxglove trickster-kissed, like most of the pipers here, but Fen doesn't deal in magic. Sayer isn't sure she's ever seen her use any herself.

At last, Fen speaks. "Tig."

It's a nickname, short for *tigren,* a jungle cat from the Farlands. Something loosens in Sayer's chest to hear it said.

"Nice duds. Pants suit you."

Sayer can't help but smile at that. "Same to you."

Fen leans back, chewing her mastic, as always. It's made from a plant that she says nullifies the effects of any alchemical someone might slip into her drink. Sayer doesn't know why, but Fen's leery of magic. Perhaps it's because she was raised by a pater, but Fen doesn't think very highly of him.

"I would've thought your new friends in Pegasus prefer you in dresses," Fen says. "Lady Leta Tangreel surely wouldn't approve."

Sayer's mouth drops open. How does Fen know about Leta?

"Don't sit there like a stunned mullet," Fen says. "You disappeared without a word to anyone. You thought I wouldn't make it my business to look?"

Sayer's cheeks flame. "How did you find me?"

"Pegasus is where your dame grew up," Fen says. "And I saw that fine-looking House lady at your dame's wake, whispering at you. I figured she was offering you something. Must have been good, for you to run away."

Sayer scowls at that. "I didn't run."

"Then what would you call it?"

"One of my dame's old friends offered me a good deal, and I took it."

"Still." Fen props her elbows on the table. "You could have said goodbye before you went."

Fen would have said not to go. Anyway, what would Sayer have told her? The Nightbirds are a secret, and she didn't want to lie to Fen.

She points down at Sayer's vest. "Where's your Stars pin?"

"Here." Sayer pulls it out of a pocket. The black beads sewn into its orange-silk foxglove glint in the chandeliers' light.

"It does you no good in your pocket, Tig."

"I know, but . . ." She looks at the flower. It's a sign of the Dark Stars' watch: their protection. A signal to other gangs that Fen sees her as one of their own. "I didn't know if I was still allowed to wear it."

Sayer makes herself look up, half expecting Fen to take the pin from her. A corner of Fen's mouth curls up.

"Don't be a ratbag. You know you are."

Sayer lets out a breath, relief blowing through her. The singer onstage hits a long, soaring note.

"So, what're you doing in the Throne?" Fen asks.

Sayer came for information. Fen is a thief, and she knows more about what happens in Simta's shadows than most. She might know something about the zealot who attacked her. But sitting here now, she realizes she really came for this: her friend. It's been a strange handful of days, and she wants to be with someone separate from the Nightbirds. Someone who likes her for herself, not for her gift.

"I came to ask you some questions," she says finally. "And to borrow a knife."

Fen frowns. "What happened to the one I gave you?"

"I stabbed someone with it."

Anyone else would have started, but Fen goes still. "And what did they do to earn the pleasure?"

Sayer swallows hard. "He tried to kill me."

That wipes away her stillness. "Let's go somewhere quieter."

She leads Sayer behind the stage and up some winding stairs that end in a small, empty room. One wall is made up of a stained-glass mural: a golden chair floating in a sea of red. Fen goes to lean against it where the light is brightest. She never has liked dark, cramped spaces.

"Do you need help drowning the body, then?"

"No. That's been taken care of." Sayer sees the zealot again, straining on top of her. She doesn't know what horrifies her more—that she stabbed someone, or how long it took her. When it counted, all Fen's sparring lessons flew away.

She wipes her hands on her pants. "I want you to help me figure out who he was and who sent him."

Fen's expression is stony. "Tell me the tale."

Ten hells. Sayer was foolish to think she could ask for help without telling Fen everything. She knows Fen can keep a secret—she's practically made up of them—but Matilde's voice whispers through her thoughts. *A sandpiper could make good money selling our secrets.* Fen would never, but still . . .

"Come now, Tig. You came to me, remember? And we're friends. At least that's what I thought."

If Leta knew, Sayer might be out on the street, out of the chance to make her fortune. But the Nightbirds aren't working, and won't until the danger's sorted. Sayer can't afford to wait.

It comes down to this: Does she trust Fen with it?

Sayer trusts her more than anyone.

So Sayer tells her about the Nightbirds. No names or details, other than what the job entails. She explains that night with the client, his words, and the vial he tried to make her drink. Telling the story brings it to life: the charred ash smell of his skin, his iron grip, his burning hate. Sayer's hands have started shaking. She balls them up to try to hold them in check.

When she's done, silence envelops them. If Fen is surprised to hear there are girls with intrinsic magic, it doesn't show.

"What's your gift?" Fen asks, surprising Sayer. "What does your magic do?"

"It lets people blend into the shadows. Invisibility."

"And you can't use it yourself?"

"No."

Fen's expression goes carefully blank, her eyes shielded. It's the look she gets when she's keeping her cards close. But there's a tension in the way she stands, arms pressed against her sides, biting down on her mastic. Part of the reason she didn't tell Fen before is because she shuns magic . . . all magic. Will she look at Sayer now and see something to dislike?

Sayer steers them back on course. "The client talked about being rewarded for bringing me to someone. But I don't think he meant the Pontifex. Have you heard anything about a new church sect? One connected to Marren?"

Fen paces the room, just once.

"They're called En Caska Dae. The Blades of Flame."

Her voice drips with venom. Fen hates churchmen. Sayer doesn't know the whole story of her childhood, but she knows the pater who ran Fen's orphanage gave her many of her scars.

"Their leader calls himself Marren's Red Hand," she goes on. "He doesn't think the law goes far enough in enforcing Prohibition. He wants to burn all magic users to the ground."

A cleansing fire to cleanse the world.

Sayer crosses her arms. She'll have to tell Leta. Hopefully knowing where the threat is coming from will help her quell it.

"At least his agent is dead," Fen says. "He won't be telling the Hand anything."

Sayer nods. "Which means he still doesn't know who we are, or how to find us."

Fen runs a hand through her flame of hair. "They found you once, Tig. And the Hand is persistent. You don't know how far he'll go."

Sayer frowns. "And you do?"

Fen's expression shutters again. Sayer can't read it. The singer's voice floats through the glass. *You're a thief, so you might as well steal the rest of me, you've already stolen my heart.*

"I'll see what I can find out about what they're up to." Fen's next words are quiet, as if she doesn't know she's even saying them. "I've let him go too far already."

Sayer's about to ask what Fen means, but she keeps going.

"You can stay at the Dark Stars club for now, or in a safe house. I have places."

"I'm not coming back to Griffin's, Fen. Not yet."

Fen is so controlled, rarely showing any anger, but Sayer sees the flash of heat.

"You want to stay?"

She steps closer. Sayer gets a whiff of her mastic, dank and acrid. Sometimes she wonders if Fen chews it just to keep people at bay.

"Blazing cats, Sayer. How can you even do it?"

Sayer stiffens. "The Madam's going to let me keep all my earnings. I'll make more in one summer than I could ever earn as a coffee girl. Enough to make whatever life I want."

She thinks again of that fantasy of her and Fen in the stone cottage. Late at night, sometimes, the image blooms in her mind. Flour on cheeks, hands in hair, Fen's full lips close . . . but it isn't real. Fen doesn't want it. The way she acted the night Sayer's dame died proved that. When she leaned in, Fen flew off the bed, as if Sayer had burned her. It makes her cheeks flame to think of it now.

Fen grimaces. "If you wanted money, you could have come to me."

"I don't want charity," Sayer snaps. "I want to make my own way. And anyway, it wasn't just about that."

"What, then?"

Her dame's words fly through her. *I wish you would join the Nightbirds. I wish you would bring us both back into the light.*

"My dame wanted me to go. I made her a promise."

"Yeah, well, I don't think she'd want you getting knifed for it."

She storms over to Fen, who presses back against the glass so no part of them touches. The movement fills Sayer with a mix of fury and dread.

"What's your problem?" she asks. "Is it that I have magic, or that I chose to join a club other than yours?"

Fen's gaze could wither fruit. "It's not a club. It's a brothel."

The words hang sharp, but Sayer refuses to be cut by them. "I didn't think you'd be one to judge."

Sayer steps back. Fen's hand comes up, but then she drops it. The air is thick with things left unsaid.

Fen blows out a breath. "All right, fine, that was a low blow. But ten hells, Tig, you love trouble more than I do."

Sayer rolls her eyes. "I'd say we're evenly matched."

SAYER LEAVES THE Throne alone. If Fen has news to share, she will send Rankin to play his trumpet by Leta's garden gate. Until then, Sayer will just have to sit tight.

Fen wanted Rankin to walk her back to the Corners, but she doesn't need an escort. She's walked these streets at night often enough. Perhaps that's why she lets herself get lost in thoughts of the Nightbirds, of her dame and Fen's anger and the mysterious En Caska Dae. She doesn't hear the footsteps until it's too late.

"Blazing cats," someone says just behind her. "Aren't you a sweet sight in pants."

Arms pin her against a broad chest. Panic threatens.

"You'd best let go," she says. "Or I'll steal the only jewels you're ever likely to own."

The arms release her.

"My. The sweet sight bites."

Someone laughs—several someones. When she turns, the first thing she sees is his flower, blue petals and choking green vines: the Kraken sigil. The face grinning down at her belongs to Gwellyn Mane. She's known him for years and wished she hadn't.

He smiles, flashing the blue-capped metal tooth that marks his high standing in the Kraken. "It's been too long, Sayer."

She tenses. "What do you want?"

"So touchy. Can't I say hello to an old flame?"

Her stomach turns. "You and I were never flames."

"Then how about we light a fire?"

All three boys laugh again. Her dame would tell her to laugh too, to smile. *Making a fuss only makes them angry.* But Sayer isn't about to pretend she's enjoying this.

She scowls. "Didn't your dame teach you not to creep up on people?"

"Probably," Gwellyn says. "But my dame's not here."

She can see his eyes, pupils slitted. He must have taken Cat Eye: a favorite alchemical with pipers. It makes your night sight feline sharp.

"Why not stay awhile?" he says. "The night's only half over."

She doesn't hold out the new knife Fen gave her, but she keeps a tight grip on it. "I have places to be."

"Fine, then. I'll let you go, for a price. How 'bout a kiss?"

There is something about the way he says it, sly and knowing. Anger roils in her blood, threaded with fear.

Gwellyn grins. "The old boss, he isn't as sharp as he used to be. When he drinks these days, he likes to talk. Sometimes about your old lady."

Sayer's heart stops.

"He told me things about the . . . favors she used to do him, in return for his watch."

Favors. Her dame's magic was a kind of liquid luck, gifting good fortune. Nadja knew better than to give it to a sandpiper, surely. But she remembers that posh man's hands on her dame's waist, his fevered whisper. *Little dove. Nothing tastes as sweet as you do.*

She goes in for the lie. "The old fool's telling you tales."

"Maybe. But his stories made me curious. And you know, I could do with a little bit of luck."

Something touches Sayer's back: the alley wall. The Kraken boys have spread out on either side, and Gwellyn's standing too close to her. Terror is a lead weight pulling her down.

He leans in. Her magic can't be taken by force, but he doesn't know that, and he can take plenty else if she doesn't move fast.

She knees him between the legs.

"You bitch!" he spits, trying not to crumple over.

His friends step forward, knives out and glinting. Her heart is throbbing, mind flooding with her fears. She sees that man in their apartment, feels the zealot's hands around her throat. She has a vision of Gwellyn dragging her into shadows she can't escape from.

But Sayer's not about to be anyone's victim. She isn't going down without a fight.

"Evening, gents," comes a voice from behind them. It's Fen, hands in pockets, as if they're at some summer picnic. *Smile on your face, knife at your back.*

"You skull too many cocktails, Gwell? Because that's a Dark Stars sigil she's wearing."

Given Fen's rank, they should back off, but all three Kraken sneer.

"Shove off, fishgut," Gwellyn growls. "You don't get to tell me what's mine for the taking."

Fen spits out her mastic and gives them a fox's feral grin. "Guess again."

She swings her blade, slicing into Gwellyn's arm. He swears and swings back, turning the alley into a blur of movement, feral kicks and flashing steel. Sayer's frozen, watching Fen, so graceful, but brutal, her knife an extension of her cold, cunning rage. No one can beat the Sly Fox in a knife fight, unless they know how the eyepatch narrows her field of vision. She hides it well, just like everything else.

Fen takes a hit to the side, shaking Sayer out of her stupor. When another Kraken tries to jump in, she kicks out his legs. The Kraken gets up fast, but she's faster, and this time there's no dress to get tripped up in. She ducks under his sloppy punch and catches him in the nose.

Blood sprays, not hers. Someone's cursing. Gwellyn raises something up—a vial.

Gwellyn smiles, blue tooth glinting like oil on water. He's in Fen's blind spot.

"Fen, look out!"

She whirls too late. Glass shatters. Grey smoke coalesces into hands that reach for Fen. Sayer doesn't want to know what they'll do if they find skin. Fear fills her chest, and she tastes thunder. It rolls through her like a sudden, violent storm.

A gust of wind rushes in, a sudden shock through the humid stillness, catching those hands and throwing them in Gwellyn's face. There is the smell of melting skin. Gwellyn screams. His friends dance around, trying to help him. Sayer can't look away.

"Tig," Fen pants, beside her now. "Let's go."

They run together, taking a right, a left, twisting and turning. Her heart is pounding so hard she can't see straight. They skid down a lane, run to the door at its end.

Fen rattles the handle, swearing. Sayer looks over her shoulder: no sign of Gwellyn, but with the Cat Eye it won't be long before they're seen. Suddenly, the door clicks. Fen must have gotten out her lock picks. She throws herself against it, but it won't open more than a crack.

Blood drips down Fen's chin. "Must be something blocking it."

Shouts come from the far end of the lane. They can't go that way.

"We have to hide," Sayer whispers.

Fen's hand is still gripping the door handle. "Where?"

She has a point. There's very little to shield them: a few stacks of old crates, an ancient cart, and the darkness.

A shout comes again. She yanks Fen over to the crates, squeezing behind them, just as footsteps echo through the lane.

"Sayerrrr," Gwellyn croons, getting closer. "Come out, come out."

She bites down on her lip. They'll have to fight, with boys who have no desire to be gentle, and Fen's injured. Sayer grips her knife and seethes.

Fen taught her the secret to tailing someone. *You have to make yourself a piece of the darkness.* If she could use her magic, that's what she would do. She asked her dame once why Nightbirds couldn't use their magic like the Fyrebirds from her bedtime stories. *It's a gift,* she said, *meant to be shared.* But what good is a gift you can only give away to others? What's the point of being powerful if you can't be strong for yourself?

One of the crates in the front of the pile is shoved aside. Someone cackles.

Her pulse picks up as a wild idea flashes.

She presses close to Fen, lips to her ear.

"Take it," she whispers. "Use it."

Fen starts to shake her head, but Sayer kisses her.

Fen's lips are firm, surprised, but then they relax a little, melting into hers. Kissing back. The lingering taste of Fen's mastic makes something in Sayer want to curl up, pull back, but the sensation fades quickly, pushed aside by something else—something strong.

Giving the magic to someone usually feels like pouring something out, slightly dizzying, but this is different. As Sayer's magic spills, something else fills her, tasting of roots and earth and iron. She feels . . . powerful.

This kiss feels like two forces colliding.

Make her a piece of the darkness, Sayer thinks, willing Fen to turn invisible. *Turn her into shadow and smoke.*

The last box is kicked aside. Sayer breaks the kiss, pressing against the wall. Gwellyn and his boys are staring straight at them. Fen's looking at her, but she quickly turns away. Sayer's heart drops: It didn't work. Fen is still visible.

Then Gwellyn says, "Where is she, Brae?"

Heart in her throat, Sayer looks down and finds . . . nothing. Her body's not gone, not quite, but cloaked in shadow, dyed the same colors as the walls and the night.

She steps noiselessly to the side. The shadows move with her. The thrill of it shivers in her chest.

"Quit playing," Fen is saying. "We both know you aren't

about to jump a piper lord in a back alley. You know what happens to boys who threaten a boss."

"You're not *my* boss," Gwellyn growls, his cheeks marked with angry purple handprints. "And Watch or no, when I find Sayer, I'm going to teach that bitch a lesson. She won't be walking straight for a week."

Something sizzles. Gwellyn's hand flies to his mouth, catching the blood gushing from it. Gwellyn's voice is so garbled Sayer can't make out what he's shouting . . . *My tooth?* Then she sees it on the stones: his blue cap, bent and bloodied. How in the dark depths did it get there?

The boys have formed a tight ring around Fen. She's breathing heavily, teeth bared. She looks wild. It's three on one—or so the Kraken think. But then Sayer starts swinging her knife. She darts between them like Fen taught her, moving like smoke, uncatchable. She carves quick cuts in forearms and shins, the back of a neck. They shout and whirl around, but all they see is the darkness. Gwellyn shrieks, high pitched, when Sayer knocks him to the ground.

He staggers up, and then the Kraken are running. The sounds of their footsteps fade away. Sayer lets out a shaky breath.

"Fen," she whispers. "Can you see me?"

Fen's words are tight. "I surely can't."

Sayer's mind is spinning, full of wonder and questions. She meant to give Fen the power to turn invisible . . . how, then, did she do it for herself? She doesn't know, but she is awake in a way she's never been before. She can almost feel the magic under her skin, flushed and tingling. And then the tidal surge of it starts to recede.

The invisibility fades. It's like her whole body, clothes included, were painted to blend in with the shadows, and now that paint is running off. It hurts Sayer's eyes to watch. It thrills her, too.

"Sayer." Fen's voice still has that tightly leashed flatness. "Was that . . . ?"

She smiles. "My magic."

The kind she isn't supposed to be able to use for herself.

Dangers lurk
in the Bluebottle Sea,
keep your eyes on the water
and just hope you don't see . . .

Hashna singing in the waves,
a mean gale a-brewin',
or a sheldar at your rival's helm
who'll bring your ship to ruin.

—"EYES ON THE WATER,"
AN ILLISH SAILORS' SONG

CHAPTER 6

WAVE TO WAVE

IT FEELS GOOD to be immersed in water. She's never bathed in anything so clear and warm. Matilde's dame, Oura, had a maid put something in the bath—a pinkish salt mixed with petals that float like tiny boats. Restwell, she called it. Æsa doubts such a thing is strong enough to calm her mind. It churns like Illan's wild tides and blue sand, so dark it looks black when the waves tumble over it. In the three days since the attacks, it hasn't stopped.

She keeps seeing Enis, the hunger in his eyes, his fingers digging into her back—the memory won't leave her. If her Hawk hadn't come, how far would he have gone?

Still, Æsa hopes he is safe. The Hawk hasn't sent her any word about him. Hawks and Sparrows only ever attend their Nightbirds in Leta's secret houses. They don't know where each lives, as that would mean knowing who they are. But the other night, before they left, Æsa wrote a note and left it in the passageway, where the Hawk was sure to see it. *Please send me word of my friend when you can.* She gave him the Dinatris address, signing her name, and ever since she has regretted it. What was she thinking, revealing herself to a boy she doesn't know? But he is her Hawk, sworn to protect her. She just has to hope that oath applies both in and out of their masks.

At least he didn't give Enis to Leta. He spun his story so smoothly when the Hawks were questioned. If she didn't know the truth, she never would have seen the lie. Matilde and Sayer lied for her, too, and she is grateful. They think she fears being sent home for her mistake, and she does—her family needs the money that being a Nightbird will bring them. But she's less fearful of that than of the question that won't leave her.

Did my magic make Enis do what he did?

She sinks down, hair floating around her face like the hashna said to haunt Illan's shores. Part woman, part fish, they lurk near rocky outcroppings, looking for sailors to sing to. They lure them in with their sweet voices, and then they drag them to their deaths.

Is her magic like that—a poison? If that is true, it would be wrong for her to be a Nightbird. It would be dangerous to kiss anyone ever again.

At least there are no clients for now, but there is Samson. Matilde's brother doesn't know about her magic. Æsa wonders if it's simply tradition, to keep the secret from male family members, or if the Dinatris ladies think he's too wild to trust. Still, that hasn't dampened his attentions. He brings her flowers and sits beside her at dinner, leaning close. Oura smiles on, clearly pleased, as Æsa should be. Mam sent her here with hopes, and there are certain expectations of a Nightbird. Yet every time she thinks of Samson stealing a kiss, she's filled with dread.

She reaches up to grasp the sea glass braided into her hair, loosened by the water. *Please,* she prays to the gods, *take it back. I don't want it.* This magic is a weight she doesn't know how to bear.

Something clicks and scratches. Æsa sits up quickly, water splashing over the sides of the tub. She's barely gotten her robe on before the sound comes again, a little louder.

Tap tap, tap tap. It's coming from her window, too regular to be a bird or a cat.

Heart crashing, she thinks of screaming for someone. Instead, she grabs the poker from beside the hearth. Night presses up against the window. Something glints there amidst the dark. She makes herself step closer, water trickling down her spine.

A voice floats in, barely audible. "It's me. Your Hawk. See?"

Æsa recognizes the thing against the glass: a feathered Hawk mask. Squinting, she can see it's him, and yet her heart won't stop pounding.

She unlatches the window and pulls it up. He's perched at the top of the rose-choked trellis, fingers gripping the sides of the sill. Gods, he must have crept through the garden and right past the parlor windows. It's a wonder none of the Dinatrises or the house guards caught him.

"What are you—?"

"Can we talk inside?" he whispers. "These thorns are very keen to impale me."

She nods, stepping back to admit him. His feet barely make a sound as his boots touch the rug. She takes in his face—the other night, she only saw it for those moments when they had their masks off. Æsa has never seen sea-colored eyes—Illish eyes—with such dark skin. His hair is dark, too, shaved at the sides and thick on top, almost curly. Paired with high cheek-bones and sensuous lips, he is striking. He might be the most beautiful boy she's ever seen.

She's been staring too long. His gaze moves between her face and the poker.

"I dearly hope you aren't still planning to use that."

She loosens her grip but doesn't put it down.

"You're lucky," she says in Illish. "I could have skewered you."

A flicker of a smile. "I believe it. You girls seem to have a knack for wielding sharp implements."

His Illish flows easily, washing over her, but his words shake her all the same. *You girls.*

"I'm sorry to surprise you like this," he says. "I couldn't figure out another way for us to talk."

Water drips from the ends of her hair. Her robe is wet, too, and clinging to her curves too closely. She feels her cheeks burst into flame.

"I need to dress. I wasn't prepared for a visitor."

"So I see." He runs a hand over his hair. "I'll wait."

She goes behind the screen next to the bath. Her pulse is still racing. She starts to pull off the robe, but hesitates. "Can you close your eyes?"

When the Hawk speaks, she thinks she hears a smile in it. "Already done, my lady."

Æsa peeks to make sure. Her gaze lingers, sweeping down the long, lean lines of his body, shown off by formfitting black clothes. She shakes herself. What is she doing? Just nights ago another, more familiar boy climbed through her window and it ended badly. The thought sobers her.

She dries herself quickly, pulling on a loose dress and a silk robe. It's a beautiful thing, all blue-green velvet waves and tassels, but just now she'd give anything for her old work dress and cloak.

Æsa steps toward the fireplace. "You can open."

The Hawk takes her in, but his gaze doesn't linger. He takes off his shoes and stalks silently to the door.

"Are there passageways between the rooms here?"

She shakes her head. His hands feel around the glass knob for the lock, pushing slowly. A thread of warning weaves its way through her chest. Her Hawk knows her name, where she lives, and with whom. It won't be much of a leap for him to guess Matilde is also a Nightbird. Matilde, who's kept her secret about Enis, and here Æsa is, unveiling hers . . .

The Hawk seems to sense her unease. He touches a thumb to his forehead, an Illish sign of respect.

"Æsa." He says her name as if it's something precious. "I swore an oath to protect you—all of you. You don't need to fear me."

But these past few days have made her fearful of everything, herself most of all.

"Perhaps I would feel better if I knew your name," she says at last. "As you know mine."

He nods. "It's Willan."

She feels the knot in her chest loosen a little. "Like the bug?"

"Go easy, now. My da gave me the name." The corner of his mouth curls. "He said it was because I was all legs."

She can't help but smile at that.

"They're strong, you know, na willans. And their music is more beautiful than any Illish fiddler can boast."

She knows. Their thrumming song used to rise from the jinny field behind her house on summer evenings. Homesickness tugs at her, a ceaseless tide.

He comes to the fireplace, leaning against its farthest edge. She should ask him about Enis, then make him go—it's a bad idea to let him linger. Or at least go and get Matilde to play their chaperone. But it feels good to speak to someone in Illish. Perhaps that's why she finds herself talking more.

She sits, motioning for him to do the same. "You're from Illan, then?"

He folds up his long legs and sits, leaving an honorable distance between them—more than he did the other night.

"I grew up there. When I was on land, anyway."

"But—" She stops.

An eyebrow lifts. "But I'm a few shades dark to be from the Sea-Whipped Isles?"

"I didn't mean . . ." She is blushing again. Why is she so flustered? "Well, yes, I did, but I don't mean to pry. It's just that you've helped me so much, and I know nothing about you."

For a moment he just watches her, touching his thumb to the tips of his fingers, back and forth in a slow, rhythmic wave.

"When I was six years old, a sailor found me in a lifeboat floating eighteen leagues from Erie, so thirsty I had no voice for days."

He leans his elbows on his knees. This close, he smells of salt and something sweeter.

"I didn't remember my parents. They're just shapes: my mam's hands mending nets, dark as foddernuts. My da's on an oar, white as foam. Something happened to their boat, I think. There'd been a storm."

Her heart constricts. "I'm sorry."

Willan looks away. "The sailor adopted me, anyway. My da taught me to sail, to tie knots, to whistle. How to fight my way out of a scrape. We had a lot of adventures."

He talks as if his da, too, is no longer living. She fights the urge to touch one of his hands.

"Was he a fisherman, then, your da?"

Willan gives her a rueful look. "Not exactly. You heard of the Serpent?"

Æsa blinks. "The pirate?"

"He would have called himself a liberator, but yes. That was him."

The Serpent was famous in Illan. Some said he was a rogue, but her da said he only raided those who could afford it. He said the Serpent took down bootleg traders, too.

"I grew up mostly on the waves," Willan says. "But we'd go to a house in Illan every summer to soak in the soil of his ancestors. Besides the sea, it's where I feel most at home."

Home. His voice holds the same fond ache that lives inside her. It makes her feel much less alone.

"So how did you end up in Simta guarding the Nightingale?"

The smile he wore before has faded. Now his eyes are full of storms.

"That's a long story, lass. And I don't think it's the one you really want to be hearing."

"All right," she begins. "What did you do with my friend?"

"I took him to a mate of mine," Willan says, careful. "A place for him to sober up before I put him on a boat back to Illan. But he kept kicking up waves, talking about things he shouldn't."

Her next words are slow to come. "Did he seem . . . unwell?"

At that, Willan frowns. "He talked as if he'd had too many bootleg cocktails. Since then he hasn't really stopped."

Her heart sinks. Is his frenzy for her a passing thing, like an illness? Or has she cursed him to walk the world in a haze?

"Where is he now?"

"Still with my friend. I can't trust anyone else to sail with him, so if you really want him home, I'll have to take him myself."

Her pulse picks up. "But . . . won't Madam Crow ask questions?"

"I told her my gran's on her deathbed. And since the Nightbirds aren't currently open for business, she wasn't overly fussed about a short leave of absence." His mouth twists, as if he's tasted something bitter. "Anyway, she's got me in a bind. She knows I'll come back."

Leta's words from their meeting rise up: *They're loyal. I've made sure of it.* Æsa has been so lost in her own fears and troubles that she's never spared a thought for what that might mean.

"Thank you for helping Enis," she says. "For helping me. I know it was a risk for you."

She should leave it at that, but something tugs at her rib cage, urging her to be brave for once. "Why did you do it?"

"Because kell ta kell, en bren to-magne."

It's an Illish saying: *Wave to wave, we ride together.* It means that Illan takes care of its own. But would he feel that kinship with her if he knew what she did? His sea-green gaze is so intense she can hardly bear it. Then he turns it on the candlelit hearth.

"The way he talked," he says at last, "he made it sound like he's your apselm."

Her eyes widen at the term. It's distinctly Illish, meaning something between *beloved* and *fated*. Apselm are pieces of a whole, two arrows aimed at each other. That bond is what compelled her mam to leave her family in Simta for an Illish fisherman she met on holiday.

"No," she says. "He's just a friend."

Willan's jaw flexes. "I don't mean to tell you your business, but the other night he didn't seem so friendly."

She touches the sea glass in her hair. "That wasn't his fault."

"You keep saying that. But surely you don't think it's yours?"

She can't tell this boy her shame—she can't tell anyone. But the pressure building in her chest won't be held back.

The story spills from her lips: the way it felt, kissing Enis back in Illan, and what he said about her magic. Enis finding her in Simta where he shouldn't have known she would be. It gives her the same rush and release as when she used to confess to Pater Toth in their church's whisperbox, except she never would have dared tell him any of this.

When she's finished, they're silent for several heartbeats. Their bodies are closer than before, almost touching, as if drawn together by some current she can't see.

"Has such a thing ever happened to the other girls?" Willan asks.

Æsa lets out a breath. "They say that clients can get . . . a little obsessive. That's why the Madam doesn't let people visit more than a few times a year. I've been told that sharing our gifts can create a kind of connection, for a short time. But this? I don't think so."

His hands are dancing again, thumb touching fingers. It seems as if he's choosing each word with care. "There was a sailor on Da's crew once. He had a penchant for a certain alchemical. He hid it for a while—he was a pious man, my da, an abstainer. But this sailor, he was more sensitive to it than other men. It scrambled him."

The thought of being someone's drug makes her shudder.

A memory rises of her and Mam in the drying shed, grinding up some starry night for a poultice. Made into a salve, the leaves will quickly ease a headache, Mam told her. But brewed into a tea, they are lethal. *A medicine can be a poison, too.*

"Do you think it's possible I scrambled Enis?"

Willan shakes his head. "His actions were his own. Nothing excuses him. What happened wasn't your fault."

Æsa wishes she could believe him.

"Your da," she says, looking away. "You said he was an abstainer. I imagine he wouldn't have approved of me."

Willan smiles a sad, rueful smile. "Please. My da would have revered you."

She starts at that.

"He used to tell great stories about the sheldars. Girls chosen by the Wellspring, he said, for great things. He always talked like they were saviors."

She thinks of her grandda's stories about those warrior women. They were always fierce and sure, but she isn't like them.

"My pater back in Illan used to say such women poisoned the Wellspring," she says. "He called them a perversion of the holy."

Willan makes a sour face. "What flotsam. Your pater must have been a real laugh come Feasttide."

Something in her expression sobers him. He leans forward.

"You must know that's not true."

She thinks of the wish she made before he came: *Take it back.* She meant it. An agitated flush creeps up her neck. "What if it's blasphemy, to give away this thing inside me? What if I poison someone else?"

"I think you're stronger than you imagine, Æsa."

He touches her then, his hand on hers a sudden plunge into the sea.

"Your magic is something rare, and no doubt powerful. But it isn't a poison."

Her throat is tight. "You can't be certain."

"I am, because it comes from you."

He is close now—so close. She should pull away, but she doesn't. She leans in, a moth drawn to a flame.

Kilventra ei'ish? he said that night. *Are you well, heart in mine?* It's a thing apselm say, but such a thing is dangerous to imagine when her kiss might be a hashna's song.

A knock at the door makes them both jump.

"Æsa?" It's Matilde's dame. "Are you done bathing?"

The doorknob jangles.

"Why is this door locked?"

Æsa's voice is too loud. "One moment!"

She pulls Willan up, tugging him over to the window.

"I'll be back to Simta soon," he whispers, pulling his shoes on. "I promise."

She feels strangely breathless. "Be careful."

"You too." He climbs back out on the trellis, quick as a mountain cat. One of his hands skims the ends of her hair. "Stay close to the other girls. Don't trust anyone but them."

Then he's climbing down into the garden. Æsa turns to see his Hawk mask on the rug. She scoops it up and stuffs it under her pillow. Hours later, when she's in bed, she pulls it out, smoothing its red-brown feathers and turning over what he said.

Your magic is something rare and no doubt powerful. But it isn't a poison . . . I know because it comes from you.

But neither of them knows what she is capable of: That's the truth of it. It scares her, just like everything that happened in the Nightbirds' rooms. They are vulnerable now: exposed. A part of her wants to climb back into the Dinatrises' bathtub and stay there. But Willan was brave enough to risk himself for her, and for the Nightbirds. Surely she can try and be the same.

PART II

Playing with Fire

Teneriffe Maylon closes his eyes, trying to figure out how he got here, both to this seedy bar in Griffin's and to this state of shabby disrepair, yet again. He should be in his club, surrounded by friends and flush with triumph, but they won't admit him. Not until he pays what he owes. Things were going so well, after that night he saw the Goldfinch. It felt as if no matter what he did, he couldn't lose. So he let himself be a little more reckless than was prudent. He bet too big and purchased too much Mermaid's Dust, the life of every party.

But then he started running out of funds. The party started to move on without him. And here he is, drinking cheap ale and fighting the desperate urge to ask his friends for more of their pocket money. He can't stomach it, just as he can't face his sire.

Tenny licks his lips, reaching in his pocket for the mask the Goldfinch gave him. Whatever magic once clung to it is spent. He didn't bother going to beg Madam Crow: He hears the Nightbirds are closed, and he doesn't have the money to see one anyway.

No matter. The Goldfinch made sure he would be able to find her.

Matilde Dinatris has exactly what he needs.

– CHAPTER 7 –
A LAYING DOWN OF CARDS

MATILDE GRABS THE carriage seat as they rumble into Dragon Quarter. Flamemoth lanterns shimmer out the window, beckoning them into the night. They wheel past the Winged Palace, pale against the purpling sky, and down the wide street that cuts through Dragon's heart. Because the Port of Simta lies in this quarter, it's never quiet. It bustles with life, the path to anywhere. They'll pass fine hotels and seedy ones, diplomats and sailors pouring out of theaters and cafes. Closer to the port, the streets will heave with navalmen and rough-and-tumble traders, heading for the bawdy houses of Smoky Row. Not that Matilde would ever be caught dead anywhere near there.

She looks at Sayer and Æsa seated across from her. It's been three days since her trip to Krastan's shop, five since the attacks on the Nightbirds, and yet this is the first time they have been alone together for more than a few fleeting moments. Sayer looks tired, and she knows Æsa hasn't been sleeping much. Truth to tell, neither has she. There have been too many questions circling her mind like flamemoths in a lantern, trying to find a crack in the glass. She likes puzzles, as a rule, but the mystery of the threats against the Nightbirds is driving her to distraction.

No other nefariousness has transpired since the attack, at least—clearly no one knows where to find them when they aren't being Nightbirds. She's heard nothing from Tenny Maylon, and Æsa's redheaded friend hasn't resurfaced. It seems the Hawk took care of him.

And yet the matriarchs are still being protective. Leta insists the Nightbirds remain closed for business. They've kept the girls mostly at home, filling their days with flower arranging and closely chaperoned teas. Gran won't even let her see her old Nightbird sisters. *No need to alarm them,* she said of the decision. *And I wouldn't want you to have to tell them untruths.* Dame has seized the opportunity to pin her and Æsa down to pore over Great House family trees, circling the most eligible bachelors. Tenny Maylon has been pointedly mentioned. She doesn't know how much more matchmaking she can take.

Matilde knows Leta is making inquiries about the zealot, but it doesn't seem as if she's gotten very far. Gran hasn't mentioned Epinine or Dennan, either. Since their meeting in Leta's study, she has only become more convinced that things are being hidden from them. She catches Gran and Leta, sometimes, engaged in heated conversation, which always dies as soon as she enters the room. When pressed, Gran insists it's all in hand, but their silence makes her anxious. Sometimes she wants to get out Alec's vial of Nightcloak and run away in a cloud of smoke.

She isn't the only one feeling caged. Sayer has been acting like a trapped cat, tense and irritable, and Æsa has managed to become even more withdrawn. Even so, there is no escaping this *thing* between them. She feels it when their hands brush or they sit close, as they are now. She assumes it's their magic, but it is yet another mystery. It feels almost like ants rushing under her skin.

She shifts in the warm air, making her outfit jangle. They are dressed to dazzle in fashionable headbands and dresses made of strings of beads. Sayer in silver, Matilde in gold, Æsa in copper: a matching set of precious metals. She hoped being alone at last might open them up, but both girls are quiet. It's time to take the situation in hand.

She puts her heels up on Sayer's knees.

"Really, ladies. Aren't you excited that we're finally out on the town?"

"Thrilled," Sayer says, pushing her off. "How did you get our jailers to let us out for the evening?"

Incessant wheedling, mostly. "Samson promised to be our chaperone." She can hear him now, laughing up in the box with one of their drivers. "My dame is keen to give him and Æsa some time together, a fact I shamelessly exploited."

Æsa's cheeks flush.

"And I let them choose the location," she goes on. "They think we're going to the theater."

Æsa frowns. "Aren't we?"

"I have something a little more exciting in mind."

She can feel the card Dennan gave her burning in her pocket, printed with the address of the Eila Loon Hotel.

Æsa tugs at the hem of her dress. "Is that a good idea?"

Matilde twirls her locket. "You won't be in any trouble, sweetness. If we get caught, my dame will know who to blame."

"No, I mean . . . it could be dangerous."

Matilde drapes herself across the seat. "There aren't going to be any paters where we're going, believe me. And anyway, it wouldn't matter if there was. They don't know the Nightbirds' true faces. The only thing anyone will see when they look at us is three Great House girls out enjoying Simta's pleasures."

Neither girl looks convinced. Matilde stifles a sigh. She used to love nights out with her old Nightbird sisters. They would swap jewelry and jokes as the city unfurled before them, opening like a friendly hand. Those girls were never afraid of taking a risk with her. Tonight, she needs Sayer and Æsa to be the same.

She claps her hands together. "Let's play a game. One secret each."

Sayer groans. "Must we?"

Matilde points. "I rescued *you* from a zealot with nothing but nerve and a fire poker, and then I helped *you* hide a boy behind a wall. Don't you think I've earned a secret?"

Sayer grumbles something about how she *had it handled*, and Æsa bites her lip and looks away. But Matilde needs them to loosen up, and to trust her. Tonight won't work unless they do.

To her surprise, Æsa goes first.

"You know how I told you my Hawk hasn't been in touch?" She tugs her dress again. "Well, I lied."

They listen as Æsa tells them about her Hawk's clandestine visit a few nights ago. Matilde can't believe she didn't know. Her friend Enis is taken care of, at least, but the Hawk saw her face, and now he knows where she lives—where they both live. Troubling.

Sayer frowns. "You're putting a lot of faith in this Hawk of yours."

"He helped me with Enis," Æsa says. "Willan's no threat. But . . ."

Matilde leans forward. "But what?"

"I—" Æsa starts, then stops. "I just hope he's all right."

Matilde doesn't know whether she means the Hawk or the redhead. Both, perhaps.

She turns to Sayer. "Your turn. Let's hear it."

There is a long pause as Sayer seems to mull on something. Her gaze, cool and assessing, makes Matilde feel skewered.

At last she sighs. "Fine. It's something you both should hear, anyway."

Matilde doesn't know what she expects Sayer to say, but certainly not that she sneaked out to go see some sandpiper in the Green Light District, at one of Simta's most clandestine clubs. A female piper lord—Matilde might be impressed if she didn't think so little of gangsters. She's surprised Sayer would call such a cutthroat her friend.

Matilde arches a brow. "And what, exactly, did you tell this dear old friend about your new life?"

Something complicated flashes through Sayer's golden eyes, turning them molten, but then they harden, honey going cold.

"Nothing revealing. I asked if she'd heard about a cult who prayed to Marren. She says they're called En Caska Dae."

The Blades of Flame. That explains the burning sword tattooed into the zealot's skin.

"Fen says their leader is some rogue pater who calls himself the Red Hand," Sayer continues. "He's been recruiting street kids to his cause, trying to turn them into soldiers."

"Soldiers for what?" Æsa asks, paler than usual.

Sayer's lips thin. "A war against magic users."

Matilde shivers. "Including, it would seem, magical girls."

A silence circles, thick with questions. Matilde asks hers aloud. "Do you think this Red Hand sent the zealot?"

Sayer leans back in her seat. "Maybe he was taking initiative. He said I would offer proof of witches: Maybe he meant proof for the Red Hand. It's possible the cult at large doesn't know about us."

It seems just as likely this Red Hand knows the Nightbirds exist, but not how to find them. Yet. She thinks back to what Alec and Krastan told her. What did Krastan say about the Wardens cracking down? *It's as if they are looking for something.* Perhaps this cult has infiltrated the Wardens. He could be sniffing them out even now . . .

"Did you tell Leta?" Æsa asks.

"Yes." Sayer blows out a breath. "Which also meant telling her how I got the information. Now she's constantly hovering. I can barely go to the privy without her wanting to follow me in."

Matilde crosses her arms. "And what did she have to say about it?"

Sayer's jaw works. "She told me to sit tight while she found out more."

Sit tight, be quiet, stay secret: It's all they seem to hear lately. Fold your wings and close your pretty eyes. Are the matriarchs simply trying to shield them from worry, or do they not want the girls to know how far from answers they are?

"Go on, then," Sayer says. "Give us your secret."

Matilde wants to dodge, to joke—it's almost second nature. But she needs to lay down some of her cards.

"Dennan Hain didn't come to the Goldfinch for a kiss," she tells them. "He came to tell me something."

She tells them about Dennan's visit in detail: Epinine Vesten's precarious position and Dennan's warning about her wanting to take the Nightbirds for herself. By the time she's done, the girls' mouths are agape.

"The Bastard Prince comes to warn you about the suzerain trying to steal us," Sayer says, "on the same night a zealot tries to do exactly that?"

Matilde nods. "I agree. It feels connected."

The rogue sect, the suzerain, the loaded silence of the matriarchs at home. It's like a spider's web: Tug on one string and the whole thing quivers.

"It makes me wonder if Epinine has allied with this rogue sect. Maybe she is using them to do her dirty work." Matilde takes a deep breath. "Which is why I want to talk with Dennan Hain. Tonight."

Æsa and Sayer both stiffen.

"You want to go and see the suzerain's brother while we . . . what?" Sayer says, tone acidic. "Act as your lookouts?"

"More or less," she says. "That and keep Samson busy. I don't need him trailing after me."

Æsa's green eyes shine with a look Matilde has never seen her wear before, as if she's peering through to things Matilde would rather not have seen. She asks, "How do you plan to ask him questions without revealing you're a Nightbird?"

Matilde swallows. If this was krellen, this would be her biggest gamble—the card that could change the whole game. "He already knows. He's known for years."

That knocks them both speechless.

"I gave my magic to him years ago, by mistake, before I understood how to control it. I thought perhaps he didn't know what passed between us, but then he showed up in the Goldfinch's room."

They say nothing, but their shocked silence speaks volumes. Matilde has to fight the flush creeping up her neck.

"Did Leta know?" Sayer asks. "When she admitted him?"

"No, but Gran does. She heard it all."

Which is why Matilde argued with Gran about going to speak with Dennan. *You must stay away,* she said, *until we can be sure of him.* But she isn't going to spend the summer sitting on her hands.

"And you trust Dennan Hain?" Æsa asks.

"If he wanted to take me to his sister, he could have. But he didn't."

"Blazing cats, Dinatris," Sayer says. "He's still a Vesten. How can you be sure he isn't playing some protracted game?"

She thinks of the earnest tilt of Dennan's voice, his conviction. Of his words when she said the Nightbird's rules would keep them safe.

Rules can also keep you in the dark.

She folds her hands together, all business. "He's kept my secret for years. And he has an inside track with Epinine. If there's some connection between this rogue sect and the suzerain, he might know it. He can help us sort out the threat."

Sayer leans back, headband glinting. "And what is he going to ask in return? Free access to you, to all three of us?"

At that, Matilde frowns. "He wouldn't do that."

"Your problem is that you think being House born gives people manners. But believe me, they're as hungry for power as any piper, and just as devious. Even covered in jewels and made of gold, a knife's a knife."

Æsa looks reproving. "You should have told us what you were planning, Matilde. Not ambushed us with it."

"I didn't think you would come with me if you knew," Matilde blurts, "and I need you. I don't want to do this by myself."

Matilde's voice comes out raw, and much too honest. It darkens the carriage like a bruise.

She tries again. "Aren't you both sick of being stuck at home, waiting for other people to make things safe for us? I'm asking you to help me sort this out."

The silence stretches, long enough to be painful.

Sayer crosses her arms. "So what, exactly, is your plan?"

Matilde tries not to exhale audibly.

She spins out her vision of the evening. It feels good to be conspiring with her new Nightbird sisters, finally. Gran would be livid if she could see them now. But Matilde is tired of waiting, cooped up at home with this restless, growing itch. She needs action.

Tonight, they will go flying on their own.

For ambitious young things and finely dressed pleasure seekers, we recommend the Liar's Club. You will need a member's invitation, but it is well worth the effort. Any lord who's anyone has his name on the rolls.

—AN EXCERPT FROM THE
VEST POCKET GUIDE TO SIMTA'S SECRET PLEASURES

CHAPTER 8

THE LIAR'S CLUB

ÆSA WATCHES AS a flamemoth lands on the velvet seat beside her. Its light makes her copper silk stockings seem to glow. She tugs at her hem, trying in vain to make it longer. She should never have let Matilde charm her into this dress, or this carriage. But they're here, and Matilde's voice is full of an unusual earnestness.

"Aren't you both sick of being stuck at home," she says, "waiting for other people to make things safe for us? I'm asking you to help me sort this out."

Their silence feels like it has teeth.

Sayer crosses her arms. "So what, exactly, is your plan?"

As Matilde explains, Æsa looks out her window. She hasn't been in this quarter since she first pulled into the Simtan port. Willan and Enis should be arriving on Illish shores in a week or so, if their vessel was a swift one. She often finds herself longing for her Hawk to come back.

Stay close to the other girls, Willan said, and she has. She feels closer to them now than ever, though not always in the way she would like. The tingling pull between them is still there; if anything, it's getting stronger. Sometimes she can feel it even when they aren't touching. It's as if their unused magic is building within them, looking for a way to get out.

Worse, she's started having dreams, strange and vivid. In one, blue glass rained down over a crowd of well-dressed gentlemen, one of whom had Matilde pressed up against a wall. Another featured Matilde in what looked like her family's garden. A man with a red handprint on his cheek was there, lunging for her, but Æsa woke up before she could see what happened next. She hasn't told the other girls—after all, they're only dreams. But they *feel* real, born of some piece of her that's long been sleeping. One she doesn't want to wake up.

"We're agreed, then?" Matilde is saying.

Æsa wipes her clammy hands on her dress. This feels dangerous, but she wants to be brave for the Nightbirds.

"Yes." She takes a deep breath and nods. "Agreed."

Sayer nods too. "Lead on, Dinatris."

The carriage jerks to a stop. Matilde peers out the window. She has as many smiles as the sea does creatures, and this one's full of mischief. "We're here."

Matilde jumps out of the carriage like she owns it—she *does* own it. Æsa's stomach flutters with nerves. She has the feeling she's forgetting something important. Those dreams have given her a dread she can't shake.

Sayer leans over, gently lifting the flamemoth from the seat and holding it out into the night. It glows in her palm for a moment before it lifts off. It doesn't go far—just to the lamppost next to the carriage. It alights on the glass cage as if wanting to get in with its fellows or find a way to let them out.

"Don't be scared," Sayer says. "I'll be with you the whole time."

In the golden glow, Sayer's lips are the same hue as the berries of the Lancer, a bush that grows wild back home in Illan. They are sweet, but difficult to harvest because of the plant's finger-long spikes. Æsa thinks Sayer might be like that. She wonders what gave her so many thorns.

"I'll tell you another secret," Sayer says, "about Simta. Everyone in this city wears a mask. They pretend they're someone braver, smarter, more cunning: whatever mask best suits them. Wear it well and no one will see you—not the real you. They'll only see what you want them to see."

Æsa isn't sure she knows how, but she promised herself she would be more courageous. She wants to feel like a sheldar for once.

"All right," she says, trying to smile. "Let's pretend."

The door opens and Samson is there. "Ladies? Shall we?"

He hands them one by one out of the carriage. Their dresses clink together as they head up the stairs. Sayer surprises her by taking her arm. The tingling feeling races over her skin, wind over waves.

The hotel before them is a grand thing the color of a cockle shell, with a lovely big dome perched on top. The Eila Loon. At the front doors, Samson argues briefly with a doorman, who at last lets them through into a soaring foyer. The furnishings are all bright wood and polished brass, but they get darker as Samson takes them into what seems like a servant's hallway. One turn, then another, a set of never-ending stairs, and then . . . a wardrobe? It looks like any other except for the small symbol etched into its side: a hand holding a match under a top hat. A burly man is leaning casually beside it.

"Young Lord Dinatris," he says. "Pleasant evening."

"Evening, Steven. It is a fine one indeed."

Matilde's smile matches her brother's. "And we're here to make it even finer."

The man, Steven, looks her up and down. "No ladies allowed, I'm afraid."

Samson shoots a glance at Æsa, then back at Steven. "Now, now, I know you make exceptions. You wouldn't deprive me of such ravishing company, would you?"

"We'll be very good," Matilde says, voice sultry. "Or bad, depending on your preference."

Steven looks unimpressed. "You look like you're going to cause me trouble."

Æsa remembers what Sayer said about masks. *Wear it well and no one will see you—not the real you. They'll only see what you want them to see.* She makes her eyes wide, her voice soft, leaning into her Illish accent.

"Oh, won't you please let us in, just this once?"

The guard and Samson both blink at her as if waking from a dream they aren't quite done with. From the corner of her eye, she sees Sayer grin.

"All right," Steven says. "But they're under your watch, Young Lord Dinatris." He opens the wardrobe. "Welcome to the Liar's Club."

He steps back, pushing a few coats aside. Music echoes from the wardrobe's innards. Surely there isn't a party through *here*?

Matilde leads the way, and Steven shuts the door behind them. All Æsa can see is their glittering dresses, but then the light changes and they step into a whole new world.

It's a swirling riot of voices, rising in waves up to the rounded golden ceiling. They must be inside the hotel's massive dome. The circular room is dim, all polished floors, sultry jazz, and plush blue velvet. Men cluster around a long bar, a collection of loosened ties and too-loud laughter. Everything is painted with a lovely blue glow. Æsa looks up at a massive chandelier made of blue glass, lit by thousands of candles. The sight makes something pull tight in her chest.

"Here we are," Matilde says. "And who knows, ladies, you might even enjoy yourselves."

Sayer snorts. "If your idea of fun is being pawed at by old men."

Samson gives them a wicked smile. "Not *just* old ones, surely."

He leads them across the floor, and many sets of eyes follow. There really aren't many girls here. There is magic, though: lapels that change color, ties that won't stay still. Understated, but still present. The bartender is pouring out a deep violet drink that smokes lazily. Above him, silvery orbs paint shifting patterns, thrown back by the mirrors that hang here and there.

"Remember," Samson says to Matilde, "Dame will murder me if she finds out I took you to my club, so no dancing on tables."

Matilde takes a mincing step, making her golden beads shimmy. "You know I don't make promises I'm not sure I can keep."

Samson sighs dramatically, putting his arm out to Æsa, and leads them over to a dimly lit booth. Two boys are there, a deck of cards set between them. Introductions are exchanged.

"Care to join us for a hand of krellen?" the boy called Maxim asks, ogling Sayer.

Sayer smiles at him darkly. "So long as you have coins you don't mind losing."

Samson's fingers press into her arm. Her heart wants to crouch behind her ribs, but now isn't the time to be timid. She can wear a mask if it means helping Matilde.

"I've never played," she says. "I don't suppose one of you might teach me?"

Samson and the other boy, West, both speak at once, scrambling over each other. Matilde gives her a smirk and a nod.

"Play a round without me," she says. "I've got to run a little errand."

Samson scoffs. "What? Where?"

An eyebrow arches. "The powder room, if you must know. I have a crimson tide to contain."

Maxim chokes on his drink. "That was more detail than we needed."

"Samson asked." She takes a sip of West's light blue drink, then makes a face. "Don't let these boys buy your cocktails."

With that, Matilde turns. On impulse, Æsa reaches out to run two fingers down her hand, a Nightbird signal. *Fly carefully.*

"Don't worry, darling." Matilde leans in close. "I always do."

She slinks off. Something about watching her go makes Æsa nervous, but she tells herself to relax. That girl's a shark in this place, not a minnow. Æsa only hopes she can swim half as fast.

MATILDE TAKES HER time. Rushing makes you look like you're doing something clandestine. No one stops her as she sashays past the bar, but heads turn. Perhaps dressing to dazzle wasn't her brightest idea. She just hopes Æsa and Sayer can keep Samson entertained for however long this takes.

She slips into a dimly lit hallway. It seems to wrap around the outskirts of the club, its curved blue walls lined with paintings of well-endowed nymphs and epic battles, all framed by potted crescent moonvines. She worried someone would try and stop her, but she sees no one as she passes several doors, most of them closed. Eventually she finds a set of wrought-iron stairs leading to the upper level. Her heels click as she climbs, emerging on a narrow gangway. The clinking of her beaded dress seems much too loud. But something else floats on the air: a tinkling music. It's coming from behind the door that reads *The Kestrel Suite.*

She checks the card Dennan gave her all those nights ago, though she's memorized its contents. Her breathing is coming faster than she'd like. There's no need to be nervous, she reasons. It's not as if she is about to unveil herself to him. But it's one thing to have your truth said aloud and another to take off the mask entirely. If she walks into this room, there will be no room for doubt. And he *is* a Vesten, brother to the suzerain, and a member of a House that openly champions Prohibition. If Gran found out about this little visit, she might never let Matilde out again.

Alec's taunt from the other day comes back, pushing her on. *You really are a sheltered bird,* he said. But not tonight—not anymore. Matilde balls up her hands. No more dawdling. She knocks: two short raps and a cascade of fingers, just like a Sparrow would do for her Nightbird. She doesn't know if Dennan will remember the code. After a pause, a deep voice says, "Come in, my lady." Lips curling at the edges, she reaches out and turns the knob. It isn't locked, as if he was expecting someone. Expecting her, perhaps.

The sumptuous room is full of flickering light and deep shadows. Candles drip on the mantel and orblights float above, pulsing like hearts. Dennan is standing by a round porthole-style window. He looks as if she's surprised him, but pleasantly so. There is an intimacy to the way his tie hangs loose, buttons open at his collar. It's as if she's caught him just about to undress.

"Young Lady Dinatris," he says, bowing. "You've come."

"You doubted me?"

"I thought you would send a note, not yourself. I should have known you'd go one better."

She sashays closer, slow, relaxed. This is a game—it's always a game with Dennan—so she's made sure to come ready to play it.

"How did you get in?" he asks. "They don't often admit women. Well . . . ladies, at any rate. The girls in these hallways tend to come courtesy of Smoky Row."

Matilde doesn't let herself react visibly to that scandalous tidbit. She puts a hand on one shimmering hip. "And why would they assume I'm a lady?"

"You look too fine to be anything else."

His smile turns the ground into waves beneath her. *Keep your wits, Dinatris.* If anyone's knees should be going weak, they're his, dash it.

The tinkling music comes again. She latches onto it.

"What is that?"

"Come and see," he says. "I think you'll like it."

She meets him at a velvet-covered card table. It holds nothing but a dark wooden box shaped like a many-pointed star. He presses his thumb to a groove in the wood and the music stops.

"It responds to the warmth of your skin," he says. "To start it again, you just . . ." He runs two fingers quickly through the candle burning beside it, then presses them to another groove. The music plays again, not loud, but so authentic, like minuscule players are hiding within.

She touches her fingers to one of the grooves. "Is it magic?"

"Not in the way you mean." He lifts a little panel in the wood, revealing a tangle of metal. "It's made of gears and levers, clever craft. Without magic, Farlands artisans have had to find other pathways to wonder. You'd be amazed what can be found in foreign ports."

Matilde wouldn't know: She's never traveled outside of Eudea. Something in his words makes her feel much too young.

"Drinks?" he asks.

She nods. He steps over to a side table and pulls out two tulip-shaped glasses. She sits, telling her jittering nerves to behave. Perhaps talking will help—after all, she's quite good at it.

"I'm surprised to find you hiding up here. Not at the bar, surrounded by favorites."

He stirs their drinks slowly, ice cubes clinking. "I make the Great House boys nervous. No one wants to get drunk with the Bastard Prince—they think I'll whisper their secrets to my sister."

"That sounds lonely."

He turns, those crysthellium-colored eyes burning into her.

"I have my crew, when I want to make a night of it. But lately I've spent my nights waiting for you."

The way he says it, he might as well be undressing her. She grips the chair where he won't see.

"And here I am," she says, "all dressed up for the occasion, and you with your tie undone."

Dennan laughs, a nice sound. "Deepest apologies."

He brings over their drinks. Hers is bubbly and violet. She sips it right away without asking what's in it. His eyes follow every move she makes.

"So," he says, sitting opposite. The orblights give his face a purple glow. "Does this visit mean you've decided I'm worth trusting?"

She swirls her drink. She *wants* to trust him. With so many threats against the Nightbirds, she also wants him on her side.

"You know, I'm rather on the fence about it."

"That won't do." He tilts his head the way he used to when they played together, waiting for her to make a move. "What else might I do to sway you?"

"Answer some questions."

The music box plays on. Dennan sips his drink, and she waits, patient, as if she has all the time in the world.

"All right," he says, leaning back. "Ask them."

She should ask for information about Epinine. Instead she asks the question that has plagued her for three years.

"Why did you leave Simta?"

He tenses. She tries to read the set of his features. Is there guilt there, or just discomfort? As always, he makes himself hard to read.

"What did you hear?"

She arches a brow. "Plenty of things, and you know I love a good intrigue. But after your kiss and run, I think I deserve to hear the real story. Don't you?"

He looks at her for several long, intense seconds. She will not be the one to look away first. Then he slides off the silver band around his wrist, etched with the dragon that is the sigil of House Vesten and set with a small amber dragonstone. The skin where it sat is shades lighter than the rest.

"My father gave me this band when I was ten. 'Wear it proudly,' he said. 'Let it remind you of who you are. One of us.' No matter what his advisers said about me being bad for the family's image, he loved me. It was the one thing I was certain of, until he lay dying."

Matilde leans forward. This isn't just a story—it's a secret. One he is entrusting to her.

"The doctors chased me from his sickbed," Dennan says, "but I lingered by a grate in the next room so I would hear him if he called. I didn't want anyone poisoning his weakened mind against me." He swallows, eyes still on that pale band of skin. "And then I heard his voice. 'Kill him, Epinine. For as long as he lives, he will spark dissension. They will use him to strip our family's power.' And she agreed."

Horror circles. She and Samson talk like they want to kill each other, but it's just playacting. They are family, and family is everything. She can't imagine what it would feel like to find out that was a lie.

"That must have burned," she says.

He looks up. "It still does."

Something flutters in her chest. Honesty suits him. The candle flames seem to lean toward him as if charmed.

"There was no time for goodbyes—no time for anything but running. So I took what I had in my pockets and left the Winged Palace." His lips quirk. "I have you to thank for how I pulled it off."

Her pulse picks up as she remembers their kiss. She has never forgotten it. They were playing hide-and-seek during a party at the Winged Palace when Dennan found her in an alcove underneath a set of stairs. *I win,* he said. *What's my prize?* She remembers the playful glint in his eyes, the unspoken words: *I dare you.* The rush she felt when she rose up and pressed her lips to his. It was her first kiss, her first time giving magic to anyone. How strange that she gave him a power she didn't yet know she had.

He leans his elbows on the table. "I didn't know what power you gave me with that kiss, but it must have understood that I had need of it. I put on a guard's uniform, hoping it would help me get out without notice. But when I happened to glance into a mirror, I looked like my guard, Timmo—exactly like him. It was easy, after that, to get out. I went and found a naval crew I had done a few trips with. I forged a notice from my sire and told them I'd been sent to take them to the Farlands. Off we sailed into the blue."

She wonders what it felt like to leave home, not knowing if he would ever come back to it. It's hard for her to even imagine.

He traces the scar on his lip with a thumbnail. "I spent those years at sea making diplomatic ties and fighting pirates. Making a reputation. Agent of the people, defender of Eudea. I knew if I built up such an image in the Vesten name, Epinine couldn't touch me. She would have to say she *sent* me. And when I finally came back, she welcomed me with open arms. At least she seemed to. With things as they are, she can't afford to have the family look fractured. I have worked ever since to make a place in her inner circle, to earn her trust, but it's not out of love for her."

The glint in his eyes is the color of hatred, but there's another shade too. She thinks it's pain.

The next question is easy to conjure.

"What is it you came back for, Dennan?"

His gaze is unflinching. "To be the suzerain this Republic deserves."

It takes a mighty effort to school her features. "Do you mean to *replace* Epinine?"

The silence stretches taut. Then he nods.

"She has made enemies of many of the Great House lords," Dennan continues. "With some of her decisions in the trade war with Teka and her push for taxes on certain imports, which she made sure the Vestens were exempt from. But mostly they don't like her growing closeness to the church. They think she lets the Pontifex wield too much power at the Table. Even the pious amongst them don't like their suzerain seeming to turn her back on the other Houses. They are more than ready to vote her out of power."

Matilde takes a sip of her drink, mind spinning. "Are you sure they would vote for you instead?"

She doesn't say *you, the Bastard Prince?* She doesn't need to. They both know the things people say behind his back.

"They might not all see me as their equal," he says, "but they're pragmatists. Since this Republic was founded, the suzerain has always been a Vesten. There is power and stability in that name. If they were to vote in someone else, there would be disquiet in Simta. There might even be riots."

She thinks of Krastan and Alec and their tales of the tension in the streets already.

"They also know," he says, "that the people would accept me. They like me better than my sister."

Bastard, sea captain, noble rogue. Of course they do.

"You would need the votes of all the House lords on the Table," she says, "to outweigh the Pontifex. I'm assuming he won't vote for you."

Dennan grimaces. "No. But I'm confident the House lords will back me. I've collected enough leverage on them all to ensure it, though I hope it doesn't come to that."

He's been planning this for years, then, perhaps since he left Simta. He always was good at the long game.

"And how would you be different from your sister?" she asks him.

He leans forward. "If there is one thing I've learned in my travels, it's that making something illegal doesn't abolish it. It only chases it into the shadows, where those who trade in it don't have to play by any rules but their own."

Her breath catches. "You would try to abolish Prohibition?"

He nods. "Not right away—it's too deeply entrenched, and there are too many people who support it. But I would work to get rid of the law, yes. It gives the church leave to morally police people through their Wardens, and it keeps the magic trade underground and corrupt. Making it taboo has weakened us . . . all of us. I would bring it back into the light."

"*All* magic?" she presses.

His comments that night in the Goldfinch's room make her think he disapproves of the secret club that is the Nightbirds. Because, like Alec, he thinks she should share her gift more widely, or because he doesn't approve of selling power for a price?

"I won't lie, I don't think any magic should be hidden," he says, careful. "And I don't like how the Houses treat you, like jewels to tuck away in a box. But your gift is yours, Matilde, no one else's. What you do with it is your choice, and yours alone."

The words make a door spring open inside her, letting a rush of warmth spill out.

It strikes her then how big a leap he is taking in laying his plans out before her. She could run to Epinine or the Pontifex tomorrow and tell them all about it if she wanted. He must know she won't, but still, he's trusting her.

She puts down her drink. "So tell me about Epinine. What is she up to?"

He drums his fingers on the velvet. "She knows the Night-birds have closed for business. I've assured her that I am working on finding you through other means. I will lead her down false trails until after Leastnight, when the vote is called. But Epinine is thorough: I wouldn't be surprised if she has others hunting for you."

Matilde's skin prickles. "I think so too."

Dennan frowns. "What makes you say that?"

She tells him, in brief, about the zealot who came to see the Ptarmigan and about the group calling themselves En Caska Dae.

"The Pontifex could have sent them," Dennan muses. "As his secret agents."

"He could have," Matilde says, "but Epinine could have too. She could be in league with the Pontifex, for all I know."

"She's said nothing of them to me," he says, "but I'll see what I can discover."

The music plays on. Dennan's gaze turns earnest.

"I promise you this," he says. "I won't ever let her have you."

The words warm her, but Sayer's warning is still circling. *You think being House born gives people manners . . . but even covered in jewels and made of gold, a knife's a knife.* She doesn't know about that, but she does know that nothing of value is ever given freely.

"And what payment do you expect for such protection?"

His hands inch across the table toward her. She tries not to hold her breath as she waits for him to speak.

"Years ago, you gave me a gift," he says. "If anything, this is me repaying you."

She steels herself. "Are you saying you wouldn't ask for access to my magic when it pleases you?"

His expression ripples, flashing what could be frustration. "I don't want to buy your favor. I want to win it. I meant what I said the other night."

She remembers. *I would rather you kiss me of your own free will.* Her eyes are caught by the scar on his lip again. They're nice lips. She wonders what it would feel like to press her own to them.

She clears her throat. "I've stayed too long," she says, standing. "I must get back before I'm missed. Will you write to me? Keep me apprised of what's happening?"

"Of course."

She smooths her dress. "There's a loose brick in the wall of our family's garden, to the left of the door. You can leave me notes there."

He walks around the table, bringing with him the scent of some smoky spice. "I have another idea."

He puts something on her palm. It's a heavy bird perched on a wafer-thin circle, both made of metal.

Matilde frowns. "What do I do with it?"

"Run your finger down its back."

She does, and the little bird ruffles its feathers, beak tipping up to meet her wide-eyed stare. It hops off its base and onto one of her fingers.

"Stick your note here," he says, indicating a slit in its belly. "Then wake it up and it will fly to me. As long as you keep that circle close, I will be able to send it back to your location."

"How do you make it sleep again?"

"Stroke it."

At her touch it stretches its wings, then settles.

Matilde laughs. "You certainly know how to keep a girl guessing."

A quirk of his roguish mouth. "I aim to please."

This close, his eyes are almost luminous. She finds herself leaning in closer still.

"I think I might just like to," she says softly.

"Like to what?"

"Kiss you again."

His gaze is hot on hers, like the candles, but she can't afford to let herself be burned.

"But not tonight."

She can feel him watching as she walks away, but she doesn't look back at him. Better that he not see the way she smiles.

———— ✢ ————

SAYER TAPS HER cards with a pinkie. Fen always teases her: It's such an easy tell.

"Is it my turn?" Æsa asks.

"It is indeed," Samson says, tipping back his newest cocktail. If you put him in a pool, he might float.

Now that she's leaned into the evening, Æsa's effervescent. The tilt of her head, the flick of her gaze, all saying *I'm so lost. Won't you help me?* Sayer is glad to see her out of her shell. Where is Matilde, though? For the fifth time, Sayer looks in the direction she disappeared to. She's having regrets about agreeing to her plans for their evening. Their veteran Nightbird is much too sure of her charms.

Tapping her foot, she looks down at her cards. The rules of krellen are simple: Collect as many valuable cards as you can before the pile in the middle runs dry. Each turn, players must pick from the pile or cast the krellen cup. Æsa opts for the cup, spilling out its contents. The seven-pointed star die clacks its way across the slippery cloth. Sayer leans in to see the roll: two hands clasped.

Æsa claps. "Oh, good. We trade!"

Samson's friend Maxim turns, smiling at Sayer from under

his unfortunate mustache. It droops like it's spent too much time in the sun.

"You won't give me a hint?" he says. "Just a tiny one?"

She shoots him a sharp-edged smirk. "You'll have to read my mind."

Maxim's eyes narrow. You can pick a card at random, but the point is to read your opponent for where she keeps what she values. The best krellen players are always good liars.

Sayer spotted Maxim's tell within two hands. He looks everywhere but at his best cards.

"Third from left," he says, pointing.

Sayer points too. "Last right."

His mustache droops farther. "Dash it all."

Normally she'd enjoy taking money from these spoiled House boys, but it's hard to relax with Matilde gone. She's taking forever. The music changes, slow and stretching, but Sayer finds herself desperate to pace.

It isn't just Matilde's plan that has her on edge. She's felt restless since that night she fought Gwellyn, when she turned herself invisible. She's practiced conjuring her Nightbird gift since then, when Leta is out and no one is looking. It comes about half of the time, but never as easily or completely as it did in the alley. It's as if something is missing, but she has no idea what.

She should probably tell the other girls what she did, but somehow it feels too personal. Perhaps because it started with a kiss. The memory of it comes to her at odd moments—during tea with the girls or as she stalks through Leta's leafy conservatory. The heady charge of it still clings to her lips.

Why did her magic come to her then, and not at some other moment? Why didn't the Ptarmigan's gift work for Fen? Does

Fen dwell on what happened as much as she does? There's no telling, as she's been silent since then. She barely said a word after Gwellyn and his boys ran from the alley. She just clung to the wall, looking at Sayer as if she'd seen a ghost. As soon as she knew the coast was clear, she practically ran from the alley. It felt like that night Sayer's dame died all over again.

Sayer grips her cards hard, thumbs turning white. Æsa must see it. She puts a hand on Sayer's elbow where the boys won't see. The touch gives her that charged feeling it always does. She feels it with Matilde, too. It isn't kinship, exactly, but something like it: a recognition. It makes her fidgety in ways she can't explain.

Someone says, *Your turn, Sayer*. She grabs the krellen cup and rolls the star. When it stops, it shows an arrow pointing past Æsa's shoulder toward the middle of the room, where a man is laughing. Recognition hits Sayer like a slap.

It's the man she spied on with Dame, that afternoon so long ago. He looks the same, if a little thicker at the waist. Burnished skin, oiled dark hair, golden rings: He fairly glistens. His suit is the purple of Eudea's finest wines. She can just make out the House sigil stitched onto the lapel, golden thread catching the blueish light. It's a Eudean timberwolf.

She knows which House it belongs to.

A terrible suspicion claws its way down her spine.

Sayer lays down her cards. "I fold."

"What?" Samson splutters. "But I'm winning. Don't be a spoilsport."

She makes herself smile. "Someone has to make sure Matilde hasn't flushed herself into a canal."

The boys all laugh but Æsa doesn't.

"Where are you going?" she whispers.

"To find Matilde." A lie. "I won't be long."

She weaves through the crush, following the man as he walks toward a doorway and slips through it. She follows, trying to stick to the shadows, but her dress is a silver, shimmering eyesore. Dash Matilde and her desire to catch all eyes!

She hurries down the curving hallway, heart racing, in time to see the man disappear into a room. Sayer creeps near enough to hear him greet another man, but she can't get closer without risking discovery. If only she could make herself disappear . . .

Pressing herself into a shadowy alcove, she calls to her magic. It might not work, but she has to follow him. She has to know.

Her eyes close.

Make me a piece of the darkness.

Turn me into shadow and smoke.

The sensation starts around her ribs, spreading outward, the featherlight scrape of a thousand knives across her skin. Her pulse picks up as dress and skin shift, turning the same blue as the walls, and the pattern of the rug paints itself across her legs.

She checks herself in a small mirror. When she moves, the illusion moves with her. It makes her think of a tigren: Those jungle cats have spots, she's been told, that help them blend with the grasses. Not quite invisible, but as good as.

A thrill shivers through her. This is so much better than Dame promised. This is a power she can fully call her own.

She creeps into the room, tucking herself behind a potted moonvine. The man is there with another, who is pouring them both glasses of something amber colored. Her hearing has gone sharp, just as it did in the alley. Blazing cats, the clink of ice against the glass is *loud*.

This close, the man who kissed her dame looks older than

158

she remembers, but he still glows from years of sumptuous prosperity. Things he had, she suspects, with help from Nadja Sant Held.

He lights a cigar. It isn't clove, like all the young lords smoke, but something dank and earthy.

"So, Antony," he says, swirling his cut-glass tumbler. "What's so important that I had to meet you *here*, and at this hour?"

Antony has a pinched, narrow face. "Bad news, I'm afraid. We haven't made much headway with the Pontifex. He says he will support the suzerain in the vote."

"Did you offer him that donation we spoke of?"

Antony wrings his drink. "I did. It wasn't well received."

The man lets out an aggravated grumble. "Perhaps we need to find something to hold against him. Even a holy man must have skeletons in his whisperbox."

"The vote is only weeks away," Antony says.

Their words seem to confirm what the Bastard Prince told the Goldfinch: These men mean to vote the suzerain out of power. Sayer has no love for Epinine Vesten, especially after what Matilde told them about her wanting to steal the Nightbirds. But who would replace her? This man who used to steal from her dame in the dark?

Antony looks around, as if someone might overhear them. Sayer presses harder into the wall.

"We could talk to Madam Crow. We need the Nightbirds' magic now, and she can't possibly deny us. After all, the Great Houses made those girls what they are."

Sayer bristles. No fancy rich man made her *anything*.

The other man's lip curls with disdain.

"We don't need them."

Antony sighs. "I know you think such things are blasphemous, but not all of us have your principles."

What principles? Sayer remembers his hands gripping Dame's waist, his fervent whisper. *Little dove. Nothing tastes as sweet as you do.*

"It *is* blasphemous. But do you know why I object, truly? It's cheating. Fortunes should be made on your feet, not on your back."

Antony looks surprised. "Really, Wyllo. You speak of them as if they're common harlots."

The name echoes through her: *Wyllo, Wyllo, Wyllo.*

Sayer feels as if she's falling through time.

She sees herself, age ten, crossing the canals for the first time, going to this man's door. She lost the nerve to lift the big knocker in the shape of a timberwolf, so she hid across the street behind a flamemoth lamppost and waited, trying not to sully her best dress. It was raining, she remembers, and she worried about getting mud on it. When he emerged from his Garden District mansion, two girls and a woman trailed behind: his legitimate family. His hat and umbrella meant she couldn't see his face. But if he saw hers, she thought, her sire would know her. She might find out for certain if Dame's rosy stories about Wyllo Regnis were true.

But he didn't look up. As their carriage passed by, someone threw Sayer a coin—a shill, worth less than a Twice Lit pastry. She grips that coin now where it's buried in her purse. Its pointed edges aren't sharp, worn down by time, but they still pierce her, just as surely as his words.

Wyllo runs a hand over his tie. "They are a vice, is what they are. A weakness. One some Houses have become much too reliant on."

She needs air. Sayer checks her camouflage and creeps out of her hiding place. Out in the hall, she finds the alcove where she turned herself into shadow and tucks herself back inside. The air is cooler here, but her thoughts are so clouded. She shuts her eyes, trying to make them coalesce.

The truth sinks in its teeth. *The man I saw kissing Dame is my sire.* He did come, just like Dame always promised, but not to save them. He came for whatever magic she still had. It wasn't enough that he used and discarded her when she was a Nightbird. He kept coming, leaving nothing but coins and empty promises. Stealing what was left of her glow.

There is a noise: footsteps. She opens her eyes to find Wyllo Regnis standing before her, staring. Her camouflage is gone.

He sees her now.

"And what might you be doing back here, young lady?"

That tone. It's almost . . . fatherly. She finds she can't quite find her voice.

"I . . ." she stammers. "I'm supposed to meet someone."

"And who might that be?"

"I can't say."

His expression changes, much less paternal. "Ah, I see. It's *that* sort of meeting. Well, I applaud your discretion."

Sayer tells herself to say something, *do something*, but she is ten years old and standing under a lamppost, wanting her sire to see and know her as his own.

He tilts his head. "You look familiar. Are we acquainted?"

Her heart drops. "No."

His eyes rove up and down her. His meaty fingers wrap around her arm.

"Perhaps we should be."

His hand on her is worse than Gwellyn's in the alley—worse

than anything. It makes wings of fear and rage beat in her chest. Something else rises with them, wild and urgent. A storm deep in her bones.

She throws out her hands and Wyllo flies backward, hitting the wall. He almost falls, but something keeps him standing, arms pinned to his sides. She can see what it is: bands of air, tinged blue and grey and black, shimmering darkly. They've found a way to harden around him, pressing him back like a giant hand.

His eyes are wide, cheeks purpling. "What sorcery is this?"

It's her magic, but not as she's ever felt it. This is a tempest bursting out of her skin.

"You want to know who I am?" Her voice is shaking. "Why don't you ask Nadja Sant Held."

At that, he goes pale.

"You can't, though, can you? Because she's dead." The air is shifting now—it tastes of lightning. Her heart is a maelstrom, roiling and dark. "And it's your fault."

Rage pulls his features taut. "I barely knew the woman. Whatever she told you about me, she lied."

Working on instinct, she closes her fists, asking the air to close around his throat and squeeze it. He gasps, eyes bulging. It feels good to see him look afraid.

"She loved you," she grits out. "And you betrayed her. You left us."

She tightens her fists, cutting off his air completely. His lips form a word: It looks like *please*.

Distantly, she knows she should stop, but it's as if the magic has been waiting for this moment. As if this is what it was designed to do.

A shattering crash comes from somewhere beyond, breaking her focus. Her hold on him drops away.

Her sire is breathing hard, eyes full of malice.

"I will make you pay for that."

But when he reaches for her, there is another crash beside them. One of the sconces on the wall bursts into angry, deep red flame.

Son, I have made some amendments to my will that might interest you.

To my wife, Maud Maylon, I leave my country house and the stocks specified in Charter XII.

To my youngest daughter, Tessa Maylon, I leave a dowry of 10,000 andels.

To my son, Teneriffe Maylon III, I leave nothing.

This could change, once you fix what you have broken, but you will have to work hard to earn back your place.

—A LETTER FROM
LORD TENERIFFE MAYLON II
TO HIS SON

CHAPTER 9

BLUE GLASS RAIN

MATILDE MAKES HER way back to the club room, her head still full of Dennan. He reminds her of a puzzle Gran gave her. It looked like a garden at first glance, but when you blurred your eyes a little it became a woman's skirt. Once you saw the true picture, you couldn't *un*see it, whereas before you never would have guessed. What would it be like to find out your life was like that puzzle? To have your family become your enemy from one breath to the next?

She's so caught up that she doesn't see him coming until he's there, blocking her exit. Her breath catches. Tie askew, hair wild, eyes red, Tenny Maylon looks ragged.

"Matilde," he says, making an awkward half bow. "Young Lady Dinatris, I mean. Pleasant evening."

It's only years of wearing masks, real and imagined, that lets her keep her expression neutral. As Gran would say, *Never let a client under your skin.*

"Can I get you something to drink, Young Lord Maylon?" she asks. "Perhaps a seltzer? You look . . . parched."

He does look thirsty, but not for anything like water. Dread coils into a tight knot in her chest.

"No." He licks his lips. "I thank you. But . . . you know, I could really use a kiss."

"From me?" She crosses her arms to hide the way her hands are shaking. "That's presumptuous."

He frowns. "After the other night, I thought . . ."

Dirty shills, she should have known he was going to cause her trouble, but she never dreamed he would accost her like this.

She straightens. "I think you're confused. You can't demand a kiss from me, Tenny."

"Perhaps not," he says, half to himself. "Not yet . . ."

She watches in horror as he drops to one knee, clutching her hand in his sweaty one.

"Matilde Dinatris, would you do me the honor—"

She tugs at him, looking around to ensure they're alone.

"Tenny, really. You must know that isn't how this works."

His expression wobbles, full of hurt and something darker. He tugs at his rumpled lapels as he stands.

"I'm in a bind, Matilde." The sconce on the wall paints strange shadows across him. "My sire is on the brink of disowning me. I need some help. I just . . . I *need* you."

She takes a steadying breath. "What you need is to kiss krellen goodbye."

He steps in, and suddenly she's pinned to the wall, his hands on either side of her.

"I could go to Madam Crow, you know. Or your family. I could tell them that you told me what you were and use it to push an engagement."

Heat flares behind her ribs. "You wouldn't dare."

"Wouldn't I?" He grinds his teeth. "Dash it, you blew me that kiss. You *asked* for this."

She didn't ask to be pawed in a hallway, trapped in the cage of someone's arms. She tries to push him away, but he leans closer, mashing his lips against hers.

She thrashes, but he holds fast, as if it's his right to take what he pleases.

How dare he do this to her.

How *dare* he.

A burst of heat rolls through her, white hot.

When her magic rises, it usually feels like petals unfurling, leaving the taste of ashes on her tongue. But this feeling is a torrent, a sudden wildfire, burning with the force of her rage.

Tenny jumps back as the wall sconce beside them shatters, revealing the shuddering flame within. It grows huge, turning from yellow to deep red. It's hers, that flame, pulsing in time with her heartbeat. She thinks she hears it whisper her name.

Another bursts down the hall, then another. She can feel them, as if they're an extension of her. Somewhere far away, there is a mighty crash.

Tenny's face is etched with horror, but Matilde feels drunk on her magic. Her whole body is alive with a fire she can't name.

ÆSA HAS HAD too many cocktails. It's hard not to when Samson keeps putting them in her hand. The other boys, Maxim and West, have gone to the bar, leaving them alone. Æsa isn't sure how much time has gone by since the other girls left, but it seems like forever. Time has turned into a slippery thing.

"Do you like it?" Samson says in her ear.

She hiccups. "What?"

"My accent."

She blinks. "I . . . Did you just say that in Illish?"

He smiles wider. "It's the cocktail. They call it the Wanderer. It has some . . . *special* ingredients . . . that help you speak another language."

Gods, she hadn't even noticed. The club has gone hot, all of a sudden. The jazz is fast, but the air is still—almost stifling.

Samson clears his throat. "You know, Æsa, that I . . . well, I think you're wonderful."

Æsa feels heat creep up her neck. "You do?"

He nods, eyes twinkling in the blue light. "I do. You rather dazzle me."

With his tousled dark hair and amber eyes, Samson is handsome. A bit frivolous, perhaps, but sweet. And he is one of Simta's imminently eligible bachelors, the kind of boy who would ensure her family never has to struggle again.

Samson leans in, breath scented by his cocktail. "Do you think you could come to feel the same about me?"

Another boy's face flashes through her mind: brown skin, blue-green eyes, full lips on the edge of a smile. A shivery feeling goes straight through her, but she can't afford to wish it was Willan sitting with her now.

She makes herself smile. "Perhaps I could."

Samson leans forward a little, an invitation. She plucks up her courage and does the same, fingers gripping the seat. Does she dare, after what happened to Enis? Will she poison Samson? No. She can kiss this boy without letting her magic out: She has to. She must find a way to be the girl everyone expects her to be.

A sudden feeling makes her gasp.

"Æsa?" Samson says, pulling back. "What is it?"

She shakes her head. Is it some effect of the cocktails? No. Something's tugging at her, as sure as fishing lines tied to her ribs. There are two of them, two strands, tingling with fear and rage that don't belong to her.

She croaks out, "Something's wrong."

Æsa has that feeling she gets on waking from one of her strange dreams: a sense of premonition. Her gaze is pulled up toward the blue-glass chandelier.

"Get under the table," she says, shoving at Samson. "Quickly."

He laughs. "What are we playing now, hide-and-seek?"

Above, there is a brilliant crashing.

Samson curses. "What in the ten bleeding hells—?"

Blue glass shatters, raining down on the heads of the men all around them. Just like what she saw in her dream. The chandelier's flames are bare now, and fairly leaping from their candles. Why are they so darkly *red*?

Men scatter and shout. Samson tries to pull her under the table, but the insistent tug at her ribs is too strong. It makes her think of the other part of her dream: Matilde pressed against the wall by a man, eyes frightened.

Suddenly Æsa knows what she must do.

She slips out of the booth. Glass rains down, drowning out Samson's shouts for her. She thinks, distantly, that she should be afraid, but there's no room for such a feeling. Not with the ocean whispering in her ear. She lets the tugging pull her through the room, around frantic arms and shouting waiters, turning a corner, weaving her way down a curved hall. Matilde is there, breathing hard and staring at the wild-looking boy who has trapped her. Æsa recognizes him from Leta's ball: Tenny Maylon. He is looking down at his vest, marked with two smoking handprints. It's as if someone took brands to the russet-colored cloth.

"You . . ." he whispers, eyes on Matilde. "You've ruined it."

Tenny is shaking, on the edge of doing something dangerous. Æsa can feel it. The ocean inside leads her on, whispering softly, urging her to make it right.

"Tenny Maylon." Her voice echoes, making it seem like it comes from all directions. The taste of brine and salt are on her tongue. "You listen."

Æsa has never seen anyone use the Nightingale's magic to shape a person's emotions. She doesn't know how such a thing is to be done. But as she takes his clammy hand, she can almost see his feelings, flowing through him like fast-moving streams. Desire and shame, anger and hurt—they need smoothing. She thinks of how the sea remakes the coastline, washing over the sand, wiping it clean.

"You aren't upset," she says. "And you aren't angry."

"But I . . ." His expression goes from enraged to doubtful, then confused. "No. Of course not."

"You care for Matilde, and you would never want to harm her."

Her words and something deeper guide the streams of his emotions, urging them down the channels where she wants them to flow.

"Yes." He sounds almost relieved. "I do care for her."

Matilde's eyes are so wide, the flame beside her head still spitting.

Down the hall, someone gasps.

Æsa turns, her concentration broken, to see a figure some ten steps away, tie hanging loose, shirt untucked.

Matilde whispers his name. "Dennan."

His purplish eyes flash in the flickering light.

He steps toward them. Tenny stumbles, his eyes glazed. Oh, gods, he looks like Enis.

What did she just *do* to him?

There is a suspended moment when it feels like they are floating underwater. Then all at once, every light gutters out.

Dennan Hain's voice floats through the darkness. "Come with me. Quickly."

Someone grabs her arm. It must be Matilde because the ocean inside Æsa crashes in response to it. Then she feels a tingling presence at her back. *Sayer?* She is moving, tugged through what feels like a sea with no edges, monsters lurking everywhere the light can't touch.

SAYER FOLLOWS THE girls, their secret shadow. It doesn't feel wise to leave Tenny Maylon behind them—he's seen too much. But so has Dennan Hain, and Matilde is still walking toward him. And her sire . . . he could be anywhere. Blazing cats, what a mess.

It's dark, but she makes sure to stay invisible. Using her magic seems to sharpen her hearing. She can make out what men are saying in the club's main room. *Didn't you feel it?* one of them says. *It was magic, I tell you. Something strong. Something strange . . .*

Others are shouting for candles, for guidance, for answers.

The three of them need to get out of here. There's only one exit that she knows of: the false wardrobe. But that isn't the direction Dennan Hain is headed in.

"Dennan." Matilde sounds dazed, all the polish knocked off her. "Where are you taking us?"

"Back to my room," he says. "To hide."

Sayer's heart beats out a warning.

"This club has protocols," he is saying, tugging them up a twisting set of wrought-iron stairs. "If there's a safety threat, they lock the exit and question everyone. Names will be taken. I don't think it's wise to let them take yours."

Sayer wants to swear aloud.

He opens a door at the end of the hallway, letting the girls through. Sayer slips in behind them before he can close it in her face. She stands by one wall, out of the way, watching Dennan watch her fellow Nightbirds. Is there a hunger in his eyes, or is that just the shifting light?

"Hello," he says, bowing to Æsa. "I don't think we've met. I'm Dennan."

Æsa looks as if she didn't hear him. "I . . . don't know what I did. To him."

"Right," Dennan says, running a hand through his hair, "about that. I'm going to get Young Lord Maylon and lock him in my other room before he speaks to anyone. And then we'll find you both a discreet way out of here."

Matilde looks ill. "Is there one?"

He nods. "A back staircase, but I need to make sure it's clear. I'm going to lock the door. Don't let anyone in but me."

He squeezes Matilde's hand, and then he's brushing past her. The door clicks behind him, and finally they're alone.

"I'm not waiting for the Bastard Prince to save us," Sayer

says. Both girls jump. "We need to get out of here before he gets back."

Matilde turns in a circle. "Sayer? Where are you?"

She steps into a shard of moonlight and lets herself become visible. Hands, then arms, then torso, shadow to light. When she turns, Æsa has sunk into a chaise, looking bewildered. Matilde is staring at Sayer like she's a puzzle that's confounding her.

"Sayer," she breathes. "Did you just use your own magic?"

It's the Ptarmigan's gift she means, but Sayer's mind turns to the way the air bent around Wyllo Regnis, changing and hardening at her command.

"I did," she says. "And so did Æsa, clearly. What in the ten hells did you just do?"

"I don't know." Matilde blinks once, twice. "But it's impossible."

They stare at each other. The room is still, but the air is full of . . . something. That charge between them, much stronger now. Ocean waves crash through her rib cage and fire licks along her veins. What *is* this? Blazing cats, what's going on?

Out in the hall, feet thunder by. Sayer's heart is pounding. Her feet hurt in her dashed heels, but still she paces.

"We can't get caught here," Sayer repeats. "We have to go. Now."

Matilde frowns. "They won't think *we* did it."

"Are you joking? It was clearly magic. The kind that used to get girls strung up by their necks."

She can almost feel them shudder.

"And even if they don't suspect, Dennan Hain knows it for certain. He could be going to get his sister right now for all you know."

Matilde shakes her head. "He won't do that. I told you."

"And what about Tenny Maylon?" Æsa's green gaze is steely. There's a strength in those eyes, Sayer sees, hidden deep. "Will he?"

Silence.

"How long has he known you're a Nightbird?" she presses.

Matilde swallows. "He came to the Goldfinch several weeks ago. Before the Season started. I did my job and sent him on his way. But then, at Leta's ball, I . . . did something I shouldn't have. I gave him a sign that made him think—"

Sayer's jaw drops. "Did you kiss him?"

"At the ball? Of course not. Just . . . flirted a little too pointedly."

Sayer knows she's kept secrets from them too—she's made mistakes—but this one raises her hackles. She balls up her hands so they can't shake.

"You're such a hypocrite," she says. "You go on about trust and sisterhood when all you do is lie to us. You preach the rules, but you don't have to follow them, do you? No, you're Matilde Dinatris. Everything's a game to you."

Matilde's voice is more command than admission. "It was an error in judgment. I thought no real harm would come of it."

Sayer is in Matilde's face, close enough to see the sweat at her hairline.

"Your problem is that you've always had your messes cleaned up for you. You've never known what it is to live in fear. You think, with your fine house and your fancy name, nothing can touch you. My dame once thought that too." Sayer's voice cracks. "But she learned better. Take the gilded blindfold from your eyes."

Sayer blinks fast, banishing the tears. This is what comes

of trusting people with her future. She won't make the same mistake again.

A whistle sounds somewhere, high and shrill, then a howl. Her skin prickles.

Matilde's eyes go wide. "It's a raid."

A bark echoes. The Wardens have brought some dogs, trained to sniff out alchemicals. But will they be able to sniff out what they've done?

"I ran across a Saluki once," Matilde says. "It couldn't scent my magic."

Sayer stiffens. "But I'll bet you hadn't just *done* magic."

Voices sound somewhere just below, coming closer, followed by a whine.

Æsa says, "We have to hide."

But where? Sayer looks around, but the room is sparsely furnished. Chairs, table, fireplace . . .

"I can disappear and make a diversion."

"No." Matilde's voice sounds far away. "I got us into this. And I know how I'm going to get us out."

Sayer frowns. "What are you—?"

"Just get out of sight." Matilde's amber eyes burn into hers. "I have this."

Æsa pulls Sayer down under the table, cowering behind its velvet cloth. She can see Matilde in the standing mirror next to the doorway, gripping something. A shirt, maybe?

"What is she doing?" Æsa whispers.

A bark and footsteps coming closer. Matilde is still just standing there.

"Matilde, get down here now."

"Dash it, *shut up*, I'm trying to concentrate."

In the mirror, Sayer watches as Matilde changes. It starts at her hands, the outlines of them going wavy, shrinking and bending like a desert mirage. No . . . like a fire, changing wood into a new shape. Body, clothes, all made new.

There is a sharp knock at the door, a jangle of keys, and then it swings wide open, revealing a hotel porter, two Wardens, and the thin white legs of a dog.

Ten hells, this is it. They've been caught.

"What is the meaning of this?"

The words come from Matilde, but her voice is someone else's. It's deeper, richer. She sounds just like—

"Lord Hain," the porter says, sweaty and flummoxed. "The Wardens have been alerted to a threat here. They would like to search your suite, if you don't mind."

"I do mind," the Bastard Prince—Matilde—says. Ten hells, she's convincing. Sayer would never guess she's just a girl wearing a mask. "And I don't appreciate my privacy being invaded."

"I don't care who you are," one Warden says. "You don't get special treatment."

"I imagine the suzerain will have something to say about that."

There is shuffling and crinkling, boots on floor, the sounds of sniffing. Æsa's nails dig into Sayer's thigh. The Saluki strains its pointy snout under the table. It barks once, then again.

A Warden leans close to the dog. "What is it, Gal?"

The tips of his boots come within inches of Sayer. Heart in her throat, she reaches for her knife.

"To doubt me is to doubt the Vestens," Matilde says, all quiet menace. "The Vestens, who have supported the Pontifex and the Wardens. So before you make a move, I would think very carefully."

There is a long pause, then some heated back and forth. Sayer holds her breath as the dog keeps sniffing. But Matilde must say something convincing, because at last the men retreat, closing the door behind them. The silence they leave in their wake seems to scream.

Then the door opens again. Sayer tenses. Someone speaks, his voice the twin of the one Matilde's stolen.

"Matilde . . . is that you?"

TENERIFFE MAYLON FALLS to his knees in the whisper-box. The back of its prayer window is etched with the sign of the four gods: a four-pointed star, one point for each Eshamein. He could really use one of their miracles now.

Please, he begs. *Forgive me. For all of it.* The gambling and cavorting, the games and the lies. Tenny has no more Mermaid's Dust, but he wishes for it. The way it makes the world seem brighter and kinder, sending you off on a euphoric cloud.

Whatever that Illish friend of Matilde's did to him was like that, banishing his fears. He wanted to bathe in it. But in the hours since, it has worn off, leaving his head throbbing and his mind sorely troubled. It was as if a part of him was being led . . . controlled. He shivers. No one should have that kind of power.

The window shifts, revealing a pair of dark eyes behind mesh. A pater. But it's his sire he sees, lips forming the last words he said to Tenny. *You are no son of mine.*

"Brother," the pater says. "What burdens have you come to lay down before the gods?"

"I—I've dishonored my House. I've gambled away my allowance and . . . more besides. Much more." He swallows, lips dry. "I have stolen from my sire and dame. I have tarnished them."

He feels a flush of shame, though it is wrapped up in fury. It's Matilde's fault that he is still in this mess. She made him promises with her teasing words, then she denied him. It's deceit, is what it is. It is betrayal.

"And what else?" the man asks, as if he's heard Tenny's thoughts.

"I bought magic," he blurts. "Well, I was given it. By a girl."

A few beats of silence. "You visited one of the girls they call Nightbirds?"

Tenny flinches, but there's no turning back now.

"I did. And . . ."

He shouldn't say what he saw—he isn't even sure what Matilde did at the Liar's Club. But his sire is an abstainer and he would want Tenny to tell the truth in this whisper box. Maybe doing so will make him worthy again.

When the pater speaks this time, his voice is different, like gravel.

"You have troubles, brother. But there can still be redemption. Just give the Wellspring this woman's name."

Tenny swallows, feeling sick. He didn't think. Didn't mean . . .

"I can't."

"You must. The gods demand it."

Tenny closes his bloodshot eyes, resting his head against the velvet. He wants a bath, some clean sheets, and a chance to start over.

"I want it all to be better," he whispers, hoarse. "*I* want to be better."

"You will be, once you unburden your soul."

And so he does.

CHAPTER 10

PINNED WINGS

MATILDE'S GARDEN IS still. It's past midnight, and Gran's night-blooming winglilies have unfurled their petals. She can smell them where she sits under a tree, fragrant and sweet. It's a peaceful place, scented with nectar and algae. But her mind is on fire with impossible things.

What happened earlier this evening at the Liar's Club goes against everything she was taught about her magic. For one, it's supposed to be invisible—powerful, but subtle. For another, Nightbirds can't use their gifts for themselves. And she did more than change her face: She commanded fire. Well, not commanded, exactly . . . It didn't feel like she was in control. A piece of her pulsed in every flame, a collective heartbeat. It's the kind of magic only a Fyrebird could claim.

She thinks of what Krastan said the last time she saw him, about Fyrebirds. *I wonder if that old magic isn't gone,* he said. *Just sleeping. If perhaps, one day soon, it will wake up.*

She and her old Nightbird sisters tried to give their magic to each other. They drank blush wine and kissed, lips tingling, but nothing happened, just as Gran said it wouldn't. Nightbirds can't give their gifts to each other: It's just the way of things. So why does it seem as if they three bring it out in each other? Every time they touch, her magic leaps inside her, growing stronger. It's as if spending time with them is waking something up.

She sighs. Why is this happening with *these* girls? These two, who don't even want to be her friends and drive her to distraction. Sayer's words whisper through her mind.

You preach the rules, but you don't have to follow them, do you? Everything's a game to you.

This evening was a gamble, to be sure, but she didn't think it would end in such disaster. Now she is exposed in a whole new way—and not just her. Both Dennan and Tenny know about Æsa. Matilde drops her head into her hands.

As Dennan smuggled them out through a secret back stairway, depositing them in the Dinatris carriage as if they were never in the club at all, she kept thinking of Tenny. She still can't quite believe what he did. She can't forget the other girls' faces when she told them: Æsa sad, Sayer betrayed.

Something crashes into the tundren palm near the edge of the fountain. She clamors to her feet as something dark flutters its wings on a leaf. It hops twice, flying toward her, landing heavy in her palm. Despite her sullen mood, a part of her still thrills to see it.

"Hello," she whispers. "What do you have to tell me?"

She sent the metal bird to Dennan hours ago, to see how things stood with Tenny and the Liar's Club. The white flash of paper in its belly must be his answer. She slides it out, the handwriting small and hard slanting. It's in a code they invented years ago, one of the simpler ones.

The Wardens searched the club for alchemicals. They found some, but not what they were truly looking for. The club's clientele is spreading rumors and wild tales already. I don't think they understand what happened here, but I would like to.

She closes her eyes. Of course he wants to know. He walked into his room and found a clone of himself. And then he watched, spellbound, as she shed the ruse. She remembers how it felt to see his imagined callouses fall away, revealing her own fingers beneath them. It was thrilling and disturbing at once.

She should be elated. Hasn't she always wanted to use the Goldfinch's gift for herself? But there is a leaden weight in her stomach, pulling her downward. How did things spill so far out of her control?

She returns to the note.

As for Tenny, he found a way out of my suite when I was taking you to your carriage. He's in the wind, but I will find him soon enough. Yours, DH

Dash it, Tenny. Where is he? Has he gone to his sire, an abstainer, and told him everything? Or as threatened, will he use what he knows to force a marriage?

She rubs at her eyes. In a moment, she is going to have to wake Gran up and tell her everything. She dreads it, but she and Leta will know how to make it right.

"What are you doing in the dark?"

Gran swishes down the veranda stairs into the garden, elegant in a grey evening robe. Matilde quickly stashes the bird and Dennan's note in her purse.

"Just . . . thinking."

"Thinking." Gran smiles. "A dangerous pastime."

"Grandsire used to say that."

"I think he meant it was dangerous when he found *me* thinking. It tended to mean trouble for him."

Gran takes a turn around the garden, touching leaves and whispering to flowers. She looks wilder amongst her creation, and younger. She could be a Nightbird still.

"I've just had an interesting conversation with your brother."

Matilde's breath catches. "Oh, really?"

Gran sits down on a bench and taps the space beside her. "Yes, really. Now I want to hear about the evening from you."

She has already been subjected to one reaming from Dame, counting crimes on her fingers: One, bringing Æsa home late and full of drink. Two, spending the evening at a gentlemen's club. Three, being wild and unforgivably wayward. But this conversation is going to be much worse.

Matilde sits down, forming the words, collecting her courage, but Gran speaks before she can.

"Samson says the hotel had a strange fire."

She taps two fingers on the back of Matilde's hand: one Nightbird calling to another.

"Tell me, dearest. Did you start it?"

Matilde's heart pounds. How could she know? Why would she guess?

"I . . ." The words are stuck in her throat. "I didn't mean to."

Gran lets out a breath. "Tell me the story."

Her instinct is to lie, but she wants answers more than she fears censure. So she spills about what she said to Tenny in the ballroom all those nights ago, then what happened in the Liar's Club. When she goes to confess the meeting with

Dennan, though, something stops her. She's already broken so many rules tonight.

When she's finished, a silence stretches. Matilde can hear the splash of the canal on the other side of the stone wall and some faraway music, but this garden is its own little world. Alec's words from the other day float back to her. *I would have you look over your garden wall and see what's happening beyond it.* Somehow, they sting more sitting here than they did then.

At last, Gran speaks. "There is so much we don't know about what Fyrebirds could truly do, in the old days. So much of what was written was burned or buried by paters, so many truths hidden or lost. All we have are the stories passed down through the Great Houses, and who knows how those have shifted. Dinatris family lore says the Fyrebird you and I are descended from could wield fire."

Matilde looks at her hands. On winter nights, she and Samson used to stick their fingers into the fireplace to see who could get closest. Hers never seemed to burn like his. Has this fire she feels always been inside her, waiting?

"It's said that all women with magic in them leaned toward an element: earth, fire, water, wind," Gran goes on, "which shaped the kinds of magic they could conjure. Such leanings shape our magic still, I think, even if we cannot see how. Sometimes a bit of that old magic bubbles up in us. A girl who can freeze water with the tip of a finger, one who can call to iron or warm a room."

"Could you ever do such things, Gran?" she blurts out. "Could you ever use your magic?"

Another silence, shorter. "Elemental magic? No. Never."

"What about your Nightbird gift?"

Gran tenses. "Have you, Matilde? Have you changed shape?"

Matilde nods. "At the club. My face, my hair, clothes, voice . . . everything."

"And the other girls?" Gran asks. "Have they?"

"Yes," Matilde says on an exhale. "All three of us."

She thought Gran would be shocked by this news, but she doesn't look it. Her hands are folded quietly in her lap. Matilde's breath quickens as her mind churns over the last few weeks and Gran and Leta's covert whispering. And Krastan . . . their exchange from the other day comes back to her.

You know I can't use my own magic.

Not yet, Stella. Not yet.

It's as if he—as if *they*—knew something she didn't.

"You knew this might happen," Matilde breathes. "Didn't you?"

"Oh, my darling." Gran closes her eyes, just for a moment. She is beautiful still, but just now she looks old. "I should have told you more."

"So tell me now."

Gran keeps her eyes on her winglilies. Their scent is so sweet, with just a whiff of decay.

"My Nightbird gift was different from yours, as you know. I was the Manakin, able to help clients appear alluring to anyone they chose to court. But the summer I was seventeen, I refused to see clients. I was like you, chafing at the idea of marrying someone chosen for me. When I stopped giving my magic away, it started coming when I called it. I could tailor my eyes or my hair, make my skin dance with illusions. The longer I went without gifting it, the more it came."

Matilde grips the bench. Some dark truth is wrapping its tendrils around her, its thorns threatening to pierce her skin.

"When I told my dame, she said I needed to keep it hidden, to gift it more and think about it less. Girls who didn't, she said, endangered the system that protected them. She was right, of course, but I grew bold. How could I not? One day, I did my magic where someone could see me. A pater."

Matilde shivers. "What happened?"

"He chased me. I escaped and ran to the boy I was seeing in secret, who hid me in the attic of his sire's shop. Then he found a way to make that pater forever silent. I never asked how . . . I didn't want to know. But I was grateful he was willing to pay such a price for my mistake."

Matilde's mind is whirring, full of questions. She just doesn't know which one to ask first.

"Grandsire was a shopkeeper's son?"

Gran laughs. "Oh, Matilde. When you love a story, you do cling to it."

The boughs of their trees seem too close, all of a sudden, the ground too soft beneath her bare feet.

"Surely the boy wasn't Krastan."

"Don't be a snob." Gran's lips curl, both fond and sad. "He was young once, as was I, and we were wild about each other. But even with what he'd done, my sire wouldn't consent to our marriage. My running away that night turned into something of a scandal, and I was quickly promised to your grandsire."

Matilde's mind tilts, tipped over by this revelation. Krastan always said he loved Gran, but she didn't think he really *meant* it. She certainly didn't think Gran loved *him*. An alchemist's son and a Great House daughter? Unthinkable. Alec's soft curls and subtle smile flash through her mind.

"But I thought you loved Grandsire."

Gran sighs. "I did, eventually, but part of my heart never left that attic room above Krastan's shop. I found things there that I have never found again."

A question forms, but it feels like one of the garden stones Samson used to delight in turning over, squealing at the creatures underneath. She is afraid of what turning this stone over might uncover, but she has to ask. Has to know.

"Is Krastan Padano my grandsire?"

Gran doesn't answer, but the silence speaks for her. Suddenly it's hard to breathe.

"Does Dame know?" Matilde asks.

"No."

"Does Krastan?"

"He suspects it."

Is that why his gaze on her has always held such fondness? All these years, he kept this secret from her too.

"You could have run away," Matilde says. "You left Krastan, after all that. And he let you?"

Gran straightens, regal as ever. "I did my duty. For women like us, duty comes first."

Something in her words makes Matilde think of her sire's butterfly collection. It still hangs above his massive oak desk. She remembers him pinning them so gently to their bed of velvet, making sure the air was dry and cool enough to keep their wings pristine. The butterflies were well loved, coveted by other collectors. She never stopped to consider how disturbing they were. Dead bugs on display, pinned down just so others could admire them. Beauty trapped forever under glass.

Matilde gets up, pacing the grass. The sweet burble of the fountain feels like a taunt to her. The cloying sweetness of the lilies makes her want to rip them out.

How has it taken her so long to discover these secrets?

About Krastan *and* about a Nightbird's magic. She could have used it for herself, all this time, and she never thought to try it. She grew up being told it couldn't be, and she believed.

"When Leta shut the Nightbirds down for business, I worried," Gran says. "I told her it was only a matter of time before you all started discovering things for yourselves."

Is this what they were always whispering about in the shadows? How best to keep their little birds in the dark?

"And yet you kept all this from me." It is their golden rule: Lie to everyone else, but not each other. "You knew and never said."

"You were always such a wild child, dearest. I didn't know what you would do if you discovered you might be able to use your gift in such a way. Some truths, I find, are better left buried."

Matilde's chest is ablaze. How can Gran say that? Tears sting. "You should have *told* me."

Gran sighs. "I didn't like keeping it from you. Truly I didn't. I thought I could protect you from my follies."

"No, you wanted to keep me tame," Matilde snaps. "A good girl. A compliant girl. Ten hells, you're no better than Dame."

The words fade into the silence, swallowed by the lily-scented air.

"It's a hard enough task keeping the Nightbirds a secret," Gran says, so calm. "When one uses her magic, it becomes harder to hide, and to surrender."

"Why *should* we surrender it? Why should we give our power away?"

Gran's eyes are fixed on her now. Even in the darkness, they glimmer.

"When the last of the Fyrebirds hid in Simta, they stopped using their elemental magic. Do you know why?"

Of course. She grew up with this story. "Because it made it hard to hide from the horrid men with flaming swords."

"It was horrible, Matilde, the things the paters did to them. But it wasn't just paters. Sometimes their neighbors hurt them, too, their friends. There are stories of people trying to harvest their magic, bottling it like some alchemist's brew. Of feudal kings finding ways to control them and wield their magic like a weapon. Others hunted them down out of fear: A woman with that kind of power is a danger. So the Houses encouraged them to keep their magic secret. The Fyrebirds didn't know it would turn inward as it did, taking strange and twisting turns, but they embraced it. It's easier to hide a thing no one can see."

Something in the words makes Matilde think of the Wardens' Salukis. Their breeders encourage certain traits in their pups, suppressing others. The Houses did the same, leaving the Nightbirds with only the gifts they could harness. Honing them into a tool and not a threat.

Gran's voice turns urgent. "It's been so long since those days that we forget why those women chose to let the Houses guide them. Why they sacrificed their magic rather than expose themselves. It's dangerous, Matilde, for us and everyone around us. Who are we to turn against the forfeits they made?"

Forfeit, honor, duty. The words feel like a cage.

"You don't like it, I know," Gran says. "But this is the system. We have to trust it. The Great Houses have gone to great lengths to keep girls from straying down that path, toward destruction. Those who don't are brought back into line, and I don't want that for you."

Matilde sucks in a breath. What does that mean? Sayer's angry words echo through her. *You think, with your fine house and your fancy name, nothing can touch you. My dame once thought that too. But she learned better.* Dame intimated that Nadja Sant Held was responsible for her own ruin. But perhaps that, too, was a lie.

"So what am I supposed to do?" Matilde whispers. "Just shove it down and forget?"

Gran stands, face painted in shadows. "We need to get you married. The sooner, the better. And you will have to seriously consider Tenny Maylon."

Matilde's stomach twists. "You must be joking."

"It will keep him quiet," Gran says. "And despite his many foibles, he's a sweet enough boy."

Matilde stares at her, mouth open in horror. Gran's eyes are sad, but she doesn't back down. Dinatris women do their duty, however unpleasant. She expects Matilde to do the same.

You think, with your fine house and your fancy name, nothing can touch you.

Take that gilded blindfold from your eyes.

It's gone now.

A sound comes from the garden door: a sort of scraping, then a wood-creaking bang.

Gran frowns. "Who could that be at this hour?"

The voice that answers is gravel and salt. "Marren's soldiers, come to mete out justice."

Gran steps in front of Matilde, pushing her toward the house.

"There is no justice here for a pater to see to."

"That is exactly what a witch would say."

A shiver shakes Matilde, dread wrapping around her.

Another scrape, another bang on the door, hard enough to shake it. The zealots are going to break it down.

SAYER STARES OUT her window at Leta's, peering into the deepening dark. It's too still in this room, too stuffy. She wishes for a wisp of a breeze, but nothing moves.

She is tired, but after the night she's just had, she can't sleep. She keeps hoping to hear Rankin's trumpet—a call to arms, a piece of news. Something to *do*. She wants to go see Fen, but Leta's been on alert since she came home. Sayer can hear her moving through the house like a ghost.

She doesn't know what to make of anything that's happened, or how to feel about it. The scene with her sire is playing through her mind again. Since she left the hotel, it hasn't stopped. She keeps remembering the way he talked about the Nightbirds, his fingers digging into her arm. The vengeful satisfaction of using her magic on him has faded, in the hours afterward, leaving nothing but a hollow, angry ache.

She didn't know what it would feel like if she ever met Wyllo Regnis. She never expected it to hurt quite so much. At least she can be fairly sure he won't tell anyone about it. He was already pretending she didn't exist when he knew better, and now that he knows about her magic . . . he's built his reputation as an abstainer. He wouldn't want anyone finding out he sired a girl like her.

I'm an orphan, Sayer thinks. *I have no family.*

She knew it before, but now it cuts her like a knife.

There is a knock. Sayer huffs out a breath. "Come in."

Leta swoops in wearing a dressing gown embroidered with black swans, her dark hair swept up neatly. They see each other every day, but it isn't often she comes to Sayer's bedroom. If she's surprised to find her ward wearing pants stolen from one of her many closets, she doesn't say.

"Good, you're awake. We need to have a chat."

Sayer pulls up her knees. Leta perches at the edge of the window seat, letting the silence curl into claws. Her code name was the Magpie once, and she gave the gift of finding things that've been buried. Her sharp stare has often made Sayer wonder if she has any of that magic left. After tonight, it doesn't seem like a stretch.

"I loved your dame, you know," Leta says.

Of all the things Sayer thought she would say, that wasn't it.

"We were Nightbirds together. Though I'm sure you must know that."

It makes sense: They were around the same age, and good friends. Leta was one of the only ones who ever came to call.

"She was a loving thing." A smile curves Leta's lips. "Brimming with sweetness. The other girls, they treated me badly at first. A girl found in a brothel would be no friend of theirs."

So the whispers about Leta are true. Matilde would be scandalized, but it makes Sayer respect her. Leta created her own Great House out of nothing. Privilege fought for is a different thing from privilege born.

"I didn't care," Leta says. "I'd survived worse things than their judgment. But the night I first met the other Nightbirds, Nadja bounced up from her seat and embraced me. 'Sister,' she said. 'We're so happy to have you.' She knew my past, but I don't believe she ever judged me. She was a warm blanket wrapped around my bitter edge."

Sayer looks away. It's a strange thing to hear, that the woman who raised you lived a whole other life before you came along.

"I told her not to let that sweetness blind her." The faint smile is gone, replaced with something brittle. "I told her the things men will say to get their way. Our madam didn't keep as tight a leash on the proceedings as I do. Your dame is why I took up the office myself. Too many visits and sweet promises lead to disaster. By the time she confessed it all to me, the damage was done."

Sayer swallows. *She* was that damage, growing inside her dame's belly. Something twists deep in her chest.

"Your grandsire assumed Wyllo would marry her. Who wouldn't want one of the Nightbirds for a bride, illicit pregnancy notwithstanding? But he was engaged already, to a very affluent family of abstainers. He didn't want the scandal. So he denied ever having slept with her. He was a man on the rise, part of a group of House nobles who professed the church was right about magic. He couldn't afford for anyone to know what a liar he was."

Leta's face is more open than Sayer's ever seen it. The fury in it matches her own.

"You said you were like sisters." Sayer's voice is tight, almost shaking. "So why didn't you help her?"

Leta's voice is sharp again. "I tried. I said I would buy a house for us, if her family rejected her. I know what it is to lose a child. The scars it leaves."

What does she mean? Sayer can't quite parse her words, or her expression.

"But she was proud, your dame," Leta goes on, "and stubborn. She wanted things her way or not at all."

That isn't how Sayer remembers her. The dame she knew would have jumped at the chance to live here. What was she thinking? Her heart aches to know she will never be able to ask.

"Her parents, the Sant Helds, would have taken her back, but they demanded she give you up." Leta looks out the window, as if seeing the past out in the darkness. "They said she could finish out her confinement with some cousins in Thirsk and let them raise you. She could go back to being a Nightbird with no one the wiser. Instead she ran away, changed her name, and hid in Griffin Quarter. Nothing I said would change her mind."

Sayer's mouth drops open. "She went to Griffin's . . . by choice?"

Leta nods. "Nadja had a powerful imagination. She thought that if she played the martyr, Wyllo would change his mind and come for her. And then, as months turned into years and he never came, she was too ashamed to admit to her mistake."

But Sayer knows the truth. He *did* come for Nadja Sant Held, but not to honor her. He came to take her power for himself. *This,* she thinks, *is what needing someone gets you.* What comes of putting your fate in other people's hands.

Something calls out in the night: a bird or an insect. The air has turned into a close-held breath.

"Why are you telling me all this?"

Leta's gaze is piercing. "Because you're keeping secrets, just like she did, and I won't make the same mistakes I did with her."

Sayer takes a breath. Maybe it's time to tell Leta what happened at the club—to trust her.

The thing outside calls again, even louder.

"Dirty shills." Leta wrinkles her nose. "Is a cat somewhere dying?"

No. It's a trumpet played badly, sounding frantic. Rankin.

Sayer stands as someone pushes open Leta's garden gate, not even trying to stay hidden. She runs out of the room, down the hall and the grand staircase, and flings open the veranda door.

"Fen, what are you *doing*?"

Fen opens her mouth just as Leta arrives.

Sayer braces herself. A sandpiper in her garden? Leta will want to arrest her. But all she does is stare, her gaze intense.

Leta tilts her head, voice strange. "Do I know you?"

"No," Fen says, barely sparing her a glance. "And you won't."

Sayer looks between them, the air pulled taut as a trip wire. What in the dear dark depths is going on?

Fen turns to her. "En Caska Dae are about to raid the Dinatris mansion."

Sayer swears. Tenny Maylon must have told them. Matilde's arrogance is coming home to roost.

"How do you know this?" Leta demands.

"No time to explain," Fen says. "And if you want to help them, Tig, there's no time to waste."

She throws Sayer a mask: the kind people wear to the Leastnight carnival in Griffin's, cheap and shiny. Fen slips on one of her own, a smiling fox.

"Wait." Sayer's thoughts are tumbling fast. "You're coming with me?"

"If you're going, I'm going," Fen says. "Like shadows stick together."

The Dark Stars oath. Sayer swallows hard.

Leta's voice is thin and tight. "You two aren't going anywhere."

Fen turns to her. "You'd leave two of your girls to a bunch of zealots?"

"I will rally the Houses."

"Then help will come too late."

Leta turns to Sayer. "Stay. I command it."

Perhaps she should—she didn't sign up to be a hero. But Sayer won't leave the girls to such a fate.

I wonder, love, if you ever dwell on those stories I found all those years ago. The ones that spoke of the Fyrebirds of old. I know you mean to protect Matilde by telling her that she can only give her magic to others. But you are keeping her weak, Frey, as you were when you left me. You clip her wings, and thus you keep her from flying.

—A LETTER, UNSENT,
FROM KRASTAN PADANO
TO LADY FREY DINATRIS

CHAPTER 11

UNMASKED

ÆSA IS WATCHING Matilde and Lady Frey from her bedroom window when boys start pouring into the garden. They are all dressed in grey robes, with an insignia on their chests she can't make out. Many have crossbows. The sight of them makes Æsa's stomach twist.

Someone grabs her arm: Matilde's dame, Oura.

"Stay here," Oura whispers. "And if they come near the house, stay hidden."

Her heart is pounding. "Who are they?"

Oura's mouth is a thin, dark-painted line. "No one good."

She rushes out into the hall. Æsa waits a moment before she follows, padding down the grand stairs and into the breakfast room. A floor-length window has been left open to the stagnant night, and she slips behind its curtains. She peeks around the frame to see Oura walking out onto the porch, fists clenched.

"This is trespassing," Lady Frey is saying. "Leave now, or there will be consequences."

"We answer to Marren and the Eshamein," the man in front says, his voice both deep and cold. "Not to you."

He is older than the rest, face pocked and thatched by scars and smeared with lines of red paint. It's as if someone dipped their hand in blood and pressed it to his cheek.

Her skin prickles—she has seen that face before, in her dreams, or what she thought were dreams. This seems more like a waking nightmare.

Samson strides onto the veranda to stand next to his dame, hair disheveled. "What's the meaning of this? Who are you?"

"I am the Red Hand of Marren," the man says. "And we are his servants, the Blades of Flame."

Æsa grips the curtain hard. Lady Frey and Matilde are inching toward the veranda, but the boys in grey are circling, closing around them like a fisherman's net.

Samson scoffs. "And what business is it you think you have here?"

"I come for the witch," the Red Hand says. He points at Matilde.

Samson lets out a choked laugh. "Have you lost your senses?"

Lady Frey faces down the men. "That is a dangerous accusation."

"That *thing* is the danger." The Red Hand's voice is like the tide, almost hypnotic. "What she wields is not hers. It was stolen from the Wellspring. It's time for her to answer for her crimes."

Oura's voice is fierce. "My daughter has committed no crime. Who are you to dare say so?"

"Not a Warden, that's for certain," Lady Frey says calmly. "You have no legal right to be here."

"That's right." Samson has made his way down the stairs, pushing past the Caska boys to face the Red Hand by the fountain. "Listen here, this is my House. Leave now or I'll make sure you regret it."

The Hand pulls back his lips, showing teeth. "We burn with purpose. Your threats mean nothing to a fire."

He twitches a finger and something flies through the air: an arrow. She watches as it punches through Samson's right shoulder. He falls and Oura screams, flying down the stairs to help him. Matilde runs toward him too.

The Red Hand lunges for Matilde, grabbing the strap of her beaded bag. Æsa can't see her face, but she can feel her fear.

"Don't you *dare*."

There is a roaring *whoosh*.

Lady Frey shouts, "Matilde, no!"

The Red Hand stumbles back. Matilde is holding something. It looks like a child's ball, but it's glowing. No . . . burning.

The boys in grey all make the sign of the Eshamein at their foreheads. Their awed, frightened eyes are full of the fireball's glow.

Matilde's expression is wild. "House Dinatris doesn't suffer trespassers. I'd suggest you leave before I burn you down."

No one moves, transfixed. The Red Hand's face is full of a strange elation. And then he says, "Take her."

A few of the braver boys move toward her. Matilde lets her fireball fly. One of them screams as it catches at his robes, the other trying to put the fire out before it spreads. Matilde is already throwing another fireball: Where are they coming from? Patches of her nightdress are singed and blackened. The flames seem to caress her skin but do not burn.

More boys in grey dance around, trying to get to her. It seems they want to capture her, not kill. But Æsa knows what will come next, because she dreamed it: the Red Hand reaching into his grey robes, scarred face twisting, something glinting in the light of Matilde's fires.

The ocean rises up in Æsa's chest.

"Matilde, look out!"

She steps through the window, flinging out her arms on instinct. Magic seems to flood through them, pouring from her in a shuddering wave. The water in the fountain rises, sliding over the lip and crashing through the garden, wrapping itself like a wall around Matilde. The Red Hand's knife comes down, but the blade lodges in the water. It's turned into a solid sheet of ice. She can see Matilde through it, eyes fixed on her in wonder.

Sea spray in her nose, waves in her ears, Æsa feels like a sheldar. Gods help her, she almost likes it.

The Red Hand looks up, all rage and triumph.

"Another one," he snarls. "Seize her!"

A few boys in grey start toward her, crossbows out. She could run into the house, but Matilde is trapped in the ice, and Frey and Oura are by the fountain, hovering over Samson. She can't abandon them.

"Come with us willingly," the Hand commands, "and no one else need suffer for your sins."

The word *sins* startles her into dropping her hands. Æsa's ice wall cracks and melts, pouring out across the grass. The boys in grey creep closer: They are going to be taken. Æsa feels a sob building in her throat.

There is a ripple of sound: a whip of wind cutting through the stillness. The Red Hand is knocked right off his feet into the grass. The boys in grey start falling, one clutching his stomach, another clawing at his throat. One swings wildly at something he can't see, then drops as if he's been punched in the jaw. Crossbows go flying from boys' hands, thrown into the bushes. There's a shimmer in the air like twisting shadows. If Æsa squints, she can almost see . . .

Sweet gods. *Sayer?*

Two masked figures are there, too, disarming the Caska before they can react. Where did they come from? One wears a fox mask, the other a badger. The badger has something in his hand—a glass orb. When two of the Caska lunge toward him, he throws it down and it shatters. Something sinuous emerges, looking like birds made of smoke. They surround the boys in grey, who start batting at them. One of them screams in high-pitched terror.

Æsa runs through the chaos to Matilde. They stumble together over to the fountain, where the Dinatrises are huddled. They should make for the house, but Samson can't seem to stand, and there are so many bodies, too many crossbows ready to shoot anything that moves.

There is a shout, and Sayer stutters into view wearing a mask like a tigress. One of her friends, the badger, trips and falls over a crossbow, rolling toward them. The fox does a graceful spin and turns toward the Hand, knife out. One of the Caska boys lunges for the badger, but Sayer raises her hand, closing a fist, and he stumbles, clawing at his throat like he can't breathe.

"Stop," the Red Hand roars. "Or we start shooting."

Sayer drops her hand, and the boy sucks in a breath. The masked boys and Sayer back toward the fountain, closer to the rest of them. A few of the Caska are still shouting and swatting at the smoke birds, but most have closed around them. There is nowhere left for them to run.

"The Pontifex wanted one as proof," the Red Hand whispers, "and I will bring him three of you. A poison hiding in plain sight."

The boys in grey touch fists to chests, whispering a prayer together. *A cleansing fire to cleanse the world.* There is such loathing on their faces. Æsa can't stop the shame from rising up.

She thinks of what Mam will think when she hears of this, what Da will say. Of Willan, who said he would come back for her. *I swore to protect you.* But he's too late.

Matilde grips her hand. With the other she reaches into her bag and pulls something out—a dark vial.

"You want poison?" she shouts. "Then here. Have some."

The vial shatters on the tiled base of the fountain. Black, thick smoke billows out like a cloud. No, not smoke, just . . . darkness. Gods, it stings her eyes something fierce. She can hear En Caska Dae shouting and coughing, but she can no longer see them.

"Into the house," Lady Frey says. "Quickly."

But which way is the house? The darkness makes it hard to tell. Matilde keeps hold of her hand, and Æsa fumbles for Sayer's, wanting to make sure she doesn't get left behind.

As soon as their hands clasp, something happens. A shiver of joining, then a sudden rush. It is like all the other times they touched were just a ripple. This is water and light, stone and earth, wind and fire, coming to life. She feels an overwhelming sense of wholeness—of rightness. But then it drops away, stealing her breath.

The ground shudders, somehow less solid beneath her. The trees groan, the sound of a ship in a storm, and something slithers near her. It's as if the whole garden has come violently to life.

When the Red Hand speaks, his voice is almost reverent. "Ana. Is that you?"

One of the Caska shouts, and then another, turning the darkness into a sea of panicked screams.

———— ✻ ————

Matilde is on fire: inside, outside. The sudden rush is like standing too close to the hearth. You want the heat, but you also know it might burn you. And then, all at once, the fire recedes.

The garden's full of sound: hissing leaves, creaking wood, curses and shouting. Something whips through the air near her head that she can't see. The Nightcloak veils everything, but it won't last. They need to make a run for it.

She reaches for Samson, but someone's already lifting him. Someone grabs her arm and they stumble for the house, up the stairs.

"I see you, little thief," the Hand shouts, over and over. "I see you!"

Matilde turns only once on the veranda, to make sure they're all with her. Her mouth drops open at what she thinks she sees. The garden is alive. Vines whip and bushes strangle. The trees have pulled up roots and wrapped themselves around the Caska like snakes. The Red Hand is pinned to the fountain, shaking with rage.

"You cannot run from me," he roars, eyes on her. "Marren will have justice!"

She runs into the house and locks the door. Her family has collapsed against a wall in the main hallway. Dame has Samson's head in her lap, pressing down on his bleeding shoulder. His eyes are glazed when they find hers.

"Tilde," he croaks. "Did I just see you make fireballs?"

She ignores him, crouching down. Dame's eyes are frightened. Is it En Caska Dae she fears, or what her daughter just did?

"My sister's magical," Samson babbles. "As is the girl I'm courting. Dirty shills, that is—"

Gran shushes him and locks eyes with Matilde. "You have to go now."

Matilde frowns. "But—"

"Listen to me. Go to Krastan. Until you hear from me, *do not* come home."

But this is her world, her family, and it's broken. "I won't leave you."

"You will," Gran says. "You must."

Dame grabs one of Matilde's hands and kisses it fervently. Gran squeezes the other.

"Fly carefully, my darling. Fly true."

Someone yanks her away and they are running.

"They have boys out the front," Sayer pants. "I can hear them trying to bang the door down."

"Then where do we go?" Æsa asks.

That shakes Matilde out of her daze. "To the roof."

They reach the top of the stairs just as the first En Caska Dae storm the foyer. She can hear them shouting at her family. "Where are they?" Her heart burns, but she can't afford to look back.

Up and up they go—has her house always had this many stairs in it?—to the ceiling hatch near Dame's room. She pulls it down and they clamor up into the attic that runs the length of the house, musty and hot.

"This way," she whispers, hurrying through Dinatris keepsakes. Sweat is collecting beneath the strap of her bag, still slung across her shoulder. Her purple satin nightgown keeps getting caught on things. Dash it, why didn't she put shoes on? She didn't think she would be running for her life in her sleep clothes. She swallows down a wild, hysterical laugh.

At the far end, she undoes the round, pink-tinged window and climbs through it, watching as the rest of them spill out onto the roof. Sayer, the fox, and the badger look like escapees from some strangely themed party. She and Æsa are the only ones with faces bare.

We're unmasked.

They run to the floating bridge, a narrow thing that swings out to connect to the next mansion over. It's there in case of fire—or, apparently, religious zealots. It's only when she and Sayer swing the thing out that she remembers it's not finished, hanging just short of the neighbor's ledge.

The fox has gone to the roof's edge and is looking at the garden. The badger goes over and tugs at his orange vest. "We have to go, boss."

The fox doesn't move. He's gone rigid, hands balled up, as if transfixed by something.

The badger boy's voice is shaking badly. "Fen? Please?"

Fen. Matilde starts at the name—the fox isn't a boy. She's Sayer's cutthroat. Fenlin Brae takes a sharp breath and turns toward them. Matilde can only see one of her eyes.

"Rankin, you first," Fen says.

The badger salutes, taking off running, a trumpet swinging where it's strapped to his back. He streaks down the bridge and flies over the gap, landing hard on the neighbor's roof. The fox goes next and turns to wave, hurrying them on, but Matilde feels unsteady. If she could just have a moment to catch her breath.

There's a ripping sound. She turns to find Sayer, knife out, slicing through Matilde's fine satin.

"Sayer, what in the—?"

"Nightgowns," Sayer growls, "weren't meant for fleeing."

The slit she's cut goes almost to Matilde's hip bone. The shouts from below are growing loud.

"Come on," the badger shouts, holding his hands out. "We'll catch you."

But Æsa is frozen at the edge of the bridge in her blue velvet night-robe, her long hair bright and wild around her face.

Footsteps come from close—too close. Panic twists and writhes in Matilde's gut. But Gran taught her to wear a mask, even when she doesn't have one—to show the world only what she wants it to see. So she grabs Sayer's arm and tugs her over to Æsa, all confidence.

"Come on, ladies. We'll jump together."

Matilde counts them down: three, two, one. Three Nightbirds flying. The gap isn't huge, but it's a long way to plummet. It feels like she is falling into some new, foreign world.

They land, almost toppling, and then are up and running, her beaded bag banging against her hip. The slick shingles make Matilde slip and the rough ones cut her feet, but she barely feels it. Her heart is beating so hard it might well burst. The setting moon paints itself on Simta's skyline as they go across the rooftops, from bridge to bridge, rushing along crests that are sometimes no wider than a forearm. Once Æsa slips, arms pinwheeling. Sayer almost pulls her robe clean off to keep her up.

Matilde keeps her arms out like wings in the darkness. She tries not to look down or back. Three more roof jumps and they reach the last house—time to go down.

The attic window is locked. The fox brings her elbow crashing down and through it, breaking the orange glass and reaching in. Matilde feels the need to say something—anything. Otherwise she might cry or scream.

"Familiar with breaking and entering, are we, Fenlin?"

The badger—Rankin?—tips back his mask and smiles, revealing a gap between his teeth. "You should see her with a set of lockpicks."

Fen grunts. "This isn't the time for finesse."

They race down through the mansion, which is mercifully empty. She used to play here with the Layton twins. It looks different from how she remembers, more menacing, but there is no time to jump at shadows. The boys in grey won't be far behind. On they go, down the stairs and through a silent garden, sneaking to the gate that leads onto the street.

"Where should we go?" Æsa whispers.

Matilde's fingers wrap around the bird Dennan gave her, still tucked in a pocket of her bag.

"My gran said go to Krastan, so that's where we should go."

"The Yellow Alchemist?" Sayer asks. "Are you sure we can trust him?"

Matilde sighs. "He knows my secret. His apprentice does, too. He made that potion we just used to escape."

"Blazing cats, Dinatris," Sayer whispers hotly. "How many people have you blabbed to?"

"About as many as you," Matilde shoots back, pointing at Fenlin and Rankin.

"Don't start," Æsa whispers. "Not now."

Fenlin speaks low, only for Sayer. "Rich girl's right. They're a safe bet. The apprentice, Alecand Padano, is on Dark Stars watch."

Matilde doesn't know what that means, but Sayer must. She sighs.

"Then let's go."

Their run through Pegasus Quarter is long, as they stick to the dimly lit back streets. It must be one or two in the morning, which means few people are out. Flamemoth lanterns scream over their heads, bright and telling. Glass and grime cut into the soles of Matilde's feet. Her stumbling steps keep time with her thoughts, always the same: *That man shot Samson. That man tried to take me away.* He invaded her home, where she thought they were protected, a sacred place no one would dare to breach. There is another thought, too: *Æsa and Sayer risked themselves to save me.* It makes it hard to catch her breath.

"This way," she gasps, pointing down a wider lane. A few people gawk from windows and porches. She just hopes none of them recognize her face.

A shout goes up behind them. Is it the Caska? Matilde veers into a sunken stairway, pressing her back against the wall. The others pile in, holding their breaths as four boys in grey run by above them.

Fenlin tips back her mask, revealing a sharp jaw, a green eyepatch, and a devastating mouth. A kissable one, if you like a dash of lethal with your trysts.

"There are more," Rankin says, peeking out. "Blazing cats, they're persistent."

Sayer scowls. "How has no one stopped them? They're not Wardens."

Fenlin shrugs. "We can't count on anyone else to get us out of this."

Matilde's mind is spinning, making plans and discarding them. "We can't let them see us near Krastan's shop. They can't know he is helping us."

Sayer slips off her mask, sweat on her brow. "I can make myself into shadow, and maybe Fen and Rankin."

Fenlin shakes her head. "No, Tig. Best you keep it for yourself."

Sayer and Rankin talk at once, and Fen says something to Æsa. Matilde grips her locket, trying not to see that horrible man, the Red Hand. And now he knows who she is and where she lives . . . He has torn her life open.

She wants to take something from him.

Matilde closes her eyes. She doesn't have anything of his to hold, to help the change, but it doesn't matter. His hands are etched into her mind, dry and papery, his dark eyes burning through that handprint on his face. Heat flickers, ashes in her mouth, and she feels a rippling heat pass over her, shimmering like a second skin.

When she opens her eyes, Rankin is staring.

"Dirty shills, miss, your *face*."

Matilde looks up and finds all eyes on her, startled. She puts a self-conscious hand to her cheek.

"Is it that bad?"

"No, it's good . . ." Sayer starts, blinking hard. "It's just uncanny."

Fenlin looks like she's seeing a ghost. "That's a sweet way of putting it."

When Matilde squints down at her hands, it's as if she can see the Red Hand's on top of them. She shudders.

"Does my voice sound like his?" she asks. "I can't tell."

They all nod. She sketches out a plan for them. Sayer doesn't like them splitting up, but Matilde convinces her it's better. Then Sayer turns into shadow, Fen and Rankin stalking behind:

She will scout ahead for them. Meanwhile, Matilde grabs Æsa's arm and prays her magic will hold.

They've only gone about a block when they meet a bunch of Caska boys. She thanks the gods the Red Hand isn't one of them.

"Sir?" one asks, expectant. "Orders?"

Matilde goes to speak, but fear chokes her.

Never take off your mask, she thinks—a Nightbird rule. *Never let them see you.*

"I have her," she says, stolen voice sure, no room for question. "The others are headed that way, toward the canal. Go and get them."

They hesitate, all eyes fixed on Æsa. *Dash it all.*

"Did you hear me?" Matilde barks. "I said *go.*"

They make a sign over their hearts and take off running.

Her stomach twists, her skin feeling as if flamemoths are crawling up it. The sensation makes it hard to think.

"Matilde," Æsa whispers. "Your real face is showing."

She wipes her hands on her skirts. "Well, then. We'd best hurry."

They creep along the lane, trying to stick to the shadows. Two more corners and they are within sight of Krastan's shop. Sayer and the others are there too, all too visible.

They run over. When Matilde turns the latch on the door, it is locked, closed for business. But Krastan will be upstairs—he has to be. She has nowhere else to go.

She pounds on the yellow door, waiting for shouts to rise behind her. Her feet are aching and her breaths come in gasps. She is just about to risk a yell when the door swings open, revealing Alec's shocked face.

"Blazing cats. Tilde?"

"Let us in. We are having a *night*."

Alec backs up, and they all fall through the doorway. A single candle is burning on the counter. The air is rich with herbs, heavy and earthen. It makes exhaustion hit her in a rush. She always thought girls who had fainting fits were merely faking it, but suddenly she feels as if she might have one.

Alec looks them over. "What's going on?"

"Krastan said to come here if I needed a port in a storm," she says. "Well, I do. We all do."

Alec's dark eyes search her like she's a finicky potion. "Who found you?"

She takes a deep breath. "Some very zealous paters."

Alec swears. "Did they follow you?"

"They tried," Rankin says. "But we lost 'em."

"Thanks for the Frightlings, mate," Fenlin cuts in, peeling off the fox mask. She seems to have recovered from her strange spell on the roof. "Worked a treat. What was that darkness potion you gave Rich Girl? You'll have to make me some."

Alec sighs. "I would, Fenlin, but who knows what you'd do with it."

How in the dear dark depths do Alec and this piper know each other? Matilde is too overwhelmed to even ask.

Alec scowls down at the floor and her bloody footprints.

"Here," he says, grabbing some battered slippers from behind the counter. "We can't have you leaving a trail of bread crumbs."

He locks the front door and leads them toward the back hallway. The slippers are too big, and she hasn't made it five steps before she trips. Alec's arm goes around her. She wants to make a joke about how he should buy her dinner first, but she's too tired. He smells so good: like smoke and frennet leaves. Something dangerously close to a sob fills her throat.

In the secret back room, Alec pulls a jar from one of the shelves near the baseboard. A whole section of the back wall swings wide, revealing a door. Another secret room—one Matilde didn't know about.

Candle in hand, Alec leads them down some rickety stairs into a basement. Few houses in Simta have them: With water levels so high, they tend to flood.

"Step back," Alec says, peeling up the corner of a carpet, revealing a round metal hatch. It is made of dark metal, etched with flowers and winged horses.

Sayer frowns. "I thought we didn't have underground tunnels anymore. They flooded."

"That," Alec says, "is one of Simta's biggest lies."

The hatch swings smoothly open on its hinges, revealing a dark hole. Alec pulls a bag out of a pocket, shakes it until it glows, and drops it into the abyss. A rope goes next, which is attached to the drain cover and the rug, somehow.

"There's usually a ladder," Alec says. "It isn't a big drop, but if I hold the lid, you can use the rope . . ."

Rankin hops up to sit on the lip of the hole. "Feet first, no problem."

He drops. Æsa gasps, but it's only a second before they hear his feet hit stone and he calls up to them. One by one, everyone follows suit until it's just her and Alec. He holds out a hand, but she can't move.

"It's safe, Tilde," he says. "I promise."

But this hole is going to take her away from her world, from her family. She can't shake the feeling that she won't be able to get back.

She swallows hard. "You first, then."

His mouth opens like he's going to argue—she almost wants him to. It would make this all feel more normal. Instead, he disappears down the hole.

She sits at the lip, clutching her purse, then her locket. One of the tattered slippers flops off and falls. Matilde used to wear Gran's slippers around the house, slapping against the wooden floors. She was all dreams, no fears, her life so sure. Pain punctures her heart, but the world won't hold still for her. So she schools her features, grits her teeth, and drops.

Alec catches her in his arms. Her ripped nightdress is high on her thighs, leaving her legs exposed.

"Put me down," she says, reddening. "No need to play the hero."

"No need to play the princess," he grumbles. "Your feet are a mess."

She struggles until he puts her down. Her heels throb, but wherever they're going, she wants to arrive there on her own two feet.

The dark tunnel stretching out in both directions isn't large: Alec could probably touch the slanted roof of it. Matilde presses a finger to one wall. They weep in places: canal water, she assumes, mixed with things she doesn't want to ponder.

"What is this place?" Sayer whispers.

Alec pulls on the rope until the hatch closes above them, clicking. The glowing bag casts a purplish light across his cheeks.

"It was used for transporting things around the city once,

we think. Then as catacombs. During the Great Revelations, it became a place to hide."

No one speaks as they walk. The tunnel smells strongly of algae, dank and mossy. She tries not to think of the city above, pressing down. Then there's light ahead. At last, they turn a corner into what Matilde thinks will be another tunnel. It's more like the inside of a church, pointed at its apex, soaring with color and dazzling light. Hundreds of orblights float above them, a cluttered starscape that makes the walls glimmer and brightens up the colorful tents. There are stalls, too, and people, all staring.

"Alec," she whispers. "Where *are* we?"

For the first time since she showed up at his door, he smiles. "Welcome to the Underground."

PART III

WHAT
HAPPENS
IN
DARKNESS

We take you as you are, and welcome.
Bring your gifts, your hurts, and your fire.

—A NOTE ETCHED INTO THE WALL
OF ONE OF THE UNDERGROUND'S TUNNELS

CHAPTER 12

BRING YOUR FIRE

For perhaps the first time in her life, Matilde is speechless. She looks to Sayer and Æsa, but they're both staring around at the dazzle. When Alec starts walking again, there is nothing to do but follow.

They wind through what looks like a bustling market, not so different from Brightwater. It's busy, given the late hour, and it seems to deal in the illicit, its sellers waving hands over rows of jars and vials. A man is explaining to a customer how his balm will keep you cool on hot evenings, while a woman is showing off artisan teas that make even the most meager meal taste like a feast. Nearby, someone is juggling glass orbs for a gaggle of children. He lets one crash to the stones and they all gasp as the gas inside takes on the shape of a galloping horse.

A full-grown tree stands in the middle of the stony thoroughfare, its branches hung with tiny orblights. Matilde reaches out to touch one of its purple leaves. It—this whole place— seems impossible. She doesn't know how anything can grow down here.

Eyes turn toward the Nightbirds, wary and wondering, but no one stops them. Alec seems to offer them safe passage. The vaulting hall goes on and on. Matilde can see smaller tunnels twisting off it, marked by quieter tents with lanterns set out at their doors. She sees a group of men playing cards, a woman rocking a fussy baby. Surely these people don't *live* in this place?

Toward the far end of the tunnel, there is a smaller archway. Alec leads them through it and toward an alcove full of chattering girls. Some of them form a ring around a girl with wild curls wearing a dingy white dress with lots of out-of-fashion frills. She is handed a slice of gulla fruit, and the dress starts changing to match it, color seeping across it until all of her is a bright sunset pink. Matilde sees no potion or charm: Just the girl, twirling and laughing. It doesn't look like any trickster work she's ever seen.

One of the others gasps as the girl's hair starts going pink to match the rest of her. She stops spinning, looking down at her arms as they change, too. She seems confused by this turn of events, but not frightened. As if turning pink is nothing about which to be concerned.

And then Matilde catches sight of another girl, fifteen, maybe younger, standing with a candle in her hand. The flame turns from red to blue, then green, as she reaches fingers toward it. Matilde wants to cry out—surely it will burn her—but when the girl pinches it, she captures a tiny piece of green fire. She passes it between her fingers like a coin, back and forth. Matilde can't look away from it. When she glances over at Sayer and Æsa, they look as nonplussed as she feels.

Matilde grabs Alec's hand. "I need to lie down. I think I'm starting to imagine things."

"It's not an illusion," he says gently. "It's real."

The girl looks her way. The moment their eyes meet is like flint on stone: a spark leaping. The green fire blossoms, shuddering to almost violent life.

The girl drops the fire, stamping it out. All the girls are staring at them now, eyes wide. The air has changed as Simta's does before a storm.

The green fire girl puts a hand to her chest. "Can you feel that?"

Many nod. There is an explosion of whispers.

Sayer reacts first. "Feel what?"

Two people walk out of a side tunnel. One is a girl with reddish hair, wearing a red robe and a knowing expression. The other has grey hair and is dressed all in yellow. Krastan's eyes, warm and kind, fall on Matilde.

"Stella. You found us."

The girl in red nods at Alec. "Just as I told you she would."

Matilde can't make sense of her words, this place, this moment. She can feel herself swaying, off-balance on her aching feet.

Krastan's eyebrows bunch. "What's happened?"

The concern in his voice makes her forced calm start to fracture.

"What is this?" she asks, waving around at the girls. "What am I looking at?"

"Girls with magic," Krastan says. "Girls like you."

"But . . ." Matilde fumbles for words. "There are no other girls like the Nightbirds."

There is a beat of silence. The girl in red arches an eyebrow.

"You truly thought you were the only ones?"

It's too much. Matilde's mask is cracking now, all in pieces, leaving her feelings bare for all to see.

Someone calls her name—Æsa, she thinks—but Matilde can't stay here. A sob is clawing its way up her throat. She stumbles toward a side tunnel, barely seeing what's in front of her. Her feet are so raw, but she keeps going, twisting and turning. Ten hells, does this labyrinth ever end?

Suddenly she's in a hallway so dark she can barely see her hands in front of her. But then the wall falls away and there's a feeling of space opening around her, enough watery light that shapes start to emerge. It's a small room, mercifully empty, with a shimmering pool at its center. Someone's put orblights in it, and they cast rippling waves of light across walls that curve and arch, rounded on all sides. It makes her think of the glass globe her sire brought back from one of his business trips to the Farlands. It sits on her bedside table even now. Filled with tiny buildings and glittering dust, it fit so neatly in her hands. But it's as if the glass has broken, and her city is spilling out between her fingers. Nothing about her life feels right. Nothing feels real.

Matilde screams. The sound echoes off the walls, raining down like the fake snow in that glass globe, until nothing remains but the ragged sound of her breath.

When was the last time she screamed? She doesn't remember, but she recalls what Dame said when she did. *Great House ladies don't make such a riot.* Such a thing is too loud, too raw, too much. They taught her to stuff her wildness down, buried where no one would see it. She didn't know, until tonight, how much of herself she kept contained.

"Tilde?"

Alec walks out of the shadows, hands in pockets. She turns quickly so he won't see her face.

"I'm fine, Alec."

One breath, two, echoing through the silence.

"You don't need to pretend." His voice is gruff. "It's just me."

That is precisely the problem. She can't lie to Alec. Or at least he always seems to see the truth.

She feels him step closer, smelling of wood ash and frennet. The nearness of him threatens to unspool her.

"Sayer told us what happened," he says. "Are you worried about your family?"

The family she left bleeding on the floor of their mansion. Her family, her world, torn to shreds.

She whirls around. "What do *you* think?"

He doesn't step back, despite her snarl. It's like he sees past the fury and straight down to the terror. Matilde can't stop seeing Gran and Dame on the floor of their house, so pale and frightened, Samson bleeding on the intricate tiles. She left them there, alone with the Caska. Alone with all of her mistakes.

"They'll be all right," he says. "Your gran is smart. And anyway, she's a Great House matron. No pater would dare do her any true harm."

But he didn't see the look in that vile man's eyes, burning with hatred. A self-righteous fire over which she has no power.

The truth slips out of her. "It's my fault."

She thought she was a jewelflower, so good at deception. She thought she had it all under control.

Alec puts a hand on her arm, just below her elbow.

"What's done is done," he says. "You're here now."

For a moment they stand there, his eyes black in the

darkness. They should feel like dark pits, but the orblights make them glisten. The softness in them beckons to be seen.

His hand slides down her arm, finding her hand.

"I'm sorry it happened this way, but it's good you're here. Maybe it's better."

She stiffens. "How could running for my life and hiding here be *better*?"

"Simta needs a change. Maybe the Nightbirds do too."

But she doesn't want change. She wants to travel back through time and unblow that kiss to Tenny Maylon, go back to when life was a game she was winning.

"You hid this from me," she says. "You, who say you don't like games."

He runs a hand over his curls.

"I wanted to tell you, but Krastan . . . he said your gran wouldn't like it. He didn't know if you were ready to hear."

For as long as Matilde can remember, she has always been sure of who she is. A Dinatris and a Nightbird, coveted, protected, and special. The keeper of a power very few would ever feel.

You really are a sheltered bird.

She shakes her head. "Alec, I . . ."

A sob escapes her.

"I want to go *home*."

But she can't. Not now, perhaps not ever.

His breath catches. "Oh, Tilde . . . don't . . ."

There's something in his voice that cuts into her. His pity is a knife in her back.

She straightens. "Just go, Alecand."

His feet shuffle. "Don't do that. Don't shut me out."

"Didn't you hear me?" She makes her voice as cold as she's able. "I don't *want you*."

It turns out she can lie to him after all.

There is a moment of silence, then his voice, all pity gone.

"Have it your way."

Only when he's gone does she let sobs overtake her, as what's left of her mask falls away.

Kinship is shaped by many forces. Sometimes it grows out of shared blood, present in the soil already. But sometimes it is forged as steel is, in the furnace of our trials.

—FROM A JOURNAL ENTRY
WRITTEN BY DELAINA DINATRIS,
ONE OF SIMTA'S FIRST NIGHTBIRDS

– CHAPTER 13 –

OCEAN FLOWERS

A<small>S SHE AND</small> Sayer walk through the Underground, Æsa marvels. She would have thought such a place would be dreary and sightless, but this one is full of life and light. And magic . . . so much of it. It overwhelms her already frayed nerves.

The scene from the garden keeps swirling through her head, in jagged pieces. She still doesn't understand the things she did. Like in the Liar's Club, the magic simply rose, hungry to push its way out of her. It made her feel almost . . . possessed.

Sayer nudges her gently. "How're you doing?"

She looks as tired as Æsa feels, but bright eyed, and more comfortable in pants than any of the dresses Æsa has seen her in. More herself.

Æsa takes a sip of the tea the girl in red—Jacinta—gave her. It tastes of honey and cinnamon.

"I'm confused. And worried."

About her family back home, for one. Will Leta keep sending them funds, even after what's happened? Will they be able to survive if she doesn't? But she's also worried about what she did in the garden, and what the Red Hand called them. *A poison hiding in plain sight.*

All her life, she has been told that to use magic is to corrupt and to be corrupted. That women with magic once tainted the Wellspring from which it sprang. But she also grew up with Grandda's stories about sheldars. He said they fought for those who couldn't speak up for themselves. She remembers the way that water rose from the fountain, wrapping around Matilde, protecting her. Surely saving a friend can't be a sin.

"And you, Sayer? What do you think of all this?"

Sayer blows out a breath. "I don't know what to think, to be honest. But we're safe, at least. For now."

They turn a corner, passing through a darkened tunnel, and emerge in the place where Alec told them Matilde would be. She is sitting with her back against the lip of a pool, legs tucked up, though Æsa can see patches of blood—her poor feet. Her long hair is loose and hopelessly tangled. Æsa has only ever known her as a smooth, polished creature. It's strange to see her frayed and unmoored.

"Be nice to her," Æsa says under her breath.

Sayer looks almost offended. "Aren't I always?"

If Æsa wasn't so tired, she might laugh.

Matilde looks up. There are dark moons under her amber eyes, but she's already smoothing out her expression. Æsa didn't know, until tonight, how much she wore a mask with them.

Sayer hands Matilde a steaming cup.

"Here. Drink."

"What is it?" Matilde asks.

"Tea," Æsa says. "The girl in red, Jacinta, says it's replenishing."

"Does she." Matilde makes a doubtful face. "I'd prefer a giant glass of port."

Sayer's mouth quirks. "Beggars can't be choosers."

Matilde sips. Sayer sits down on the floor beside her, not quite touching. Æsa perches behind her on the lip of the pool. She can almost feel the pool's subtle movements, swaying in time with her breath. It makes sense that she might have some connection with water. Hasn't the ocean always called to her, an old friend? But she knows how quickly a tide can turn against you.

She thinks again of the Dinatris garden when she raised her hands and the magic poured out. The feeling that came with it reminded her of the first time she kissed Enis. It felt good—too good. And that felt dangerous. Her cheeks heat with shame, but it is hidden by the dark.

In the low light and their silence, sounds of the Underground float toward them. Someone is playing slow, mournful jazz on a trumpet. Running footsteps echo distantly, and then a laugh.

"So, Sayer," Matilde says at last. "How long has that sandpiper of yours known our secret?"

Sayer crosses her arms. "Not nearly as long as Krastan and Alecand Padano."

Matilde sniffs. "*They* don't run with thugs who sell bootleg. What were you thinking?"

Sayer snaps back, "If it wasn't for Fen, you might be dead."

"Would you two *stop*?" Æsa blows out a frustrated breath. "We are in this together. If we can't trust each other now, then when?"

Silence envelops them again. There are a thousand things they could discuss—how they got into this mess, how they're going to get out of it—but the night has been too full. Too shattering.

"I suppose I should thank you," Matilde says, voice quiet. "For coming to rescue us."

Sayer shifts against the side of the pool.

"I'm the reason you had to," Matilde says. "This is my fault. And I'm sorry for it."

Her words hang, impossibly loud.

"A thank-you *and* an apology from Matilde Dinatris," Sayer quips. "Have you been drinking? Are you ill?"

A hiccupping sound, laugh or sob, is all the reply they get.

On impulse, Æsa runs her fingers through Matilde's hair, unsnarling the tangles. Then she starts to comb it back into a braid. Matilde lets out a sigh, head tilting back.

"Let's play a game," she says after a while. "One secret each. I'll go first."

The pause Matilde leaves is brief but loaded.

"I just found out Krastan Padano is my grandsire."

Æsa is shocked speechless.

Sayer makes a choking sound. "Lady Frey . . . and the Yellow Alchemist?"

Matilde sighs. "Apparently."

Æsa assumes she won't explain further. This seems like the kind of thing most Great House girls would take to their graves. But then Matilde relates a talk she had, just hours ago, with Lady Frey about her past. She is sorry for Matilde, who's just had her life ripped away from her. She understands the way such wounds can ache.

Matilde's voice fades.

"Does it bother you?" Sayer asks. "That he's low born?"

"No." Matilde rearranges her tattered nightgown. "Not really. It bothers me that Gran lied."

"For what it's worth," Æsa says, "he seems like a kind man."

Matilde takes a shaking breath. "I know. He is."

Sayer stretches out her long legs. "At least Alecand is adopted, yes? You don't have to worry."

Matilde bristles. "Why would I worry?"

Æsa can just see Sayer's small grin. "No reason."

Another silence, lighter than the last. The orbs in the pool cast their faces in shadow. It's so much easier to speak freely in the dark.

Finally, Sayer says, "The reason I left the booth at the Liar's Club is because I saw my sire."

Her voice sounds raw, almost wounded. Æsa reaches to touch her but hesitates.

It's Matilde who speaks. "Will you tell us the story of your parents, Sayer?"

The silence goes on for long enough that music drifts in again from the hallway, bouncing off the rounded walls.

"It starts," Sayer says, "with a girl falling in love with a monster."

She weaves a tale about a Nightbird and the client who seduced her, then walked away from the promises he made. Of a woman who let herself be used, over and over, and a girl holding a coin her estranged sire tossed. And then of that girl grown up, listening to her sire spout poison.

"He caught me skulking in the club's hallway," Sayer says, voice strangely flat. "He didn't recognize me, though, even up close. I think he thought I was a girl for hire."

"Ten hells," Matilde says. "What a horrid piece of flotsam."

Æsa knows how her own da feels about people who use magic. She doesn't want to find out what he might think of hers. Still, she can't imagine him ever treating her so cruelly.

She lets her hand rest on Sayer's shoulder. "I'm so sorry."

Sayer flinches a little but doesn't move away.

"Your dame deserved better," Matilde says, quiet and fierce. "From him, and from the Houses."

Sayer says nothing, but the air shifts, getting warmer.

"And you, Æsa?" Matilde says. "What's your secret?"

She speaks without thinking, too tired to hide. "At the club, I almost kissed your brother."

Matilde twists around. "Wait. Ew. *My* brother?"

"In her defense," Sayer says, "those cocktails were strong."

There's a pause, and then they all burst into laughter. They laugh and laugh, a beautiful release. When they finally stop, Æsa takes a deep breath. It must be very late—it might even be morning. Down here there is no way to know for sure.

"Let's have no more secrets." Matilde says it like a vow, a prayer. "No more lies. I don't know what's coming next, but we three need to stick together."

Her words are weighty in the watery darkness.

"Agreed," Sayer says. "We stick together."

Æsa takes their hands, a warmth humming between them. Of magic, yes, but something else too.

"Agreed."

They get quiet then. Æsa moves to sit on the floor beside Sayer. Suddenly her eyelids don't want to stay aloft. Her head droops onto Sayer's shoulder. Matilde lets out a soft, kittenish snore.

There is a plant that dwells near Illish coves. It floats free, its long tendrils attached to nothing, until it finds another of its kind. They twine their roots, forming huge, connected clusters. It is only then that they unfurl their blooms.

This moment feels like that. As frightening as the evening has been, Æsa feels more at home than she has in a long time, tangled up with these girls. Three ocean flowers.

THE PONTIFEX FOLDS his hands. They used to be chapped when he served as a pater in Griffin Quarter, fighting the good fight on behalf of the gods, but now they're soft. He uses a cream made of goat's milk and estaflower petals to keep them supple. After all, he no longer has to toil for what he wants. He is the voice of the gods, and men like the one currently babbling too loudly are meant to be his will and his justice. But his acolytes don't always do as they are told.

The audience chamber at Augustain's church is high ceilinged, richly furnished, and elaborate. The Brethren, his advisers, each sit in a straight-backed, gilded chair. The Pontifex is raised above them all, of course, placed on a dais. He tries not to show his vexation as Brother Dorisall raves on.

"I found them," Dorisall is saying. His red face paint is smeared—the Pontifex wishes he had cleaned himself up before this unplanned audience. He looks unhinged. "At last, I *found* them. And now we know the Great Houses have been hiding them all along."

Witches, he means. The thought sends a thrill through the Pontifex. He has long suspected the Great Houses are keeping sacrilegious secrets, and now he knows it for certain. He longs to leverage their betrayal against the gods to strip some of their power, but this pater has made rather a mess of things . . .

The Pontifex holds up a hand. "I sent you, Brother Dorisall, to find proof of these witches. I see no proof."

"I saw them do magic, Pontifex. My acolytes can vouch for it."

His acolytes. The man is getting too big for his robes. "I'm afraid the words of a bunch of overzealous boys and their master are not enough to take to the Table. Their hackles will be up, after what you've just done."

Dorisall scowls, waving at the ceiling to the cells where the Dinatrises and the House Maylon lordling are waiting. "The boy, Teneriffe, will give you answers freely. As for the witch's family, interrogate them."

A wave of distaste ripples through the Pontifex. He has never liked Lady Frey Dinatris. A woman should never be the head of any house. But still, she is an influential member of one of Simta's wealthiest families. He cannot pour a truth potion down her throat without consequences. If only Brother Dorisall understood politics, or discretion.

"I asked you to investigate the rumors *quietly*." He draws out the word, making it sharp. "To bring anything you learned to me. Instead, you invaded a Great House mansion without permission, and without any Wardens, and then lost the witches of which you speak."

Dorisall's face purples. "I answered Marren's call."

"You answered your *own* call for glory. And in doing so, you have made a mess that I will have to clean up."

Brother Dorisall's mouth opens and closes, gawping like a just-caught fish.

The Pontifex stands, his purple robes swishing. The Brethren follow his lead.

"Brothers," he says, "we must tread carefully now. This is a delicate situation."

One of the Brethren frowns. "Surely you don't mean to let the Dinatrises go, Pontifex."

"No, brother. We will press our advantage, while we have it, but we will have to question our prisoners with our softest gloves on. Which means they are unlikely to give us what we need."

"The Maylon boy, though," another says. "He sounds promising."

"Indeed." His testimony might be enough to justify a thorough search of the Houses, and a chance to air out all their dirty laundry on the Pontifex's righteous way through their halls. Those families are rife with corruption and wield far too much influence on the Table. "But we also need to find a way to coax the witches out of whatever hole they're crouching in."

The Pontifex presses his hands together, making them into an open book.

"The thing about setting a trap is that one must walk away from it, or seem to. The quarry must believe they are safe. One must wait until they have a leg fully within it. And then . . ." He snaps his soft palms closed. "Then, we strike."

———

LADY FREY DINATRIS straightens her spine. This stone cell clearly wasn't designed to make anyone comfortable. It is a place for penance—for confessions. The Pontifex will get none out of her.

Beside her, Oura is weeping silently, smoothing Samson's hair where he lies in her lap. His bleeding has slowed, but the paters haven't sent a doctor to tend to him. Frey adds it to her list of grievances to be avenged.

"Will they put us through inquisition?" Oura whispers. "Surely they wouldn't dare to."

"Oh, yes," Lady Frey whispers back. "I think they might."

She only saw the Pontifex briefly, when the Red Hand dragged them through Augustain's and made them stand before the Brethren like the catch of the day. The man knows how to hide his emotions—he never could have risen so high if he didn't —and yet she still saw the satisfaction in him. The hunger.

She closes her eyes. Where are the girls now? she wonders. Not captured, or else they would be here. She sends out a silent plea to the man she's never quite stopped loving. His warm eyes and ready smile.

Please, Krastan. Watch over her.

Because if these men get ahold of Matilde, she will die.

"I've heard they use truth serums on people," Samson croaks. "Is that true, Gran?"

She has also heard the church uses alchemical serums in their proceedings. A little hypocritical, but anything can be claimed as holy when it's done in the name of the gods.

"Perhaps they do." But since her younger days, Frey has made sure to keep a variety of potions hidden on her person, woven into her underdress where no one would dare search. She slips one of them out: It's called the Judge, and it nullifies the effects of any alchemical. Krastan made it for her himself. "But take heart, darling. They will find that we have nothing to hide."

"You might as well confess," a tired voice says from the next cell over. "The bird's out of the bag already."

Samson sits up, wincing. "Tenny? Is that you?"

The boy groans. They can't see him, but it is clear he's feeling worse for wear.

"I'm sorry, Sam," he says. "I didn't mean for you to end up dragged into this. Or myself, for that matter."

Frey stands. "If you wish to make amends, Teneriffe Maylon, then tell me what happened. All of it."

There is a pause, and then the story tumbles out of him. Matilde's blown kiss at Leta's ball, his rise and fall in fortune, his behavior at the Liar's Club, and Dennan Hain in the middle of it all. *Dash it, Tilde.* Why doesn't she listen? Because she is as Frey was once: blind to what recklessness can cost.

Frey weighs Tenny's words, sifting and sorting, trying to understand what kind of threat he might pose. He is not strong-willed, this boy, that much is certain. If he is put to inquisition by the Pontifex, he will break.

Frey sits close to the bars. "If you promise not to tell the Pontifex any of this, I will help you with your debts and with your sire. My husband and he were friends. If I speak, he will listen."

"But . . ." Tenny sighs. "It's all gone too far. I can't lie to the Pontifex."

A sound echoes through the hall, not far away: a door unlocking. It's time to make a choice.

She looks through the bars to make sure no one is watching, then holds out a vial.

"Here," she says, making sure to sound motherly. "It's whiskey and estaflower syrup. To calm your nerves."

Frey holds her breath, fearing he won't drink it. But she is a sweet old lady, like his own gran, offering him comfort. At last, she hears him swallow hard.

For a few seconds, all is silence. Then Tenny Maylon starts to pant. He makes a choking noise, banging a hand against the wall, and then goes still again.

When he speaks, his voice is like a child's. "Where am I? What . . . is this?"

The color drains from Samson's face. "Gran, what did you do?"

Her voice is calm—assured. "I protected us."

Frey would do anything for her family. For women like her, duty comes first.

CHAPTER 14

FLEDGLINGS

MATILDE SIPS A thoroughly mediocre coffee, trying not to scratch at her eyes or around the collar of her dress. It's borrowed, and the cheap weave of the cloth chafes something fierce around the neckline. She never realized how fine her dresses were until she had them taken away from her. Her closet, her house, her family . . . She drinks the coffee down to its bitter dregs.

Last night—was it only last night?—the three of them fell asleep next to that pool. At some point, Krastan came and led them to a hallway lined with cots. She only vaguely remembers him pulling a blanket up over her. When she woke, stiff and sore and still exhausted, he was waiting in a chair beside her. The first thing she asked was if her family was all right. *I've sent some people to go and see,* he told her gently, but they still haven't brought any word back about the Dinatrises. She has to fight the urge to go and see for herself. But Gran told her to stay away, so she tries to focus on the scene in front of her. She can only tackle one life-altering crisis at a time.

She, Sayer, and Æsa sit together in a long, high-ceilinged

space that reminds Matilde of a ballroom. Orblights and candles are clustered in each corner, painting the walls with a flickering glow. The trumpet boy from last night, Rankin, is leaning on the wall just behind them. He's been hovering around Sayer since he found them having breakfast. Matilde wonders if Fenlin Brae, conspicuously absent, put him up to it. No one else seems bothered by having a sandpiper in their midst.

The room is crowded. Krastan is standing by the doorway near Alec, who is sitting on an upturned crate and ignoring her. That girl Jacinta, though. From her perch beside Alec, her stare is sharp and annoyingly insistent. It makes Matilde feel like a bug squashed under glass for further study.

And then there are the girls, a little over a dozen of them, lined up along the opposite wall. Matilde remembers some of them from the alcove last night, but there seem to be more than she remembers. They're staring at the Nightbirds with a look like hungry fledglings waiting for a worm to be dropped into their nest.

"What do you think this is about?" Æsa says, sipping her tea. She's wearing a borrowed dress, too, though hers is more becoming. Sayer looks annoyingly comfortable in a loose shirt and trousers.

Matilde yawns. "I don't know, but pass me that hideous coffee. I feel like death warmed over."

Sayer tips her mug at Matilde. "You look more like a canal rat cooked over coals."

"Rude."

Sayer smiles. "I thought we said no more lying to each other."

Matilde sniffs. "I'd like to think I smell a good deal better."

Æsa makes a face. "Do Simtans eat rats?"

"I never have," Sayer says. "But Fen says if you douse it in garnam sauce and close your eyes, it could almost be pork loin."

Matilde bites back her sharp retort. *If a cutthroat says it, then of course it must be so.*

She knows Fenlin Brae helped the Nightbirds get away from the Caska. But still, she's a sandpiper, and aren't they all cut from the same criminal cloth? Matilde is suspicious of Fen, but Sayer seems to share things with her freely. Secrets and stories that she's never shared with Matilde.

At least her fellow Nightbirds are here, and safe, and speaking to her. She's going to count her stars where they fall.

Krastan walks over. He looks crumpled and friendly, same as always, but Matilde can't help but search for pieces of herself in his face. The nose, perhaps? The tilt of his jaw?

"I still can't believe this place," Sayer says to him. "How do you keep it a secret?"

"A lot of charms and spells, upkept constantly," Krastan says. "Glamours on the tunnel hatches to make them look like walls."

"But who built it to begin with?" Matilde asks. "What did they even build it for?"

"We don't know," he says. "The Underground is very old, but like so much from before the Great Revelations, most of its history has been lost to us. All we can do is read the hints they left behind."

He gestures at the murals that wrap around the room. They *look* old, their flaking silvered outlines glowing faintly with the sway of the candles, but still bright. The scenes seem to tell a story, all storm and war and danger, and women feature prominently in them all. At Augustain's church, the murals turn girls into evil witches or helpless damsels, but these are different. These women seem more like warrior queens.

"It's a good place to practice our magic," Jacinta says, standing up. Her hair, a blackish red, suggests some ancestor from the Illish Isles. The shade is pretty against her tawny Simtan skin. "We thought it would be a good space for a little show-and-tell."

Matilde crosses her arms. "What makes you think we have anything to show you?"

"There's no need to be shy," Jacinta says. "And no point. I know what you are. Just as I saw you coming."

Her knowing tone grates. "Is that your gift, then? You're some kind of fortune-teller?"

Matilde means it as a jest, but Æsa stiffens.

Jacinta pulls a pack of what look like oracle cards out of the folds of her skirts. "I see things. Glimpses of the future. Sometimes they're just vague suggestions, but lately they've become very clear."

Matilde's lips purse. One of Dame's friends used to hire a fortune-teller for parties. She made a big show of telling everyone about their great loves and untimely deaths.

"I kept seeing you all showing up here," Jacinta says. "Pulsing with power. Brimming with it. And here you are, stirring everything up."

The Underground girls start whispering heatedly to each other. Æsa and Sayer exchange a questioning glance.

Matilde looks to Krastan.

"I came to you," she says, voice quiet. "Whatever this is, I want you to explain it. I want the truths you've been keeping from me."

His gaze sharpens as he searches her face, but she keeps her expression unreadable. He lets out a sigh, nodding once.

"Your gran told me the story you grew up with. That the

last of the most powerful witches, the ones they called Fyrebirds, fled to Simta and hid with the families that would become the Great Houses. They stopped using their magic, gifting only their more subtle gifts to their protectors, passing them down to new girls as the generations passed."

With time, the magic changed, getting smaller and smaller. *It's easier to hide a thing no one can see.*

Matilde grips her coffee. "That's why Nightbirds always come from the Houses. The magic runs through our blood."

Jacinta arches her infernal eyebrow. "You never wondered if there were girls who didn't trust themselves to your so-called Great Houses?"

"I had no reason to. I never heard of any."

"It must sting to learn you're not as special as you thought."

"Cin," Alec says, shaking his head. "Go easy."

She smiles back at him. "Oh, please. I am."

Alec gives her a look, a corner of his mouth curling. Something about it makes Matilde want to light Jacinta's pretty hair on fire.

"I suspect there have always been girls with intrinsic magic in Simta," Krastan says. "Rare, still, but not as rare as you were taught."

Even with the evidence standing in front of her, Matilde struggles to accept it. All her life, she was told she was a rare bird.

It must sting to learn you're not as special as you thought.

She pins Krastan with a look. "And you didn't tell me this before because . . . ?"

Krastan spreads his hands. "Such girls take great pains to keep their magic hidden, just as you do. I didn't know about them until a few years ago."

Years. *Years* he's known and never said a word to her. What about Gran? Did he tell her?

Matilde lowers her voice. "And . . . can they bestow their gifts as we do?"

"With a kiss?" Krastan nods. "Yes, if they so choose. But they can't give it to each other."

Just like the Nightbirds.

"Most of us keep it close," one of the girls pipes up. Her long hair falls about her shoulders in tangled waves. "When we give it away, it gets depleted . . . harder to conjure."

"Apparently *they* were never told they couldn't use it for themselves," Sayer grumbles.

It seems impossible now that Matilde ever believed it. But she was brought up with certain rules, unbreakable. She thought she understood the game she played.

Jacinta taps her painted nails against her stack of cards. "There didn't use to be so many of us. Before a few months ago, I had only ever met a few others. But something's changing."

A crease forms between Æsa's delicate brows. "What kind of something?"

Krastan's eyes gleam. "Stella, do you remember in the shop the other day, when I said that I thought the old magic has simply been sleeping? That perhaps it might be waking up?" He points to the line of girls. "These girls are proof of it. We find more of them with every passing day. Most didn't know they had intrinsic magic in their bloodlines. It flared up in the past few months, as if something lit a match to it."

The green fire girl pipes up. "I didn't use to be able to do more than create a few sparks between my fingers. But now . . . it's getting stronger."

Sayer's golden eyes meet Matilde's, and for once she can read them. *Just like ours.*

She thinks of Sayer seeming to call to the wind in the garden, of Æsa commanding the water in the fountain, of the fireballs floating just above her own hands. A few months ago, she would have laughed if someone told her they could do such things. To her knowledge, none of her old Nightbird sisters ever could. *Sometimes a bit of that old magic bubbles up in us,* Gran told her. But that was here and there, in pieces . . . This feels more like a rising tide.

"But why?" she asks, frustration edging her words. "Why now? Why is this *happening?*"

Krastan shrugs. "It's hard to say. The paters burned too many books during the Great Revelations, at the height of the witch hunts. Outside of rumor and legend, we don't know much about what the women of old could do, and how it worked."

"Lucky for you all," Alec says, "it's always been one of Krastan's areas of interest."

Krastan smiles. "Too true, my boy."

He pulls a tattered book out of his satchel. It has splotches on the front that look like grimmberry juice, or blood, or both.

"Most alchemists are lazy," he says. "They craft with what they have and what they know to be sure. But I've spent years hunting for books on magic, trying to glean what I could and understand its workings. Alchemical and . . . other kinds as well."

He looks at Matilde again, secrets in his eyes. Can he sense that she knows them?

He puts the book down on the end of a barrel, opening it to a well-worn page. All three of the Nightbirds lean forward to see. Krastan runs a finger across an illustration, painstakingly painted. It resembles the symbol etched into prayer books: a four-pointed star cut into quadrants by the lines of an X.

"It looks like the Points of the Eshamein," Æsa says. "But the symbols are different."

She's right. The symbols in each point aren't those of the four gods. Instead they are a leaf, clouds, waves, and a flame.

"This is an old symbol," Krastan says. "The Points was appropriated for the four gods, but as far as I can tell it goes back much further."

Krastan touches the very center of the X, decorated with lines that make it look as if it's shining. "Imagine that this, here, is the heart of the Wellspring. The spiritual place from which all magic flows. The points represent each of the four elements. From what we can tell, girls with magic in them can only access one of them. Whatever element they lean toward shapes the kind of magic they can do."

It fits what Gran told her. She said that every Nightbird leans toward one of the elements. Earth, water, wind . . . fire.

Sayer looks up at the girls along the far wall. "What kinds of things can you all do, then?"

Jacinta smiles. "Girls, why don't you show her?"

A ripple of excitement passes through the Underground girls. As they stand, Matilde is reminded, absurdly, of the beginning of a ball, that heady moment when all the dancers take their places. There is a moment of breath-held silence. Then they begin.

One girl holds out a handful of coins. They're copper shills, worth very little. They start to soften and melt into liquid pools.

Another scoops a handful of water out of a bowl she brought with her. It should run through her fingers, but instead it takes the shape of a rabbit and hops across the floor. It lands in Æsa's lap, twitching its nose. Æsa lets out a startled laugh.

The green fire girl shows them a flame that seems to wrap around her arm, changing color from green to black to purple. It writhes like a snake, almost alive.

The girl with long, wild hair is stretching a thin thread between her palms, crackling like lightning—Matilde thinks it might actually *be* lightning. It fills the air with the smell of iron.

Rankin has stepped away from the wall, mouth hanging open.

"Blazing cats, you girls can do some cracking tricks."

"And you?" Sayer says to the cluster of girls who haven't shown off any magic. She seems delighted by all of this, when Matilde can barely take it in. "What can you do?"

One of them blushes. "Our gifts are harder to show."

"Every girl's gift is different," Jacinta says. "There are physical powers like these, manipulations. And then there are ones that are more . . . complex. Like Lili's, for example. She can compel someone to tell the truth."

A girl with a brassy bob steps forward.

"It doesn't work on other girls with magic," Lili says. "They seem immune to it."

Rankin strides over, thumbs in his vest pockets. "Go ahead, then. Try and break me."

Lili wraps her fingers around his wrist. Matilde expects the girl to ask him a question, but she just waits as Rankin's mouth works. It seems like it's taking him some effort not to open it. When it does, words tumble out.

"I've always liked posh girls." His face flushes pink, but it seems he can't stop talking. "That Dinatris girl probably thinks I'm too young for her, but I reckon I might be in with a chance."

Sayer laughs. Lili drops Rankin's wrist and he rubs at it,

scowling. Matilde's eyes land on Alec, who's looking back at her with an odd expression. Flustered, she turns her gaze away. Beside her, Æsa is looking pensive.

"Which element do you lean toward?" she asks Jacinta.

"I'm a water girl."

"But what does seeing the future have to do with water?"

"Our bodies are full of it," Jacinta says. "And water's a conduit. The seers of old used it to scry."

Æsa grips the folds of her skirts: She looks troubled. Matilde's about to ask why when Krastan speaks. "Sometimes the connection to an element isn't obvious," he says, excited now. "The Wellspring's magic manifests differently in every girl, shaped by her needs and personality."

Alec chimes in. "It seems it's heightened by emotion, too."

Jacinta nods. "It's often strong emotion that first brings the magic out. Layla here got angry at her fellow baker's apprentice and almost burned him to a crisp."

The green fire girl shrugs, unrepentant. "Trust me when I say he had it coming."

Ten hells, how have these girls stayed a secret?

"Perhaps that's why your magic came out at the club," Æsa says, low, just for Matilde. "You were frightened."

Matilde sniffs. "I was furious, mostly."

But she's right: In that moment when Tenny pressed her to the wall, emotions swelled, and with them her magic. These people seem to know so much more about it than she does.

"So?" Jacinta says, turning to Sayer. "Are you going to show us what you can do?"

Matilde shoots her fellow Nightbird a look—*don't you dare.* Sayer shoots her one back. *Why not?*

Sayer's eyes close. The room changes, smelling of wind and the air before a storm. And then she is gone, melting into the room's shifting shadows. It's a shocking thing, still, to watch her disappear. Though if Matilde squints, she can almost see the shape of her. Not true invisibility, but a trick of the light.

Alec looks like someone just dunked him in cold water. "That's a new one."

"Turning to shadow. Bending the air," Jacinta murmurs. "That has to be air, surely."

"I can do other things with it too," Sayer says. When did she become so dashed chatty? "I can harden it to hold something in place. Or . . . someone."

When did she do *that*? It's becoming quite clear that Sayer knew before last night that she could use her own magic. Matilde looks at her sharply, but she won't catch her eye.

"And you?" Jacinta asks Æsa. "What can you do?"

"Well . . ." Æsa fidgets, clearly uncomfortable. "A few things."

Jacinta waits, but Æsa doesn't explain further. She certainly doesn't mention her Nightbird gift. Matilde thinks of the way she seemed to mold Tenny's thoughts at the Liar's Club, her voice swimming around him like a school of clever fish. It was one thing to know what the Nightingale's gift was and another to see it in action. It makes Matilde shiver to think of it now.

Jacinta turns that too-knowing gaze on Matilde. "And you?"

She knows there is no point in hiding, but she doesn't like the feeling of being dissected. Of Nightbird business laid out for all to see.

"She can shift to look like someone else!" Rankin blurts. "Clothes, face, everything. I almost soiled my socks to see it."

Matilde shoots him a venomous look, and he withers. Both of Jacinta's infernal brows shoot up.

"A phoenix rising from her ashes. I'd love to see it."

Matilde would rather strip naked and swim in the canals.

"I'm not going to splash out my magic for you."

Jacinta rolls her eyes. "No need to be a prude. After all, you're a Nightbird, aren't you?"

Matilde stiffens. "Your point being?"

"Just that I wouldn't have expected someone who sells kisses to strangers to be so reserved."

Something sparks in Matilde, hot and untamed. "I don't like your tone."

"And I don't much like the Nightbirds' way of doing business. Do you know what most of the people in this city would do if they found us? We've all had to fight to keep hidden, and you're showing our magic to whoever can pay."

The words are a slap. Æsa looks stricken. Sayer looks like she might dig out the knife she's no doubt got under her shirt.

"Jacinta," Krastan warns. "That's enough."

"What? Is she too delicate to hear the truth, then?"

The temperature in the ballroom seems to rise.

"Don't pretend to understand who we are," Matilde warns. "You know nothing about the Nightbirds."

Jacinta looks at Alec. "You didn't tell me how difficult she was."

Something scorches her tongue, tasting of fury and ashes. Matilde is going to burn the girl to sticky ash. The candles around the room throb, turning white and then dark red as she stands, ready to rush at her. Æsa and Sayer both reach out to hold her back.

A tingling rush swells inside her like it did last night, in the garden, when Sayer and Æsa's magic seemed to collide with hers. Their touch makes her magic expand inside her, beyond her, rippling outward in a hot, shimmering wave.

Several of the other girls gasp. The one who melted the copper coins is staring at the liquid pools she is still holding, watching as they transmute into what looks like gold. The green fire girl, Layla, smiles as her flames form a halo around her. The air around them all seems to pulse.

And then Sayer and Æsa let go, severing the connection between them. The rippling sensation dies away.

The girls are all whispering, fast and urgent.

Did you feel it? And you, and you?

Matilde looks at Sayer, who looks as shaken as she does. Æsa has a hand pressed to her chest as if to keep her heart inside. Krastan, Alec, and Rankin all look confused. Whatever just happened, it seems only the magical girls could feel it.

Jacinta's eyes have gone wide. "How did you do that?"

"What is it?" Krastan asks. "What did you feel?"

"My magic flared," Layla says. "Like when the Nightbirds first arrived, but . . . stronger."

All the other girls start talking at once.

"I don't understand." Matilde looks at Sayer and Æsa. "What *is* this?"

"I don't know," Sayer says, "but I think we'd better figure it out."

Matilde looks at the mural on the closest wall. It depicts a woman in armor, hair floating around her, surrounded by soldiers and a wild-looking storm. Is the army fighting for her or against her? It's hard to tell, from this vantage, but she looks so confident. Matilde wishes she could reach up and grasp onto her surety, because she has never felt quite so out of her depth.

I have made up a tincture from the herb mentioned in some of Marren's more obscure works. The text seems to suggest that the bark of weil breamus *might allow one to draw magic out. I will test it on the girl, as always. She has proven resistant to my attempts thus far, but I will crack her open. Females, I find, have the thinnest of skins.*

—NOTES FROM A JOURNAL
KEPT BY PATER DORISALL, OTHERWISE KNOWN
AS THE RED HAND

– CHAPTER 15 –

LEAVES WHISPER

ÆSA WENDS HER way through a magical garden. It must be, as no plants could grow in this place without help. The only illumination comes from violet-glass lanterns hung from hooks, yet everything seems to be thriving. Bright moss creeps around shelves full of greenery. Vines wrap up rope tied to the room's arched ceiling, forming a verdant curtain. It's impossible and beautiful, like so much of what lives down here.

It's hard to know how much time has passed since they first came to the Underground. Down here, it's difficult to tell day from night. Some of their new friends have been slipping in and out, trying to get a read on what's happening above them. Very little of it sounds good. It seems the Red Hand went to the Pontifex the night they fled and told him what happened in the garden. It makes her cringe to think of him describing what she did to the head of the Eudean church. He took the Dinatrises in for inquisition, too. She is sorry to have subjected Matilde's family to such a horror. Leta and a few other heads of Great Houses swooped in within hours, and the Pontifex didn't have enough evidence to hold them further. It's the Red Hand's claims against those of the Dinatris family, but Æsa fears her and Matilde's disappearance is speaking loudly for itself.

The church has made no public announcement, at least, and the Red Hand has gone quiet. *It seems,* Sayer mused, *the church has put him on a leash.* But how long will it hold him? She saw the fervor in the man's eyes, the conviction. Is he up above right now, telling tales of the witches who could conjure fire and water? How long will it be before stories of that night start to spread?

She sighs, picking at a blue petal that just landed on her dress. It is a relief to be alone, just for a moment. These past handful of days, the Underground girls are always there, gazes full of too much reverence. Matilde has taken to calling them *our fledglings* for the way they follow the Nightbirds around. Every day, they all practice together in the Underground ball-room, honing their magic. When she watches the other girls, she can't see evil in their play.

The Nightbirds seem to amplify them all, somehow, and each other. Sayer can disappear as easily as breathing now, and Matilde can change the color of her eyes or the shape of her face with ease. They are both getting better at commanding their elements, beckoning to air and fire in a myriad of ways. Æsa practices, too, though mostly because she wants to learn how to contain it, parting water, making it freeze, turning it into mist. She'll only do the smallest of things, no matter how the girls press her. It's easier to trust them with such power than herself.

Sayer scowls. *It isn't going to go away just because you don't like it.*

Matilde purses her lips. *Wouldn't it be better to own it, rather than let it own you?*

But she can't forget the Red Hand's words about them being a poison. For her, the church's lessons aren't so easily unlearned.

Anyway, she doesn't want to practice that thing she did to Teneriffe Maylon. She can still feel the streams of his emotions, there for her to bend and beckon. The way she was able to touch his mind as well—how good it felt.

It reminded her too much of kissing Enis: that wild, insatiable hunger. Of the hashna, with their long hair and glistening scales and pointed teeth. Their song is like a drug, luring hapless sailors to the water, but now she wonders if the hashna don't mean to drag them to their deaths. Perhaps they simply want someone to love, to cherish, only realizing humans have no gills when it's too late.

She doesn't want to hurt anyone else, that's for certain. And that means learning how to keep the magic in, to keep it tame.

Footsteps echo through the garden. She watches from behind a tall fern as Fenlin Brae walks in, tread light as a cat's.

Sayer's friend has made herself scarce since they arrived here. Unlike Rankin, she never seems to want to watch the girls practice their powers. Sayer told her that Fen doesn't like dark, cramped places—perhaps that's it. But Matilde has darker notions. *I'm telling you,* she's whispered more than once when Sayer's back is turned. *That girl is up to no good. I don't trust her.* Fenlin has secrets, clearly, but Æsa doesn't think she means to harm them. It feels more like she's trying to keep the world from harming her.

Fen goes to a workbench in one corner, heaped with jars and vials. A sheen of sweat covers her brow, as if she's been running. The deep green of her eyepatch blends in with the vines.

Matilde insists there's something off about Fen: something suspicious. Perhaps because she can't read Fen like she does

254

everyone else. It's as if she wears armor, making it so no one can touch her. But here, where she thinks no one is watching, she seems less guarded. Æsa can see her tension, frustration, and fear. There is something almost inviting about her in this moment. Almost . . . familiar. It pulls Æsa forward, like a moth to a flame.

Covertly, Fen reaches underneath the bench, freeing a jar from some hidden place there. She pinches out some of its contents, mixes it with a pale, sticky-looking substance, then puts it all in the silver tin Æsa has seen her pulling out of her vest. It must be the mastic she is always chewing. Matilde says it smells like rotting algae, which is true: It's repulsive. And yet Fen shoves some in her mouth and bites down hard. Hands pressed to the wood, her one eye closes, her whole body relaxing. She takes a long, uneven breath.

The pull Æsa feels bleeds away, leaving a truth bare in its wake. An understanding. She steps closer.

"Does Sayer know?"

Fen's lips thin, but that is all the sign she gives of being surprised to see Æsa.

"Know what?"

Æsa lets the silence stretch, filling the verdant air between them.

"That you knew about the Underground before we came here."

It makes sense. Why else would Krastan, Jacinta, and the rest seem so unthreatened by a sandpiper amongst them?

Fen looks her up and down, weighing and measuring. Then she runs a hand through her short twist of hair.

"My crew deals in finding things that have been buried. Treasures, secrets . . . Simta has no better thieves. But I've been moving the Dark Stars away from that, into the rare-plant business. Ingredients that most alchemists can't get, and that Prohibition keeps flowing in at a trickle, we offer." She gestures at the garden at large. "This is how."

Æsa's eyes widen. "Where did it all come from?"

"I smuggled seeds in from the Callistan," Fen says. "And then I worked with Alecand Padano to come up with ways to grow them down here. In exchange for his help keeping it thriving, my crew, the Dark Stars, help keep this place out of the other gangs' eyelines."

Fen's voice is relaxed, but her hand is clutched around the silver tin, as if she fears Æsa might take it.

"I'm surprised," she says. "Sayer says you don't like magic."

Fen shrugs. "These plants aren't just used just for alchemicals. There are things for treating wounds and easing pains."

Æsa looks at the scars on her neck, just visible above her collar. She wonders how many pains Fen's had occasion to numb.

"Matilde doesn't like you much, you know," Æsa says.

Fen lets out something like a laugh. "Of course she doesn't. I'm a piper. I'll bet Rich Girl finds pond scum more appealing."

Æsa comes close to the bench. "It's not that. It's that Sayer is yours. She belongs to you. More than she belongs to us."

Emotions flicker through Fen's brown eye, hot and tangled.

"Matilde thinks Sayer's blinded by her feelings for you," Æsa continues.

Fen's posture is rigid, as if she's wrapped in thorns. "And what you do think?"

I think that you're afraid, just like me.

She touches Fen's hand, as softly as a sea breeze. "Does Sayer know?"

Fen's face hardens, shutting her out, saying *no closer*. But Æsa sees . . .

"You should tell her."

A voice floats out of the darkness. "Tell me what?"

———————————

SAYER LIKES TO wander through the Underground, letting her senses guide her. She still can't believe how vast it is. Alec told her the tunnels used to be mostly an illicit market and a place to hide out from the Wardens, but as Prohibition's enforcement has grown harsher, people have started staying. Some live down here, while others come and go. So many opportunities for word to bleed out, and yet it hasn't. It seems the Nightbirds weren't Simta's best-kept secret after all.

Today she's found a secret garden. It's stuffed to the brim with rows of plants with broad, dark leaves. She brushes by a table full of serpent orchids, much like the ones Leta grows in her conservatory. Their flowers are the same caramel brown as Fen's eye. Sayer wants to talk to her friend about the Underground, about everything, but it seems like Fen's avoiding her. Again. Ever since that night they saved the other Nightbirds, she's been guarded. Is it because Sayer offered her and Rankin kisses so they could blend into the shadows? *No, Tig. Better you keep it for yourself.* But why? She knows Fen has always shunned magic, but Sayer's power isn't some trickster alchemical. Is that how Fen sees her? Or as something even worse?

Sayer relishes the chance to explore her magic, to stretch it. She can call to the wind or deepen shadows, hear conversations in other rooms and muffle sound. It's still hard to control, especially when she's feeling any potent emotion. *All magic has limits,*

Krastan says. *Even the kind that lives inside.* It is strongest when the Nightbirds are together, skin to skin. They seem to make the air sing with some charge that none of them can name. Æsa is worried about the ways their magic is growing, but Sayer likes it. It's a weapon she wants to learn how to wield.

Without thinking, she reaches into her pocket for the shill her sire once tossed her. The one she kept as a reminder not to seek him out again. But as she runs her fingers over its blunt points, she thinks about the havoc she could wreak on his life now. How she could steal in and ruin it, a vengeful ghost.

Voices float through the garden's leaves, low and clandestine. Sayer moves toward them, but she stops at the sound of her name.

"Does Sayer know?"

Sayer peeks through the leaves to see Fen looking down at where Æsa is touching her.

"You should tell her."

Sayer wants to wait, to hear, but something makes her interrupt.

"Tell me what?"

Æsa steps back. Fen's hands clench.

"Tig. Fancy meeting you here."

Sayer walks out of the leaves and over to the workbench. "Fancy meeting you at all."

Æsa's green eyes bounce between them. She gets this look sometimes, as if she's seeing things that no one else can. Maybe she is. It's a disconcerting thought.

"I'm going to find Matilde," she says. Before she goes, she leans close enough to Fen to whisper something. Fen's face becomes a blank mask, pointedly unreadable, but Sayer can see something roiling underneath.

As Æsa leaves, Sayer perches on a moss-crusted ledge set into the wall.

"What was all that about?" she asks Fen.

"Nothing," she says, putting her silver case back in her pocket. "She just wants everyone to be friends, is all."

Sayer pulls a leaf off a nearby vine. "You two seem friendly enough."

Fen smiles a little. Sayer rips the leaf to shreds.

"So?" Sayer asks. "Where have you been?"

Fen picks up a vial of something viscous, holding it up to the light. "Tending to business. The Stars doesn't run itself, you know."

Sayer looks away. "Did you take Leta my message?"

She couldn't tell Leta where she was, but she didn't want her to worry.

Fen nods, tight. "I went to see her."

"Is she all right?"

"She's fine. She's telling people she sent you up to Thirsk for your health. Your secret is still safe."

But not Matilde or Æsa's. The city at large might not know about them yet, but the Caska does. And the Pontifex, though he hasn't put the word out on the street yet. What is he waiting for?

Sayer lets out a breath. "What else did she say?"

"She asked what you're going to do next. I said I didn't know."

A silence wraps around them as Fen steps around the bench, coming closer.

"So?" she says, voice low. "What're you thinking?"

The same thing that's been circling her head for days, since their trip to the Liar's Club.

"I'm going to get revenge."

Fen cuts her a look. "On who? The Hand?"

"He's on my list. But I meant my sire."

Sayer hasn't told anyone the full truth about what happened between her and Wyllo Regnis in the club. She doesn't want them to know how badly she tipped her hand to him. Who can guess what he might do with what he knows. She can still see the fury in his eyes as she used her magic to bind him. *I will make you pay for that*. But he's the one who is going to pay—for all of it.

"His bill's past due," she says to Fen. "It's time someone made him pay it."

Fen looks incredulous. "That's what you want to use your power for?"

"Why not?" she shoots back. "He left my dame in the gutter. You don't know the half of what he's done."

"I'm sure that's true, but we've got bigger fish to fry. Surely your revenge can wait."

But her dame waited: hours, months, years. She died waiting. Sayer isn't going to do the same.

Fen stalks toward her, slow and graceful. The garden seems to hold its breath.

"And what about the other girls?" Fen asks.

Sayer frowns. "The Nightbirds?"

"No, the others. You must know that for every magical girl that's found her way to the Underground there'll be one who is still up there, without protection."

Fen's voice is pulled taut by some unnamable emotion.

"The more there are, the more likely they are to let their magic slip in front of someone and be found by the Caska or a Warden. Or a piper, which is just as bad. Can you imagine if someone like Gwellyn found one? A renewable source of magic, forever on tap. A girl like that would sell for a fortune."

A vision forms of Gwellyn with a girl on a leash, tugging her behind him. Sayer shivers.

"What do you want me to do about it?"

"Join the Dark Stars for real," Fen says. "Help me keep the girls hidden."

"I can do that *and* ruin my sire." And dash it, it's her life, her magic. She isn't going to be told what it's for. "I owe it to my dame's memory."

Fen's tone softens. "You know she wouldn't want that."

Sayer grits her teeth. "But I *do*."

Fen is close now, just an arm's length away. Sayer can see the scars on her neck she tries so hard to keep hidden, and beneath them her rapid pulse.

"You don't understand what he is. What he did. He needs to suffer."

Otherwise this angry hollowness will never leave her. She can feel it eating her alive.

Fen's voice is full of heat. "You think I don't know what it is to want revenge? I was raised by a pater who hated me. Who denied me meals and locked me in the dark."

She rips at the collar of her shirt, as if it's chafing. Her bright brown eye holds a haunted edge.

"My first years on the street, revenge is all I thought about. So one night I got a message to the kids still in the orphanage, telling them to be out by midnight, and I lit the place on fire."

Sayer doesn't move. She doesn't dare breathe, lest Fen stop talking.

"He got out," Fen says. "Badly burned, but he made it. But the fire spread through the street, too fast for the people sleeping in the upper levels. Five people died before they could get it under control."

Fen looks away, but Sayer can see her remorse.

"That man is a more dangerous monster now than ever, and it's my fault. I *made* him."

Fen cuts herself off, but some silent confession hovers. It rubs at Sayer's skin like an itch.

"Fen," Sayer says. "What you trying to tell me?"

Fen presses her hands to the wall on either side of Sayer. The way she moves makes Sayer think of a coiled spring begging for release. No part of them is touching—when was the last time? It feels like years ago.

"Just that revenge doesn't fix what's past. It doesn't heal what's broken. It just blinds you to what matters."

Sayer can smell the acrid stink of her mastic. It isn't enough to make her want to pull away. She wants to touch Fen's scars and press her lips to them. To peel off every layer between them until there's nothing left.

Sayer leans in, just a fraction.

Fen's lush lips part as her gaze lands on Sayer's mouth.

She doesn't mean to call up a wind. It weaves through the garden, making all the plants shiver.

Fen cocks her head. "Are you doing that?"

Sayer nods.

"I've always liked that sound," Fen says, eyes closing. "Leaves in a breeze."

It feels like a confession. Sayer can feel it in her, trying to take root.

They're so close. With a tilt of Sayer's chin, they could be kissing. But they're friends . . . just friends. There is nothing else between them.

The leaves around them seem to whisper. *Liar.*

One of them pulls away—Sayer doesn't know who. It doesn't matter. Her dame put her heart in someone else's hands, and it ruined her. Maybe it's better to keep hers safe in her own chest, untouched.

*Don't worry about me. All's well, by which
I mean I'm still breathing. ~M*

---

*What happened after you left me at the club?
Where are you now? ~D*

---

*I can't say. As for the rest . . . well. En Caska Dae
stormed my family's garden, and things got . . . heated.
The Nightbirds had to find a place to hide. ~M*

---

*You shouldn't have to hide. Let's talk—
just tell me where to meet you. ~D*

---

*What we do next isn't only my
decision to make. ~M*

---

*It's your choice, but I am here when you're ready.
You and I can find a way to make this right. ~D*

—A SERIES OF NOTES PASSED BETWEEN
DENNAN HAIN AND MATILDE DINATRIS

CHAPTER 16

A SLOW BURN

W**HEN MATILDE FINALLY** gets Alec alone, it's in one of the quieter sections of the Underground. The walls here are jagged, a rough-cut gemstone, stalactites hanging down like dried lines of candle wax. Even after several days in these tunnels, this place continues to surprise her. To think it's been here all her life, beneath her feet.

She watches Alec from the doorway of what seems like a makeshift workshop, lit by tiny lanterns. They shine steadily, tinged orange by what must be some kind of alchemical, casting a warm glow over the room. She's tried to seek him out this past handful of days, to make things right between them, but half the time he's in the shop, or talking with Jacinta. Not that Matilde cares. Not at all.

Alec picks up a glass vial off a battered wooden table, covered in mortars and jars of who knows what. There is something comforting about him with his sleeves rolled up, mixing herbs with a steaming cup of frennet beside him. A familiar sight amidst the current riot of her life.

She breezes in, keeping her voice light. "What trouble are you brewing?"

He looks up. There is an intensity in the way he takes her in, those dark eyes gleaming. It makes her want to fidget as it never did before.

"Your hair," he says, eyebrows rising.

She twirls, showing off her stylish bob. One of their fledglings cut it. "What do you think?"

A corner of Alec's mouth curls. "It suits you."

Something flutters in her chest. "Yes, well. Everything else about my life has changed. I figured I might as well style to match."

She doesn't tell him that she had to fight back tears as they cut it. How seeing the dark waves fall around her made her feel more severed from her life than before. Dame would hate the bob, she's sure. Matilde can imagine her pursed lips, Gran's sly smile, Samson's easy laugh at her rebellion. Her family feels so close, and a thousand leagues away.

Krastan assured her they're all right, but Matilde wasn't satisfied with secondhand information, so she snuck out, changed her face, and went to see for herself. The other Nightbirds—and Krastan, and Alec—wouldn't like her trips above, but she's never really in danger. Not when she looks like someone else. That first time, she went to stand by their garden gate. She could see her family through the windows, just barely, but she didn't dare linger. Not with Wardens patrolling the canal right by the house. It seems strange that the Pontifex let her family go, and that he hasn't called her out publicly, but then he is only one voice around the Table. Politics—and the collective might of the Houses—seem to have stalled him. That or he's following some secret plan, biding his time. Either way, his silence won't hold forever: She is sure of it. When he publishes her name, what happens then? Will Epinine Vesten find some way to get to her, and through her the other Nightbirds? Will the church make it so that none of them will ever be safe?

Alec shakes her out of her thoughts.

"Are you just going to stand there looking pretty, or are you going to come and help me?"

She grins, skirting around to Alec's side of the table.

"Where do you want me?"

"Right here." He pushes a mortar her way, and a pile of slender leaves. "Grind these."

She picks up the pestle. The herbs smell sharp, almost spicy. She wonders how well they might burn.

"Why aren't you brewing in the shop?" she asks.

Alec shrugs. "Krastan doesn't come back here that often, and there are projects I'd rather he not know about."

She bumps his hip with hers. "There you go again, living dangerously."

He bumps her back. "I'm a man of hidden depths."

They work in silence for a time. When they were younger, they used to bicker while they did this, but now she doesn't know what to say. Things have changed.

"So," he says at last. "How does it feel?"

Her heart picks up its rhythm. "How does what feel?"

"Using your magic."

The words touch on a tangle of emotions. How does she feel? A bit . . . unmoored.

"It's overwhelming." These days Matilde feels like a dancer who's had the floor go soft beneath her, making her unsteady on her usually sure feet. "But thrilling, too."

She likes the way her magic makes her feel, powerful and

potent. But the more she uses it, the surer she is that she can never go back to her life the way it was. She feels like something has been taken from her—a certainty. She knew who she was and how she fit, before. She was a Nightbird and she was a Dinatris. Who is she now, without that? Without them?

"And how does it feel to know other girls share your talents?" Alec asks. "Layla seems pretty taken with you."

The green fire girl. Matilde smiles. "She's rather growing on me. They all are."

It was strange to find out that, as Jacinta so delicately put it, Matilde wasn't quite as special as she grew up believing. It still sits like an ill-fitting coat, a little tight. Especially since none of them are House born. Hetty, one of the air girls, is a blacksmith's daughter, and Layla . . . well. Matilde gets the impression that some sailor left her on a dock and sailed back off again. A few weeks ago she wouldn't have given them a second glance, thinking they had nothing in common. But the fledglings could have been Nightbirds, had they been born in different circumstances. They're all the same, down here in the dark.

"I understand what you meant now," she says, not looking at Alec. "About my being a sheltered bird. I didn't know the way some of these girls lived."

"Well," he says. "You had no reason to know it."

A bitter taste crosses her tongue.

The silence stretches, begging for a confession. She finds she doesn't want to hide from him.

"Truth to tell, I miss my old life," she says, low. "And my family. I feel a little lost without them."

Alec frowns. "Would you go back to being a Nightbird?"

She isn't sure she could return to giving pieces of herself away to others.

"No." She tries for a lighter tone. "But I would go back to having regular access to a bathtub. You know how I love a little luxury."

"Change can be good." Alec's eyes meet hers. "It means new possibilities."

Possibilities. Matilde reaches into her pocket, gripping Dennan's metal bird. When she first changed her face and went to check on her family, she also sent Dennan a message. *Don't worry about me. All's well, by which I mean I'm still breathing.* The next day, when she went to where she hid its base on the roof up at Krastan's, she found the bird waiting.

What happened after you left me in the club? Dennan wrote. *Where are you now?*

I can't say, she wrote back. *As for the rest . . .*

She relishes her clandestine trips above, those brief moments standing in the sunshine. But they stir her fears and her frustration, too. She can't hide in the Underground forever, but she also can't slide right back into her life. She needs a plan first—a way to protect her family, the Nightbirds, and her name.

Dennan's last note is warm between her fingers.

It's your choice, but I am here when you're ready. You and I can find a way to make this right.

Matilde wants to believe him, but her next steps might make or break her future. She doesn't know which ones to take.

Alec nods down at where she's listlessly pounding at the mortar. "Your technique is terrible, Tilde."

She reverts to flirtation. "Show me how it's done, then."

She says it as a dare, knowing he won't rise to it. But then he steps behind her, bracketing her body with his own.

"Don't pound at it like that," he says, his soft curls brushing her cheek. "You have to swirl it."

He puts his hand over hers on the pestle, tilting its angle. His calluses rub against her skin.

"Me, I like change," Alec says, the hard planes of his chest touching her back. "That's what alchemy is. You combine two things, thinking you know what will happen, but just one change to their conditions can shift the whole game."

Her magic stirs, heating the room, warming her blood. "I didn't think you liked games."

His lips are close to her ear. "Games, no. But I don't mind risks. Taking chances. Forging new paths."

They've stopped grinding the herbs and are just standing there, leaning against each other. She breathes in his scent of frennet and ash.

Gran's words from the garden come back to her.

Part of my heart never left that attic room above Krastan's shop. I found things there that I have never found again.

And yet she walked away from him then, and let her family make her choices for her.

For women like us, duty comes first.

Krastan was an alchemist's apprentice, Gran a Great House daughter, born and bred to belong in different worlds. But down here, such lines seem softer than they were before. Matilde doesn't feel as bound by those rules.

She turns her head, her temple brushing Alec's cheekbone. "Why didn't you ever kiss me?"

He swallows and she feels it everywhere.

"All these years. You knew what I was," she presses. "You knew I had magic. Why didn't you ever ask?"

His chin dips down, lips hovering so near her neck that she can feel the heat of them. But then he pushes away, leaving her cold.

When she turns around, his expression is one of befuddled amusement.

"I don't know," he says. "I never really thought about it."

The words sting, but she won't let him see it.

"Well, it's not as if you could have afforded me."

It's meant to be a quip, but it comes out too pointed. A shadow passes over his face.

"I have to go," he says. "Just . . . put those herbs into a jar and seal it tight, would you?"

And then Alec's gone, leaving Matilde more uncertain than ever, the orange lights flickering, a slow burn.

To the Great Houses of Simta,

The church has received reports that you hide witches amongst you. The Pontifex is sure this can't be true. But in service to the four gods, and to the souls of all Eudeans, the Wardens will conduct a thorough search of all Great Houses. Those who cooperate will be treated kindly, and those who are honest will receive a reward.

This is the will of the gods. We are dedicated to ripping out any corruption that may have rooted amongst us. We will honor the Wellspring and let it cleanse us of our stains.

—A NOTE SENT TO EVERY GREAT HOUSE,
SIGNED BY THE PONTIFEX

– CHAPTER 17 –
FATE'S MANY STREAMS

ÆSA WEAVES THROUGH the Underground market, underneath the purple tree growing in its middle and past stalls filled with alchemical magic. They don't scandalize her as much as they once did. Much of it is medicine, potions meant to ease pain and make food last longer. There are people back in Illan who would gladly pay the price for such things, she thinks, no matter what Pater Toth might say.

People nod as she passes, some tipping their hats at her. She reaches up to touch one of the pieces of sea glass braided into her hair. It's become a fashion amongst the fledglings, since she told some of them her grandda's stories about the Illish sheldars. They asked Æsa to weave them in herself. She still misses Illan: her family, the cliffs, the constant song of the sea. But somehow, down here with these girls, it hurts her less.

They also make her less fearful of her magic. With them, it feels more like a gift than a curse. After all, she didn't steal it from the Wellspring: It was given to her. Surely the gods wouldn't have done it unless they thought it should be so.

So more and more, she tries to hone and control it, but there is one piece of her magic that refuses to be tamed. Her visions started as dreams, coming only when she was sleeping. But the more she works with water, the more they come while she's awake. Alecand said the seers of old used to scry with bowls of water, their minds wandering off to different times and places. He made it sound like a choice—hers is not. She will pass a shallow pool and find her mind tumbling into it, the feeling of being tossed from a ship in a storm. It's dark water churning around her, thick and clouded. She can never tell where the surface might be.

She takes a left down a side tunnel and stops in front of a canvas tent. Before she can decide if she's really going to enter, a voice floats out.

"Come in, Æsa."

Jacinta is sitting on a large cushion, reading. A thick rug covers the cold stones. The tent is littered with books and colorful glass lanterns, with tiny mirrors hanging from strings that shine like stars. It feels lived in.

Jacinta smiles. "What brings you to my humble abode?"

Æsa swallows. What with Jacinta's ability to see snippets of the future, she thought she might already know why she's come.

"I was hoping you might tell me how you use your cards to decipher your visions."

I was hoping you might tell me how to read mine, too.

She has seen all sorts of things: Matilde in a ballroom with fiery wings stretched out behind her. Sayer in a fine dress with a rope around her wrists. Each vision wrings her heart with dread, but she can't make sense of them. What good is seeing the future when it's such a jumbled mess?

She still hasn't told the other girls. She doesn't want to scare them. But Jacinta is comfortable with her gift, it seems, and owns it fully. If anyone can help, it's her.

"Come here." Jacinta pats the cushion beside her. "I'll show you."

Æsa sits, and Jacinta pulls out the hand-painted cards she reads fortunes with, spreading them across the rug.

"Pick three," Jacinta says. "Only three."

Æsa lets her hand hover over them. Without thinking, she lets her fingers decide. Jacinta flips them faceup, laying them on top of the others. A spider's web, a serpent, and a fiery bird.

Jacinta narrows her eyes, rearranging the cards for no reason Æsa can discern.

"I painted these cards myself," she says, tapping them with dark-painted nails. "Each card has a central meaning. I just have to lay them out and let my magic weave them together, wait for the connection between them to emerge."

She thinks of her da, who always seems to know where the fish will be on any given morning. There's no magic in it. *The sea has a pattern,* he says—*you just have to learn how to read it.* But if her visions have a pattern, she can't find it. This ocean inside her seems to make its own tides.

Jacinta's gaze has gone soft, as if she's looking at something Æsa can't see. She seems so comfortable in her power. It's as if no one ever told her that such a thing might corrupt her, or she didn't believe them if they did. Æsa almost envies her.

"You will go on a journey soon," she says at last. "I see three sharp hills on a coastline."

Æsa's breath catches. It sounds like the Three Sisters, off the southern coast of Illan.

"How far into the future will that be?"

"Time is difficult to measure. It could be tomorrow or years from now."

She had a vision of Willan on a ship, standing behind her. Is he a part of that future?

There's a crease between Jacinta's brows. "You will take a winding path. But eventually it will bring you home again."

Home. She longs for it, but the thought of going home also makes her feel strange. What does it mean that she might be leaving Simta? Where will her other Nightbirds be?

She takes a deep breath. "The futures you see, Jacinta. Do they always happen? Are they fixed things, or can they be changed?"

Jacinta stares at her for several moments. Then she lets her fingers dance over the cards. She plucks one out of the pile, not looking, and turns it over. It holds the outline of a woman in fine armor, no helmet, one hand placed over her heart. The Knight.

"When I read for myself, this card represents someone I love. Someone I lost."

Æsa glances at Jacinta's dress, the same dark red she's always wearing. In Simta, it's a color for widows.

"I read for Tom often. I always saw the same things in his cards. Ambition and risk, reward and trial. His readings always had so much life in them."

She strokes the card as you might a cheek, so lovingly.

"He had a small sloop, which he used to run bootleg potions to boats off the coastline. He built a special compartment in the hull. It's dangerous work, especially for someone operating outside the piper gangs, but Tom was very good at it. One day, I saw a fall in the cards. I didn't want to believe it, and I couldn't quite see how it might go down. It was a possibility—one version of the future. So I warned him to be careful, and then I chose to forget. But the Wardens caught him, and there's no trial for repeat offenders. I only got to Gallows Row in time to watch."

Her voice is hard, both full and hollow, honed to a point by her loss.

"I'm sorry, Jacinta," Æsa says.

She waves away the words. "I'm just trying to answer your question. The future's an unpredictable thing. Fortunes change, depending on decisions made on the road toward them. Sometimes every road leads to the same place, but I don't think any future is immutable. We have choices. Our fates have many different streams."

Æsa takes a breath and reaches toward the pile of cards, letting her fingers hover. She can do this. When she feels a subtle spark, she picks one up.

The card is all sharp lines, dark paint, and two eyes burning. The robed man almost looks like a pater. One word is etched beneath him: DEATH.

Her vision swims, and then she's tumbling into darkness. Within it, she sees someone light a spark. She tries to see, to understand, but it's hazy. There is noise, loud, and a torrent of water. The ground shakes with a low, ominous roar.

With a gasp, her mind comes back into her body, her heart still screaming with the force of the dream.

"Æsa?" Jacinta is saying. "What is it?"

She opens her mouth to tell Jacinta, but then the tent flap is raked back, the space flooding with people. Matilde and Alecand, Sayer and Krastan. The air they bring into the tent with them is charged.

"It's a foolish idea," Alec is saying, "and you know it."

Matilde tilts up her chin. "I disagree."

The grief on Jacinta's face is gone, replaced by cool amusement. She and Matilde have more in common than she thinks.

"What's this, then?" Jacinta asks.

Alecand turns. "Matilde thinks it's time to give the Pontifex a talking-to."

Matilde scowls, arms akimbo. "You think I'm just going to ignore what he's done?"

Jacinta's eyes narrow. "Ignore what, exactly?"

Alec hands Jacinta a note. "These are being sent to all the Great Houses."

The thin paper is marked with the Points of the Eshamein and the Pontifex's sigil.

The church has received reports that you hide witches amongst you. The Pontifex is sure this can't be true. But in service to the four gods, and to the souls of all Eudeans, the Wardens will conduct a thorough search of all Great Houses. Those who cooperate will be treated kindly, and those who are honest will receive a reward.

This is the will of the gods. We are dedicated to ripping out any corruption that may have rooted amongst us. We will honor the Wellspring and let it cleanse us of our stains.

Sayer turns to Matilde. "At least he didn't publish your names. That's something."

"He might as well have." Matilde's voice is calm, but every line of her is tense and quivering. "Everyone knows my family is at the heart of this, and I've vanished. Those who don't know Æsa and I are Nightbirds must guess."

Dread fills Æsa. "Will they really submit all the Houses to inquisition?"

"It seems so." Krastan takes off his yellow cap, scrunching it between his hands. "The suzerain has thrown her weight behind it. Her word, combined with that of the church, is enough."

"Epinine Vesten isn't supporting the church because she's pious," Matilde says. "She's playing at something."

Alec makes a frustrated noise. "And what do you think you're going to do about it? March up there and demand an audience with the Pontifex? Tell him there's been some misunderstanding and go back to life as it was?"

"All he has is the Red Hand's words," Matilde says. "He can't prove I have magic. They can't force it out of me against my will."

"You can't know that, Stella," Krastan says softly. "There are stories of the feudal kings of old controlling girls with magic. Of Marren finding tools to subdue the Fyrebirds other than a sword."

Æsa's chest constricts. Is there a way someone could control this thing inside her? Take it from her?

"I don't know how they did it," Krastan continues, "but the church has archives. We don't know what kinds of knowledge they might hold."

Matilde's fists clench around the note. "They will interrogate my friends, past Nightbirds. I can't just sit on my hands down here."

Æsa can almost see her thoughts whirring, a card player trying to figure out her next move.

"Perhaps there is another way to fix this."

Sayer frowns. "Such as?"

"The Pontifex has power," Matilde says. "Especially with the suzerain standing by him. They're both a threat. But a Table vote is coming up. If we could depose Epinine and replace her with someone of our choosing . . . someone who cares about our interests . . ."

Sayer's expression is inscrutable. "You're thinking of Dennan Hain."

Alec makes a choking sound. "The Bastard Prince?"

Matilde stiffens. "He wants the same thing as you—to bring magic out of hiding. He doesn't believe in Prohibition. He doesn't share his sister's views."

Jacinta's eyes have narrowed to slits. "And you would trust him with our secrets?"

Matilde looks at Sayer and Æsa. "We trusted him once before. Why not again?"

Perhaps Matilde is right. The other night, Dennan did help them. But can he shield them from whatever dangers come their way?

"We need a powerful friend," Matilde says. "One who isn't afraid to change things."

Alec tugs at his curls. "He's a *Vesten*. He won't change things. He just wants his sister's power for himself."

"He's not like that." Matilde's voice is all heat. "You don't know him."

Alec's almost shouting now. "What, and you do?"

The tension in the air is thick enough to hang from. One of the mirrors above them turns, flashing with light.

"I know him well enough to be sure he means us no harm," Matilde says. "He will protect us."

"You, maybe." Jacinta's tone is scathing. "But what about

the rest of us? If you go to Dennan Hain, we'll be exposed. This place. All of us."

"How would staying here help?" Matilde throws up her hands. "What would you have me do, Jacinta?"

"You can't go." Jacinta stands. "We're so close. I can feel it."

Sayer's voice takes on a wary edge. "Close to what?"

"Krastan, tell them what you found," Alec says. "Or I will."

Silence falls again. Whatever's coming, Æsa isn't sure they are ready for it.

Matilde turns to her grandsire. "Krastan?"

Emotion flashes in his eyes, fondness and sadness, and something that has the flavor of regret.

He lets out a breath. "There is a story. I found it years ago, but never thought much of it. But now . . . well. Things have changed."

Prickles rise on the back of Æsa's neck.

"It speaks of something that happened, now and then, between Fyrebirds. Once in a very rare while, a special set of four would rise. They each leaned toward one of the four elements— earth, air, water, fire. And they were powerful. More powerful than all the others."

Æsa leans in, closer to Krastan. The silence beats like a stuttering heart.

"But these four were bound, too," he continues. "Called to each other, drawn together by an unstoppable pull. The story uses an old Eudean word for it: *Dendeal*."

Sayer's face seems paler than before. "What does that mean?"

"Heart tied."

Æsa thinks of the tingling sensation she feels when she touches her fellow Nightbirds. She assumed that girls with magic in them always felt it, but she doesn't with the fledglings. It is fullness and, more and more, an absence. A feeling that, somehow, they aren't yet whole.

Krastan goes on. "The closer they get, these four, in both body and spirit, the more they amplify the Wellspring's magic in each other. And when they join—truly combine their powers— it's like they drop a stone into the Wellspring's waters, making it ripple through everyone touched by it. That's how Fyrebirds were once able to part seas and move mountains. Together, they were strong enough to shake the world."

Æsa has the feeling she gets before she is pulled into a vision, thrown into the riotous unknown.

"Blazing cats," Sayer breathes. "You can't think we're like those Fyrebirds."

"Why not?" Alec says. "The signs are there."

Seconds pass, speaking volumes. The lights flicker with what Æsa thinks might be Matilde's rising pulse.

"It's just a story," Matilde says. "What makes you think it's true?"

"I've seen you, Stella," Krastan says. "All three of you, amplifying the other girls. I've seen how you make each other stronger."

"We're all stronger with you here," Jacinta presses. "And every day, more girls with magic find their way to us. It's as if something is calling to them."

As if something is waking their magic up. Could it be them?

"But you said four," Sayer says to Krastan. "*Four* girls."

"I believe your earth girl is close," he says. "Perhaps even in these tunnels."

Something ripples through Æsa, sharp and sudden. A knowing.

"The Wellspring brought you together," Jacinta says. "It gave you this power that hasn't risen in centuries. There has to be some reason for it."

Sayer's voice has turned suspicious. "What is it you want from us?"

"We've never had the power to truly change things in Simta," Jacinta says. "But with Fyrebirds on our side, making us stronger, we could finally start."

Matilde stiffens. "Start *what*?"

It's Alec who answers. "A revolution."

The silence circles, thin and razor-edged.

"Fyrebirds used their power to shape the world once," Krastan says. "To make it better."

"We're not flamemoths," Sayer says, her voice a warning. "You can't just throw us in a jar and use us as your guiding light."

Æsa thinks of Grandda saying she has a sheldar within her. *You just have to listen for her song and have the courage to answer.* If she does, could she become like one of those women painted on the walls of the underground ballroom? With the other girls beside her, perhaps . . .

Beneath her slippered feet, the ground trembles. The sense of knowing comes again as ice-cold fear floods her chest.

"Oh, gods," she whispers.

Sayer grabs her hand. "What is it, Æsa?"

She looks down at the card still in her hand. "It's Death."

A BOY IN grey crawls through a tunnel that smells of jawbone algae. Eli knows he should be scared, but he feels lit from within. He can still feel the Red Hand's fingers on his forehead, blessing his quest. Eli will be dead soon—his mortal body. But his soul will have flown into Marren's embrace.

Crouching down, he sets his tools out, careful not to let the water touch them. The fuse must stay dry to do its holy work. Eli lights it fast, hands shaking only slightly. He is ready. One second, two, and then a spark . . . a righteous fire. *A cleansing fire to cleanse the world.*

CHAPTER 18

HEART TIED

T HE UNDERGROUND IS flooding," Æsa tells them.

"It happens," Alec says. "We'll go and close the leak."

"You can't close it." She can still see the hole, huge and ragged, and the water rushing through. "Someone has blown a hole in one of the tunnels. Right under one of the main canals."

Sayer swears. "Who?"

Æsa makes herself say it. "One of the Caska."

They are all up then, rushing out of the tent into the tunnel. It quakes ominously beneath their feet. People on either side are stumbling out of their tents, too, grabbing belongings, hands, and children. They have escape hatches, she knows, in case anything happens to these tunnels, but no one knows which one to run to. The rumble seems to come from everywhere.

Krastan grabs Matilde's arm. "Up to the shop, all of you. Quickly."

They run with the rest of the crowd into the soaring market. Out here, the rumble is more like a roar. People rush out of its side tunnels, shouting names and grabbing what they can. Tentpoles are knocked askew and tables topple, making herbs and powders cloud the air. Someone knocks Æsa's shoulder, but Sayer catches her.

"Come on," Sayer pants. "We have to hurry."

But something has Æsa by the ribs, holding her fast.

A wave crashes into view at the far end of the arched tunnel. Æsa had hoped it would be a trickle in this vast space, but it's a torrent, roaring like some wrathful god. She watches in horror as it swallows one body, then another, as they try to outrun it. How many tunnels has it rushed down to get here? How long before it swallows them too?

The wave only parts for the market's tree, which bends hard under its current, bright purple leaves ripped free.

"Æsa!" someone shouts. Sayer tugs hard at her hand, but they cannot outrun this, and she is so tired of running scared.

Willan's words slip past her fear. *I think you're stronger than you imagine.* Her grandda's too. Perhaps there *is* a sheldar singing through her, and water is her element.

Æsa will listen to her song now, come what may.

She lets the ocean inside her swell, filling her to brimming. She steps in front of her friends and throws out her hands.

"Dwen!" she roars in Illish.

Stop.

Her magic pours out of her. It rises from her bones, her blood, as if it's been waiting for this moment, spilling out on an invisible tide. It seems to crash into the wave, halting some of its momentum so that it moves more like syrup than a sea. She can feel the weight of the water, pushing back against her power. She strains, arms shaking. There is so much of it, and more is flooding in from the canal above.

Fingers wrap around her arm: it's Sayer. Matilde grips Sayer's other hand. Their magic twines together like strands of rope, making them stronger. She tastes a storm on her tongue, fire in her veins.

The water slows, then stops as if it's hit an invisible barrier. It climbs through the air in a sheet, almost as tall as she is—taller. A curtain of water creeping up a wall of air. *Sayer*. She has a hand up, twisting and turning as if she's shaping it. The dark water beyond it is filled with tents and clothes, chairs and barrels, and—oh, gods—bodies. A few hit the barrier, arms and legs flailing. Alec and Krastan run up to the water, trying to reach through. But the wall of air is too thick, and it seems to be rising, trying to keep up with the water filling the tunnel. Soon it will turn the market into a sealed tomb.

Æsa's heart is in her throat. "It's too much. I can't hold it!"

"Neither can I," Sayer pants. Little cracks are forming in the invisible wall, water dribbling out of them. "I'm trying, but . . ."

"If you let go," Matilde grits out, "we all drown."

A few of the fledglings have appeared, gathering around them, hands out, but they can't fix this. They need their fourth. Their missing piece.

There is a presence in the tunnel, wrapping around her like a vine, tighter and tighter. Æsa can barely breathe under its pull. It's their fourth, and she is coming closer. And yet it isn't close enough.

Æsa turns, holding out a shaking hand. "Fenlin."

Fen's hair is wild, her hands clenched in tight fists. "What . . ."

She wasn't there in the tent when Krastan told them that legend, but surely she can feel its truth.

"Fen," Æsa says again. "Please. We need you."

Fen shakes her head hard. Æsa has never seen her expression so raw before.

Out beyond the wall of air, someone screams.

Æsa turns back toward the wave to see someone hanging from one of the half-drowned tree's branches, just above the waterline. It's Rankin, yanking Verony—one of the air girls—out of the churning froth. They cling together, choking on the murky water. Rankin looks up at them, eyes huge and frightened.

"Fen!" he screams again. "Help!"

Fen spits out her mastic and steps forward, face as grim as any mourner's.

"Blazing cats and dash it *all.*"

She grabs Æsa's wrist. Magic pulses through her. No: It rages. Leaves shake, fire kindles, air blows, water crashes, a force too vast for her body to contain. She has tasted this power before, in the Dinatris garden, but that was only a ripple. This is the stone that makes the waves. And with it comes a sense of profound and utter rightness. It's as if she has been missing pieces all her life, and now she's whole. *Heart tied.*

She focuses on the water again and it stops churning, curling in on itself like a sleepy cat. The cracks in Sayer's wall close up, and no more water spills over the lip of it. Fen is breathing fast, glaring at that tree out in the deep. Its branches move, groaning as they stretch toward the invisible barrier, dropping Rankin and Verony near the edge of the water. Krastan and Alec rush to catch them as they struggle over the lip of the wall.

Matilde and Sayer are staring at Fen, mouths hanging open. Fen's gaze is focused on Rankin standing by the invisible wall.

"Don't stand there like a stunned mullet," Fen growls. "Help those people."

Rankin shakes himself and turns back toward the water. People are swimming up to the barrier, fighting to get their bodies over it. Alec, Krastan, and Rankin all help them as they fall the several feet onto the stones, gasping. Verony comes to stand by Sayer. Æsa can see other bodies, lifeless, swaying in time with the water. She prays that most of the Underground's inhabitants are behind her, fleeing, instead of drowning in the dark.

"We have to go," Æsa pants. She's starting to shake badly. "It's a lot of water. I don't know how long we can hold it."

"You can't push it back?" Alec asks. "Or freeze it?"

"It's not like there's a guidebook," Sayer grinds out. "How should we know?"

"It feels like too much to freeze," Æsa says. "But I don't feel like we can just leave it, either. If we let go, it won't hold."

The people they helped out of the wave are getting up now. Verony's tight curls are plastered to her cheeks, eyes wide. Æsa looks over her shoulder to see that other people have stopped running to stare. Young faces, old faces, some fledglings, all looking at the four of them as if they can save them from disaster. She badly wants to prove their faith.

"We can't let the wave go," Æsa says, thinking fast. "Which means we have to take it with us."

"What?" Matilde asks. "Just . . . drag it behind us like a dog on a lead?"

Æsa nods. "We hold it until everyone's out."

Krastan whispers swiftly to Alec, then they are both running, herding the crowd away.

"Make haste!" Krastan shouts. "Everyone out! You have minutes only."

With that, feet pound and the people shout as they pour out of the market at its dry end to run for whatever escape routes they can find. Before long there is only the four of them, plus Jacinta, and a sopping wet Rankin and Verony. The light is strange, as if they're all underwater. Errant orblights bob out on the wave's surface, glowing like ghosts.

"It's time to go," Æsa says, trying to sound certain. "Are you ready?"

Matilde huffs out a breath. "As I will ever be."

Æsa looks at Fen, who is eyeing the water as if she'd like to knife it, and Sayer, who is staring at her friend.

"Sayer? Fen?"

They both nod, saying nothing. Then the four of them take a slow step back. The wave and the wall of air follow behind them. Its restless murmuring reverberates off the stone.

They take another step, another, and the water follows. Jacinta, Rankin, and Verony follow beside. Krastan and Alec run ahead, shouting down side tunnels to anyone who might be left there. Stragglers emerge, gaping as they try to understand what they are seeing. One man trips, sprawling on stone, and Alec has to help him. His eyes on them are stunned . . . perhaps afraid.

Æsa can feel the water's pressure building; it wants to push its fingers deeper into the Underground, but she won't let it. Containing it to just the market tunnel is taking everything she has. It's what a sheldar would do, so she will do it. Perhaps her magic was meant to save, and not to hurt, after all.

They have almost reached the end of the market, where it branches off in a T. The right branch goes toward the garden where she talked to Fen the other day. The other will take them to Krastan's shop.

Matilde is out of breath. "Can we make a wave turn a corner?"

Sayer says, "Only one way to find out."

They have just started to pivot down the left-hand tunnel, the wave hovering on the edge of the market, when screams ricochet off the walls. A clutch of people run out from the right-hand tunnel, almost running into the Nightbirds. They're being chased by three boys in grey.

En Caska Dae.

One points his crossbow at the four of them. "That's them! Take them!"

Verony throws herself in front of Sayer, hands extended. "Leave them *alone*."

Something sparks over her palms like lightning. It flickers, crackling loudly as she hurls it, wrapping around one of the Caska like a net. He falls down, twitching, and there's a moment of stillness.

An arrow punches right through Verony's chest.

Sayer shouts her name as Verony crumples. Jacinta bends down, putting her hands around the arrow, but too much blood is leaking out. Verony's eyes find Æsa's, filled with fear and yawning horror. *Make it stop,* they seem to say. *Make it right.* Then she is gone.

The boy whose arrow hit Verony crows, as if he has just achieved some kind of greatness. As if this is a hunt and Verony is his prize. The Caska haven't yet seen the wall of water churning at the edge of the market. Or the ocean in her chest, now full of rage.

A tendril of water breaks through Sayer's wall, as thick around as she is, sliding across the stones like a serpent. It knocks the crossbows out of the hands of the two boys still standing. She wills it to reach for the one who shot Verony, wrapping around his torso, squeezing him in a tightening fist.

He claws at the serpent, but his fingers slide through it. As she tightens its grip a rib snaps, and he shrieks.

"We are Marren's hands," the other boy shouts. "Our mission is holy!"

The song inside is so loud Æsa can't hear any other. The sheldar bares her teeth, thirsty for blood.

"You are *not* men of the gods."

She wills the serpent to return to where it came from. It jerks the Caska with it through Sayer's barrier, throwing him into the watery depths. His fists pound—once, twice, fingers splaying out against it. Then he is gone, floating away through the dark.

Her anger bleeds away. She can't stop staring at the place where the boy's hands just were. Oh, gods. What has she done?

She stumbles. Behind the wall of air, the wave shudders.

"Come now, darling," Matilde says, voice thin but controlled. "It's just a little farther."

The other two Caska boys are up, stumbling away, back in the direction they came from. Jacinta closes Verony's eyes, whispers a prayer.

They make the turn and walk toward Krastan's, the wave dragging behind them. More and more water is slipping through the cracks in Sayer's wall. Æsa feels like she is cracking, too, her concentration fractured. There are so few lights, and the water is so dark.

After what feels like an eternity, they are beneath the hatch that leads to Krastan's shop. Alec pulls the ladder out from the wall, yanks on a rope, and the hatch opens. He's holding one of his glowing light bags, which paints them all in purple light.

"You all go first," Sayer gasps. "We'll follow."

Alec looks to Krastan. "But—"

"You don't do us any favors by dawdling, Padano," Fen growls. "So move."

They do, Krastan, Jacinta, and Rankin disappearing up the ladder and through the hatchway. Alec ties a string to the purple light and puts it around Matilde's neck. He hurries up, and now it is just the four of them.

"Don't let go," Æsa gasps. The wave is heavy, enough of it leaking out to swirl up to their knees. "I don't think I can hold it without you touching me."

"How are we supposed to climb holding on to each other?" Matilde says.

As if in answer, a rope tumbles down to them. Fen grabs it with her free hand and ties it around each of their waists.

"We do it quickly."

She shouts at those above to hold on, then starts to climb the ladder. Æsa gasps as she is yanked up behind. More water slips free—it's gushing now. Sayer is staring down the wall of air, but it's failing. Æsa can feel them all getting tired.

Matilde screams, "Dash it, go *faster*!"

The rope around Æsa's middle burns as it tightens. Her hand on Matilde's starts to slip as someone above shouts, *"Pull."* The water rises, tearing at her skirts, tumbling her thoughts. She fumbles to climb, but the metal rungs of the ladder are slippery. She feels like she is being ripped apart.

The air barrier breaks and the wave roars, crashing into the ladder. Æsa screams as Matilde and Sayer both disappear under the froth. The rope yanks hard, stealing her air, but she manages to grab on to the metal footholds built into the inside of the hatchway.

Someone is screaming from above.

"Climb, Æsa!"

She can't see, can barely breathe. Matilde and Sayer are a dead weight dragging behind her. If she doesn't get them out, they will die. She fumbles blindly for another metal hold, yanking them upward. One hand, two. She tries to breathe, but everything hurts.

Hands go under her armpits, yanking so hard that she loses all balance. Someone cushions her as they collapse into a shaking heap on the basement floor. With a flurry of footsteps and grunts, the rope eases. Sayer lands beside her, spitting up water, but Matilde is silent. By the glow of the strange light, Æsa sees Alecand fall to his knees.

"Tilde?" he says, shaking her roughly. "Dash it, Tilde, *stop playing.*"

He lays her down, putting his ear to her lips, then kisses her roughly. No: breathes into her. One breath, two. She doesn't speak. Matilde, who is always talking and teasing, coaxing the world into the shapes she likes best. But she has to wake up. If she doesn't, it feels as if Æsa will lose something . . . vital. Some part of herself she can't yet name.

And then Matilde rolls onto her side, throwing up water. Alec lets out a long, jagged breath.

There is the scrape of someone closing the hatch cover, sealing them off from the Underground. The purple light sputters and dies; the basement is suddenly in darkness. All Æsa can hear are trembling coughs, waterlogged breaths, and the trickle of water pushing through the holes in the hatch cover. She hopes the wave isn't going to follow them. If it does, she might just let it take her away.

She closes her eyes, seeing that Caska boy's fists pounding against Sayer's barrier. She watched him drown and didn't care. Her magic took her rage and twisted it, turning it into something monstrous. Something she couldn't push down or hold back.

She sobs, once, in the darkness.

You have a sheldar singing through you. But it's a hashna's song, laced with death and destruction.

It seems she's been a poison all along.

SOMETHING RIPPLES THROUGH Simta, silent and sudden, but it's a tide that only certain girls can feel. They will describe the sensation in dozens of ways: as a flint struck between ribs, a shudder like thunder, a shiver passing through their blood. But all will say it stirred something deep inside them, bringing it up into the light.

SOMEWHERE IN GRIFFIN Quarter, two sisters pause halfway through a game of Twelve Star. The rope between them stills, but in their chests, something shakes. No, it *quivers*, like the canals do when the weather changes, dragging a storm in from the sea.

"Did you feel that?" one says, touching her collarbone, half expecting to find it vibrating.

"I think so," says the other. "It tickles."

They both laugh, nervous and a little bit excited. Then they pack their rope away and go inside to play their favorite game, the secret one. Usually they have to try very hard to call up enough wind to slide a coin across the attic floor. Today they lift the coin up without touching it. It floats there, like a promise, on the air.

SOMEWHERE IN DRAGON Quarter, a girl closes her eyes, wishing herself away from this Smoky Row brothel. Her sire isn't coming to fetch her home, though; she knows it. He sold her to settle debts he could not pay. She rests her hands against the narrow windowsill, leaning into the street noise. There is no point in wishing for a savior—none is coming. But then something rolls through her, hot as embers. It kindles a strange sort of blaze in her hands. When she pulls them away, the wood is charred.

Did *she* do that?

She presses a shaking finger to the sill again. The wood sizzles. She sears her name into it, a dark brand. *Iona was here.*

Downstairs, the madam shouts her name. It's a sound she dreads, and yet she is smiling.

———

SOMEWHERE IN THE Garden District, a dark-haired girl sits on the roof outside her bedroom, hands cupped around a pot full of dirt. She thought she might be able to make the seedling grow if she sang to it. The flowers in their hothouse have been singing to her, lately, in voices no one else seems to hear.

In a tingling rush, something unfurls inside her. It's like sun peeking between the leaves in her family's garden, a sudden burst of warmth in the gloom. She scrunches up her nose, willing the estaflower to grow for her. Its velvet-soft petals curl up around her thumbs. It seems to sing her name: *Jolena Regnis.*

Wyllo Regnis's youngest daughter makes a sound of pure delight.

– CHAPTER 19 –

INTO THE LIGHT

MATILDE HAS NEVER felt so angry at daylight. It forces her to see things she would rather ignore. The water streaming from their clothes and their haunted expressions, all bathed in a brightness that hurts her stinging eyes.

She clears her throat. It's still raw from the brackish water. Every Simtan learns to swim, and she is good at it, but her skill made no difference in that tunnel. If not for the rope and these people, she would be dead. The wave must be filling the Underground, and that ballroom where she and the other girls practiced. All those murals of powerful women, drowned in the dark. It feels like part of her is down there with them, lost forever. The part that thought the world was fair and made for her.

Alec and Krastan stalk through the shop's secret back room. They are all holding their breaths, waiting to see if anyone is poised to ensnare them. The shop is too quiet, the air too calm.

En Caska Dae wants to kill us. Even after the attack in her family's garden, a part of her refused to believe it. But in the tunnels, she watched a boy in grey shoot Verony right in front of them. Then she watched Æsa drag him into the watery deep. Beside her now, Æsa is shivering, her green eyes vacant. It's hard to believe the kind of power she just wielded—that they all wielded. The kind that will only make the paters want to hunt them more.

Krastan's voice cuts through her thoughts.

"We're alone. For now, at least."

No one moves. Matilde works her parched tongue, trying to smooth her voice into its normal cadence. "We need new clothes. And then we need to make a plan."

No one argues. They file wearily through the secret door and behind the front counter, up the narrow, creaking stairs to the Padanos' apartments, leaving wet footprints in their wake. Matilde clutches her locket, grateful for the familiar weight. Exhaustion beckons, but she can't give in to it. She has to stay alert and awake.

Krastan points to two doors on opposite sides of the hallway. "Ladies in here. Boys in there."

Sayer stalks in first, fists clenched, pointedly not looking at Fenlin. Æsa follows her numbly. Alec goes with Krastan into the other room, leaving the door open. Rankin lingers as if he might say something to Fen, but her face is a wall, closed off and uninviting. After a breath, he slouches off.

Matilde stares at Fenlin Brae glowering down at the floorboards. She's always thought the girl was suspicious, and no wonder . . . she's been keeping more secrets than anyone else. Fen, the sandpiper girl Matilde has never warmed to, is one of them. And their supposed fourth, if what Krastan said about those Fyrebirds is true. Ten hells.

How did she hide it? Matilde can feel the tingling pull of

magic with Sayer and Æsa, but never Fenlin. It's as if the piper is surrounded by some unseen, malevolent wall. That wall is gone now. Matilde can feel the magic pulsing under her skin, green and growing. She tilts her head, trying to catch Fen's eye.

"Care to join us, Fenlin?"

Every line of Fen's body is rigid. "I surely don't."

Well, then. "Suit yourself."

Matilde turns to Jacinta.

"There's another room down there." She points. "We three need a moment, if you don't mind."

She doesn't wait to find out if she does.

The door snicks shut. Sayer and Æsa are standing next to the tiny yellow-glass window, each looking lost in her own haunted thoughts. Matilde should say something. But what words are there for what they've just seen . . . what they've done?

She keeps seeing Verony stepping in front of them, as if she might protect them from the Caska. That arrow bursting through her chest and out the other side. The way that Caska boy shouted in triumph, as if her life had no value . . . only her death.

But now isn't the time to sink into such horrors. She pushes the memory down, slipping on her calmest mask.

"Let's change," she says. "Whatever comes, we don't want to meet it stinking of canal water."

Sayer's movements are all contained fury. She throws open the closet door hard enough to shake the floor. Matilde gives her room to rummage, going to sit on the narrow, neatly made bed. It's been years since she was last in Alec's room. There's a table full of instruments she doesn't know the names of, a colorful woven rug, a tightly tucked coverlet, a stack of alchemical books next to the bed. Something trails out from one of them: a bunch of braided silk ribbons. They're faded, but she recognizes them just the same. Alec let her weave them into his hair once, when he still wore it down to his shoulders. When he caught his reflection, he promptly made her take them out. *Fine,* she said, braiding the ribbons together. *I'll make you something to hold when you're missing me.*

She assumed he threw it away, but here it is, marking his place for him. Something about it threatens to rip her calm away. It's the kind of calm, she thinks, that might actually be shock, or exhaustion. She feels wrung out, but even so, more alive. It's as if joining with the other three to stop that wave has awoken something deep inside her: a new and thrilling kind of fire.

She feels a new awareness of the girls, too. No . . . a bond. She can hear Fen shifting her feet out in the hallway and sense Sayer's emotions raging through her chest. She can almost see Æsa's guilt, blooming in blue clouds around her. They're all a part of her now. She is a part of them.

Krastan said that a rare few Fyrebirds used to feel this pull toward each other. That when they joined, they became something more. *That's how Fyrebirds were once able to part seas and move mountains. Together, they were strong enough to shake the world.*

"Here." Sayer throws a bundle of clothes at her. "Take these."

They must have shucked their own wet clothes while Matilde was lost in thought, as both are wearing pants and rough-spun shirts in varying shades of yellow. Æsa keeps yanking at the wet strands of hair around her neck. She looks very much like her skin is the only thing holding her together. Matilde would do anything to wipe the bleakness from her face.

"These are pants, Sayer."

Sayer's expression darkens. "If you were hoping for a gown, Alecand is fresh out."

She shouldn't joke, but if she doesn't, she will scream. "But what am I supposed to *do* with them?"

"One leg in each hole," Sayer growls. "It's pretty self-explanatory."

She looks like she wants to punch everything, Matilde included, but she knows Sayer well enough now not to be stung by it. Anger is her favorite mask.

Matilde peels off the dress, but she leaves on her underclothes. They may be wet, but at least they're hers. She never realized how much control her finely tailored dresses gave her. They made it clear who she was: a Great House daughter, protected, untouchable. None of that is true anymore.

Alec's pants are tight around her hips. The shirt smells of him: woodsmoke, ashes, frennet. She touches her lips, thinking of him breathing air back into her lungs. He kept an arm around her all the way up the stairs, but in the light, he walked away from her, just like that afternoon in his underground lab.

But she has more pressing concerns than Alecand Padano's mixed signals. Matilde gets up, the pants rubbing strangely between her thighs, and walks over to Æsa. She runs two fingers down the back of her hand.

"A shill for your thoughts, darling."

One breath, two. Æsa's shoulders shudder. "I killed him."

Matilde doesn't have to ask who she means.

"He killed one of our girls," Matilde says, swallowing down the pain of it.

Sayer closes the closet door roughly. "If you hadn't done it, believe me, I would have. That boy got what he deserved."

Æsa looks up at that, her eyes a sea-colored ruin.

"He was just a boy following the wrong star. Now he won't ever have a chance to find another."

Matilde thinks that boy reaped what he sowed, but that doesn't make it less ugly.

"I know we're all overwrought," she says, "but we need to talk about—"

Sayer says, "No."

"You don't even know what I was going to say."

"Just . . . no."

Sayer glances toward the door, too distraught to hide her feelings. She clearly didn't know Fen's secret, either, though it seems Æsa did.

"We need to move fast," Matilde presses. "We need to talk to Dennan."

Sayer turns, expression incredulous. "We just watched the Underground get flooded, and you want to go play politics?"

The edge in her voice makes Matilde flinch. "The Caska know who we are. And if those two Caska boys escaped the wave, then they also know what we four can do together. They saw us. We have to take control of this situation before it takes control of us."

"I'm going to tear them all apart for what they did." Sayer is pacing now. "I'll make them pay for this."

"So your plan is . . . what?" Matilde asks. "March out into the streets and start killing paters?"

"They seem more than willing to do it to us."

Verony's memory is there, hovering between them.

"The church has poured poison into people's ears about girls with magic since before the three of us were born," Matilde insists. "There will always be people who fear what's inside us. What do you think will happen if we start burning churches down?"

"They will see us for what we truly are," Æsa whispers. "Monsters."

Matilde looks to Æsa, shocked by her words, but Sayer isn't finished.

"Don't you get it? We're the reason the Underground was raided. They've stayed hidden for years. And then we go down there, and within days the Caska find it. You're telling me you think that's a coincidence? Those people lost everything because of us. We owe them justice."

Matilde reaches for Dennan's bird in her pocket, but then remembers she sent it to him yesterday. Something dark and tangled rises within her. But she didn't tell him where they were, just that she wanted to talk to him about the future. He wouldn't give them up to the Caska. She's sure.

"And what happens after we take vengeance?" Matilde asks. "Do you think the Pontifex is going to shrug and say all's well? That the city is going to throw us a party?"

Sayer scowls. "After what the Caska did to your family, I'm surprised to find you such a coward."

Matilde grits her teeth. "My family can't afford for me to turn outlaw. It will endanger them. It's easy for you to do what you want, Sayer. You don't have any more family to lose."

The silence that descends is like a tear, rough and jagged. Matilde wishes she could take the words back.

"I'm sorry. I just . . . I want my life back," Matilde says, hushed. "And my family. But first, we have to make it safe. We have to show people that the church is wrong about us."

"But are they?" Æsa says, more to herself than to them. "Sheldars are supposed to be saviors. All we seem to do is cause pain."

But they *did* save people, didn't they? Pulled them out of the water and stopped that wave long enough for more to escape. And there's more to discover between them—she feels it. They could remake their world as they see fit.

"There will be people who fear us no matter what we do. We need protection. We need a champion who will fight to change the law, and fight for our interests. Dennan is by far the best bet, for all of us."

"Fine. Go and flirt with the Bastard Prince," Sayer snaps. "I won't stop you. You only ever do what you want, anyway."

I, you. Sayer speaks as if the four of them aren't tied irreparably together.

Matilde thinks of her old Nightbird sisters who she laughed with and schemed with, sharing flirtations and impossible dreams. They were so close, and yet they never shared this kind of kinship. The tie between them isn't love, or even choice, but something deeper. It is more than just the magic in their veins.

These frustrating, impossible girls are her sisters. She isn't going to let them slip away. Not now.

"I don't understand this thing between us," Matilde says. "But I know that being together makes us stronger. I need you both. We need each other."

Sayer's voice is hot and cold at once. "I didn't *ask* for this. I don't want it."

The words cut all the way through her.

"And you, Æsa? What do you want?"

But Matilde can see the fight she showed in the tunnels has left her. Her voice is the smallest thing in the room.

"I want to go home."

Matilde looks at her sisters. Except they aren't, because they have chosen not to be.

"Fine." She storms past them toward the door, refusing to look back. "I suppose that means I'm flying on my own."

My daughter is like I was, but she doesn't want to see it. She refuses to become the brilliant Nightbird she could be. The trouble, I think, is that she doesn't attend to all the pieces of my stories. She only hears the part about what others will take. I feel for her: She has never known what it is to have sisters. Girls who hold the deepest parts of you, who share your dreams. It's a bond that holds a power she has never truly known.

—EXCERPT FROM NADJA SANT HELD'S
PRIVATE JOURNAL

CHAPTER 20

SHADOW NO MORE

SAYER STALKS DOWN the hallway, which is blessedly empty. It seems like everyone has changed and gone downstairs. She's glad for the shadows and this temporary quiet. She keeps sucking down air but can't quite seem to catch her breath.

A burst of queasiness has her leaning against the wall. It's the herb smell of the shop, smoky and acrid, and vaguely familiar. Or maybe she just swallowed too much water down below. Her magic feels muted, as tired and heartsick as the rest of her. Even so, she can feel the other Nightbirds and Fen. She can hear their breaths and feel their heartbeats like an echo. It's as if a piece of each girl wrapped itself around her ribs and won't let go.

Sayer meant what she said to Matilde: She doesn't want this. She didn't come to the Nightbirds to get tangled up in other lives. Such bonds weigh you down, turning into a danger. They only cause you pain when they break.

She thinks of Fen, the one she trusted not to lie—not to her. But she has magic, and she's kept it from Sayer. Memories coalesce as she leans against the wall, heart beating hard. She remembers that moment in the alley when they kissed. She was trying to give Fen her magic, but it didn't work because Fen had her own. Still, the kiss made something rise up in Sayer, charged and singing. Was it Fen's magic that amplified hers that night, allowing her to turn into smoke?

It makes sense now why Fen has been so cagey. Why she seemed reticent to touch Sayer ever since. Fen must have some way of masking her magic, keeping it hidden. Still, she should have known—should have seen. She thinks of Æsa reaching back for Fen's hand, as if she knew already. Betrayal rips at Sayer's chest, making it ache.

Æsa pads out into the hall in Alec's yellow shirt and rough-spun pants, face paler than usual. At least her eyes are clearer now.

Sayer crosses her arms. "All right?"

She winces. "My stomach's just hurting."

Sayer's, too. "Simta's canal water never does go down smooth."

They pause at the top of the stairs. Matilde is walking down them. Back in the Underground, Sayer would've laughed at how awkward she looks in pants, but now she doesn't have the heart for it. Especially when she sees who's at the bottom of the stairs. Fen stands against the wall, in the shadows of a towering book-shelf. Her wet hair is slicked back, her one eye a fiery lantern. When their gazes meet, Sayer's heart shudders. No, it *burns*.

A war wages in her chest. One side says she's Fenlin Brae, her oldest friend and her truest. The other side insists she doesn't know Fen at all.

Sayer wants to look away but can't seem to. Fen's lips part, forming a silent word.

Run.

Something crawls up Sayer's spine. She didn't notice before how strange the air is, full of a poised silence and some kind of sickly smell.

Æsa squeezes her arm. "Oh, gods, it's—"

But Sayer knows already. The Red Hand's voice is one she could never forget.

"Come down, witch," he says to Matilde. "Come and join us."

For a moment, Matilde stands frozen. Sayer waits for a crossbow to skewer her. One second, two, but no arrows come. In the Underground, the Hand's soldiers shot first and asked questions never. What game is he playing now? Matilde seems to know, because she is smiling like she's just spotted a friend she hasn't seen in ages. Sayer doesn't know how she can play pretend so well, even now.

"Well met," she says. "*Such* a pleasure. Have I kept you waiting long?"

Sayer reaches for her magic, but it's dull and stunted. They've discovered it has limits, running low when they try to use too much. Maybe they used up their reserves on the wave and it needs time to build again. She needs a way to see down into the shop without being seen. She looks around. There: to the right, a cramped galley full of unpacked crates. She grabs Æsa's elbow, crouching down and crawling slowly, silently, toward it.

"The time of reckoning has come, witch," the Red Hand says.

Sayer can almost feel Matilde's eye roll. Dirty shills, the girl's got brass.

"Reckonings are best had on a full stomach, and I haven't eaten a morsel. How about I set you alight instead?"

Can Matilde conjure fire? Sayer's magic won't come, even

with Æsa beside her. Perhaps she's trying to throw the Hand off his game.

Sayer wriggles through the crates, trying to get a clear view. What she sees makes her want to curse long and loud. The front room of the shop is full of Caska, all pointing their crossbows. Krastan has his back pressed up against the client's side of the wooden counter. Alec is behind it, hand on Jacinta's shoulder to keep her down and out of view. Fen is pressed so hard against the wall it's as if she is trying to push through it. From where the boys in grey are standing, it's possible they might not see her. Especially through Rankin, who's turned as if he means to shield Fen from view.

The Red Hand looks the same as she remembers: scarred cheeks marked with a red handprint, a shaved head and eyebrows, that unwavering gaze. Otherworldly. He swings a copper censer, which emits a blue-tinged trail of smoke.

"Go ahead, witch," he says. "I would love to see you try it."

Matilde's voice is less playful. "If you think I have qualms about burning a man of the church, I truly don't."

"If anything happens to me, my boys will start shooting. Demon that you are, I don't believe you want these people's blood on your hands."

Sayer looks into the open crates nearest her. Maybe one of them holds something she can use to create a diversion. There has to be some way to get them out of this.

"It seems you aren't in a hurry to kill me," Matilde says. "So tell me. Why flood the tunnels? I could have died, and dead girls can't do magic. Isn't that what you wanted me for? As proof?"

The Hand's mouth twists. "The explosion was meant to flush you out and drive you above, where we could catch you. Brother Eli was a little overeager, but no matter. Everyone down there was either a witch or a blasphemer. I am glad to do Marren's holy work."

There is such conviction in his eyes, a fervent light that sends a chill right through Sayer.

"How did you know I would be here?" Matilde asks, voice flat and strange.

The corner of the Hand's mouth twitches. "A little bird told me."

What Sayer can see of Matilde's face goes ashen. Sayer's queasy feeling deepens further still.

"Come with me quietly, now," the Hand says, "and nothing else will happen to these friends of yours."

Someone's crossbow clicks.

"Shoot anyone here," Matilde says, "and it's murder. You will hang for it."

The Hand flashes his teeth. "What makes you so sure?"

Silence descends, sharp as a blade. There is a smug edge to the Hand's expression that makes Sayer want to lunge for him. She wills her magic to rise, for some plan to present itself: nothing. Just that coiled, oily feeling of sickness in her gut.

The Hand moves forward. Krastan steps in front of Matilde, shielding her from him, but something by the stairs has caught his eye.

"Little Johnny Rankin," he says. "Is that you? You've grown taller."

The boy balls up his fists, but Sayer can still see they're shaking. "It's Rankin to you. Don't you come any closer."

Fen steps away from the wall then, putting a hand on Rankin's shoulder. The Hand's expression changes, equal parts triumph and rage.

He smiles like a wolf. "Ah, Ana. At last."

Fen looks so shaken, face beaded with sweat. "You're confused, old man. My name isn't Ana."

The Red Hand touches one of his cheeks. "Oh, I could never forget you, little thief. You who led me down this path."

I see you, little thief. Isn't that what the Hand shouted in the Dinatris garden? Sayer looks with new eyes at the Hand's scars. They're swirling and shiny, like long-ago burns. Fen burned down the orphanage she and Rankin grew up in, in hopes of killing the pater inside it. The one who made their lives a living hell.

Sayer looks from the Hand to Fen, who isn't moving, paralyzed by this nightmare from her past.

Matilde lifts her hands. Some of the boys in grey shake their crossbows, but the Hand makes a staying gesture. Then he opens his censer and lets its contents spill onto the floor. Matilde clutches her stomach as Sayer feels a wave of nausea sweep through her. What she can feel of her magic just . . . dies, a light snuffed out.

"What . . ." Matilde gasps. "What have you done to me?"

The boys in grey look relieved, but the Red Hand looks elated. He claps his hands in glee.

"Marren knew that every poison has an antidote. He traveled the land until he found a plant that tamped down a witch's magic. The other paters thought the story a myth. But I hunted it down, and for years worked to extract the secrets of its usage. It seems I've finally found them out. You've been breathing Marren's witchbane all this while."

Ten hells, it *hurts*, like someone's trying to squeeze out Sayer's insides. Matilde grips the counter as Æsa lets out a quiet, muffled moan.

An hour ago, they were strong enough to stop a tidal wave. Now the Red Hand has stolen their power.

The Caska are looking at their leader, whispering the candle prayer. *A cleansing fire to cleanse the world.*

Sayer catches sight of Alec using his foot to pull open a drawer behind the counter. He is pointing covertly, prompting Jacinta to sort through it.

"Tell me where the other witches are," the Red Hand says, "or these people will suffer."

Sayer braces for Matilde to say, *They're upstairs.*

"No," Matilde croaks. "I won't give my sisters up."

The Hand steps forward. "I think you will change your mind in time."

Horror fills Sayer as two Caska advance, crossbows ready. Two more edge closer to Rankin and Fen. Something flies, hitting one of the Caska. He falls, gripping the small blade in his leg, and Rankin smiles.

"Told you to stay back," he says.

"Enough," the Red Hand commands. He points at Matilde and Fen. "Come with me now, or my boys will start shooting."

There is a pause, a breath held. Æsa kisses Sayer's cheek.

She stands up, revealing herself before Sayer can stop her.

"You don't need them," she says, putting up her hands, voice calm. "I will come."

In the shocked silence, the Hand looks up. Someone lunges for him: It's Krastan, something clutched in his fist. An arrow flies. Matilde screams.

Krastan crumples. He reaches for Matilde, mouth moving as he bleeds on the floorboards. Matilde drops to her knees and lets out a strangled sob.

"Take them all!" the Hand screams.

Alec crouches down and grabs a vial from Jacinta, quickly pouring a dark powder down its mouth. He whispers a few words, and the vial starts to simmer. He roars as he hurls it through the air.

It shatters on the Hand's robes. Something sinuous and bright slithers out of it. A creature with talons made of angry greenish flames.

. . . The battle raged with a terrible fury,
rivers of blood wending their way through the grass.
They parted around her, alone and in armor,
untouched by arrow, spear or spell.
When she raised her arms, both armies quivered.
For this was a time when the Fyrebirds
commanded men and moved mountains.
It was an age when they still ruled the world.

—THE SICLID CYCLE,
BOOK II

CHAPTER 21

THROUGH FLAMES

MATILDE CAN'T BREATHE. There's too much smoke, so much pain.

The creature Alec made looks like a dragon, long and sinuous, flashing teeth made of sickly greenish fire. It licks hungrily up the Hand's clothes, wrapping around him. He claws at the dragon with a bloodcurdling scream.

The boys in grey rush to put him out, but they fear the raging dragon. Matilde leans over Krastan. His hand is on her cheek, smeared in blood. There is so much.

"Can you stand?" she asks. "We need to—"

"Be brave, my Stella," he says, hoarse. "Be strong. Take care of Alec. And tell Frey . . . tell her . . ."

She puts her hand over his on her cheek, pressing it tighter.

"I should never have let her go," he whispers.

His hand goes limp. She squeezes it.

"Krastan?"

His eyes glow in the firelight, but she sees nothing in them. He is gone. Gone, and she never got to tell him that she knew who he was to her. She thought they would have time.

The room around them is chaos as the fire dragon flies, knocking into wooden beams and bouncing off crowded shelving, showering sparks and trailing smoke. It crashes into the pile of witchbane on the floor and the censer, burning it to nothing. In the smoke, she can no longer tell friend from foe.

She should get up, but her breath won't come. Someone crashes down beside her: It's Alec, pressing down on Krastan's wound, grabbing a handful of his shirt.

"We have to go." His voice is shaking. "Krastan? *Krastan*."

But Krastan has flown somewhere they can't reach him. Matilde fights down a sob.

"Alec, he's gone."

There is a whoosh and the sound of something exploding. There's such pain in Alec's eyes.

Someone shouts: She thinks it might be Jacinta, though the smoke makes it hard to see faces. An arrow hits one of the shelves.

"We have to go," Alec croaks.

Matilde's heart aches. "I don't want to leave him."

A tear streaks down Alec's cheek, fast as a star. "Neither do I."

He takes her hand. She must have twisted her ankle when she fell, because it buckles. He holds her as she tries to find the front door. It's just visible through the smoke, offering the promise of sunlight, but she knows it isn't freedom that awaits them there. It's a cage.

Alec pulls her toward it.

"We can't go out that way," she gasps. "They'll take me."

And they are likely to shoot Alec.

"We can't go back below," he says. "That leaves . . ."

Matilde glances at the stairs, not yet touched by the flame dragon. They hobble together over shards of yellow glass. He half helps, half drags her up the stairs and into his bedroom, then sets her down onto his bed.

As he goes to the yellow-glass window, Matilde's thoughts are in pieces. At least Sayer and Æsa aren't up here, which is good. They must have gotten out—she hopes they did, and Fen, hidden by the smoke and chaos. She hopes they're running far and fast. She thinks of Æsa standing up with an expression of defeat, of acceptance. What was she thinking? Matilde isn't sure she understands her Nightbird sisters at all.

Alec fights with the window's latch. Smoke creeps under the door. Everything in here looks as it did . . . Was that minutes ago, or a lifetime? Before they knew their magic could be stolen. Before Krastan . . . before . . .

She grabs the ribbons tucked in Alec's book, needing something to hold on to. He curses loudly, making her look up.

"What is it?"

"It won't open."

"Ten hells, just break it."

He grabs some instrument off his worktable and hurls it through the yellow glass. Blood trickles down his arm as he clears out the shards. Her heart sinks: There's no way Alec's shoulders will fit through the opening. Coming up here was a mistake. One of many.

She hobbles to the door and opens it. The fire has caught the bottom of the stairs, forming a sickly green wall.

She curses. "Isn't there some way to tame your dragon?"

"A design flaw," he grunts. "I was working on it."

The dragon comes flying up the stairs. She throws her hands up without thinking, flinching as it glances off her palm. All she feels is warmth, a tickling sensation. She blinks down at them as the dragon flies away. She didn't burn.

Deep inside, she can feel something stirring. Is it her magic coming back again? It feels faint, but perhaps it can still save them. She turns, a new hope blooming in her chest.

She hobbles over to Alec, tugging at his arm.

"Do you remember what you said?" she asks, tying the ribbons around his wrist and knotting them. "About how you never thought about kissing me?"

She touches his face, smooths back his hair.

"I think you lied."

His lips crash into hers. Their kiss is like the first taste of air after being underwater. Lips part as they drink each other in, bodies pressed close. His arms pull her in as she grips a handful of his dark curls, which are as soft as she remembers. Their desperate want brings her magic bubbling up.

Alec starts, feeling it too, but she holds on. Her magic will save them—it has to. She lets some of it pour out and into him.

When she pulls back, they're both gasping.

"What did you do?" he pants.

She takes his hand. "Do you trust me, Alec?"

"That feels like a dangerous question."

She picks a shirt up from the floor. "Just follow me."

They go out into the hall, Alec partly supporting her. The wall of fire has crept almost to the top of the stairs. But she can feel her magic in them both, and fire is her element. She just has to bend it to her will.

She raises her free hand and asks it to part for them. The fire fights, unwilling to curb its grasping thirst. For a moment, she doesn't think it will obey, but then it slinks backward, making a path for them.

"We have to go fast," she says. "I don't know how long the stairs will hold."

"We'll burn," he says, muffled as she ties the shirt around his mouth and nose.

"We won't." At least she hopes so. "My magic is in you. Imagine it sitting on your skin like armor might."

That's what she does as they hurry down the stairs, the flames a tunnel around them. It is dangerously warm, singeing her sleeves. A ball of flames drips down to brush Alec's arm, but slides off without burning. His eyes are wide, tinted green by the fire.

The dragon is circling the shop, still roaring. She sees people running, feels her sisters somewhere in the smoke, but she can't see. Matilde can just make out the outlines of Krastan's body. It takes everything she has to step around him. Alec says nothing, but his hand tightens in hers.

A beam falls, coming close. She has to concentrate to keep the fire away from them. There's a hunger in the air, like the dragon smells blood. One step, two. Their joined hands are all that is keeping her focused. Where's the door? There: She stumbles toward it. Choking, they stagger out into the light of day.

She sucks in the outside air, lungs screaming. A seething crowd surrounds the shop, forming a circle in front of it. Some are pointing at her and Alec. Someone shouts.

"It's her!"

She sees some boys in grey sprinting toward them. Alec tenses, ready to step in front of her, just as Krastan did. But Matilde can't stand to lose them both.

She kisses his cheek. "Try not to miss me this time."

Then she pushes him toward the crowd. They shrink back, but when she lights a fireball in her palm, all eyes are back on her. Someone grabs Alec by the shoulders, pulling him into the sea of people: It's Fenlin. Matilde mouths *go* and takes a shuddering breath. The crowd is slowing the Caska down, forming a barrier, but it won't hold. The flames are swallowing Krastan's shop. If the fire spreads, half of the quarter could burn with it.

She thinks of Krastan then, saying how the Fyrebirds were saviors. Krastan, still in that shop he loved so much.

She raises her hands. Gran taught her how to be commanding without shouting. It's that voice she conjures as she closes her fists and says, "Come."

The fire pulls in, disappearing from the upstairs window, collecting in the front room of the shop. Then the dragon's green head appears in the doorway, scales shimmering so brightly—most of the crowd has to turn and look away. It slithers out into the street on wicked claws, dragging the whole fire with it. Screams rise, but it doesn't turn its fiery head. It crouches down at her feet, where it bows to her. When she claps her hands together, it turns to ash. The fire is out.

The street is strangely silent. There's just the hiss of charred wood and Matilde's rasping breaths. Then the whispers start to ripple through the crowd. *Witch,* some hiss. *Fyrebird,* others murmur. A few people shake their fists, and others drop to their knees.

Matilde doesn't know what she is, but she feels like a phoenix, remade by those flames . . . forever changed by them.

A hand clamps around her wrists, pulling her hands behind her. Something foul smelling is smeared under her nose.

"You're coming with us," one of the Caska boys growls. "Don't fight it."

Matilde is pushed from behind. The crowd is breaking, shoving, shouting, seething. Someone calls her a name. Another shouts, "She saved us all!"

Then something is pulled over her eyes. Not a mask—a bag of some sort. A choking, terrible cage.

One for the lost,
one for the lonely,
one for the sick and the stray.

The Stars pour out equal parts
justice and vengeance
to wash its enemies away.

—A **DARK STARS** DRINKING SONG

– CHAPTER 22 –
'SPRING-STAINED SECRETS

THE GARDEN DISTRICT smells as it always does, of flowers. Sayer gulps it down, but it can't clean the stink of the fire from her. There is an ache in her chest that feels like more than just smoke.

Dash it, how did she lose them? She had Æsa as they ran down the stairs, but someone wrenched them apart. The smoke was so thick, shrouding everything. If Fen hadn't found her, she may never have gotten out.

Outside the shop, people were shouting and running, making a screen for her and Fen and Rankin to hide in. Sayer craned her neck, trying to find the girls, the Hand . . . too late. She caught a glimpse of Æsa and Jacinta by a waiting carriage, being bagged and bound by three Caska boys. Jacinta fought, but Æsa didn't struggle at all.

She watched as Matilde and Alec emerged. Sayer will never forget the way the fire parted, making a path for them. And then Matilde pushed Alec into the crowd. Fen lunged for him, but Sayer couldn't look away from her fellow Nightbird. All eyes were on her, hands raised, bobbed hair flying wild. She called that fire dragon to heel, in front of all those people. Commanded it as if it were hers.

Sayer tried to reach her, but the Caska were faster. They smeared something under her nose and threw a bag over her head. She was shoved into an unmarked carriage, but not the same one as Æsa. Why were they split up? She couldn't see the Red Hand in either of them. Everything was chaos and smoke. And she did nothing—just stood there and watched the Nightbirds roll away.

Sayer knocks on Leta's back door, praying someone answers quickly. Alec looks about three breaths from full collapse.

Behind her, Fen's voice is husky from the smoke. "I don't like this. It's too risky."

"Leave, then," Sayer says, not looking back. "I won't stop you."

Fen says nothing. Sayer raises her fist to knock again when the door swings open.

"Mistress Sayer." It's Alice, the sweet-faced young housekeeper. To her credit, her eyes widen only slightly at what must be a shocking sight. "Thank the Wellspring. Lady Leta has been looking everywhere for you."

She ushers them into Leta's large, pristine kitchen. She keeps few staff, all of them women, and they all seem to be standing near the giant oven. The cook drops a pan with a clang.

"The lady is out," Alice says, leading them through. "Shall I send someone to fetch her?"

Sayer lets out a breath. "No, it's fine."

Alice surprises Sayer by touching her shoulder. "Go into the study while I round up some things for you."

"Maybe some food, miss?" Rankin croaks. "Those pies back there looked pretty lonely."

Alice smiles. "Of course, young sir. Just you rest while I cut them."

She leaves them at the door of Leta's study. It feels too quiet, too calm, too clean.

"Nice house," Rankin whispers. "Is this where you been living, Say?"

She nods, though that feels like another life, another Sayer. The last time she was in this room was with the other girls. She can still see Matilde lounging on the couch, teasing Æsa as she sips daintily at her coffee. They look up at her, expectant ghosts.

Alec stumbles, yanking her out of her reverie. Fen and Rankin guide him over to one of the armchairs.

Sayer grabs a jug of water and a glass from a side table. Alec doesn't look up when she holds the water out.

"Come on, drink," she says. "Your throat must hurt."

He screamed so loud when they dragged him away from the shop that Fen had to cover his mouth, but he hasn't said a word since then.

"Alec," she says again, louder.

He looks up, but his eyes are glassy and unfocused. And then he lets out a strange, high-pitched laugh. Fen swears, getting down on one knee.

"What's wrong with him?" Rankin asks.

"His sugar's low," Fen says. "He needs his frennet. He'll go into a coma without it."

Alec laughs again, saying something in a whisper, gripping the bright ribbons tied around his wrist.

"It's gone. All gone."

Fen rummages through the pockets of Alec's vest, then his pants. She holds her palm out to the light: There are seeds there.

"Are those them?" Rankin says. "Can he eat them?"

Fen sighs. "No. It has to be the leaves."

Sayer's pulse is racing. "Leta has all sorts of plants in her conservatory. Rare things. She might have some. I'll go—"

In Fen's palm, the seeds have started sprouting. The frennet's purplish leaves are shaped like stars, but then they open into moons. They turn their faces toward Fen, as if she is the sun to them. Their roots wrap her fingers in a delicate embrace.

Rankin swallows hard, but doesn't look shocked to see Fen do magic. Ten hells, he knew, just like Æsa. Could everyone see Fen clearly but her?

Fen rips some leaves free and shoves them into Alec's mouth.

"Chew, Padano. Be quick about it."

Alec chews. It's the only sound, other than the fire crackling. Fen puts the plant in Rankin's hands.

"He should be fine in about ten minutes. If he still seems dazed, make him chew a few more."

Fen turns to go. Rankin frowns.

"Where are you going?"

"To get some air."

"I'll go too—"

"*Stay*, Rankin."

Rankin flinches, but Fen doesn't turn to see it. She leaves the room without a backward glance.

Sayer looks Rankin over. His cheeks are covered in ash, his clothes as torn as one of the worst-off urchins in Griffin's. His Dark Stars ribbons are limp and charred at his lapel. When he tilts up his sooty face, his brown eyes are huge and bewildered. He looks so young to her just then.

"What's gonna happen, Say? To the other girls?"

She swallows. How is she supposed to know?

"Stay with Alec," she says. "And when Alice comes, eat a pie. Eat two. I'll be back."

He nods. Sayer slips into the hall, stalks through the house. There is no trail to tell her where Fen went, and yet she isn't hard to follow. After all, they're tied now. Maybe they always were.

The air is warm in Leta's conservatory. It's large, some thirty strides across, though with all the plants it feels smaller. Exotic palms and creepers climb the glass-and-copper walls. The domed ceiling is made of amber-colored glass, meant to keep the leaves from scorching. The reddish light paints itself across the tiles.

Fen is standing by the pond, so still she could almost be a part of it. Then she leans forward, dipping her hands into the water, using it to slick back her hair. She tips her head back, water running down her neck into her collar. The palm leaves seem to lean toward her. Recognizing her in a way Sayer never did.

"Out with it, Tig." Fen's voice is tight and emotionless. "Say what it is you came to say."

She thought she knew, but she feels choked, her words all tangled.

"I told you everything, Fen. All you ever did was lie."

Fen turns then. "I didn't lie about anything that mattered."

Anger surges. "Really, *Ana*?"

Fen looks away. "Don't call me that."

"But it's your real name, isn't it?"

A flash of heat. "It's the name the orphanage gave me. Not the one I chose for myself."

But Sly Fox isn't a name—it's a mask she wears so no one

will see her. Sayer thought she knew the person underneath.

"How long have you had magic?" she asks.

Silence.

"How long have you known about mine?"

More silence. She's hiding from Sayer, even now.

Sayer closes her eyes. The quiet is so thick that she can hear her own heartbeat, the sound like wings beating against glass.

"I don't know who my dame was," Fen says. "Or my sire. I don't remember them. The Red Hand was the only parent I had."

Sayer shivers.

"He told me once that my parents gave me up because they thought I had a curse on me."

Sayer frowns. "Why would he say that?"

The moment stretches out, green and delicate. Fen raises a hand.

"Because of this."

Slowly, she peels away her eyepatch. Sayer's breath catches in her throat. She's spent years wondering what's under it: a wicked scar, an empty hole, a glass orb. But it's an eye, green as leaves, shockingly vivid. A riotous color that doesn't match the caramel brown of the other. Eudeans have a name for such eyes: *'spring stained*. A mark that someone has been touched by the Wellspring, which isn't something most Simtan girls would want to wear.

Fen squints, like even this low light hurts it.

"He wasn't the Red Hand then. He was Pater Dorisall, but his beliefs were as they are now. He hated how people used magic. It was robbing from the sacred, he told us. He said that if it wasn't checked, the old evils would start rising again.

Witches, specifically. He was fixated on the idea that they were hiding amongst us already. He wanted proof, and there I was, with my 'spring-stained eyes."

The conservatory's leaves seem to hold their breaths, waiting. Fen's voice drops, so quiet Sayer can hardly hear.

"It didn't start until I was ten, maybe eleven. He found some old church text that said strong emotion tended to bring out a witch's magic. So he found ways to try to scare me, provoke me."

Fen's shoulders pull in, tucking in tight around her. The ferns near the fountain seem to curl around her too.

"All the orphanage kids knew there were monsters in the rectory's basement. We'd hear them at night sometimes, creaking and moaning. He started locking me there alone for hours, in the dark. The first time, I prayed for one of the gods to save me from the monsters. The next time, I gripped a butter knife I'd nicked from the kitchen and swore I'd kill them all if they came near. By the time my magic came I knew there were no monsters, but I still hated that basement. I melted the butter knife and re-formed it into a lock pick."

"How old were you?" Sayer asks.

"I was twelve."

Years younger than Sayer was the first time she felt her magic stirring. At least she had a dame who could explain what was happening, who would never beat her or lock her down in the dark.

"That basement is where I first learned how to break out of places. 'Little thief,' Dorisall said when he found me. 'Stealing your penance from the gods.' "

"He didn't know you'd used magic?"

Fen shakes her head. "After that first time, I made sure never to use it. I buried it down as deep as it would go. But then . . ."

Sayer waits. The air is humid around them, scented with dirt and striving life.

"I got older." Fen licks her lips. Her face looks different when she isn't chewing her mastic—somehow softer. "And he became more intense, more obsessed with his mission to find witches. His tactics got a lot more severe. 'Pain and deprivation are the true path to the Wellspring,' he'd say. 'It is only when you strip a tree of its leaves that you can see its strength.' He had this whip he kept above the doorframe in the schoolroom. He used it more on me than anyone else. It's like he thought pain would force any magic I had to show itself."

Fen reaches up, running a finger down one of her scars. "I had a rule for when he got the whip down. Don't scream. Don't cry. When that got hard, I'd close my eyes and imagine myself rowing through the Callistan. I'd seen a painting of those everglades once, and it stuck with me. The ghost moss, the tangled trees . . . I don't know. It felt . . . familiar."

Of course it did: Fen's an earth girl. Sayer stays still, but she can feel the world tilting.

"This one beating, though. It went on forever. I had blood in my ears, my nose. In my eyes, Sayer. And then Dorisall commanded Rankin to step up beside me. He was nine then, and Dorisall knew he was a brother to me. The fear on Rankin's face made something inside me just . . . snap. I went to my imaginary glade and begged it to help us. When my magic rose, I didn't push it down."

Sayer's skin prickles. "What happened?"

A muscle in Fen's jaw ticks. "He kept this crown-of-thorns bush in a corner of our schoolroom. It burst out of its pot, wrapping around me and Rankin like a shield. Dorisall's face— I'd never seen such disgust on it, or such excitement."

Sayer remembers Fen's face when the Red Hand recognized her at Krastan's. The fear. It's like his presence stripped her of all her hard-earned certainty, the same way Wyllo Regnis did to her.

"What did you do then?"

"I made the crown of thorns attack him. As he fended it off, I grabbed Rankin and ran. I knew I could never let him find us. I knew I had to hide. But Griffin's was my home—I didn't want to leave it. So I covered up my eye, took a new name, and made a life. A truer one. I did work for the Quick Cuts, then other gangs, building a rep for getting into well-locked places."

"You used your magic?"

Fen shakes her head, tight and fast. "No. Never."

Sayer frowns, confused. "Why not?"

"Because all it ever did was bring me pain."

Sayer can feel that pain in the bond between them, the cuts that run deeper than she ever knew. Is this why Fen's always held her cards so close? Never fully cut loose, never let anyone in. Except for that night her dame died and Fen stayed, curling up with her on top of Sayer's covers. When she let Sayer in just enough to hold her close.

"I didn't want to need it to get ahead," Fen says. "And I couldn't let any of the other piper lords find out I had it. It's hard enough, holding my place in their ranks. Can you imagine if they knew? They'd say I cheated my way into the business. It would threaten everything I've built. Or worse. Most of them trade in bootleg—the rarer and more exclusive, the better. That's how they'd see me. As something worth collecting. So I vowed to push it down and forget. But then . . ."

Fen's gaze finds Sayer's. The full force of her two-toned eyes is still a shock.

"I hadn't met anyone else like me, with magic. But there

were rumors about your dame, how she might once have had some. I told myself it didn't matter; I could keep my magic in, even if you had some of your own. But you never showed any signs—never mentioned it. Then that night your dame died, I felt something, when we almost . . ."

Kissed. So that's why Fen got up and left so abruptly. Sayer thought it was just her.

"When you left Griffin's, I told myself it was for the best. You were back with your dame's people. I could keep busy with Dark Stars business. I told myself it would all be fine."

"And then I kissed you," Sayer says, "that night in the alley."

Fen clenches her fists. "I keep a tight leash on my magic. So tight I mostly forget it's even there. But with that kiss, I couldn't control it. It's like it took on a life of its own."

Sayer remembers how it felt, that kiss, the taste of storm and iron, the charge that filled her. Earth and air crashing together in a heady, tingling rush.

She thinks of Gwellyn in the alley, grabbing his face and screaming, *My tooth.* His blue cap, made of metal, on the cobbles, strangely twisted.

"Gwellyn's tooth," she breathes. "That was you?"

A flicker of a smile. "Like I said, I didn't mean to, but I can't say I'm sorry to have melted the ugly thing out of his mouth."

Fen's expression turns grave. "My magic had never slipped out of my control like that. It felt dangerous. So I stayed away, hoping it would fade, given time."

So this is why Fen has kept her distance. This is why she hasn't touched Sayer since.

Fen runs a hand through her damp hair. "I did look into the Red Hand, like I promised, to try and find out what he was doing. Truth to tell, I didn't look as hard as I should have. I thought there was no way he would find you, and I didn't want to get tangled up with him. I should have known how far he'd go. Where it could lead. Then Rankin intercepted a note talking about that attack on the Dinatris mansion. I couldn't let him get his hands on girls with magic. Not again."

The air is too warm in the room, too close. Sayer feels like it might smother her. But she doesn't move, barely breathes. She needs to hear.

"You grabbed my hand, when Matilde used Alec's Night-cloak," Fen says. "It was like your magic was calling out to mine. I could feel the other girls, too. And the garden. The roots, the leaves . . . it's like they were an extension of my body. The magic got away from me again."

Sayer remembers Fen yanking her hand back, then the sound of branches whipping, of roots ripping from the earth. Fen did that. Fen stood next to her and did magic, and Sayer still didn't know. Couldn't see.

Fen's face has taken on a sickly pallor. She's touching the scars on her neck again. "The trees responded to my fear, just like the crown of thorns all those years ago. And even though he couldn't see my face, he knew. Dorisall *knew*."

What is it the Red Hand shouted as they ran from the garden? *I see you, little thief. I see you.* Sayer's skin prickles.

Fen falls silent. They stand there, watching each other. The handful of steps that lie between them feel like an ocean in the amber-tinted light.

Fen was the friend Sayer chose—her found family. Now she wonders if it was ever a choice at all. Some Fyrebirds rise in sets, Krastan said, pulled toward each other. Heart tied. Has it always been magic, this thing between them? Are any of her feelings even real?

Sayer crosses her arms. "How did you keep your magic hidden in the first place? How come I could never feel it when we touched?"

Fen reaches for the silver snuff tin in her vest pocket. It shines dully. "The Hand was always poring over tomes from Augustain's great library, trying to find the herbs that Marren mentions in some of the old texts. There was one, he said, that was supposed to take a witch's magic from her, but the text wasn't specific. So he started collecting rare plants from all over to try and figure out which one it was. I would sneak samples when he wasn't looking. I trialed them on myself."

Sayer's breath catches. "They could've hurt you, Fen. Or killed you."

"Around that time, I wouldn't have minded if they did."

That startles Sayer back into silence. Fen takes a long, slow breath.

"Eventually I found one that seemed to work, if I chewed it," she says, weighing the tin in her palm. "*Weil breamus*, it's called. Fresh leaves were okay, but dried were best. I stole cuttings, and when I ran, I took them with me. I made sure I'd always have a steady supply."

"Your mastic," Sayer breathes. The gum that Fen is forever chewing, with its dank and acrid smell. She smelled it again in Krastan's shop, floating out of the Red Hand's censer. "It's got witchbane in it."

Fen nods, not quite meeting her eyes. "Just a little. Just enough to keep my magic tamped down."

Sayer's hand goes to her stomach as she remembers how it felt to breathe that herbal smoke. The sick, twisted feeling, and then the hollowness, as if a piece of her soul had been removed.

Tears collect at the corners of Sayer's eyes, hot and sudden.

The Red Hand hurt Fen so badly that she would rather poison herself than face what lives inside.

"Why didn't you tell me?" Sayer whispers.

"Because I don't tell anyone. I barely acknowledge it to myself half the time."

"But why didn't you tell *me*?"

The night her dame died was Sayer's darkest. *I'm alone,* she sobbed, but then Fen's arms went around her, her hand pressed against the back of her neck. *That's not true.* She's tried to safeguard her heart, but that night she took it out and let Fen hold it. Now she knows Fen never did the same for her.

Her magic rises on the tide of her hurt, conjuring a wind that ruffles the leaves and sends the scent of loam circling. She feels exposed.

"You didn't trust me." Sayer swallows, trying to keep her voice from shaking. "And now it feels like I never really knew you."

Fen stalks toward her. She only stops when they're a hand's breadth apart.

"Don't say that, Tig."

She lifts Sayer's hand and presses it flat to her chest, just above her breastbone. She can feel Fen's heart pounding, loud, as if it's trying to speak.

"I've shown you more of me than anyone."

The raw edge in Fen's voice cuts her open. A tear streaks down Sayer's face.

"I'm tired of lies."

Sayer walks away, fast. The house's shadows press in as she rushes blindly through the ballroom, into the foyer at the front of the house. She leans against the wall next to a vase full of ghostvines, tall and silent. Tears are carving hot paths down her cheeks.

"Sayer."

Her head snaps up. It's Leta. She looks nothing like Nadja Sant Held, but seeing her makes Sayer miss her dame so fiercely. The ache of it fractures something deep in her chest.

Leta opens her arms. Sayer steps into them and lets her tears flow freely.

"It's all right," Leta whispers. "You're home."

She closes her eyes, pretending Leta *is* her dame, just for a moment. What would Sayer ask her if she could?

How did I get here? She crossed the canals to honor a promise, make some money, and forge a life all her own. She didn't come here to make friends or to get caught up in their problems. How did all these girls' fates get so tangled up with hers? She has the wild urge to fade into shadow and leave. To be free.

But she can still hear Matilde in the shop: *I won't give up my sisters.*

She can feel Æsa kissing her softly on the cheek.

She can see the raw need in Fen's two-toned eyes. *I've shown you more of me than anyone.*

And their fledglings, looking to the Nightbirds for hope, for answers. Where are all of those girls now?

It would be easier to walk away, but her friends need her. She isn't going to leave them now.

In storm and siege we stand unmoved.
When threatened, we breathe fire.

—THE HOUSE VESTEN CREED

CHAPTER 23

A GILDED CAGE

MATILDE'S CAPTORS ARE rough and thorough with their bindings. The carriage bumps, pulling the rope taut around her wrists.

"Careful," she croaks. "You wouldn't want to give me rope burn."

"We're s'posed to bring you alive," one of them says. "No one cares if you bruise."

She tilts up her chin, though with the bag over her head they won't see it. There was a time when these boys wouldn't have dared touch her, but they don't see her as a Great House girl anymore. She is a witch.

The stench of the paste they smeared above her lip is overwhelming. It must be made out of the Red Hand's witchbane. Her magic is silent in her bones, barely there. Minutes ago, she made fire bow before her. Now she's being taken to the Pontifex on a leash.

She breathes in slow, shallow gasps, but panic still grips her, so she turns her mind to plans of revenge. She's going to have every Caska stripped down to his underthings and roasted. If the Red Hand isn't dead, she's going to ignite him again. Anger hones her focus, so much easier to carry than grief is. She thinks she might finally understand Sayer Sant Held.

But anger can't squash the memories rising within her. She keeps seeing Krastan, feeling his calloused hand against her cheek. The way he whispered, *Be brave, my Stella. Be strong.* But she wasn't strong enough to save him. Matilde swallows a sob before it can escape.

The neck of Alec's shirt rubs against her collarbone. She can still feel his curls between her fingers, his lips pressed hungrily to hers. He kissed her, finally, and not because he wanted her magic. Just because he wanted her.

Take care of Alec. Those were some of Krastan's last words. She tried, but all she ever seems to do is cause him trouble. And now he is alone, and so is she . . .

The carriage jerks and the rope pulls tight again. She takes a sharp breath. Now isn't the time for such thoughts: They will only unravel her. She needs her wits for whatever's next.

The carriage stops. Rough hands drag her into the sunlight. They pull the rope hard, but she makes sure not to stumble. She'll claim whatever dignities she can.

She is tugged up some stairs. They must be taking her to Augustain's church, to the Pontifex. She doesn't feel either of her Nightbird sisters near her; she hopes they got away, but she can't see, can't know.

The sunlight drops away as they walk into a space that echoes. She expects it to smell like incense and candle wax, and instead it's silver polish and cold marble. Shadows press against the rough cloth over her eyes. Eventually they stop and someone knocks on a door in a specific rhythm. Hinges creak and someone's skirts flutter at her feet.

There is a pause.

"She's a mess," someone says: a woman. Strange. "What happened?"

"There was a fire," one of the boys says. "We barely got her out of there."

"And the other girls? Where are they?"

The other Nightbirds, she means. Matilde's skin crawls.

"Don't know. It was madness at the alchemist's. The Caska got at least one of them."

The Caska. She thought these men *were* the Caska. Who are they if not that?

"And the herb is effective?" the woman says. "You're sure?"

Another boy sniffs. "It got us here, didn't it?"

Panic rises again. Who are these people? She doesn't know what twisted game she's landed in.

She is pulled forward, a door closing behind her. Then the bag is yanked away and she can finally see. The room is small, scrubbed clean of any distinguishing features. It must be one of the holding cells at Augustain's.

The woman's older, perhaps Dame's age, dressed in a dark green dress. She takes in Matilde's sooty face and shop boy's clothes. Her pants are covered in blood. Krastan's blood . . .

"We can't present you in that state," the woman says.

"Present me to whom?"

The woman doesn't answer. Just says, "Listen carefully, now. There is no point trying to fight me. There are guards outside the doors, and you won't be able to get past them. This will all go much more smoothly if you do as you're told."

She raises a pair of scissors and cuts the rope. Matilde rubs her wrists, sore from the bindings, and looks to the doors at either end of the room. She wants to run, but will likely have only one chance at it, and this doesn't feel like a promising moment. Maybe she should have taken Sayer up on her offer of sparring lessons after all.

"Clothes off," the woman says. "Those are ruined."

Matilde takes a step back. "Excuse me?"

The woman sighs. "Take them off or I will have to do it for you."

Matilde strips off Alec's shirt, then his pants. They reek of smoke, but she resents having to part with them. Finally, she is down to her underthings and her locket. The woman reaches for the golden orb.

"Don't touch that," Matilde snaps.

The woman's mouth thins. "I'll give it back when it's emptied."

Matilde watches as the woman dumps her Estra Doole into a basin. Krastan made that potion with his stained, patient hands. They will never make her anything again.

She bites her tongue, swallowing back tears.

More herb-laced paste is smeared under her nose. It smells awful, the witchbane. She wonders where and how the Red Hand found it, and how far its powers to subdue her might extend. Her magic came back to her in the shop: Perhaps the fire dragon burned through all the witchbane. What would happen if they made her ingest it? Is it strong enough to take her magic for good?

The woman puts her into a fashionable drop-waisted sheath, dark gold and shimmering, and pins her bobbed hair back. Gilded gloves sweep up her arms. Such finery. Matilde doesn't understand it.

"Tell me," Matilde says. "Does the Pontifex dress up all his prisoners?"

The woman tuts. "You're not a prisoner. You're a guest."

What in the dear dark depths is going on here?

The woman opens one of the doors onto a narrow, darkened hallway. There is a guard there, but he isn't wearing the uniform of a Warden. His tunic is dark green, like the woman's. There is a sigil on his chest: a sinuous dragon wrapped around a verda bloom. Matilde is filled with a fierce and sudden dread.

And then she's following the guard through shadows until she's standing at a dark green door carved with interlocking dragons. The woman whispers to the guardsman, who knocks a special rhythm. On the other side, a female voice calls out. Distant, but familiar. Matilde's chest shrinks, but she remembers the first rule of being a Nightbird: *Never take off your mask. Never let them see you.* She straightens, hiding her fear away.

The doors open, revealing an opulent room. Its walls are pink, turned bright as jewels by the light streaming through the long red-glass windows. They bathe the suzerain in a violent streak of crimson.

"Matilde Dinatris," Epinine Vesten says, smiling. "It's been an age."

She is only a few years older than Matilde, with fine-boned features. Unlike Dennan's eyes, hers are quite dark. Her hair is dark, too, and glossy, done up in a complicated twist. She wears a ring set with a yellow dragonstone, a symbol of House Vesten. It watches Matilde like a third, uncanny eye.

"Do sit," she says, gesturing to Matilde. "You must be famished after all your misadventures."

Does the suzerain know about what happened at Krastan's? Does she know about what Matilde did to the fire? She wishes she had a better hold on what's happening. The stink of witchbane makes it hard to think.

"That paste on your face," the suzerain says. "It's rather unsightly. Do wipe it off."

Matilde blinks in confusion.

The woman in green clears her throat. "But Lady Suzerain . . . her magic . . ."

Epinine waves, a flick of delicate fingers. "She won't cause any trouble. Will you, Matilde?"

Epinine is bold, she'll give her that. "I wouldn't dream of it."

"There you have it. Now leave us."

As the maid takes her leave, Matilde sits down at the table, wetting a napkin in a glass of water and wiping the paste off her face. She hopes her magic will come roaring back, but it doesn't. Her gaze fixes on the lavish spread. Cold meats, soft bread, bright fruit. Epinine had it all prepared, ready for Matilde to be brought here. The thought makes her stomach twist.

"I hope my men weren't too rough," the suzerain says. "I'm glad to see you're well, considering."

Matilde has the wild urge to laugh. "Yes, being tied up and kidnapped is *wonderful* for the complexion. You should try it."

Epinine leans back in her throne-like chair. "One of them told me what happened at the alchemist's. It's all been rather messier than I was hoping."

To play this game, she must mark every gesture, every muscle twitch and tip of the chin. But rage is clawing its way through Matilde's composure. Rage and fear of what's to come.

"Your men?" she says. "I thought they were the Red Hand's."

Epinine sighs. "Yes, I imagine you must be confused about what's happened. Shall I enlighten you?"

Matilde balls her hands under the table. "Do tell."

"After the Red Hand took your family to the Pontifex, I

think he expected to be patted on the head for his initiative. After all, it was the Pontifex who sent him looking for you in the first place."

So the Pontifex *was* involved in the attack on the Nightbirds. Matilde fights back a shiver.

"The Hand was supposed to do it on the quiet. And then he took four Great House members hostage, with no tangible proof of his claims other than the word of his followers. It caused quite a political quagmire for the church, I can tell you. The House members of the Table called an emergency meeting. They said the church had no right to hold the Dinatrises, and they were furious about Young Lord Teneriffe Maylon. He was injured while in church custody, it seems—quite addled. Such a shame."

Oh, Tenny. What did they do to him? Matilde swallows hard.

"In the end, the Pontifex had to release them. But as the head of the church, and commander of the Wardens, it was within his rights to call a full investigation of the Houses. To find out if the stories about the Nightbirds were true."

Matilde's expression sours. Epinine's thin lips pucker.

"Oh, yes, the man's a toad," she goes on, "without question. But he's also a supporter of mine—a better one than the Houses, lately. So I backed his decision, just as I have backed the Prohibition he and my sire pushed into law. But I had no interest in letting him find you.

"The Pontifex told the Red Hand to lie low, to behave. But I saw an opportunity in his ambition. So we struck a deal, he and I. I would support him in looking for you in secret. I would also give him something he wanted if he brought you all to me alive."

Matilde's jaw clenches. "Barely. He almost killed us."

Epinine picks up her glass, swirling its contents. Her fingers look like a spider's legs.

"Yes, well. That's what I get for sending men to do a job, isn't it? They love to swing at a problem with a hammer. Had I known, I would have told them to be more discreet."

Such genteel words for mass murder. She thinks of Krastan's eyes, always so filled with life, empty forever. Her fists beneath the table start to shake.

"Luckily I had my own men embedded in the Caska," Epinine goes on. "To ensure things went my way. And now here you are, safe and sound."

Matilde leans forward. "When the rest of the Table finds out that you allied with a zealous sect and set it loose on Simta's people, they will make you pay for it."

Epinine smiles, delighted. "But I didn't send them. En Caska Dae acted alone, against orders, and they will be punished. Once the Pontifex is apprised of their behavior, which he will be shortly, he'll make sure of it."

Matilde's head is spinning. "But you made a deal with the Red Hand. He'll tell everyone."

Epinine makes a dismissive noise. "No one will believe him. The Red Hand has angered the Great Houses, and he is dangerous to the church's reputation. Really, he made it easy to assign him all the blame."

Matilde takes a slow breath. Her magic is still dull, barely there, but something else is building in her. Something that might burn, but she has to ask . . . has to know.

"How did you know where we were? How to find us?"

The suzerain leans forward, as if they are two friends sharing secrets. "A little bird whispered in my ear."

A little bird: Those are the same words the Red Hand used at Krastan's. Heat rushes up her neck, then icy cold.

Epinine lifts the cover off a tray with a flourish, revealing a dark metal disk and a bird perched on top. Dennan's bird. The one they've been sending back and forth, full of questions and promises.

Epinine picks it up between two fingers. "It's quite an ingenious little thing. It doesn't just deliver messages, did you know? It can lead one back over the route it's taken."

A sinking feeling pools in Matilde's stomach.

"Oh, I see." The suzerain frowns. "Dennan forgot to mention that part?"

Epinine pulls Matilde's last note out of its belly, waving it like a traitorous flag.

"He kept promising he would find me a Nightbird. But he was being so slow, and so secretive. I knew he was hiding something from me. So I had him up for dinner last night, and we had a nice, long chat about it. He told me everything. We've had our differences, Dennan and I, but I knew he would deliver in the end."

Matilde held on to that bird all through their time in the Underground. Something to remind her of the promises he made. But his bird was like that leash the Caska put around her wrists . . . a tether. A lie that's put her in this cage.

"He was working for you."

Epinine's gaze darkens. "Of course. He is my brother."

But it doesn't make sense. He could have taken her to Epinine at any time—he knew where to find her. And that night at the Liar's Club, he helped them escape.

"Why isn't he here, then?"

Epinine sips her wine. "He's resting. It's been a trying day for everyone."

Matilde wonders if *resting* really means *captured* . . . or dead.

She wants to burn, but her magic won't come back to her. She tries to keep her expression as unruffled as she can. "Well, I'm here, and you've gone to a lot of trouble to find me. So what is it you want?"

Epinine tilts her head, assessing. "Ah, Matilde. I want us to be friends."

Matilde tries to wipe any reaction from her face, but her shock must bleed through.

"I grew up as I imagine you did, Matilde." Epinine puts her delicate chin in her hand, propped on the table. "Privileged, protected, told to behave by certain rules. I was made to sit through endless lectures about Eudea's history, the Vestens of old, and the mighty deeds of the Eshamein. They were meant to make me see Prohibition's value, but I must say they had the opposite effect. I wanted to be like one of the Fyrebirds. Strong enough that no one would dare interrupt me, and no one could stand in my way."

Epinine sighs.

"But men don't like powerful women unless they can control them, especially in the realm of politics. It doesn't matter to the rest of the Houses that my sire wanted me to follow him into the position of suzerain. A female suzerain? She will be too emotional. Too irrational."

Her mouth twists. "Oh, they were willing to go along at first, when they thought I would bow to them. And then, when I wouldn't, they started pressuring me. They had the gall to say they would vote my way, when the time came, if I agreed to marry a Great House lord of their choosing. If I didn't, they would vote me out of the position entirely. They meant to take out this dragon's fangs."

Epinine's fingers have gone white on her glass.

"They wouldn't pull such tricks if I were a man, of course. But a woman has to work twice as hard to make people respect or fear her. She has to be much tougher than the men."

Matilde grips the edge of the table. "And then you found out about the Nightbirds."

Epinine smiles. "There have always been rumors, and I knew there had to be something to them. Such girls would have to be Great House protected. How else could they rise so high, claim so much power? I knew their threats would mean nothing if I had their treasured girls in my possession. They wouldn't dare to touch me then."

Epinine leans forward.

"At first I simply thought to hold you all hostage. But when the Red Hand told me what you and your friends did in that garden . . . I was intrigued. That kind of magic hasn't been seen in centuries. With such power at my fingertips, I could do much more than hang on to my seat at the Table. Perhaps I could rule it. Become a queen."

Matilde's skin prickles.

"I already know about your sweet Illish housemate. She was supposed to be brought in with you, but vexingly, things didn't go as planned. No matter: I will get my hands on her soon enough. Now all we need is for you to give me the names of the other two. Help me find them."

Sweat trickles down Matilde's spine. "Why? You have one. Surely that's enough to serve your purposes."

Epinine's eyes are shining with a cold, glinting light.

"Because one of the boys in grey came to see me, a few hours ago. He told me about what the four of you did in that tunnel, stopping that wave. The boy was quite distraught about his friend being drowned, but I must admit, I wasn't. I was rather thrilled by the tale."

Oh, gods: She knows. Epinine knows what the four of them can do together. She didn't say anything about the fledglings, but it's only a matter of time before she finds out there are other girls with magic. Before everyone does.

"I'm no tame bird," Matilde says. "I won't sing for you just because you demand it."

Epinine's voice drops down to a caress. "Really, Matilde. I only want to protect them. Your lives don't even have to change. I'm simply asking you to transfer your allegiance from the other Houses to mine—just mine. You will be my silent partner. A sister, really."

The word makes Matilde think of Æsa and Sayer. Frustrating, confounding, contrary . . . She misses them so badly she can't breathe.

"I'm going to set a meeting of the Table," Epinine says. "The Pontifex will be left out, of course. I can't afford to lose the church's support at such a moment. I will tell the House members that I have their magical girls, and that I will keep them unless they vote me in as suzerain. Not that I plan to give you back, mind. We will move you all somewhere discreet. After what you did at the alchemist's, I don't think we can keep you in the city. You can all live safe and quiet, and serve your suzerain. You won't ever have to kiss some puffed-up lordling again."

Matilde lifts her chin. "And why would I agree to help you?"

"Because you love your friends. And your family, of course."

Matilde's heart is screaming in her chest. "What have you done with my family?"

"Oh, don't worry. They are perfectly safe, tucked in a secret location. It's a tense time. I didn't want anything bad to befall them."

Horror fills her to think of Gran and Dame and Samson in some dank room, as trapped as she is. Epinine has taken her family. Her choices.

Matilde forces a smile. "I must say, I always thought you were boring, Epinine. But you're more crooked than a sandpiper lord."

She laughs, high and bell-like. "Now, now. You will see them just as soon as you've proved your fealty. Tell me: Where are the other Nightbirds?"

Matilde swallows hard. "I don't know."

It's the truth. She saw Æsa pulled into a carriage but doesn't know where she was taken. The last time she saw Sayer and Fen was in the crowd . . .

"I imagine they've left the city," Matilde says, hoping it's true.

"Oh, I doubt it. I've had the port locked down and the Neck closed to outbound traffic until after Leastnight. This city is tied up tighter than a wineskin."

Matilde's throat constricts.

"Really, Matilde. Why are you fighting me? Those girls are vulnerable out there. Better they join us, and together we can shape this world to our liking. We girls must look out for each other."

Matilde tries not to let her voice quaver. "It's been a very tiring day. I need time to think on it."

"Certainly," Epinine purrs. "But Leastnight and the vote are only two days away, so think quickly."

Matilde thought having to marry someone she didn't choose was the worst fate that could befall her. She thought she understood what it meant to feel tied. But this helplessness is worse than the rope around her wrists, and just as biting. This is a game she doesn't know how to win.

Marren looked upon the witch kneeling before him
and asked if she would give the magic
back to the Wellspring.
Such power, *he said,* was never meant for you.

———

She said only these words:
I cannot give it back. It is a part of me.
And so Marren performed his miracle.
His sword burst into flame, white hot and 'spring-gifted,
and he used the holy fire to cut the magic out.

—*The Book of Eshamein Marren*
2:5–10

CHAPTER 24

TOO MUCH TO HOLD

ÆSA LISTENS AS men argue around her. With the bag over her head, she can't see who they are.

"We've brought them here on behalf of the Red Hand," one is saying.

"I don't answer to the Red Hand," snaps another. "And if these are his prisoners, then where is he?"

Æsa didn't see the Red Hand in the smoke outside the shop. When one of the Caska put this sack over her eyes, she didn't fight him. She felt too heavy, too shocked, to do anything.

The men's argument blurs, becoming nothing but a gentle shushing, moving in and out like a wave. She tries to sail away into memories of home, into numbness, but Jacinta's urgent whisper keeps her moored.

"If we get separated," she says, clutching for Æsa's bound hands, "don't tell them anything. Don't show them—"

"Quiet, witch," one of the men commands. Jacinta stiffens. Æsa can't seem to feel anything at all.

Fight, a voice says in her mind, sounding like her friends. *Fight this, Æsa.* But every time she tries, the magic inside her turns monstrous. Perhaps her time of reckoning has come.

They're pulled forward, footsteps echoing off stone. Light flickers through the sack, but it isn't enough to see much. She can't tell if they are walking through a prison or a house. Doors creak open and closed. The floor turns from stone to soft carpet. The scent of incense pierces through her haze. It smells like her church in Illan on an Eshamein's day. Pater Toth's oft-said words rise up: *In mortal hands, magic turns into a vice, and then a poison.* She is a poison. Willan told her such a thing couldn't be true, and she wanted to believe him. But she killed that Caska boy in cold blood. She can see him, banging his fists against Sayer's wall, but it's too late to save him. Too late to save her soul. Too late.

They come to a stop. The light is brighter here, the air cleaner. Someone is holding a hushed conversation, interrupted only by the sound of rustling sleeves. The greasy pain in Æsa's stomach is gone now. Wherever they are, no one is burning witchbane. Perhaps they aren't in the Caska's lair after all.

At last, a voice echoes through the room, low and resonant. "Remove the blindfolds," a man says. "Let us see."

The sack comes off. Æsa blinks against the sudden brightness. Shafts of light spear down, making it hard to see anything but gilded shapes. A vaulted ceiling comes slowly into focus, lined with panes of colorless glass. There is only one type of building in Simta where the glass isn't colored, letting the gods see clearly through it. Her heart, so heavy, threatens to crack.

She looks to the line of chairs before them, which hold a row of men in purple robes. The one in the middle is about her grandda's age, his robe a lighter shade than the others. The golden staff he holds glints in the light. Her breath catches:

She knows that staff, though only from sermons and stories. A man once used it to conjure miracles before he died, becoming a god.

"Kneel," someone intones, "before the Pontifex."

Æsa drops to her knees. Jacinta is pushed down onto hers by a Warden. There are several of them ranged about the room, all armed, though they too kneel, touching their fists to the upturned cups stitched onto their uniforms. The Caska boys who brought them here are nowhere to be seen.

"So," the Pontifex says. "It appears the Red Hand has sent us witches, at last."

There is whispering amongst the Wardens. One of the men sitting behind the Pontifex speaks into his ear. They must be his Council of Brethren, his advisers. Their eyes on her are like a dozen searing swords.

"Please, Pontifex," Jacinta says, voice small and trembling. She's as good an actress as Matilde. "We were shopping near the alchemist's shop when the fire broke out. There was a crush of people, and some boys just grabbed us. We don't know anything about any witches."

"Remember where you are, child," the Pontifex says, pointing to the clear-glass windows. "And that the gods are watching."

Jacinta doesn't back down. "This is a terrible mistake. I swear it."

The Pontifex's gaze lands on Æsa, cool and assessing. She keeps her eyes cast down on the carpet as he moves. She waits, breath held, for him to condemn her. This man who speaks with gods—who speaks for them.

Fingers touch her chin, their skin so soft.

"Don't hide your face, child."

His tone catches her off guard. It's warm—almost fatherly. A bright shaft of light haloes his creased face and hairless head.

"This is the gods' house," he goes on. "There is nothing they don't see."

Something shivers through Æsa.

"But it is also a house of cleansing. Do you not want to be washed of your sins?"

They are the same words Pater Toth would use when she confessed her sins in their church's whisperbox. The transgressions she used to confess seem so small now. Coveting what others had and she didn't, hungering for things she couldn't name. Since then, her sins have become as vast as the ocean. She is afraid she will never feel truly clean again.

He cups her chin. "Come, now. Tell me the truth of it. Have you stolen from the Wellspring?"

Matilde would dissemble. Sayer would refuse to speak at all. But Æsa was taught to revere this man, who speaks for all that is holy. Surely confessing to him will ease her heavy guilt.

"I asked the gods to take it back," she whispers. "But it was just . . . there. Inside me."

Shoulders stiffen, whispers circle. Jacinta shoots her a look that says to stop talking, but Æsa makes herself go on.

"I never meant to hurt anyone." A tear streaks down her cheek. "I thought I could control it."

She thought she could use her power for good.

"It isn't your fault." The Pontifex's voice has the sweetness of fruit just on the edge of turning rotten. "You are a woman, run by emotion. Of course you could not control it. It is a sacred power, too much for you to hold."

His words make her cheeks flush with shame.

"You have done wrong," he goes on, his dark eyes burning. "But the gods may yet forgive you, if you are willing to serve them."

Her breath catches. "What must I do?"

"Give me the names of the other witches. The ones who have been hiding amongst the Great Houses, especially."

Dread seizes her. "I . . . I can't."

She is willing to take her punishment, but she will not bring down the other girls.

"You think I will hurt them?" The Pontifex smiles, indulgent. "I know the old wives' tales about what paters used to do to witches. But the church's archives contain other tales, and other options. There is no need to hurt a girl with magic in her veins."

Æsa's head is spinning. "What do you mean?"

He leans in closer. "What if I told you there was a way to extract the magic? A way to separate it from your mortal flesh?"

In this moment, she wants to believe him. If she could rip out this thing and give it to this man, she thinks she would.

"We won't kill your friends, child," the Pontifex whispers. "We will simply take back what they have stolen."

Jacinta's voice is low and taut. "You're a liar."

His fatherly expression curdles. "You dare to question me?"

"He can't take your magic from you, Æsa." Jacinta's eyes are on her, brimming with emotion. "It's a part of you. A gift, and wholly yours."

"Magic is holy," the Pontifex seethes. "Girls like you make it a poison."

"These men are the poison." One of the Wardens tries to restrain Jacinta as she crawls toward Æsa. "Don't let them tell you who you are. Remember the other girls. Remember—"

The Pontifex slaps Jacinta. The sound shudders through Æsa, breaking her out of what feels like a trance.

Jacinta crashes to the rug, blood dripping down her cheekbone. The Pontifex turns away, back toward Æsa, as if she isn't there at all. What can she do? She doesn't know, but this man no longer seems holy. Nothing about this feels like the will of any god.

"I know you want to serve the Wellspring," the Pontifex says. "You don't want to continue to poison a power that was never yours to hold."

It isn't posed as a question, but an answer, writing over any she might give. He sounds like Enis when he said they were meant for each other, like the man in Leta's ballroom when he commanded her to dance. All different men, but their words served the same purpose. To tell her who she is, what she is for. To drown her voice.

But this man speaks for the gods. Is he right about her, about them? Jacinta's eyes are on her again, so bright. *Remember the other girls. Remember.* She thinks of the fledglings, brave and hopeful. Of Matilde's sly smile, Sayer's laugh, and Fen's hand, joining the four of them together. Making her strong enough to stop that wave and save them all.

She says the word that has been building inside her.

"No."

The Pontifex's cheeks redden. "What did you say?"

"*No.* Do as you will with me, but I can't give you what you want. I won't."

The Brethren mumble to each other. The Pontifex's face tightens.

"I have other ways of getting what I want, you know. And they are painful."

Fear threads through her, but the sheldars of old were courageous. She wants to believe she might be one of them still.

"Fine," the Pontifex says. "I will give you a night to come to your senses. Meanwhile . . ." He points to Jacinta. "She will undergo inquisition."

A few Wardens step forward, pulling Jacinta up roughly. Her eyes flash with fear.

"Wait," Æsa shouts. "I—"

"Don't," Jacinta says. "I can take it."

What can she do? There are so many Wardens, all armed, and no water to call on. No Nightbird sisters to help make her strong.

"Tomorrow evening is Leastnight," the Pontifex is saying. "I will give you until the morning after to make your confession. If you do, the gods will be merciful. If you don't, I will execute this witch. Her fate is in your hands."

As two Wardens drag her away, down hallways and through a series of dark tunnels, Æsa reaches up into her hair. A piece of sea glass is still there, buried deep within a braid she plaited days ago. She rubs it hard, making a wish.

Make me a sheldar. Help me find a way to save us all.

In ancient times, it's said, Eudea was filled with winged creatures. Wrathful dragons, fiery phoenixes, mighty griffins, and graceful pegasi. They were coveted: After all, who amongst us hasn't dreamed of flying? Many reached for them with hand and rope and spear, wanting to claim their power, to own it. But winged creatures cannot bear the weight of chains.

—INTRODUCTION FROM
A COMPENDIUM OF OLD EUDEAN CREATURES
BY KRASTAN PADANO

– CHAPTER 25 –

NEW RULES

THE TOWER BEDROOM they locked Matilde in is a mockery. It has a plush twin bed draped with silks from Teka, but that is where all pleasantries end. The walls aren't smooth paper but rough-hewn stone, half covered by sun-bleached tapestries. It isn't a cell, but it is still a prison. It smells of mildew, dust, and fear.

She stands by the window. It isn't barred, but only someone with wings could escape through it. She is in one of the spindle-thin towers of the Winged Palace, high enough up that no one below will hear her. The people entering and exiting the palace look like insects. None of them glance up. She is alone.

The sky is classic Simtan summer evening, streaked with bruised and bloody clouds. She can see most of the city, from the Corners to the Edges. Across the water, she can just make out a mothman filling lanterns in the Garden District, going on as if nothing has changed.

Her chest burns with frustration. Her stomach writhes and twists. They've had a smoking brazier of witchbane outside the door all day, stealing her magic. Even if she could use the Goldfinch's gift to change shape, she doesn't have Fen's skill for picking locks. Anyway, how can she leave when Epinine has hold of her family? She can't risk them being hurt again on her account.

Matilde doesn't want to be used as a pawn in Epinine's game, or anyone else's. She wishes she knew what was happening in the city outside. Where did that carriage whisk Æsa off to? Are Sayer and Fen safe? And Alec, too? After the flood, where did their fledglings go? If the suzerain knows about the Underground girls, she hasn't said. But their secret is out now, especially after what she did in front of Krastan's. The story is bound to spread like wildfire.

She closes her eyes, trying to think, but she's so tired. When was the last time she slept? She has passed the hours trying to conjure a plan that will protect both the Nightbirds and her family, but she has no idea what comes next.

To her left, there is a quiet creaking. Her eyes fly open as one of the tapestries moves. It pushes away from the wall as if a ghost is moving behind it. She backs away, curling her fists.

Dennan steps out from behind the tapestry. His hair is mussed, eyes fever bright.

"How?" It's all she can manage: The breath seems to have left her. Her heart is a wild, frantic bird.

He takes a step, slow. "I used to play up here when I was young. Epinine never wanted to join me, so she doesn't know about the old servants' halls that run between the rooms."

Emotion swirls. She is too tired to conceal it.

"Why not just use the main door? I imagine that's the traditional mode for a jailer wanting to speak to a prisoner."

He frowns, confused. "You must know I'm her prisoner, too."

His crysthellium-colored eyes are so earnest. Is the hope she feels the truth, or a lie?

His voice is strained. "What did Epinine tell you?"

"That you're the one who told her where to find us. You and your bird."

"Did she mention what she did to me to get that information?"

Matilde looks at him again. He looks fine: no bruises. "It doesn't look like she had to beat you for it."

"She could've had me beaten to a pulp, and I still wouldn't have spilled that secret."

Her breath hitches. What is he saying?

Dennan scrubs a hand through his hair. "She called me to the palace last night. I didn't think it wise to risk not showing up. Stupidly, I drank the wine she gave me. The truth serum she laced it with was strong—I think it's the kind the church uses. It hurt to lie, but I tried, Matilde. I *tried*. I never wanted her to find you." A loaded pause. "Say you believe me."

She used to be so good at picking pretense from sincerity, but right now she doesn't trust herself. "I don't know if I can."

A muscle in his jaw ticks. "Why would I come and warn you about Epinine all those nights ago? Or help you escape the Liar's Club, for that matter, if I was just planning to turn you over to her?"

Her chest is blazing now. "Then why did you give me that dashed bird?"

At that, he winces. "I only wanted to be able to keep in touch. I swore to myself I'd never use it to follow you. But dash it, Matilde, perhaps I should have." There is an edge to his voice, laced with frustration. "Why didn't you come to me after En Caska Dae raided your house? I could have protected you."

"And how would you have done that?" she says, throwing

her hands out. "Hidden us under a table in the club we'd only just escaped?"

She went to Krastan instead because she knew he would help her. Now she will never see his smiling face again.

Her chin quivers. She should hold her feelings in, but she is sick of games, too tired for masks.

"That bird didn't just give me away. It ruined lives." She fights down a sob. "People died."

Dennan closes his eyes. The sun's dying light paints his face a glowing amber. He looks as tired as she feels.

"None of this was supposed to happen. I never wanted to see you trapped like this."

And yet here she is, a caged bird.

But then, in a way, she always has been. Alec told her she lived in a gilded cage once, and she didn't believe him. Now she knows she was too close to the bars to see them. Too enamored of their shine.

Alec's question from the Underground comes back to her: *Would you go back to being a Nightbird?* She wasn't sure before—not really. But now she knows there is no going back. Not for her.

In the silence, Dennan closes the distance between them. He touches her hand. She doesn't pull away. Instead she thinks of that night he came to see the Goldfinch, knowing it was her behind the mask. He didn't ask her for a kiss. Instead, he gave *her* something, then walked away and let her decide what to do.

What did he say in the club? *I don't want to buy your favor. I want to win it.* He's never tried to force her hand, like Epinine. Or her family, pushing her to wed, be a good girl—a quiet girl.

"Epinine has my family," she whispers. "She will hurt them if I don't give her what she wants."

"And will you?"

She looks at him. "It doesn't feel like I have much of a choice."

"There's always a choice." Dennan runs his calloused fingers over hers. "You asked me once what I truly wanted. So tell me. What do you want, Matilde?"

The humid air hums around them, ripe for confessions. Somewhere in the clouds, a bird cries out.

"I want to make it so no one can hurt me," she whispers. "Or my family, my friends. I'm sick of running. I want to make it so I never have to do it again."

His thumb brushes her cheek, wiping a tear away. "All right, then."

Dizzy and raw, she makes herself step back. "What?"

"I meant everything I told you," he says. "I want to be suzerain. I want to bring magic aboveground. I can still get a majority of the votes on the Table, if we can best Epinine before the vote happens."

It feels like years ago, instead of hours, that she argued with Alec and the rest about how Dennan might be their best bet at safety. That with him as suzerain, girls like them would have a better chance. Does she still believe it?

She clears her throat. "Do you have a plan?"

He nods. "The beginnings of one. But it won't work without you."

Her mind reels as he tells her his plan, seeing possibilities and pitfalls. Together, they start to hone a way out. It feels almost like it did, years ago, when they played together, making up grand games and new worlds.

What would Gran do, or Leta? Nightbirds are supposed to follow the rules and wear a mask. But those rules didn't protect her or Æsa or Sayer. Perhaps it's time she made new ones.

"I should go," Dennan says, "before the guards bring our dinners. I'll come back later."

He turns to go. Her battered heart has started racing. "Dennan, wait."

She doesn't know what she intends until she is before him. She tilts up her chin, pressing her lips against his. His arms go around her, pulling her close. His mouth devours her. She forgets everything but the feel of his tongue brushing hers. Alec flashes through her mind, sparking grief and guilt and confusion. She ignores it. Right now, she needs this intoxicating fire.

Dennan's lips roam down her neck and across her collarbone. By the time they rejoin hers, her breaths are gasps. Her magic won't rise, with the witchbane burning, but there's freedom in kissing someone without it. It reminds her she isn't alone—not anymore.

He pulls back, breaths heavy. "What have I done to win such favor?"

You let me choose my own path.

She smiles. "It's that scar on your lip. I've always longed to kiss a pirate."

He laughs, and some of her pain flies away on it. With him by her side, perhaps she can still win.

PART IV

WINGS
SPREAD
WIDE

~ SUZERAIN EPININE VESTEN ~

CORDIALLY INVITES YOU
TO THE

LEASTNIGHT
MASQUERADE BALL

BEGINNING AT DUSK, ENDING AT DAWN,
THIS LEASTNIGHT'S THEME IS

LEGACY.

COME DRESSED IN TRIBUTE
TO THE HOUSE THAT SHAPED YOU,
THE LAND THAT MADE YOU,

–OR–

THE HALLOWED NAME YOU BEAR.

– CHAPTER 26 –
POISON IN THE GUISE OF SOMETHING SWEET

MATILDE WALKS DOWN the hall behind one of Epinine's guards. It's a relief to feel her magic again instead of the hollow nausea from the witchbane. Her power can't be muzzled if Epinine is to taste it. It shows how thoroughly the suzerain thinks she's won.

They stop at the same green dragon doors she was led to yesterday morning, when she was first brought to the palace. The guard knocks and a voice floats out.

"Do come in."

The room looks the same as the last time she was here, except now it's evening. The candles cast strange shadows on the mauve-colored walls. This time, there is no food on the long, polished table. Just a white, glittering mask beside three full crystal glasses. Matilde wonders who that third glass might be for.

Epinine is dressed to kill, made to look like one of the dragons that is the symbol of House Vesten. Her dress is made of overlapping leather scales in colors that range from pale chalk to old bone. A fine mesh frill juts out from her collar, stiff as a wing. She looks impenetrable. Matilde commands her nerves to lie still.

"Nice dress," she says, trying to sound bored. "Reptile suits you."

Epinine purses her lips. "Don't pout just because you weren't invited."

Matilde is still wearing the golden sheath the maid first dressed her in when she came here. It's a costume, too, letting Epinine pretend Matilde is here of her own volition. Two friends drinking wine, conspiring together.

Matilde gives a mocking curtsy. "As you wish, my suzerain. Your will is my command."

Epinine gestures for her to sit. Matilde does, although she doesn't think she can stay still. Her heart is beating fast, but she can't let Epinine sense her urgency. She has to wear her most convincing mask.

"Let's have a toast," Epinine says. "To us, and to the future."

Matilde raises her glass but doesn't let it touch her lips.

"Now," Epinine says. "I've set a meeting with some of the Great House members of the Table for later this evening, after I open the ball. I have told them that you're in my keeping, but they'll want proof."

Matilde nods. "Which is where my kiss comes in."

Epinine smiles, white teeth behind dark lips. "They will want to know your location, of course. But by then you will have been escorted out of Simta, to a secure location. The other Nightbirds will join you there in time."

Matilde fights the urge to touch her locket. She is starting to feel dizzy. "And my family?"

Epinine claps her fine-boned hands. "Oh, yes! About that. I have a little surprise for you. Something to make you feel surer of our friendship."

She pulls out a little bell and rings it. The doors at the back of the room crack open, revealing one of Epinine's maids and a woman . . .

Matilde's heart gets lodged in her throat. It's Gran.

She is wearing a deep blue gown, composed and regal as always. But she looks different than Matilde remembers: thinner. Her eyes, red rimmed, look a little bit wild.

Matilde is up in an instant, closing the distance between them. Gran folds her in her arms, pulling her close.

"Gran," she whispers. "I thought . . . Did they hurt you?"

Gran takes a shuddering breath. "I'm not so easy to break."

Gran smells different, too, more like stone than the flowers in their garden. Matilde hadn't realized how deeply she missed her. She never wants to let her go.

"I'm sorry," Matilde whispers. "For all of it."

Gran holds her tighter. "I am too, darling. I am too."

"There, now," Epinine says. "See? I am a woman of my word. She is safe. And if you behave, the rest of your family will stay that way."

Matilde makes herself hesitate, as if she's still deciding.

"I will tell you how to find the other Nightbirds. But not tonight."

Epinine raises a brow. "You think you are in a position to bargain, do you?"

Matilde tilts up her chin. "My magic can't be taken by force: It must be freely given. So if you want it before your meeting, then yes, I am."

Gran runs two fingers down her palm: *Fly carefully*. Matilde squeezes her hand.

"Fine." Epinine's gaze, usually cool, has turned thirsty. "Come here, then."

She walks to the suzerain, leaning down before her. Epinine tilts up her face, eyes on Matilde's lips. She isn't even seeing her—not really. She's focused on the gift her kiss will give. Like all clients, she sees Matilde as a cup to be drunk from. But tonight, she isn't just a pretty vessel. She is poison in the guise of something sweet.

FASTEN:
This won't be the end of us, will it?

GULE:
No. He knew too much, so I paid him a visit.

FASTEN:
And how did you silence his tongue in his head?

GULE:
I went pleading mercy, then I killed him instead.

—PART 3, ACT 4 OF
THE *SIMTAN COMEDIES*

CHAPTER 27

THE DRAGON'S DEN

SAYER SWEEPS UP the palace steps, trying not to touch her mask. The smoke-colored swath leaves nothing but her mouth and jaw visible, but she still feels more exposed than she'd like.

Most of Simta will stay out late tonight, celebrating the shortest night of the year with cool citrine and summer ale. People in Griffin's usually wear cheap masks on Leastnight, made to look like mythical creatures. Not this crowd, though: They are made of more sophisticated stuff. She shouldn't be surprised so many Great House lords and ladies have come to the suzerain's party, despite her supporting the church's investigation of the Houses. They hide their true feelings behind their masks, as always. Tonight, so does she.

The partygoers are all wearing costumes meant to celebrate their legacy. Glittering fins have been sewn onto jackets and flowers tucked into elaborate hair. Leta's glittering and feathered: a black swan, her House's symbol. Though, swathed in black, she could also be a crow. Sayer's gown speaks of a legacy no one here will know the meaning of. Gauzy and loose, it's the dark grey of storm clouds and shadows. A shimmering grey capelet drips down her back, split so that it almost looks like wings.

Sayer catches sight of someone in a fox mask. It isn't Fen—she's on her own mission tonight—but her heart still does a swooping turn. They've barely spoken since Leta's conservatory. Last night, lying awake, Sayer felt the gnawing ache of all the things she left unsaid between them. Of something lost she isn't sure she can get back.

Leta touches her arm. "Are you ready to walk into the dragon's den?"

Sayer frowns. "I still think we should have gone with my plan."

Leta arches a brow above her mask. "The smash and grab? Not very elegant."

"Alec's the one who suggested smashing," she mutters.

Sayer just wanted to blend in with the shadows, sneak into the Winged Palace, find Matilde, and get her out. Simple. She doesn't know why she has to dress up and pretend.

Leta laughs, playing a part for anyone who might be watching. "Your plan was reckless. You have no idea what we're going to find in there."

Madam Crow spoke to the Great House lords on the Table, who told her Epinine is holding Matilde hostage. She plans to use her to ensure tomorrow's vote goes her way. Madam Crow assured them she would get Matilde away before that happened, and they assured her they would vote Epinine out. They will elect a new suzerain, someone who will protect the Dinatris family and the Nightbirds. It all seems straightforward enough, but it isn't sitting well with Sayer.

The House lords spoke of setting things to rights—making

them as they were before. But some secrets, once revealed, can't be reburied. The church knows there are girls with magic in them now. Have the Caska boys who escaped the Underground told the Pontifex what they saw? Plenty of people saw Matilde tame the fire in front of Krastan's—hundreds of them. The tale of it is already flowing through Simta faster than a flooded canal. She has no doubt the sandpiper lords have heard it: boys like Gwellyn, who already suspects Sayer has magic. Men who will want to try to bottle such riches and use them for themselves. Those who don't covet such girls will fear them—even hunt them.

The fledglings are in the wind, and more vulnerable than ever. Voting in another rich, Great House–born suzerain enamored of the status quo won't change that.

"I know you don't like working with the House lords," Leta says. "I don't particularly like it either. But our priority right now is to ensure the girls' safety. We must get them out of sight and harm's way while we still can."

Sayer blows out a breath. "I still don't see why we have to attend the ball, though."

"The palace will be full of masked guests coming and going," Leta says. "If you get caught somewhere you aren't supposed to be, you can claim you got lost. Besides, we don't know what kinds of precautions they've taken. Better to walk in the old-fashioned way and assess the situation from inside."

She's right, Sayer knows. Epinine could have witchbane burning in the hallways, mixed into the drinks . . . anywhere. It seems likely she knows about the herb. How else could she have kept Matilde from changing faces and escaping on her own? But then, there could be another reason. No one knows where the Dinatrises are. They've vanished, as has Dennan Hain. Leta suspects the suzerain has Matilde's family and will use them to ensure she does Epinine's bidding. Leta and Fen's palace informants haven't seen them, but they've heard whispers of a girl locked in one of the towers.

Sayer clenches her fists. They can't be sure Matilde is still there; for all they know, Epinine could have sent her out of Simta. Sayer has no way of being sure. All she can do is hope she finds Matilde in the madness. Tonight, Sayer is going to get her out of this mess.

They're almost to the top of the pale stone steps, where some officials stand waiting. This party will likely be crawling with Wardens. It's the other reason Sayer can't just turn to shadows and sneak in. She doesn't know if their Salukis can scent her brand of magic, but she doesn't want to risk them catching her while she's invisible. Better to walk in looking like an ordinary girl.

Leta touches her again. "Smile, darling. Now isn't the time to look like a viper."

Sayer tries to act bored as their invitations are pored over.

"Welcome," one official intones, making a note in his ledger. "The Wardens will inspect you before you enter."

She looks to where he points, about ten paces into the soaring foyer. It's an effort not to gasp at what she sees. It's the Warden from the Liar's Club—the one who almost found them under Dennan's table. It must be. She recognizes his dog, brindle and white. It tips up its slender snout, sniffing the air in her direction. Can it smell her magic even when she isn't using it?

"Really," Leta drawls as the Warden pats her down. "Is this necessary?"

"Afraid so," he says. "The suzerain and the Pontifex demand it."

Sayer keeps her face impassive as the Warden searches her. A bead of sweat runs down her spine. His eyes roam, but he won't recognize her—he never even saw her. His Saluki whines again, louder now.

The Warden's expression darkens. "If you have anything illicit on you, best give it to me."

Sayer makes herself laugh, breathy and light. "Oh, dash it, I forgot."

She opens her clutch and holds out the dried fish she hid there.

"I always have them on me. My dogs love them."

The Saluki is still sniffing at her, not the treat, but the Warden doesn't notice. He's too busy smiling at her.

"A girl after my own heart."

Then they're in, swept forward by the crowd, out of the Warden's eyeline. Sayer lets out a long, low breath.

She can't help but be impressed by her first glimpse inside the Winged Palace. The vaulted ceiling of the reception hall is the blue of a summer sky, filled with paintings of winged creatures. They stare down at her, their eyes unnerving, but they don't know the power she holds. Unlike Matilde and Æsa, her identity is still a secret, at least from the fancy people here.

Leta whisks a champagne glass off a tray, holding it before her lips. "Do you feel anything?"

Witchbane, she means. Sayer breathes deep.

"No. I feel fine."

Leta pulls Sayer in then. Her swan mask presses up against Sayer's.

"Find her," she whispers. "And fly carefully back to me."

Sayer swallows down the strange lump in her throat.

With that, she turns and weaves deeper into the crowd and down the lofty Hall of Countenance, past candles that gild the space a rosy gold. Art and mirrors line the walls, as do palace guards and more Wardens. Conversation echoes off the marble floor.

She takes a breath and reaches, trying to find that thread that connects her to Matilde. She hasn't felt it for days, perhaps because the other girls aren't in close enough proximity, or because they've been drugged with witchbane. She worries it's because they're hurt, or worse . . . but no. Matilde is fine. Sayer just has to try harder.

Something catches on her ribs, full of that prickling recognition. It seems to beckon her and lead her on. She follows it through the Hall of Countenance, past the swiftly filling ballroom and toward its farther end. There are palace guards posted there, clearly meant to keep anyone from getting to the inner layers of the palace. Sayer just has to find a place to turn to shadow where no one will see.

Tracking back, she finds a door that leads into what looks like a sitting room. A heavy curtain shrouds an archway along one wall. Leta told her these alcoves are scattered throughout the palace's public rooms, a space meant for prayer. She just hopes no one's in this one.

She slips in and finds the space mercifully empty. A single candle burns in a wall sconce framed with wings, casting dancing shadows. Eyes closed, she prepares to fade in with them.

But then a voice comes from behind. "Hello, lovely stranger."

She whirls, heart thrashing, to see the Warden from the palace doors.

"Remember me?" he asks.

Panic claws at Sayer's ribs, but she makes herself smile.

"The one with the handsome dog."

"That's right." He leans against a side of the prayer space.

"I've just gotten off shift and saw you wander in here. I thought I might beg for a dance when the party starts."

She tries to look relaxed. "You weren't worried you would interrupt my prayers?"

"Not really." He smirks. "No one hides away in these during parties to do anything so chaste as talk to gods."

She bites back a sharp retort, going for mildly offended.

"Perhaps they should try it. We could use a little prayer in these times."

Sayer hopes her chastening tone will make him back off, but he only steps closer.

"Something tells me you aren't as pious as you sound, my lady."

Before she can reply, he grips her hand and pulls her toward him. Lips and teeth collide with hers. Thought flies away and all she wants is this boy off of her. And then he is, eyes thrown wide as a hard wind pushes him back against the alcove wall.

"You," he chokes, face going red. She's got bands of air wrapped around him, just like she did with her sire all those nights ago. "You're . . ."

"Not interested," she says. "Which you would know if you had bothered asking."

The Warden opens his mouth, but she concentrates her magic around it, forming an invisible bubble of air. She practiced this with Rankin in the Underground: He would shout, but her bubble dampened and contained it. When the Warden tries to scream now, all she hears is a sigh.

"Wren?" someone says from the other side of the curtain. "Are you in here?"

The Warden thrashes.

Ten hells, she doesn't have *time* for this.

Sayer knows the bands of air won't hold unless she stays to hold them, but she can't be found with him like this. She concentrates, making her body fade into the shadows. The Warden looks like he's going to be sick.

Footsteps come closer, closer, closer.

The curtain is thrown back by another Warden and a dog.

"What're you doing in here?" he asks. "I thought we were meeting by the . . ."

He trails off as he sees his friend struggling against some invisible barrier. Sayer backs away, trying not to make a sound. The new Warden steps forward, coming within inches of her. She holds her breath, heart in her throat.

The Saluki strains at its leash, sniffing hard. It is looking right at Sayer.

She needs to get out of here, now.

The dog snarls, and her control slips. The Warden raises a shaking finger toward her.

He chokes out, "It's a witch!"

Sayer breaks into a run, rushing back into the main hall, making sure her invisibility is still in place. But what good is being a shadow in a crowded hall? She weaves through as quickly as she can, wincing every time she brushes someone's body. She can't be caught here like this. She won't.

"Move! Out of our way."

She risks a look back to see the two Wardens heading toward her. The dog has its snout up, sniffing intently. Can it pick up her scent amidst all these people? To her horror, it seems that it can. It pulls the Warden across the hall, right for her. Sayer strains to see over the heads around her, trying to figure out where to go. There are guards in front of every door that guests aren't meant to go through. The front entrance is filled with people: She can't go back that way. She won't leave until she finds Matilde. The Wardens are getting closer with every second she hesitates.

Sayer turns, colliding with a woman in purple.

"Barnaby!" the woman shrieks to the man beside her. "You almost toppled me."

He frowns. "Are you daft? That wasn't me."

She hurries away, so focused on not knocking anyone else over that she doesn't realize she's entered the ballroom until the light changes. She looks around, trying to find some side door, some escape, but there is none. The Saluki barks again, too close behind.

Sayer looks in time to see someone scolding the Wardens. A palace guard, and he's clearly telling them to stop creating a scene. The Warden she used her magic on, still red faced, is pointing in her general direction. The palace guard looks unimpressed and unmoved. And then they're being forced out of the ballroom. How long, though, before they explain what they saw to a pater . . . perhaps even the Pontifex? How much more time does she have before they sound the alarm?

She needs to get Matilde out of this palace before that happens.

And then, up on the stage, the music swells.

"The world is what it is," says the girl. "I can't make something real just by thinking it."

"In that other world, perhaps," says Brown Malkin. "But here, thoughts have the power to change the course of rivers. The minds of others, too, if you can make their rivers tame."

—EXCERPT FROM
ADVENTURES ON THE UNDERSIDE

– CHAPTER 28 –
TAMING RIVERS

I**T IS EVENING,** Æsa thinks, though the day's heat still lingers. It hugs her like an old, oppressive coat. It is hard to tell exactly how long she has been in this cell, but she thinks it's been one night and most of a day. The Wardens have taken her to what she assumes is the infamous Jawbone Prison. Matilde told her, once, they have a special sector just for Prohibition breakers, but somehow she never pictured it this dank. It smells, Æsa thinks, like the Underground turned rotten. It's as if something has crawled into a hollow stone and died.

She doesn't know where they have taken Jacinta. When she asks her Warden guards, they look away. Now and then, Æsa thinks she hears strangled cries from somewhere, distinctly female. It never fails to make her chest ache.

If it has been a day, then that means tonight is Leastnight. Tomorrow the Pontifex will ask for her to make her confession, and if she doesn't give it, Jacinta will be led to the scaffold. She knows that she is running out of time.

These many hours have been spent thinking up escape plans.

Strangely, it seems the Wardens don't know about witchbane, or at least they aren't using it. Perhaps the Red Hand is keeping that secret to himself. For all her magic, she doesn't have the power to cut through iron bars or break locks. But there is one secret skill they don't know she can wield.

She counts the bells: seven, eight, nine. What if he isn't on duty this evening? But then, at last, the fresh-faced Warden arrives and takes up his post. As he leans against the wall, she smooths her features into something sweet and mournful. It's time to put Sayer and Matilde's lessons on wearing masks to good use.

She gives him a little wave. "Hello."

He straightens his collar. There is a nick just above it where he cut himself shaving, though he doesn't look like he has much hair to shave. "Hello there."

The other Wardens barely acknowledge her, but this boy is different. She sees the way his gaze flicks toward her and stays. It's as if she is a damaged flamemoth he wants to pick up and cradle. So when he's near, she's made sure to look like a damsel in distress. It isn't hard.

Æsa stands, making sure to wobble a little. "Do you mind if I come to the bars? The cool eases my headache."

A crease forms between his brows. "Are you unwell?"

She looks down at her hands. "I'm sure it's nothing."

After a moment, he nods. "Go on, then."

Her hands wrap around the bars, eyes closing as she presses her forehead to the metal. She can feel his eyes roaming, taking advantage of the fact that she won't see.

"This will be over soon," he says. "Just tell them what they want to know. You'll feel better."

She sighs, making it sad. "I know. I'm just so tired."

"I believe it. This place could drive Eshamein to drink."

She wants to rush him along, but she has to be careful. There will only be one chance to get this right.

"It's quiet tonight." Just as she hoped. "Are many of the Wardens at the Leastnight Ball?"

The boy pulls a flask off his belt. "Everyone wanted to get assigned to the party, but some of us had to stay here. I drew a short straw."

She smiles shyly, looking up at him through her lashes.

"I've heard stories of Simta's Leastnight festivities," she says, wistful. "But I've never been to them."

The boy runs a hand through his hair. It is badly cut, as if with blunted scissors. "I haven't been to the suzerain's ball, but my older brother says it's mostly fancy lords and ladies dressed up in costumes. The parties around the city are epic, though."

How would Matilde lure him in? She heaves a sigh, pushing her ample chest against the bars a little. His eyes slide well below her face.

"I wish I was dancing the night away."

She tries to look lost in the image of it.

"Well, perhaps we can have a little party of our own."

Her breath catches as he takes a step toward the bars, then another. He puts the flask on the floor and slides it toward her. The other Wardens never get this close.

"Cherry wine," he says. "My dame's. She brews it fine."

Æsa puts it to her lips. It stings, and she is glad for the sensation. Perhaps it will help her keep wearing this mask.

"You're very sweet." She steels herself: This next part is a gamble. "Maybe I could give you something, for your kindness."

"Like what?"

"Well . . . like a kiss."

He stiffens. "I'm a Warden. An abstainer."

"I know," she soothes. "I didn't mean a kiss like that. I just meant . . . well, a regular one."

Her cheeks start to flush, and she lets them. Her heart is beating hard enough to break.

He shakes his head, but his eyes are shining in the dimness. He takes another step. She reaches out a hand between the bars. One breath, two, three. He isn't going to do it.

Then he whispers, "Dash it," and he's right beside the bars.

She wraps her fingers around his wrist, just as she did with Tenny Maylon. She sees the waters of his feelings, different streams braiding themselves into a river. She just has to coax them to flow the way she wants.

"I don't belong in this cell," she says, voice doubling, tripling, echoing strangely off the stone. "I am not a witch, and you know it."

"I do." He blinks once, twice. "I do?"

She wishes she had practiced this particular magic as Matilde and Sayer urged her. His emotions are slippery. They wriggle like wet fish between her hands.

"You have the keys," she says. "You know the way. You can free me. You *want* to free me. To be my savior."

She wills her words to sink in, her feelings to become his. His eyes have glazed over. At last, he nods. "Let's get you out of here."

As he fumbles for the keys, she stays close. She doesn't know how long her hold on him will last, or even if it will if she's not touching him. As the door creaks open, she reaches around for his other hand, untangling herself from the bars. Then she's out into the hallway. It's a slender, vaulting space, cast in flickering shadows. She can't see any other cells or Wardens. The hall is empty, at least for now.

"Where is Jacinta?" she asks.

He frowns. "Who?"

"The other girl who came here with me. You want to free her too."

"Oh. Well . . . she's at the far end of the Wardens' sector. It's near the wing that holds the regular prisoners."

She concentrates, pushing her conviction into him. "You want to rescue her as well. You want to be a hero."

"I . . . well, yes," the boy says, sounding drunk. "Yes. I do."

They walk down the curved hall, nothing but wall sconces to guide them, their candles made of some foul-smelling fat. Their light casts ghoulish shadows that Æsa has to work not to jump at, but now is not a time for fear.

They reach a crossroads. Their way is bisected by a much larger hallway, wide enough to pass a carriage through. Slender, clear-glass windows let in the last violet gasps of sunset. Once they step into the light, there will be nowhere to hide.

Oh, gods: She sees two Wardens coming toward them. She presses back into the shadows, hoping they won't be seen. But if they turn their heads a little to the left . . .

Their steps ring on stone. She sees the flash of their uniforms, hears one of them chuckling. The other says something about a dog. Then their voices are fading. Æsa lets out a slow breath.

"Come on," her mesmerized Warden says. "We should hurry."

She doesn't argue as they rush across the large hall and into a smaller one. They take one turn, two, and the light grows dimmer. She thought her cell was grim, but the ones here are much worse. The stench of urine and sweat could peel paint off a boat's hull. A few grimy hands reach out between bars, but Æsa doesn't recognize the people crouched within them. And then she hears girls' voices, low and frightened. Her heart wants to fly out of her chest.

The cell Æsa stops at is no wider than an arm's length. She knows the two faces behind its bars, despite the dirt and grime. They're Layla and Belle, two girls from the Underground. How did the Pontifex and his Wardens find them? Jacinta would die rather than give up their names, Æsa is certain. But what if they *made* her tell them? What if, what if . . .

"Æsa?" Layla whispers.

"Shh," she says, trying not to lose her grip on her Warden's thoughts. "Don't worry. We are going to get you out of here."

Her Warden obligingly gets out his keys and unlocks the cell door. They move down the hall and to the next. One more girl, then two, are let out of cells. She knows them all. Where is Jacinta? She has to be here. She has to be all right.

They come to the last cell. The tang of blood folds around her. A body hangs suspended from two chains, arms out like a broken starfish. Her eyes are closed, hair loose and tangled. Her dress is torn.

"Jacinta."

She doesn't look up. Æsa can't tell if she is breathing.

She pushes urgency into her Warden's mind, trying not to send panic with it, but she is too frantic for subtlety. His hands on the key ring shake.

As soon as the door clicks, Æsa rushes forward. Streaks of red mar Jacinta's cheeks, leaving trails through the dust.

"Cin?" Æsa presses her hands to her cheeks. What did they do to her? "Wake up, *please*."

She stirs. "Æsa?"

Relief buckles her knees. "I'm here."

"Good," she croaks. "I hope you killed them. All of them."

Her voice is strange, both hot and hollow. Æsa wipes away some of the blood.

There's a strangled noise behind her. Layla and Belle have their hands on the Warden, as if to keep him from running. He shakes his head like someone waking from a dream.

"This is wrong," he says.

She goes over to take his wrist again. "No. It's justice. You are determined not to leave without this last innocent girl."

The Warden shakes his head again, harder. "I don't have the keys to those manacles."

Her heart stops. "You must have them."

"No," the boy says. And then, a little louder, *"No."*

He is wrestling with her now. She's thrown off-balance, and they both fall back into a rancid pile of straw. He is over her, hands at her throat, and panic swamps her.

There is a sudden clang and the boy is falling sideways, eyes closing. Belle has hit him with a bucket. The other girls are clustered together, panting in shallow, frightened breaths.

They need to leave before any other Wardens find them. But which way to run? Æsa doesn't know the way out of Jawbone. She is as likely to take them deeper into it as out, and Jacinta is still chained to the wall—they can't leave her.

"I can burn through the chains, I think," Layla says, a little green flame floating over her fingers. "I'll just need a minute."

A shout comes from somewhere down the hall.

Æsa says, "I don't know if we have one to spare."

There is another noise: fast footsteps, growing louder. They're about to be trapped in this dank hall of horrors. Æsa steps in front of the other girls, reaching for whatever water might cling to the stones, for anything she can use to defend them.

A Warden comes sprinting into the cell, his face cast in shadow. She puts her hands up, trying not to let them shake.

"Stay back," she says, making her voice hard. "I don't want to hurt you, but gods help me, I *will*."

The Warden speaks, voice strangely soft.

"It's just me, lass."

Æsa's breath catches.

"Willan?"

Nothing burns as hot as the desire for vengeance.
No fuel shines as bright, or for so long.

—A SYTHIAN PROVERB

CHAPTER 29

PLAYING THE GAME

MATILDE WIPES ROUGHLY at her lips, trying to remove what remains of the elixir she painted there. Some has made its way in, burning bitter on her tongue.

"Matilde?" Gran says, grabbing her arm. "What's wrong?"

She can't answer. Dennan told her not to put the potion on until the last possible moment, but he didn't say it would work quite like this.

Epinine goes for the green doors, yanking the handle. They are locked from the outside.

"Bren!" she shouts to the guard. "Get in here!"

But the doors don't open. There is a thump out in the hall. Epinine stumbles toward the other doors, but they are locked.

Matilde's vision tilts. Her throat feels like it's closing. She finds her knees buckling, folding her down onto the floor.

"Tilde," Gran says, crouching down. "Talk to me."

Matilde grasps for her necklace. Her hands are shaking badly. "I—the locket. Give me what's in it. All of it."

Gran yanks the golden orb free and unscrews it. Epinine

sees and lunges, but Matilde has already swallowed the anti-dote down.

Epinine doubles over, her cheeks as white as her dress. "What have you done to me?"

"You took my power," Matilde croaks. "I'm just returning the favor."

Epinine yanks at her opal-colored frill. "How did you do this? How *could* you?"

But there is no need to answer. The dragon door clicks, swinging open, and Dennan steps into the room. His hair is slicked back, everything about him immaculate. Dark green verda blooms shine at his lapel, the floral sigil of House Vesten. He is dazzling.

"Secure the hall," Dennan says to the guard at his shoulder. "We don't want anyone wandering back here."

He nods. "Yes, Captain."

The other set of doors open then. Matilde sees more guards—or Dennan's crew, dressed as guards. Dennan got word to them through one of their more sympathetic jailers. They've done it. Matilde lets out a shaking breath.

"All clear, Captain," he says to Dennan, "and no one the wiser."

Dennan makes some sailor's sign to him. Then he stalks over to the suzerain, who has clawed her way back into her chair. His expression is cold and full of righteous fury. The way he moves makes Matilde think of a predator.

"You did this," Epinine wheezes. "Even now, you betray me."

"Well, *sister*." Dennan spits the word. "It's only fitting. After all, you betrayed me first."

Epinine's expression changes, rage shifting to disbelief.

"You think to take my place, don't you?" Her words come out on a strangled laugh. "The Table won't accept you. You are the Bastard Prince to them, not a Vesten. You will never be our sire's true heir."

Dennan's knuckles go white on the arms of her chair.

"I will show them what a Vesten is supposed to look like. Before long, they won't even remember your name."

Epinine tries to spit at him, but it comes out a red dribble. Is that . . . blood?

Dennan's voice loses its sharp edge. "It could have been different, you know. If you had treated me like a brother."

Her eyes flash. "I should have killed you like our sire told me to do."

Dennan sneers, his handsome face turning ugly. "He wasn't himself when he said that. You poisoned him against me."

Epinine laughs. The sound of it scrapes along Matilde's skin. "He just saw you for what you were, in the end. And so do I."

Matilde doesn't understand. The potion is supposed to send Epinine into a deep, drugged sleep, knocking her out until they've sorted things out with the Table. So why does blood keep trickling from her mouth?

"Give her the antidote, Dennan," Matilde says. He barely even turns his head. "Something's wrong with her."

"No," he says. "Everything is finally going right."

Matilde stands, going over to touch his shoulder. Dennan is shaking, vibrating like a tuning fork. She looks at Epinine again—blood at her mouth, fear in her eyes—and understands. She is dying.

"You said she would fall asleep," Matilde whispers. "This isn't what you promised."

"She hurt you," he says. "She's hurt us both. And you would let her live?"

Matilde touches her lips, which are still stinging. She doesn't want to be a murderer.

"Don't do this," she says, almost begging. "Dennan, *please*."

There is a taut, glittering moment when she thinks he will listen. Then he slams a palm down on the table.

"I have waited too long," he growls. "I need this."

Dennan looks back at his sister, but Epinine's eyes are locked on Matilde.

"You're a fool to think he is your savior," she croaks. "He cares for no one but himself."

The suzerain takes a jagged breath, and then the life gutters out of her. Her eyes, once bright, are pale and still. Horror flickers through Matilde: Epinine Vesten is dead. Dennan killed her . . . *she* killed her. Matilde's kiss sent the suzerain to the depths.

One heartbeat passes, two. The candles flicker.

"She was too big a threat, Matilde."

He steps toward her, all bright eyes and earnestness. He looks like the Dennan she kissed in the tower.

"Think of what she did to us," he says, "and to your family. None of you were going to be safe while she lived."

At Dennan's signal, one of his guards scoops up Epinine's body. Dennan shoves an empty vial and a note down the front of her dress. There's something horrible about the way her body sways, then goes still.

"Put her in her bed," he says. "It will look like she took her own life. She knew the Table was going to vote her out, and she couldn't take it. The strain of it all was too much."

Matilde thinks of Epinine's words about how a woman has

to work twice as hard to prove her mettle . . . how people are so quick to believe she is weak.

"You lied to me," she whispers.

The skin between his eyebrows creases. "I didn't want her death weighing on your conscience. It was me who chose to kill Epinine, not you."

But he did it through her, using her as his vessel, a means to his own ends.

"It's done now," he is saying. "This will be better for us both. I promise."

Dennan promised many things, and she still wants to believe them, but now she knows he's lied to her. And lies are like swamp beetles that burrow into canal boats: Where there's one, there are bound to be many, eating the boards from the inside out.

Gran grips her hand. "Tilde. Tell me you haven't struck a deal with him."

"Epinine was dangerous, Gran," Matilde says. "Someone had to stop her."

"You think *he* isn't a danger?" Gran's face is a mask of fury. "He's the one who brought En Caska Dae to our door."

Dread rises in Matilde's chest. "Tenny Maylon is the one who gave them my name."

"Yes," Gran says. "He was at Augustain's that night the Red Hand took us in. When I asked why he did it, he broke down in tears. He told me someone took him to a church and encouraged him to give your name to that pater."

"Dennan?" Matilde says, wheeling around. "Is this true?"

Dennan sighs. "It's not the way she makes it sound."

Her thoughts are in tatters, refusing to make sense.

"You said Tenny escaped your rooms. *You* took him to the Red Hand?"

"I took him to a church. I took him to confess to a pater. I had no idea he was the zealot who attacked your friend." His voice takes on a pleading, desperate edge. "I thought the pater would go directly to the Pontifex with the story. He may be head of the church, but he's also a political animal—I knew he wouldn't make any rash moves before I could warn you. I never dreamed he would invade your family's house."

Betrayal is a beast roaring inside her, clawing through the shock.

"But . . . why, Dennan?"

He throws out his hands. "Because you needed a push, Matilde. Even after the attack on the Nightbirds, you still weren't ready to walk away from the system. I thought if I broke you out, you would see it. I just wanted you to be free."

Free? If anything, she feels more caged than ever. All this time, he has only pretended to give her choices. But he's been leading her down a path, and she has followed blindly. He's been playing his own game.

He takes one of her hands. "I know I've made mistakes. I do. But we can't dwell on what's past—we have to move forward. We're in this together. You and I are going to shape this world into what we want it to be."

Gran steps between them. "If you're our ally, then where is the rest of our family?"

"I don't know," he says. "Yet. But as soon as I can, I will send my men out looking. They will be free soon. That's a promise."

They are good words, sweet words, but now his promises feel hollow.

"And how am I supposed to trust you now?"

The moment stretches out, thick and heated. Then Dennan gets down on one knee and presses one of her hands between his.

"We're so close," he says. "We've come this far together. Will you step with me into the light?"

He's giving her a choice, it seems, but is he? Because he's right: She has come this far already. Her old life is gone, her secret out.

At last, she nods.

"I'd like a moment with my gran before we go," she says.

"Of course," he says after a moment. "I'll be outside."

With that, he leaves the room, shutting the door softly behind him.

"My darling." Gran takes Matilde's face between her hands, her gaze so tender. "What are you going to do?"

She isn't sure. She only knows she can't go back—only forward. Matilde doesn't want to run from whatever comes next.

She takes a shaking breath. "I'm going to make Simta safe for us."

It feels more like a wish than a certainty. All she can do is hope for the strength to make it come true.

Someone called from the waves,
Her voice bright and face fair,
He followed the sound
Of his dearest one there,
She looked at him softly,
The wind in her hair,
And sang, Kiss me before
We reach mooring.

—"THE BALLAD OF BALLENA ROCK"

CHAPTER 30

BREAKING CHAINS

WILLAN'S LIPS CURL, and his smile is the same one she remembers. Æsa takes a shuddering breath.

"How are you here?" she asks. "How did you find us?"

He nods toward the door. "I had some help."

Another, shorter Warden comes into the cell, steps light and catlike. Something throbs in Æsa's chest, a knowing ache.

"Blazing cats," one of the girls breathes. "Is that you, Fenlin?"

Fen takes off the Warden's cap and smooths her flame of hair. "In the flesh."

The throb inside Æsa is a living thing, pulsing between them. Æsa throws her arms around Fen. She stiffens, but doesn't pull away.

"You're here," Æsa says, holding tight. "I can't believe it. But how—?"

"Later." Fen pulls back. "We're on a schedule."

Willan nods. "We'd best get moving. I don't know about you, but this place gives me the crawls."

Behind them, Jacinta moans.

"The chains," Æsa breathes.

Layla is pushing up her sleeves. "I can do it."

Fen lets out a breath. "You're tired. Let me."

Her face looks different, somehow. Æsa thinks it's that she isn't chewing her mastic. She thinks Fen might use her magic to manipulate the metal, but instead she gets out a set of lock picks. It's only a moment before one of Jacinta's manacles clicks and swings open. Willan holds her while Fen takes care of the other. She drops into Willan's arms, barely able to keep her feet. Relief floods Æsa, but she doesn't speak. No one does.

Fen pulls a jar out of her stolen Warden's jacket.

"Chins up," she says, scooping a dark gel out of its innards.

One of the girls wrinkles her nose. "What is it?"

"Alec made it. He says it'll help muffle our sounds."

She smears it on their necks. It smells like rotting fruit and stagnant water, but Æsa has more pressing worries. Jacinta's shallow breaths, for one; someone catching them another.

Fen locks the real Warden in the cell as they leave it. Æsa looks back at him, still unconscious on the straw. The boy will hate her now, or girls like her. The thought gives her a pang of remorse.

"Stay close," Fen says. "Nobody dawdle."

Æsa frowns. "But the Wardens . . . Surely we will run into some."

Fen's gaze is piercing. "We've taken care of it. Trust me."

They walk in silence through the shadows, the girls all keeping close to Æsa, Willan half carrying Jacinta just in front. Æsa still can't quite believe that he is here. Fen leads them back in the direction they came, knife out, steps quiet. They don't meet any Wardens as they wind down a narrow stairwell and enter another hall, just as dark as the one above. Fen uses her picks to open cell doors as they pass, to the amazement of the crumpled forms within. Some stagger out, blinking hard.

"Is that a good idea?" Willan whispers.

"The more prisoners we let out, the more divided the Wardens' efforts, as well as the regular prison guards." Fen's jaw tightens. "And no one, thief or beggar, deserves to spend their days in here."

Willan nods in agreement. "True enough."

They stop at a closed door. Fen opens it, and they follow her through what looks like a barracks. It's rooms full of bunks, Warden uniforms hung on hooks, boots lined up in doorways. But where are all the Wardens? They can't all be out at the Leastnight Ball or patrolling the streets.

After a time, they stop at a door with a small sign that says *Vittles Room*. Fen fishes out a cloth, tying it around her mouth.

"Stay here. And no one breathe too deeply."

She opens the door and hurries through, darting over what look like piles of laundry. No . . . they're bodies. Wardens, heads down on their arms at a long wooden table, some on their backs on the floor. A few Saluki dogs lie beside them, long legs fixed as if frozen mid-run.

"Willan," she whispers. "Are they . . . ?"

"No," he says. "Look at their chests."

They rise and fall, as if sleeping. None of them seem anywhere close to waking up.

Fen drags a body through the mess by the collar. Back out in the hall, door firmly closed, she gives the boy a shake.

"I asked myself, what's the best way to knock out as many Wardens as possible?" Fen says. "It being Leastnight, I knew they'd be in the mood to party, and they'd likely forgo their usual precautions if they had the right incentive. So someone gave them a crate of fine Illish whiskey and hired Rankin to play a few tunes."

Oh, gods, it *is* Rankin. His face is so ashen. Fen smears a paste under his nose and gives the boy a light slap. One breath, two, then he starts coughing and sputtering, clutching his trumpet. Æsa can feel Fen's relief as if it's hers.

"Bodies all go down as planned, Rankin?"

"Yeah, boss." He smiles, flashing the gap in his teeth. "The resin inside my trumpet's bell worked a treat. I was halfway through a tune when they passed right out. Alec's a wizard."

"That he is," Fen says. "Can you walk?"

" 'Course."

"Right, then. We'll have to hustle. It isn't going to last much longer."

They wind through more tunnels, pausing at blind corners. Æsa's hands are cold with sweat, breaths coming fast. Every time they reach a locked door, she thinks it might be the end of them, but Fen makes quick work of them all with her picks. Finally, they emerge into the night air and a small walled courtyard, the moon turning the stones a silvery blue.

"What now?" Layla whispers.

"I open that," Fen says, pointing to the huge wood-and-iron door opposite. "Then we get out of here."

"Just don't anyone forget," Rankin says, "about them."

Æsa follows his finger to find prison guards some twenty feet above them, walking the perimeter of an outer wall. They wear the coats of regular prison guards, not Wardens, but it doesn't matter. She has no doubt they will shoot them just the same.

"Alec's paste will help muffle the sound of our steps, but it won't hide us," Fen whispers. "So stick close to the wall."

Fen leads the way. One by one, they each edge out, sliding with their backs against the stone wall. Æsa can hear guards shifting their feet on the walkway above, checking their crossbows. She holds her breath until she can't anymore.

Fen is at the huge door, head tilted like she's listening to something. But there's another sound, too—someone above them is singing.

"Fair lady, lady fair, your queendom sweet to know . . ."

She looks up to see the tips of two boots edge over the lip of the walkway.

". . . won't you let me climb your tower, explore the land below . . ."

Something rains down as he sings, streaming around them. Belle edges out of the way, making a face. If he looks down, the guard will see them. There is nowhere to hide, nowhere to run.

The song is cut off by a deep-throated ringing. The guard swears, then his boots are pounding away. More boots follow, all headed back inside the prison. They think whoever the alarm is ringing for is still inside trying to get out.

They hurry over to Fen. Beads of sweat run down her face and she seems winded, but the door is open. They slip out into the street, rounding a corner to find a carriage waiting. Rankin jumps up onto the driver's perch. The carriage is black and mauve, pulled by four dark horses.

"This is Leta's carriage," she says. "How do you have Leta's carriage?"

Fen helps Willan lift Jacinta in. "Climb in and I'll explain."

They all pile in quickly, filling the carriage with fast breaths and the smell of jawbone algae. It's so crowded that a few of the girls sit on the floor. Fen bangs on the top and the horses take off. The curtains are closed, but Jacinta leans into the small opening between them, sucking in air as if to clear her lungs of where they've been.

Æsa speaks first. "Explain, please."

Fen smiles, but there's a brittleness to it. "Word on the street was that the Pontifex had some magical girls locked up for inquisition. I knew one of them had to be you. We figured that Leastnight would be the best time to get you out, since the Pontifex would be up at the palace, and a bunch of the Wardens too."

"But how did you know where we would be?"

Willan speaks then. "A Jawbone guard owed me a favor. I asked him to draw some Xs on a prison map, no questions asked, and give me the Wardens' shift change timetable."

Æsa looks between him and Fen. "But how did the two of you even meet?"

"When I got back to Simta a few days ago," Willan says, "I went to find you. Instead I found the Dinatris house dark. I went to the Madam, prepared to barter for answers, but it turned out she wanted to strike a deal. She said if I helped break you out, she would pay off my fines and get my da's ship out of embargo."

Æsa remembers what he said all those nights ago in her room, about how Leta had made sure he was tied to the Nightbirds. He came back for his ship, then, not for her.

"She thought she had to bribe me," Willan says in Illish. "But I would have come for you regardless."

The intensity in his sea-colored eyes lights up the dark.

"So what happens now?"

Willan smiles. "I'm sailing you all out of here."

Fen speaks up. "The deal was that we'd get his ship out of impound if he and his crew agreed to sail a bunch of magical girls past port patrols."

"You put out the call?" Jacinta croaks, voice rusted.

Fen nods. "I put the word out through Underground channels that any girls who want out of Simta should meet us at a particular dockyard. They should be in the ship's hold by now."

Æsa's pulse is racing. "But what about Matilde? Where is Sayer?"

A muscle twitches in Fen's jaw. "The suzerain has Matilde."

Æsa feels sick. *What?*

"Sayer's gone up to the palace to get her. By the time we get to the docks, they should be there."

"What if they aren't?"

"Then you'll have to sail away without them."

Jacinta huffs out a breath. "It's not—"

The carriage explodes with sound. Glass shatters, flying in every direction. Pain sears Æsa's cheek as something hits it, breaking her vision into shards. When it comes back together, there is an arrow sticking out of the seat inches from where Willan's head just was, flaming and smoking. Willan bats the fire out as the carriage careens too fast around a corner. Æsa can't seem to make her arms work.

"Blast it all," Fen growls. "Who is it? Jawbone guards? Wardens?"

Layla's face is all grim lines as she peeks out. "No. It's worse."

Once in a generation rise four Fyrebirds who are heart tied. Once joined, they are forever bound, strongest together, sending ripples through the world.

—A PASSAGE FROM CANTON'S
SECRET HISTORIES

– CHAPTER 31 –

INCANDESCENCE

SAYER PRESSES HERSELF against one wall of the ballroom, still invisible, as Dennan Hain steps out from behind a curtain and takes the half-moon-shaped stage. The crowd erupts in surprised murmurs: They didn't expect him. What does it mean that he's here instead of Epinine?

"Pleasant evening, all, and happy Leastnight. Suzerain Epinine and I are so pleased you're here."

The Bastard Prince is standing center stage, where the candlelight is brightest, in front of the chairs that ring its outer edge. The people in them are masked, but Sayer knows who they are. The ones clustered to the left are delegates from foreign nations, who always sail in for Leastnight. The ones to the right are Table members: five Great House lords and the Pontifex. Their faces are all turned toward Dennan Hain, but Sayer can't stop looking at the curtain. She can't see Matilde, but Sayer knows she's behind it—she can feel her. There, and just out of her reach.

One of the Table members says something to Dennan, but

they're too far away to hear. Sayer reaches for one of the skills she honed in the Underground, making a tunnel of air between her and the stage that will amplify their voices.

"Where is the suzerain?" the Pontifex is demanding, his purple robe swallowing the light. "I wasn't informed of any changes to the program."

"She is feeling poorly," Dennan says. "She sends her deepest apologies. I am here to act in her stead."

With the masks, Sayer can't see anyone's expressions, but she can feel their tension.

"You have no authority here," the Pontifex intones. "You aren't a member of the Table."

Dennan's bright eyes flash. "I am a Vesten. Epinine can choose to share her seat at the Table with me if she likes."

The Table members erupt into whispers and questions. The crowd shifts, uneasy now.

Dennan steps forward, lifting his voice for the room.

"We come here to celebrate the shortest night of the year together. It's a time for banishing shadows, and it seems to me we've let them reign in Simta for too long."

The whispers are gone now, replaced with absolute silence. Dennan has them in his thrall.

"Those shadows have protected the corrupt, giving them room to grow and prosper. They helped hide the violent actions of the rogue sect known as En Caska Dae. They've fed on the darkness in our Republic, spreading lies, spreading hate, and attacking one of our most prominent families. All in the name of our holy church."

The Pontifex stands, hands going out. "They did not act on the church's authority. And yet it must be said, they did it in service of the gods." He points a finger at the other Table members. "You speak of darkness? The church has done its best to lead us all away from temptation, but our Great Houses have been hiding girls with magic for a very long time."

The foreign delegates lean close, whispering swiftly to each other. The crowd murmurs, their voices threaded with confusion, anger, fear.

"I grow weary of rumors," Dennan says. "Let's let the subject of so much of this gossip speak for herself."

Matilde appears through a slit in the curtain. Something inside Sayer seizes, making her chest feel hot. Matilde is wearing a golden dress that almost burns in the candlelight, her short hair styled to perfection, the picture of poise. And yet Sayer can feel confusion in her, and doubt—even fear.

The Pontifex looks enraged. "*You* have the witch?"

"What game is this?" one of the House lords asks, quiet enough that Sayer has to strain to hear. "She isn't yours to parade around as it suits you. Give her back."

Matilde's expression darkens. "I'm here of my own volition, thank you, and I don't belong to you. *Any* of you."

"She is under Vesten protection," Dennan says, hand on her back. "Someone needed to safeguard her, after such persecution. The Houses, it seems, weren't up to the task."

Matilde steps forward, lifting her voice for the crowd. "The church preaches they hunted down all girls with magic in them long ago. That isn't so. I'm living proof."

At the back of the ballroom, Salukis are whining. The crowd jostles and whispers. The room has the feel of a storm about to break.

"I have magic inside me, gifted by the Wellspring. Girls like me don't deserve to be hunted. The power I hold shouldn't be scorned."

Sayer can't see the foreign delegates' faces clearly, but their interest is palpable. Their hungry eyes devour Matilde.

"No woman is meant to hold the holy," the Pontifex says, cheeks flushed. "That is blasphemy. You corrupt it."

Sayer feels Matilde's surge of anger. "You're just jealous such power is mine instead of yours."

What is Matilde *doing*? She shouldn't be up there. She should be with Sayer, fleeing this place.

"Matilde Dinatris has taught my sister and I an important lesson," Dennan is saying. "Magic runs deep in Eudea's waters, and it is one of our greatest strengths. Prohibiting it is what corrupts it. Perhaps it's time we found another way."

Dennan looks at Matilde, as if yielding the stage to her.

Sayer feels the bond within her pull tight.

All around the ballroom, candles flicker. Their flames pulse and stretch, bathing everything in their light. And then a sudden, fiery glow envelops Matilde. Flames unfurl behind her, seeming to sprout from her shoulders like twin vines of living fire. No . . . they're wings. Their roiling light catches the chandeliers, incandescent, making their crystal orbs shine blindingly bright. Some members of the crowd make the sign of the Eshamein at their foreheads, clearly shaken. Others simply stare at her, awed.

"Witch!" The Pontifex's voice is wild. "How dare you flaunt what you stole from the Wellspring."

"I didn't steal anything." Matilde's voice is as hot as the flames. "I was born with it. And I'm tired of men like you preaching such a thing is some grand sin."

Sayer can't stop looking at her wings. At Matilde, standing bravely in front of all these eyes and the Wardens' pointed crossbows. Sayer doesn't know whether to cheer or scream.

"Wardens," the Pontifex shouts. "Take her."

Several push forward, but a few Vesten guardsmen step from the edges of the stage to stop them. Sayer is wondering if a fight is about to break out when a girl, a maid, stumbles onto the stage, clutching her skirts.

"The suzerain is dead!" she shouts.

Matilde's fiery wings sputter out as the crowd takes a long, collective gasp.

"What did you say?" the Pontifex demands.

"She is dead." The maid's chin wobbles. "She . . . she did herself in."

Dennan's face is all shock, but Sayer can feel Matilde's unease. This isn't a surprise to her. Ten hells, Epinine Vesten is dead?

The maid holds out a roll of paper. "She left a note."

A moment, two, as one of the Table members reads it. The room is so quiet Sayer doesn't have to work to hear the men onstage.

The House delegate's voice is slow and measured. "This says that her dying wish is that her brother serve as suzerain after her."

Dennan touches a hand to his heart. "If the Table will have me, I am ready and willing to serve."

The palace guards flanking Dennan drop to one knee, touching fists to chests. Around the room, other guards do the same, though some just glower.

"No—" The Pontifex's voice is strangled. "There is a process for electing the suzerain. Tomorrow there will be a vote."

Dennan nods. "Yes, of course. And I feel confident the other members of the Table will vote for whomever they think best."

The way he says it makes Sayer think he's threatening those other lords, or perhaps reminding them of some prior arrangement. How long has Dennan Hain been planning this? A few of them nod at him, as if in agreement. The Pontifex must sense the turning tide.

"The bastard and the witch want to ruin Eudea," he shouts. He looks unhinged. "They openly defy the gods. *Arrest them.*"

Some Wardens raise their crossbows, clearly ready to use them, but several palace guards step in their paths. There is a shout and a scuffle. A crossbow goes off, and the people near it start running. Someone jostles Sayer, so caught up in the action they don't see the invisible girl they just touched.

A flash of purple pulls Sayer's attention to the stage: It's the Pontifex. His eyes are wild as he slides something from under his robes.

Sayer tastes lightning.

She doesn't want these glittering people to see her. She doesn't want to be caught and put in chains. But Matilde fought for her once—more than that. Now Sayer wants to fight for her.

Sayer's hands rise, her invisibility fading. Someone near her turns and shrieks. She draws on the air, asking it to gather. The ballroom shakes, booming with a growl of thunder that seems to come from everywhere. A wind circles the room, blowing out many of the candles. At last, Matilde turns, and they lock eyes. Sayer's magic leaps, responding to Matilde's, echo and answer, filling her with certainty—with strength.

Dame told her once that Nightbirds are like sisters. When she said it, Sayer didn't believe it was true. But she feels it now, the bond between them. A kinship that goes deeper than anything she's ever known. Forged not just by magic, but by secrets shared in darkness, by sacrifice and laughter and blood.

The Pontifex is moving toward Matilde, teeth gritted, blade shining.

Sayer's voice booms, more storm than girl. "Leave her *alone*."

She lifts her hands high, moving on instinct as the magic thunders through her. The wind she conjured howls, drowning out people's shouts. The Pontifex is lifted up, trapped by the whirling maelstrom. He screams and kicks, but it won't let him go.

People are pointing at her now. She needs to go, to run, but it's too late for that. There's nothing left to do but stand and fight, whatever comes.

A cloud of darkness bursts into being at one side of the ballroom. Her wind drops away as a dark orb flies through the air and breaks, darkness billowing out of it, spilling like a cloud of ink.

Another erupts onstage. Matilde starts reaching out a hand, reaching for Sayer, just before a burst of darkness swallows her whole.

Ten hells, Alecand. It must be his dashed Nightcloak. She *told* him to stay out of sight.

The ballroom is in total chaos. Patrons scream and scatter, jostling for a way out. The surging crowd lifts Sayer off her feet and drops her into a cloud of Nightcloak. She tries to get up, but boots step on her dress, almost crushing her fingers. She can barely see her hands splayed on the floor.

She has to get to Matilde, and quickly. But which way is the stage? She crawls, elbowing someone's leg, finally reaching the cloud's edge. She stands, trying to get her bearings. And then a set of arms wrap around her, pulling her back into the cloud. She tries to fight, but his grip is rough and painful. It's all she can do to suck in a breath. Something's being smeared under her nose: It smells familiar. Fear and an oily sickness make her gag.

He throws her to the floor, the wind rushing out of her. She is fighting for breath as a knee digs into her back. Her captor smells of clove smoke and a cloying cologne. Horror seizes her.

"How does it feel," Wyllo Regnis hisses, "to be the one brought to your knees?"

ORCHIDS, RARE

NAME:

Morbus gordiala

DESCRIPTION:

This orchid is one of the rarest in all of Eudea. Some maintain it is a myth. Most swampland orchids flower during certain moon phases, but this one keeps its own, elusive schedule. It seems only to unfurl its pale blooms in thick mists, but no one truly understands it. The people of the Callistan call it the Ghost in the Mist.

—AN ENTRY FROM
EUDEAN FLORA AND FAUNA

CHAPTER 32

WILD AND GREEN

ÆSA **TRIES TO** steady herself, but her vision is spinning. The carriage bashes against a wall, shrieking as it scrapes against stone.

Willan reaches for her. "Stay down! They're still firing."

"Who?" she shouts.

Fen swears. "En Caska Dae."

Another flaming arrow lands on the roof, burning a hole through it. One of the girls snuffs it out before it can catch. Æsa pushes up to the window, looking out and behind them. She catches a flash of grey on horseback—several of them.

"How did the Caska know?" she shouts. "How did they find us?"

Fen is rummaging around the girls, trying to find something. "They must have been watching the prison, or they had a mole inside it. I don't know."

Buildings blur by, windows lit up in the darkness. There are a lot of people in the streets. Many wear masks, but she can still see their terror as the carriage nearly hits them. Æsa hears their screams as they race past.

She grips Willan's arm. "We're going to kill someone!"

"Not if they kill us first." Fen yanks a bag from beneath one of the seats. "Which is clearly what they're aiming for."

She pulls a small glass sphere out of the bag, its smoky contents shifting like restless clouds. It looks like the same kind Rankin used in the Dinatris garden. Fen hurls it out the window, and it crashes next to one of the Caska's horses, exploding in a swirling burst of smoke. It makes strange shapes—fangs or talons, wings or scythes—that curl around him, rising up to obscure the rider's eyes.

His horse rears as the boy shrieks, clawing the air.

"Ten hells," Jacinta breathes. "What is it?"

"Alec calls them Frightlings," Fen says. "The powder makes you see nightmares."

Layla bares her teeth. "Got any more?"

Fen fishes some out of her bag, handing them around. More orbs are thrown, and more Caska flail at imaginary monsters, but they keep coming, nipping at their heels through ever-narrower streets.

When they run out of orbs, Fen dumps the bag's contents, throwing something into each of their laps. Masks.

"We can't let them follow us to the port," Fen says. "Which means we have to lose them. If we can't do that with the carriage, we'll have to split up and go on foot."

Fen holds up a mask: It's like the shiny ones Æsa's seen people in the street wearing. Hers is a Pegasus, Willan's is a phoenix, Jacinta's a dragon, Fen's a fox.

"These will help us blend in," Fen says. "It's hard to find drops of water in a sea."

Æsa slips on the mask. The carriage lurches. She grabs for Willan as they plow through a market stall, sending ceramic mugs and a vat of some sweet-smelling liquid flying.

Jacinta grips the seat, looking too pale. "But how are we going to—"

Something crashes into the side of the carriage. Willan wraps his arms around her as they swerve wildly, spinning in what feels like a circle before coming to a sudden, shuddering halt.

For a moment, all is still. Æsa's ears are ringing. The door nearest her is yanked open.

"Get out, quick!" Rankin shouts. "It's on fire!"

They all tumble out onto the cobbles. Æsa heaves herself up from where she fell, gripping her mask tightly, looking for somewhere to run. All she sees is high walls. To the left, to the right, all walls and windows. Their pursuers have trapped them in a courtyard. There is only one way out, and the Caska are blocking it, crossbows raised.

They huddle behind the smoking carriage as arrows rain down. One of the horses shrieks: Rankin has a knife out and is slicing at their bindings. One breaks free and runs, eyes wide and wild. Bystanders press against the walls, caught in the madness. One girl, about her age, clutches a small boy in a phoenix mask. She looks as terrified as Æsa feels.

There is the sound of wheels against stone, and then a creak as another carriage door opens. The arrows cease. Æsa risks a glance through the carriage's broken windows and sees two figures, supporting a third between them. When he turns, her pulse lurches.

Oh, gods. The Red Hand.

Even from this distance, she can see the burns Alec's fire dragon gave him. They mar his face, making it look almost half melted, but Æsa is more frightened by what burns in his eyes.

"You thought you could run," he shouts. "But Marren won't let you. I am going to make you pay for your sins against his will."

He hobbles forward with help from the two boys, who are also swinging censers, drawing dread-inducing shapes in the air. She cannot feel it yet, but soon the witchbane will find its way to them. She has to do something before it steals her magic away.

"Surrender," the Hand roars, "and I may just show you mercy."

"Mercy?" Fen growls, loud enough for him to hear. "Since when did you know anything about that?"

There is a loaded pause, the crackle of fire starting to catch on the carriage.

"Ah, Ana." The Hand laughs. "You know I only ever wanted to save you from yourself."

Æsa can feel Fen's emotions, roiling like those terrible Frightlings. Disgust and rage, defiance and fear. She pulls something out of a pocket and hurls it over the carriage. When it shatters, darkness rolls across the cobbles, engulfing the Caska. It must be Nightcloak. It has bought them a sliver of time, but no more.

"Let's run, quick!" one of the girls yells.

Willan nods. "Maybe we can skirt around them before the darkness clears."

But Æsa's eyes are fixed on Fen, who has gone to kneel beside the closest wall. She's breathing hard as she puts her hands down on the cobbles, pushing down as if she's trying to stanch a wound. She looks up, her one eye wild behind her mask.

Æsa, help me.

She doesn't say it out loud, but Æsa hears.

She runs and stacks her hands on top of Fen's, calling up her magic. Earth twines with ocean, surging and rushing. Fen's fingers shake under hers.

"It's all right." Æsa doesn't know how she knows Fen needs to hear it. Perhaps it's what they both need to believe. "To let it out."

Fen presses down harder, her body vibrating. A roar is ripped out of her throat. Something shoots up between their hands: a vine, growing so swiftly it hurts Æsa's eyes to watch it. Roots slither, cracking stone, making the ground around them break. The vine grows arms, branching out against the building, its fibrous fingers gripping on. Tendrils plunge through windows and strangle pipes in its frenzy, covered in dark green flowers shaped like stars.

"Climb!" Fen shouts. "All of you."

A few of the girls start scaling the vine, its many tangled loops and coils giving them handholds. When Layla slips, a tendril shoots out to keep her steady. With a quick look at Fen, Rankin starts climbing. An arrow whistles close to his head, but the vine slaps it away. It's as if Fen has filled the plant with her desire to protect them.

Jacinta lets out a shriek as a branch wraps around her waist, lifting her up and toward the roof of the building. Æsa stares, too shocked to move.

Willan reaches for her. "Come on. Hurry."

The vine has grown all the way to the top of the building and is still growing. She can see her friends rising with it, clambering onto the roof. On the ground, the Nightcloak is starting to clear.

"Come on," she says to Fen. "We'll climb together."

"There's no time," Fen pants. "If I don't lift you out, you'll never make it."

Æsa grips Fen's sleeve. "I won't leave you."

Some emotion flickers through Fen's eye, there and gone.

Something grips Æsa's waist. It's a vine, wrapped tight around her. She tries to pry it away, but it won't let her go.

"Get to the ship," Fen growls. "Get out of Simta. And if anyone tries to stop you, dash it, *fight*."

Æsa is lifted through the air, above the Nightcloak and the carriage. Fen's name is on her lips, lost to the wind.

Like shadows stick together.

—THE DARK STARS OATH

– CHAPTER 33 –

LIKE SHADOWS

S AYER FIGHTS, BUT Wyllo has her off-balance. Something cinches around her wrists, pulling tight.

"What are you doing?" she gasps, eyes stinging from the Nightcloak.

"I told you I'd make you pay," he says. "That bill's come due."

He tugs her along, out of the madness of the ballroom, through more clouds of darkness and into a cramped hall. Anytime someone runs by, he dodges through side doors. Dazed, she tries to fight, but he is yanking her along so quickly, and her magic is tamped down, buried within. How did Wyllo Regnis find out about witchbane? How did he *get* some? Her heart is screaming too loud to think.

"What you did at the Liar's Club was bad enough," he hisses. "And then you had to go and commit blasphemy in front of all of Simta. I shouldn't be surprised. Your dame was reckless, too. I thought you would have learned from her mistakes."

Rage sparks, but her terror is brighter. She tries to keep her feet underneath her, find some way to break his hold, but the witchbane is messing with her senses. It feels like she can't breathe beyond its reek.

"I should take you to Augustain's and be done with it," he growls. "But I don't trust you not to tell lies about your parentage in some last-ditch attempt to stain my name."

She tastes blood on her lips. "So what, then? You're going to kill me?"

"Rather that than anyone find out I have a witch for a daughter."

It's the first time she has ever heard him call her that: daughter. It makes bile rise in her throat.

They're in a cramped passage now. Sayer kicks out, trying to scream, but he yanks hard on the rope at her wrists, twisting one of her shoulders.

"Or perhaps I should hide you away at the country house," he says. "Instead of being a plague to me, you can finally be some dashed *use*."

Sayer would rather go to the depths than give him her magic.

She shouts down the bonds between her and the other girls, even though the witchbane has muted them. She sends them all the feelings she's kept hidden, buried in her secret depths. Her yearning for a family, after Dame died. Her surprise and gratitude at finding sisters in the darkness, a kinship where before she had none.

She reaches for Fen, crying out to her.

I need you.

Wyllo drags her out into a courtyard that looks like an old carriage graveyard. The stars above are nothing but cold, distant fires. Leta said she was a star once—one meant for wishing. Her dame was always wishing for this man. She taught

Sayer that needing others spells ruin, so she vowed to make herself a different future. There was a time when she thought she would be stronger alone.

As her sire pulls her down a set of stone steps, she sends a wish into the darkness.

Please let my friends hear me.

But she pushed them all away—she is alone.

Suddenly, the pressure around her wrists eases. She stumbles as her sire lets out a bellow. Blinking, Sayer tries to understand what she is seeing. Crates groan as nails pull free of their moorings, tools rise from the ground, spokes come free from wheels. Their metal turns liquid, streaking like a thousand shooting stars through the air only to collide with each other, forming long, liquid bands. Her sire puts up his hands, but he is helpless as the metal bands wrap around his body. He goes rigid as they harden, trapping him within.

He and his metal trap topple, ringing as they hit the stones.

"Let me out of here," he shrieks, voice laced with panic. "You devil!"

She works the rope off her wrists and wipes the witchbane from her face.

"No thanks. I like you better in a cage."

She stalks closer, leaning down over the man she has feared and loathed and longed for. Her sire in blood, never in name.

"I'm coming for you, Wyllo Regnis," she whispers. "Not tonight, but someday."

She takes the coin out of her pocket, the one he tossed from his carriage all those years ago. She drops it into his mouth, as one might do for the dead.

He shouts something around it, almost choking, but she

turns away. She's done with him—for now. Something else in this courtyard is tugging at her, wrapping itself around her heart.

A Warden steps out of the shadows of a broken carriage. Sayer tenses on instinct, but then she sees past the uniform, ripped and filthy, to the brassy flame of hair.

Sayer goes to Fen, steps a little unsteady. She's lost her eyepatch, leaving her green eye to gleam through the dark. Blood is smeared across her shirt and neck.

"You're hurt," Sayer gasps.

"It's fine." Fen tries to smile. "I'll live, probably."

She grips Fen's hand, holding her tight. "How did you find me?"

"Doesn't matter. Like shadows stick together." She presses her forehead to Sayer's. "I'll always find you. You're my shadow, Tig. And I am yours."

Sayer takes a breath, letting herself feel the truth of it.

"Fen, I—"

Fen's eyes roll back and she collapses to the stones.

Wind bends, waves listen.
The fields bow low and elkhounds swiften
To meet the Sheldar when she calls.

Bears rear up and flowers sway,
A shield in hand, keeping darkness at bay
To aid the Sheldar when she calls.

—EXCERPT FROM AN ILLISH LYRIC POEM,
"THE SHELDAR WHEN SHE CALLS"

– CHAPTER 34 –

A SHELDAR'S COURAGE

ÆSA STANDS AT the prow of Willan's ship. She can just see the figurehead: a woman with wild hair and arms thrown back against the bow, its protector. Æsa wonders if she has the strength to do the same.

Willan is at the wheel, making hand gestures to the crew rushing around them. At his command, they raise and tie the ship's dark green sails. It's frantic, but they do it all in silence. They can't afford to make undue noise.

Willan's men—his da's, once—have taken care of the nearby patrols, but that doesn't mean they are safe from discovery. The alarm bells of Jawbone Prison are no doubt still tolling; watchful eyes are everywhere. They are in the crescent-moon-shaped port's farthest berth, where the Simtan navy keeps all confiscated craft. The waters of the Whispering Lagoon are quiet— too quiet. At least the sun is gone, and the heavens are dark.

Ships stretch to her left, filling the port all the way to its farthest end, topped by a watchtower. The end closest to them has one, too. There are two more perched at either end of the

Simtan Rim, the thin spit of land that protects the port from breakers. No doubt all four hold navalmen with spyglasses. But this is a pirate ship, built for secrecy and stealth.

A collection of the Underground girls are stowed away belowdecks. She tried to make Jacinta go down there, too, but she wouldn't. The sight of her, bruised and bleeding, makes Æsa's chest ache. But what hurts even more is that the other girls are missing. It makes her feel panicked and strangely bereft. What happened to Fen after Æsa left her in that courtyard? Where are Matilde and Sayer? Why aren't they here?

Jacinta leans hard on the rail beside her. The water laps at the oars as they're lowered—with so little wind, they will need to row out.

Æsa swallows past the lump in her throat. "We have to wait for them."

"If we're caught, we're dead," Jacinta says. "You must know that. The rest of your girls can hold their own."

Your girls. Matilde, Sayer, and Fen, all out there, perhaps in trouble, but every second they remain makes it more likely they'll be dragged back to Jawbone. Truth to tell, she wants to put Simta behind her. So why does it feel so terribly wrong?

A fire flares to life on the horizon. No: It's from one of the watchtowers on the tip of the Rim. Moments later the tower opposite on the mainland ignites, and then the others. Angry bells begin to toll.

"Crew," Willan shouts, "cast off!"

Time stretches strangely as they shove away from their mooring. Oarsmen heave and whisper, both too quiet and too loud. They glide through the waves, farther and farther, but they are moving too slowly. She grips the rail, heart in her throat.

Minutes pass. The bells are wearing at her composure. One of the men gives a shout.

Æsa squints through the darkness. "What is that?"

Jacinta's eyes are wide. "A naval ship."

Æsa can see its glowing lights and hulking outline. It looms in the water between two of the towers, a giant on the waves.

"We have to turn," Jacinta says. "We won't be able to get past them."

But Willan's already shouting orders, trying to steer them toward the far side of the Rim. There's a boat there, too, smaller, but still a naval vessel. She can just make out figures running on its decks. Then something flies toward them, burning bright against the darkness, slamming into the waves beside them. She watches it hiss and swim under their hull.

"Firebolts!" Willan shouts. "And that wasn't a warning shot."

The navy is *firing* on them?

"Why would they do that?" she asks Jacinta. "We could be anyone."

Jacinta's gaze stays fixed on the ship in front of them. "They must know about the jailbreak."

The naval crew on the closest ship are at the railing, ready to fire what look like huge crossbows. Willan steers the ship left, right, making them a more difficult target, but both sides of the port are blocked by the warships. How are they going to get out?

Another firebolt sails toward them. Æsa feels the heat of it on her cheeks, far too close.

Jacinta grips her hand. "They're going to sink us, Æsa."

Æsa swallows. "Willan knows what he's doing."

"He can't do what you can."

"And what is it you think I can do?"

"Water is your element, isn't it? And you're a Fyrebird."

But this isn't a fountain's worth of water or a single rushing wave. This is the ocean, and she doesn't have Matilde, Sayer, and Fen here. Those girls are so much stronger than she knows how to be.

"It's too much," she whispers. "I can't do it."

Jacinta's gaze is unwavering. "But for me, for the girls on this ship, you can try."

She looks over her shoulder at Willan at the wheel, face grave and determined. At the girls pouring onto the deck from below. Fen told her to fight, and she won't stand here helpless. She raises her hands, closes her eyes, and lets go. She lets the magic wrap around her bones, offering no resistance, only welcome. It overflows in waves of liquid light.

And yet a part of her still cowers—that part that gave herself up to the Red Hand and the Pontifex. The part that still fears she has poison in her blood.

Her grandda always said she had a sheldar singing through her. *Just listen for her tune and have the courage to answer.* Perhaps courage is a thing you choose, like friendship. It's choosing to have faith in the voice within.

The water whispers her name. She can feel it not as a boat does, but as a fish, all around her. It waits for her to speak. What will she say?

Another firebolt appears, flying straight for them. The waves churn and foam around their hull. She calls a wave up from that foam, long and slender. No . . . It's a head, huge and sleek. When it turns, its watery teeth glisten in the moonlight. It snaps the firebolt right out of the air.

Someone screams, but the sea is vast and depthless. She can't turn away or she will lose her grip.

Æsa wills her water serpent to protect their ship, stopping firebolts as they come. She *is* the serpent, seeing the world through its watery eyes, feeling the firebolts melt on her tongue. But it isn't enough—the closest naval ship is in their way.

Her serpent dives through the water toward it, growing bigger and fiercer with every plunge and rise. Through its eyes, she sees navalmen pointing and shouting, full of terror. The serpent's going to crash into their ship and drown them all.

No. She doesn't want to kill anyone else, but she can't stop it. The magic is controlling her. Except she can feel the other girls at her back, reminding her of her body, and Willan with his hand on her spine, keeping her moored.

Æsa takes a breath and reaches down, down, into the sea of her soul, the truest part of her, and wishes for the courage to protect and save, not to destroy.

A groan escapes her lips as the serpent dives under the naval ship. There is a moment of weighted stillness before the whole thing rises on one mighty, rumbling wave. Her chest heaves as she wills the serpent up, holding the ship, trying to keep it from tipping. If she can just raise it high enough . . .

"You're doing it," Willan breathes. "Keep going, Æsa."

She wills the serpent higher, a mountain moving through the darkness. With every breath it gets closer to the cliffs on the Rim. But it's so heavy—oh, gods. Something in her falters. Jacinta grabs her hand and squeezes hard.

The serpent stutters and foams, but she gives everything she has to it. She asks the sea, and herself, for what she needs.

The ship comes down with a crack on the cliffs, just below

the shining watchtower. It leans drunkenly against the rocks, but holds firm.

"Yes, Æsa," someone says. *"Yes."*

Someone catches her waist as she falls, but Æsa is no longer with her body. She is her serpent, swimming away into the deep. She dives, and the water brushes her scales as they soften. Then she breaks, becoming a part of the waves.

Flamemoths come together in great clusters, drawn to each other's shining. It is not a mating instinct, it seems, but a desire for communion. They always burn brightest when joined together in the dark.

—ENCYCLOPEDIA OF EUDEAN INSECTS

– CHAPTER 35 –

LIGHTS IN THE DARK

MATILDE FEELS HERSELF yanked through the cloud of stinging darkness, through the curtain at the back of the stage. When her vision clears, she sees a boy wearing the Vesten's livery: Is he one of Dennan's? But then her gaze catches on his curls.

"Alec?" Of course: It was Nightcloak that just shrouded the ballroom. Matilde's heart feels like it's caught in her throat. "What in the dear dark depths—"

He shushes her. "What do you think? I'm getting you out of here."

Her thoughts are like spilled wine—she can't seem to get ahold of them.

"But—"

His grip tightens on her arm. "Come on, Tilde."

He pulls her through a doorway and down a set of winding stairs. They emerge into a deserted hallway lined with shelves of pots and pans—they must be near the kitchens. She knows this is Alec, her friend, come to her rescue, but she is tired of people dragging her around.

"Alec, wait."

He keeps pulling her forward. "The boat is going to leave soon. I don't know how much time we have. We need to—"

"*Dash it*, Alec."

She pulls him through an open doorway. The room is narrow, full of rows of shelves and baskets: a pantry. A flamemoth lantern burns brightly on a stool.

She looks at Alec, eyes wild, chest heaving. Then she throws her arms around his neck, breathing him in. He still smells of herbs and frennet, but it isn't the same perfume she remembers. There's something bitter to it now.

"We can't stop," he says, but his arms go around her. "We have to get to the ship, and quickly. Most of the Underground girls are already stowed in the hold."

"What boat?" Matilde's thoughts won't stand still for her. "Going where?"

"Out of Simta. Out of danger. Fen went to break Æsa and Jacinta out of Jawbone. If all went well, they should be down there."

Her chest constricts. Æsa was in Jawbone Prison? But there's no time to dwell.

"But Sayer isn't down there," she says. "I just saw her."

She thinks of Sayer in the crowd, raising her hands, saving Matilde from the Pontifex. Showing everyone in Simta the kind of power she can wield.

"She'll meet us down there," he says. "But we have to *go*, Tilde. *Now*."

"But Epinine closed the port. They won't make it."

"It's a chance we're going to have to take."

He means for them to run again, like criminals. To hide in shadow . . . but she's already stepped into the light.

"I can't," she says. "I can't leave Simta."

"What? Why?"

"Because my family is here, and they need me."

"Your family would want you to be out of harm's way."

"Don't you get it?" she shouts. "I'm tired of *running*, Alec."

Her voice disturbs the flamemoths in their lantern. Alec's cheeks flicker in their frantic light.

"If I run away now, it will look like the Pontifex is right about us being dangerous. He will twist the things we've done. He will turn people against us. If I run now, I'll be running forever."

Alec's face is a mask of confusion.

"So, what? You're going to stay here . . . with Dennan Hain?"

She stiffens. "I'm not staying for him. It isn't *about* him."

After everything that happened tonight, she can't trust Dennan, but perhaps she can steer him, and the Table, in the direction she wants them to go.

What is it Dennan said before? *We can't dwell on what's past. We have to move forward.* It's time to carve out the future she wants for herself. But to do that, she has to stay here, at the heart of things. She has to be a player in this game.

"You're the one who said you wanted change. You . . . Krastan." She tries not to choke on his name. "You wanted me to look outside my garden gate. Well, I'm looking, and the secret of girls with magic is out now, Alec. I have a chance to change the rules for all of us. To make things right."

Alec throws out his hands. "Are you doing this because you want to make things better? Or because you want to be a queen?"

How can he even think that? She wants to cry into his shirt, to scream, to tell him everything that's happened. But his eyes are tired, hard, and full of things she isn't ready to see.

He puts his hands on the shelves to either side of her, bringing his scent of herbs and smoke.

"Tilde, Krastan is gone," he whispers. "The shop is gone. I need you."

She touches his face, voice gentle. "And I need you to leave before someone finds us here."

He steps back as if struck. "You're really going to stay and be his Nightbird?"

"That's not what this is." Why can't he trust her? "Alec—"

"Krastan would shudder to see you play a Vesten's whore."

His words are a brand, making her burn. She turns away from him.

"Think what you want, then. Just go. I don't need rescuing."

A part of her longs for him to see past the mask—to reach out for her.

"Yes, I forgot," he says. "You never do."

And then he's gone. All is silent. For a long time, she simply stares at the flamemoths in their cage. At last, she clicks open the latch and swings the glass door open. The moths are quick to fly out, but they only seem to want to circle back to each other. They land on her gold dress one by one, making it shimmer. Lending her their lights in the dark.

Leave me, *said the Woman of the Waters.*
No, *said the Woman of the Winds.*
This cord between us can't be severed.
Though we are of two bodies,
our hearts beat as one.

—FRAGMENT OF A LOST POEM

CHAPTER 36

MOTHS ON THE WIND

ATILDE'S LIFE IS a thousand layers of secrets. Some live under her skin, conjured up when she needs them. A flicker in her palm, a pair of smoldering wings. Others are buried deep: Her fears, her aches, her uncertainties. She hides them all behind a mask she can't take off.

She walks down one of the Winged Palace's many halls through its private section. Guards nod as she passes. The Wardens and their dogs are gone, replaced by men who were once sailors on Dennan's crew and others he's recruited from the ranks of the navy. They all seem to worship him.

The doors to the new suzerain's study have been left open, but Dennan isn't within. He will be somewhere in the palace, planning his next moves. In the three days since Leastnight, she doesn't think he's slept at all. Neither has she.

The day after the ball, at the meeting of the Table, they officially voted him in as suzerain. Matilde was a little surprised that so many of the Houses chose to back him, but he did say he had leverage with them all. Besides, one of their own House daughters—and a Nightbird—stands beside him. They thought it prudent to do the same, for now. None of them seem concerned by the old suzerain's suspicious death.

They wouldn't pull such tricks if I were a man.

She shoves the memory away. Matilde makes it a point not to think about Epinine while awake. The woman haunts her dreams often enough as it is.

Of course, not all the Houses are pleased to have Dennan as their new suzerain. His words at the ball about wanting to end Prohibition have caused an uproar amongst the most pious; others see Dennan as a path to limiting the church's power. The church, of course, has condemned him, though the Pontifex wasn't at the meeting of the Table. He was arrested after the ball for attempting to kill Matilde, odious man. But she knows there are people in Simta cheering his name for it. Some of them have taken to protesting outside the palace, raising signs that range from Honor the Wellspring to Kill the Witch.

The city is picking sides, and tension is rising. She almost tastes war on the air.

She walks into the apartments Dennan had cleared out for her family. Dame is at a desk, writing a letter, and Samson is lounging on a divan, inhaling a plate of something fragrant. Since regaining his freedom, all he seems to want to do is eat.

"Tilde," he says, mouth full. "Set fire to anyone while you were out?"

Their dame tsks. "Samson, really."

"Not today," Matilde teases. "But I might try it if you test me."

Samson rolls his eyes. He's taken her magic and their new situation in stride with more finesse than she would have given him credit for. It's still a shock and a relief to have them back by her side. Dennan found them the day after the ball, in a dilapidated house in Dragon Quarter, and brought them to the palace. Her family seem the same, but also different. More wary. Or perhaps that's only her.

Dennan thinks it's safer, for now, that they all stay here instead of going home. Someone has tried to set the Dinatris house ablaze once already—a message. As little as she trusts Dennan now, she agrees with him on this matter. She wants to keep her family close.

She heads for the covered balcony where Gran has taken to spending much of her time. She has been quiet since Matilde told her everything that happened. When she choked out the part about Krastan, silent tears spilled down Gran's cheeks.

It's my fault, Matilde said, *that he's gone.*

Kras would've done anything to save you, darling. He loved you.

He didn't deserve what happened to him. And the man who killed him is still free. No one can find the Red Hand and his acolytes, but she has no doubt he is far from finished making trouble. One of the many threats she will have to try to contain.

She steps onto the balcony, which faces the Corners, its outlook framed by arched stone wings that form windows all along it. Moonlight is scattered across the water like a thousand sequins. Simta looks beautiful, but Matilde sees its shadows in a way she never did before. She wonders how many magical girls might still be hiding in them.

At the sound of her approach, Gran turns, smiling. The flamemoth lantern she has set on the sill paints her in shifting light.

"You know," she says, looking Matilde over, "I don't think I've ever seen you in pants before."

A small laugh escapes her. "Blame Sayer for that—she's a bad influence."

Thinking of Sayer makes her chest ache.

Matilde has gone over that moment between them in the ballroom many times: Sayer's hands thrown out, lightning crackling around her, exposing herself for Matilde's sake. All the next day, after the chaos, she was so afraid that some Warden had caught her. But the next night, she found a note in their apartments. *I hope you know what you're doing, Dinatris.* Matilde is annoyed at her for creeping through shadows and not staying to talk. They need to, and soon.

She wonders if Sayer and Fen are together somewhere. She knows Æsa escaped the city, leaving quite a memento in her wake. The girl they're calling the Wave Witch left a monstrous ship atop the Rim, lying on the cliffs like a beached whale. It's being talked about throughout Simta and, she's sure, beyond.

It isn't the only mark the Nightbirds left behind. There are scorch marks all through Hester Street in Pegasus Quarter, and lightning-made cracks in the palace's ballroom floor. She's heard there is a massive vine in Phoenix Quarter clinging to the wall of a courtyard. *It grew all at once,* one of her new maids whispered, *under the command of someone in a fox mask.* It's the kind of magic that hasn't been seen for centuries. *The old magic is rising again,* the whispers say. *Dangerous magic.* If only people knew what the four of them can do when they join.

But that secret died with Epinine—mostly. Some people in the Underground saw what they could do, and those two Caska boys. Who knows who they've told the tale to. At least Dennan doesn't know, and she isn't about to tell him. Some secrets are better left buried . . . for now, at least.

Late at night, she lies awake thinking of those murals in the Underground. Those Fyrebirds of old, so powerful: How did they fall? She wants to know their secrets and their stories. There is so much about the Fyrebirds they still don't know.

She's glad the other girls are safe, but she misses how it feels when they're together. The place where their bonds should be is now a hollow ache. She remembers what it felt like when they joined hands, becoming stronger. What else could they do together? What could they be?

"Are you sure about this, Tilde?" Gran says, bringing her back to the moment.

"Sure of what?"

"Of this path you've chosen."

She means choosing to stay in the palace and ally with Dennan Hain, or at least appearing to. Every time she stands beside him, Alec's angry words come back. *Krastan would shudder to see you play a Vesten's whore.* In the last few days, Dennan has tried to mend what's broken between them, including her in many of his meetings, calling her his adviser on magical matters. He seems genuine in wanting her to be his partner, but she can't forget how good he is at telling lies. She can't trust him—instead, she plans to use him. And so she is back to wearing a mask.

"Becoming the public face of girls with magic is turning you into a target," Gran continues. "I would rather you be hidden and safe."

Sometimes, in her weaker moments, Matilde longs for that old life, all private jokes and glistening evenings, but she isn't a Nightbird anymore—that life is gone. It's time to make a new one. Not just for herself, but for Alec, and their fledglings, and all the people in the Underground. If she can't find a way to make things better, then who will?

"Things are changing, Gran," she says. "We have powers

not seen in generations. More and more girls are rising who have magic in them, too. If I play my cards right, I can make it safe for us. All of us."

Gran frowns. "People fear power, especially when it's held by a woman. You're playing with fire."

Matilde's lips quirk. "It *is* my element."

As confident as she sounds, she's plagued with doubts.

She looks out over the Corners, wishing she was on a boat sailing across them. She hasn't left the palace since the day Epinine had her brought here. But she isn't a prisoner now: She could leave anytime she wanted. Staying is a choice, and yet sometimes she feels trapped.

But even caged birds have choices, don't they? They can squawk and bang their wings against the bars, trying to break them, or pretend to be tame until someone opens the door.

"Krastan thought I was meant for something," she says, swallowing her tears. "I don't want to disappoint him."

"You won't," Gran whispers. "You never could."

But Krastan thought she was a Fyrebird. Even now, she isn't sure if she believes him, but his faith is like a flame inside her. Bright enough, almost, to burn.

———⟡———

SAYER STANDS BENEATH a flamemoth lamppost in the Garden District. She stood in this same spot years ago, waiting to see if her sire would recognize her. Now she wreaths herself in shadow to ensure he won't.

Across the street, she can just make out the knocker on House Regnis's dark blue door. It's a timberwolf's head, its mouth gripping a ring made for knocking. It looks like a monster from where she stands. A wounded monster, she hopes. She had to leave her sire behind on Leastnight to drag an unconscious Fen away to safety. He must have lain there for hours, maybe all night. Sayer can't imagine what story he spun for whoever found him. And now he's back in his comfortable mansion as if he didn't threaten to kill her. In Simta, all the wrong people suffer.

She puts a hand to her wrist. It stills hurts from the rope he wrapped around it—even the memory makes her feel sick. But not as sick as the witchbane. Sayer still doesn't know how Wyllo found out about it. Could he have gotten it from the Red Hand? She doesn't see why that zealot would keep it secret from the rest of the church but give it freely to a Great House magnate. It seems the herb isn't yet common knowledge in Simta, but Sayer wonders how long that will hold.

She stalks over to the front steps, invisible, and takes a deep breath: no witchbane. Ear to the door, she works her lock picks out of her pocket. It doesn't take long to get it open. The well-oiled hinges don't make a sound.

The front foyer is high and many-sided, like a cut gem, mirrors hanging from every dark blue wall. The tile mosaic on the floor features a timberwolf on the hunt, chasing down a host of winged creatures. It can't stop her from creeping farther into the house. She tiptoes past vases full of flowers and gilded family portraits. In a different version of her life, she might have been one of those faces. But she has no family.

At least not one defined by blood.

She works her way from dining to sitting room, steps light and careful. And then, at last, she finds her sire. He's sitting at a desk in a windowless study, poring over a ledger. The room smells of clove smoke and wood polish. Some beast's antlers are mounted on the wall above his head.

Sayer steps closer, closer, until she is beside him, making

sure her invisibility is still in place. There is some satisfaction in seeing the bruise on his cheek, but it isn't enough—not nearly. She slips the knife out of its sheath.

She's spent days thinking of what she's going to say right before she stabs him. But other people's words are always circling, too loud.

Her dame's: *You were meant for beauty and light, not violence.*

And Fen's. *Revenge doesn't fix what's past. It just blinds you to what matters.*

She raises the knife. One swing and this will be over. He's earned this. She is ready to be free of him.

Her hands shake. *Ten hells. Just do it, Sayer.*

Wyllo looks up, anger simmering in his glare.

He shouts, "Minna!"

Sayer jumps. A moment later, his wife appears in the doorway. She looks younger than she did in those oil paintings, more fragile.

"Yes, dear?"

"Our books suggest that you've had *gardening trousers* made for Jolena."

Minna's voice is laced with what Sayer thinks might be fear.

"It seemed better than letting her dirty all her day dresses."

A fist comes down on the desk with a crack. Minna flinches.

"I will not have my offspring playing in the dirt like an urchin. She should be spending that time attending to the lessons I pay so dearly for."

"I've told her," Minna says. "But you know our daughter. She has her own ideas."

"You promised me boys, and all I got were girls with *ideas.*"

Sayer wants to stab him right then—perhaps Minna wouldn't even mind it. Instead, she finds herself easing silently back.

It isn't just that she doesn't want to stab Wyllo in front of this fine-boned woman. It's that Fen was right: Her dame wouldn't want this. And what would it achieve, anyway? When she takes her revenge, she wants him to see her coming. He deserves to suffer slowly before she sends him to the deep.

Sayer turns and slides out of the room, past Minna, tiptoeing her way around the edges of the house. She might not be stabbing Wyllo tonight, but she's too angry to leave yet, and dash it if she isn't going to steal some of his fancy knickknacks.

She passes an open window facing onto a walled garden. The smell of the greenery makes her think of Fen. She slept for two days straight at Leta's. Sayer cleaned her wounds and sat by her, reliving that night in her mind's eye. The way Fen called to the metal in the courtyard, sending it flying. Her whispered words: *You're my shadow, Tig, and I am yours.*

But when Sayer woke this morning, Fen was gone, left without a word, just like Sayer did months ago. She supposes that's fair enough. They need to talk, but something has kept her from going looking. How can she when she doesn't know what she wants or what they are? Tied, that's for certain.

She shakes away the thought as she climbs the grand staircase. Slowly, slowly, trying not to make a sound. When she gets to the top, she walks past bedrooms toward the end of the hall. A sweet voice floats out of an open doorway, full of frustration.

"Dash it *all*."

Curious, Sayer sneaks in. The bedroom is all frills and pastel colors, but it's empty. Out an open window, Sayer sees a flash of pale nightdress. A girl is sitting on the roof just outside. This must be the gardening girl, Jolena. She is in profile from where Sayer is standing. It shouldn't surprise her that the girl looks a little bit like her, and yet it does. She is maybe thirteen, scrubbed and polished. Even the ribbon in her hair speaks of a plush life without worry. Sayer's lip twists, a bitter taste on her tongue.

But the girl's hands are dirty. There are dark crescents under her nails, and she's got them cupped around what looks like a pile of dirt. She is staring down at it, as if expecting something to happen. Something prickles along the skin of Sayer's arms.

The girl's mouth puckers, then she swears again. What is she doing?

Sayer carefully climbs out the window, creeping closer. The girl is looking down at the dirt again, eyebrows scrunched. She's singing a little song under her breath. She gasps as something rises from the dirt. It's a plant, unfurling jagged leaves as Sayer watches, growing fast . . . almost like magic. It *is* magic.

Wyllo Regnis has two magical daughters.

Blazing cats, how it would burn him to know.

She should leave, but instead she sits to the girl's right, still wreathed in shadows. Jolena stiffens and stills.

"Hello?" she whispers.

Sayer holds her breath, debating.

"Is it you? The Storm Witch?"

Sayer's lips curl. She's heard that is what Simta's rumor mill is calling her, after what she did up at the palace. They still don't know her true name. No one does, except the people she trusts and the horrible man downstairs.

The girl is still talking. "I think they mean it as an insult, but I like it. It's fearsome."

Sayer says, "I rather think so too."

Jolena gasps. Sayer shouldn't reveal herself here, to this girl. But with a glance back at the window to make sure she can't be seen from the doorway, she makes herself visible again.

The girl's smile is wide, unreserved. Freckles dot her cheeks like a sky full of stars.

"I knew it was you. Did you really make a storm inside the palace?" she asks, as if there's nothing strange about a girl appearing on her roof out of thin air. "Did you really throw the Pontifex up in the air?"

Sayer nods.

"Ten hells," the girl swears. "I wish I'd seen it."

Sayer looks down at the plant Jolena's sprouted. "It looks like you have your own special talents."

Jolena frowns. "I only did it for the first time a few weeks ago. I don't understand quite how it works yet, but I will."

But the more power a girl has, the more people want to take it from her. Sayer knows that all too well.

Matilde wants to change the system from the inside. Sayer understands that. But the wheels of politics always turn slowly, while rumor and fear move fast. The church is making noise about hunting down girls with magic, no matter what the Table has to say about it. People are looking for girls like this one, either to use or subdue, and there aren't any laws to protect them. Out in the streets, it's every girl on her own.

Jolena runs a finger down the plant she's just sprouted. It has unfurled a tiny white flower, its petals edged in red.

She looks up. "Have you come to show me how to use my magic?"

"I came to tell you to be careful where you practice. Out here, someone might see."

Jolena's eyes flash. Sayer can see some of herself in them. "I don't care what anyone says. I'm not ashamed."

There's a knot in Sayer's chest that wasn't there before.

"I wish I could go invisible." The girl's expression darkens. "My sire doesn't let me do anything. He says I have to learn how to behave like a lady, so I'm always locked inside."

Locked in this house, with a man who has already tried to hurt one magical daughter. What would he do if he knew one was living under his roof? She's a member of his family—the one he chose to honor. But Sayer can't forget the feeling of being dragged by her wrists. *I'd rather kill you than anyone find out I have a witch for a daughter.* How many other sires in Simta feel the same?

"Does he know what you can do? Your sire?"

"No," Jolena says. "I don't like keeping secrets, but Dame says I can't ever tell."

Sayer wonders how many of the fledglings are still in Simta. They can't all have gotten away with Æsa on that ship. How many new girls are there like Jolena, just finding their magic, and with no Underground to run to? Who is going to look out for them now?

"I can't teach you how to turn into shadow," she says, pulling her knife free. "But maybe I can teach you something else."

Sayer flips her knife end over end, blade flashing. It stops and hovers in the air above her hand.

Jolena's mouth makes an O. "How to make things float?"

"No." Sayer smiles. "I mean to teach you how to fight."

Later, she leaves the knife with Jolena, and a note the girl promised to put on her sire's desk.

I will be watching you, Wyllo Regnis. If I see you hurt one more girl with magic, I will send you to the depths.
Sincerely,
The Storm Witch

She walks back out to the flamemoth lamppost. Its golden light flickers in a way that makes her think of Matilde. Sayer doesn't understand what she thinks she's going to achieve up at that palace, talking and maneuvering. She clearly thinks she can change things by stepping into the light.

Things do need to change—Sayer can see that. She might even believe that she should have a hand in changing them. But she isn't going to do it in plain sight, with all of Simta watching. She is going to be a knife in the dark.

FEN KEEPS HER hands flat on the table. She wants to itch at the half-formed scab on her shoulder—to pick at it—but she's learned not to call attention to her hurts. Especially not around this table in the attic of the Throne Room, in front of the other piper bosses. She already feels too dashed exposed.

She swills her shot of Illish whiskey. Fen doesn't drink, not really, but she has a lot of pains to dull. Three nights ago, she barely escaped Dorisall and his cronies in that courtyard in Phoenix Quarter. The arrow through her shoulder made it so she had to climb her vine one-handed, heart thrashing, as Dorisall screamed her name below. And now he's in the wind, again, licking his wounds, gathering strength. She fights a shudder. Fen should have killed him years ago. But every time he's near, she feels like a kid again, trapped in that basement. Blazing cats, she's Fenlin Brae: She's not afraid of anything.

Which is the biggest lie she's ever sold.

The boss of the Quick Cuts raps his knuckles on the table. "Let's get going, gents. Lots to discuss."

Simta's seven gang lords are all here, dressed in their usual finery. Fen's got her best orange vest on, a new patch covering her green eye. Their seconds are perched in chairs just to their right. Olsa's a good second: loyal, but doesn't ask too many questions. Gwellyn, the second of the old boss of the Kraken, is glowering at her across the table's polished wood. He can stare all he likes—Fen has bigger problems. Her Underground garden is gone, washed away, as well as all the money she sank into it. The Dark Stars are strapped for cash, and she has to find some way to fix it. She doesn't have the time to obsess about Sayer. And yet Fen can't stop thinking of her, and the other night outside the palace. The memory of it throbs like a wound that won't heal. *I'll always find you. You're my shadow, Tig, and I am yours.* Fen might as well have taken her heart out and laid it on the cobbles. That night she let too many of her secrets slip.

The Quick Cuts boss pulls her out of her thoughts.

"Things are changing in Simta, quicklike. We need to change with them. Discuss terms on how we're dealing with these magical girls."

How to control them, he means. To use them. Disgust washes through her, but she can't let it show.

"We don't want war between us," the Deep Seas boss rumbles. "So it needs to be civilized. No poaching girls from other gangs. And we need clear rules on claiming them."

"How about a finders keepers rule," Gwellyn chimes in. "You find one of these girls, you get to keep her, no matter whose patch she's on."

Fen makes sure to keep her voice free of emotion. "You talk like they're bottles of bootleg, Gwell, that you can just pick up and put in your pocket. They're people."

Gwellyn grins, showing the gap where his blue tooth should be. "I see why you'd say that, given your . . . associations."

Hackles of tension rise at the back of Fen's neck. Sayer, he means. He might not know for sure that she has magic, but he suspects it. He means the comment to cut Fen, and it does.

"You all know you can't force the magic out of them," Fen says. "They have to give it freely."

The boss of the Dreadlots leans forward. "And how would you be knowing that, then, Fenlin? You got information you want to share with the group?"

Fen shrugs, pushing her panic down deep. "It's just what I heard. Word on the street."

She reaches for her tin of mastic, ripping off a tiny pinch. She doesn't have much left, and her main supply is drowned under the city. Another problem to be dealt with. But if life has taught her anything, it's how to survive.

It's all right, Æsa said that night, before Fen lifted her to safety. *To let it out.*

Easy for her to say. She's never lived in Griffin's. If these men knew what she could do, they'd use it against her. They'd tear apart the life she's built, the gang she loves. But they *don't* know, and that's how Fen is going to keep it.

"We're not talking about taking them by force," the old Kraken boss wheezes. "There are plenty of reasons a girl with such powers might want the protection of the pipers. I'll bet most of them would work for us for free."

But in Simta, nothing's free, and there are plenty of ways to induce someone to do your bidding. The pipers do it all the time. She has a vision of one of the Quick Cuts' brothels, filled with girls selling magical kisses and handing all their earnings to the gang. Fen's skin crawls. She has the urge to scream, but she makes herself lean back, unbothered. She can't afford to stand against them on this.

She also can't ignore it. That's what she did with the Red

Hand, and look what happened there. She's part of how he became what he became, and the reason why witchbane is now a wider problem. Who knows how long that's going to stay hidden from men like the ones at this table. Who knows how long Fen can keep her secrets close . . .

She thinks of all the girls in Griffin's who are as she was once: scared, and full of a power that turns them into a target. *Like shadows stick together.* But it feels like she has too many shadows to tend.

ÆSA CLOSES HER eyes, letting the sea spray paint her eyelids. The ship's prow bobs gently on the waves. All Illish think of the ocean as a living thing, with moods and opinions, but it's alive to her as never before.

She wraps her hands around the ship's railing. Sailors work to either side, but none come near. Since she woke up from her spell, they've kept their distance. They bow their heads and make the Illish sign of respect at their foreheads. It's as if they see her as a symbol now, instead of a girl. She understands. After giving herself fully to the magic, she feels removed from everything around her. Of this world, but somehow still under the waves.

The sun slinks down toward the horizon, but it's hard not to think about what lies behind. It's been several days since they fled Simta. She keeps thinking of Matilde, Sayer, and Fen. Are they all right? Were they able to rescue each other? She has tried reaching for the bonds between them, but they've gone quiet. Perhaps they only come alive when they're close.

Jacinta and most of the other girls are down below. When Æsa can, she avoids them. They all look to her like she knows what their future holds. She spends most of her time on deck, listening to seabirds call to each other. They hover on the air, careless and free.

"Fine day for sailing."

Willan steps up beside her. Unlike his crew, he doesn't bow his head. He looks at her with the same steady, warm gaze she remembers from before he left her in Simta.

He leans into the wind, looking at home on the water. Handsome, too, glowing in the setting sun.

"We should catch sight of it in the next hour or so."

The Illish Isles, he means. It should fill her with elation, but nothing feels the way she thought it would.

Willan looks at her as if she's said her thoughts aloud.

"Going back to Illan always makes me smile," he says. "The place reminds me of some of my happiest moments. But it makes me sad, too, because it never feels the same without my da. I wonder, after the first time you leave home, if you can never truly go back again."

She swallows, throat tight. "For so long, going home was all I wanted. But now . . ."

He waits for her, expectant.

"I suppose I'm afraid of what my parents will think."

Her da, especially. She knows now that her magic can't be pushed away. It's a part of her, and it doesn't have to be a bad one, no matter what the Pontifex or the Red Hand might say. But will her da be disappointed to have a sheldar for a daughter? Will he see her as something to fear?

"You never know," Willan says. "They might surprise you."

Their eyes lock. How is it that this boy makes her feel both anchored *and* unsteady?

"What will you do, when we land?" she says, trying to keep her voice light. "Go to your da's for a while? Or sail onward?"

Willan is staring at her like she is the horizon he's sailing toward.

"Wave to wave, we ride together, Æsa."

The words hold the weight of a vow, a solemn promise. This current between them only seems to gain strength. Her mam used to tell her the story of how she met Da—her apselm, her beloved. Their eyes met as they danced around an Eventide bonfire, and she said she could almost see their future in the flames. Their story was already written; she simply had to decide if she was going to walk toward it.

But does she dare?

Æsa reaches out, threading their fingers together. She has time to see him smile before a vision overtakes her. It's some future Willan, leaning in to kiss her fiercely, salt and sea spray on his lips. When he pulls away, there is blood. It's everywhere, coating his jacket. He looks at her as if she made the wound.

She startles back into the present. Willan's brows are creased.

"What is it, Æsa?"

She blinks hard, pulling her hand away. "I don't want to hurt you."

"Why would you worry about that?"

Because she's hurt a boy before. And she's a sheldar now, or something like it. It's what the girls below need her to be. They're vulnerable, some of them without their families, heading to a land most of them have never seen. It's possible that Simta's navy will come hunting for them. If not them, then others will. If he stays with her, Willan will become a target. Perhaps she can't be a sheldar and an apselm too.

She tries to make her voice indifferent. "Anyway, I've decided I'm done with kissing. I don't know what you would be staying for."

She expects him to look stung, but instead he only smiles a little.

"Nice try, kilventra. But if you want to be rid of me, you're going to have to try harder than that."

With that he walks away, toward the wheel.

Watching him gives her a strange sensation. She's seen this moment before, in her dreams. It was one of the first visions she had in Simta: Willan on a boat, walking away into the sunset. She wonders if the future she just saw of him has to come true. Is it written in sand, shifting and changeable, or is it destined to happen? How much difference do any of her choices make?

Three dark shapes appear on the horizon, ringed by birds. It's the Three Sisters: The cliffs that greet all travelers who approach Illan from the south. Elation swells, but there's something else, too.

Æsa thinks back to that day Jacinta read her fortune. *You will take a winding path,* she said, *but eventually it will bring you home again.* But now Illan isn't the only place her heart lives. She left a part of it behind, with three girls in Simta. Her future's far from clear, but she can't shake the feeling it will bring them back together. That they are waiting for her on that now-distant shore.

– TO BE CONTINUED –

– ACKNOWLEDGMENTS –

I'VE OFTEN FANTASIZED about writing my very first acknowledgments. It's a glorious thing to have so many people to thank.

Much love to my agent, Josh Adams (and his co-pilot, Tracey), for believing in me and in this story. Thanks, Josh, for being my calm port in a storm. I owe you some IKEA meatballs. Thanks also to the foreign agents who helped this book fly around the world, finding homes in places I can't wait to explore.

May much sparkly confetti rain down on everyone at Penguin Teen and Nancy Paulsen Books. What an incredible crew to get to ride with. I'm especially grateful to my talented editor, Stacey Barney, for loving my magical girls so fiercely and helping me turn this story into the best version of itself. I thank my lucky stars for you. Thanks to Jennifer Klonsky, an early enthusiast, and Nancy Paulsen for their continued support, and to everyone who's poured their expertise and hard work into this book's making and promotion, including Caitlin Tutterow who is always there when I need her, Felicity Valence and the digital marketing team, my lovely publicist Olivia Russo, and the incredible copyeditors and proofreaders who saved me from myself more times than I can count: Laurel Robinson, Janet Rosenberg, and Cindy Howle. My gratitude, as well, to all the people behind the scenes I don't know to thank yet. I see you and thank you from the bottom of my heart.

A round of magical cocktails goes to the very talented humans who made this book look so beautiful. Aykut Aydoğdu, whose fierce art graces the cover (pinch me), and Jessica Jenkins, who turned that cover into the stuff of my dreams. Sveta Dorosheva, who transformed my made-up world into the most glorious maps ever, and Suki Boynton, who made the internal pages shine so bright. I am a very lucky author.

To all the librarians, booksellers, teachers, bloggers, 'tubers, 'grammers, 'Tokers, and other bookish people who've hyped this book and helped spread the word about it: You do incredible work. Thank you forever. Thanks also to Miranda, one of the book's OG fangirls, whose excitement kept me going, and to Carly, whose cheerleading and era-appropriate funnies made me laugh when I needed it most. And of course, thank you to everyone who's listened to *Pub Dates*, the podcast where I cataloged this book's journey to publication. I've loved having you with me on this wild, magical ride. Thank you, too, reader, for taking a chance on my novel. You're the reason I get to do this thing I love.

Thank you to all *The Exploress* fans out there. When I first started the show, it was just me, a mic, and a desire to tell stories about women MY way, but you've helped me turn it into something much bigger. Your enthusiasm helped shape this novel, too. I'm grateful to all the women of the past whose shoulders I stand on, and to my women's history podcast friends whose work keeps me inspired, especially Beckett and Susan, Olivia and Katie, Genn and Jenny, and Katy and Nathan (YAS, queens).

Endless love and all the brownies to my long-time critique partner, Ryan Graudin. You've made me a better writer, no question. Thank you for holding my hand for over a decade and never letting go. To Amie Kaufman: publishing Yoda, voice of reason, ride-or-die friend. I would be lost without you. To the House of Progress crew for being genuinely wonderful, with special thanks to Lili Wilkinson, magic system sorceress, and Ellie Marney for their critique and support.

I'm lucky to have an incredible friend in Kaitlin Seifert, whose enthusiasm kept me from setting this novel on fire more than once. I think you've maybe read this story more times than I have, and it wouldn't be as good without our late-night chats about magic and feelings. And Layla Seifert, my first Real Teen reader: Thanks for giving my fledglings such cool powers! My gratitude also goes to Cath Gablonski for her eagle-eyed editorial prowess and constant cheerleading.

To all the friends who've cheered me on through the years: Eve and the Sparkle Girls, Lyndsey, Nadja, Lori, Tori, Claire, Misty, Bel, Loran, Anna, Smeds, Goldman . . . the list goes on, and I'm grateful. To my friends in the Nest and my students at Charles E. Smith Jewish Day School: I can't tell you how thoroughly you all inspired me. A special thanks to Steven Reichel and Alison Kraner, who made me feel like my writing might be worthy of them.

I've been lucky to have some magnificent teachers, without whom I'm not sure this book would exist. Mrs. Rapson, who hung my poem above her desk and told me to keep writing. Aaron Sacks and Jeff Rosinski, who lit a fire in me for both history and literature and changed my life in more ways than they can possibly know. Jay Paul, the world's best creative writing professor, and Kim Wilkins, who I still want to be when I grow up.

To my family, who have always been my most fervent supporters: my dad (who has probably bought more copies of this book than is prudent), Carol, John (you'll have to read this book thoroughly to see all the pieces of you I stole, bro), Beth, the Chevaliers and the Gablonskis, including Elizabeth (put that pencil away, I see you), and all my favorite Canadians. A special shout-out to Ray—I wish we could pour out some red wine and celebrate this moment together—and to my niece, Victoria: I can't wait to talk about this book with you, and for the day when you publish one of your own. To Grams, Great-Uncle Jack, and Grandpa Chev, who all inspired my creative journey. I hope you're watching.

A gigantic thank-you to my mom, Edie Chevalier. You've been there every step of the way, from reading early pages and shouting at me to keep going to making me dinner every night as I got through my edits. Thank you for teaching me to love stories and for insisting that mine are worth sharing.

And to Paul, my husband, best friend, and partner in all my adventures. I couldn't have done any of this without you. I love you.